T0287098

LEGACY OF THE BLUE MOUNTAINS

Legacy of the Blue Mountains

A Novel

LYNN GALVIN

UNIVERSITY OF NEVADA PRESS | *Reno & Las Vegas*

University of Nevada Press | Reno, Nevada 89557 USA
www.unpress.nevada.edu
Copyright © 2025 by University of Nevada Press
All rights reserved

Manufactured in the United States of America

First Printing

Cover design: Rebecca Lown Design
Cover photograph: Shutterstock / oasisamuel

Library of Congress Cataloging-in-Publication Data
Names: Galvin, Lynn, author.
Title: Legacy of the blue mountains : a novel / Lynn Galvin.
Description: Reno, Nevada : University of Nevada Press, 2025.
Summary: "In Legacy of the Blue Mountains, author Lynn Galvin
    asks: What might happen to a group of Apache children, born
    in present times, yet living as if in the past and marooned in the
    Sierra Madre mountains of Mexico when their last renegade
    adult dies? As they attempt to reach their nearest, last known
    family members, they embark on a journey to a place none of
    them has ever seen or visited before. Will they be able to remain
    undetected while following a memorized path laid out in previous
    centuries that will lead them into the modern world? As the last
    remaining Apache children confront the challenges of survival in
    unfamiliar lands, will they endure long enough to reunite with
    their remaining relatives?"—Provided by publisher.
Identifiers: LCCN 2024032128 | ISBN 9781647791933 (paperback)
    | ISBN 9781647791940 (ebook)
Subjects: LCGFT: Novels.
Classification: LCC PS3607.A42585 L44 2025 | DDC 813/.6—
    dc23/eng/20240712
LC record available at https://lccn.loc.gov/2024032128

ISBN 9781647791933 (paper)
ISBN 9781647791940 (ebook)
LCCN: 2024032128

The paper used in this book meets the requirements of American
National Standard for Information Sciences—Permanence of Paper
for Printed Library Materials, ANSI/NISO Z.48-1992 (R2002).

To those Apache who chose to remain in the Blue Mountains and to their descendants, wherever they may be today.

And to Ray and Alex—Always.

When the past disappears, so do the trails and paths, the location of safe camps, water, and food. Without the memory of the ancestors, all must be discovered anew. That is why the stories of the ancestors must be remembered and honored. Why the "mind maps" handed down from the ancestors are so valuable.

PREFACE

THIS BOOK IS A work of fiction. However, its inspiration grew from historic events, and many of the characters are based on actual human experience, both modern and historic. Geronimo's surrender to the U.S. Cavalry with his hold-out band of "Bronco," wild Apache, commenced from the Sierra Madre of Sonora and Chihuahua, Mexico, in March 1886. Geronimo's third (and final) surrender to the U.S. government included a small group of fewer than fifty men, women, and children, who chose to follow him into captivity.

Both the Mexican villagers of the northern Sierra Madre, and the border residents of what is primarily today *Cochise* County, Arizona, and Hidalgo County, New Mexico, experienced the worst of residual Apache frustration and anger, in this final organized resistance of native people in the U.S. Indian Wars. To be accurate, all parties to the final termination of hostilities, whether Apache, Mexican, or American, shared culpability in ruthlessness and barbarity.

Border residents breathed a sigh of relief when Geronimo, *Naiche* (youngest son of *Cochise*), *Lozen* (the famous Apache woman warrior), and others were placed on a train and transported east to Florida as prisoners of war (their destiny for twenty-seven years). In time the band was transferred to Alabama, and eventually returned to a reservation in Oklahoma, where a choice was offered: stay in Oklahoma or accept refuge with the *Mescalero* Apache in New Mexico. Today, descendants of the *Ndee Nnaahi* (the Nameless Ones, so called because they could not claim membership in any specific band) predominantly live in both New Mexico and Oklahoma.

Initially after the Apache group's removal only a few Mexican villages recognized that not all Apache had departed. No one knows how many decided to remain behind when Geronimo left. Estimates have varied from one hundred to (an overwrought) one thousand. What is known is that the remaining Apache population divided into small groups that lived separately and met infrequently. Small children were placed with older women who raised and trained children apart from the fighting groups. Raiding continued without pause in northern Mexico and southern Arizona (although generally went unreported in the United States) into the 1940s. There was some continuing contact, eventually lost, between the Sierra Madre Broncos and the U.S. reservation Apache. As clashes occurred between the Broncos and Mexicans it became clear that Apache men were eliminated first, as they led and defended in raiding, leaving primarily women and children to fend for themselves. By the late 1930s Mexican newspapers and other reports usually mentioned encounters only with women and children. Reports of raids into Arizona ceased in the late 1920s, but violent contact continued to make provincial headlines in Mexico until World War II. After that, the written record goes quiet.

This captured my imagination: unconquered Apache, living off the land (and its inhabitants) almost halfway into the twentieth century? Who could dream of it?

As I learned of documented kidnappings involving American, Mexican, and Apache children by one another's people, of their frequently violent deaths, sometimes amazing life stories, my creative side stirred to ask: What if Apaches left behind did not all disappear by the end of WWII? What if the very last of them (ending with women and children) lived into the next century? Who would they be now? What would they know about survival and the world around them? Where would they go if they had to leave the Sierra Madre?

One more note: I am not the only person to speculate that Bronco Apache might still live in the Sierra Madre of Mexico. Expeditions have been mounted to search for them, books have been written, even movies made. Ethnologists such as Grenville Goodwin gathered proof, before his untimely death in 1940, that Bronco Apache continued to survive. In 1988 a small group of *Chiricahua* Apache from the *Mescalero* Apache Reservation arranged to visit the general locations (learned and passed down from Geronimo-era ancestors) in the Sierra Madre. Visited sites included *Juh's Nednhi* band Stronghold, a flat-topped mesa of land approachable from only two ways, one a steep "zig zag" trail that could be controlled by one or two warriors, and the other a thin stretch of land that could be easily defended, called "the skillet." Specific ancient cliff dwellings where Apache left caches of food and supplies; where springs, trails, and landmarks, taught and learned by rote memory, worked to anchor "mind maps." Apache skills in rapidly covering distances and surviving well, even in places they'd never previously visited, long received notice and wonder in western U.S. historic sources. The 1988 Chiricahua expedition camped and danced in such places, built bonfires announcing their presence, and used traditional drums and songs to invite any still-resident Apache to approach.

No one came.

I ask the reader to suspend belief in what is known, and enjoy a "what if" tale that is less than a century away from historic fact that some Bronco Apache refused to surrender and leave their mountain stronghold in the northern Sierra Madre.

It is unlikely that a remnant Apache population lives in the Sierra Madre today. But it's almost certain a few aged individuals remain alive who began life as Apache children, experienced kidnapping (or rescue, depending on the viewpoint), and grew up among the Mexicans or possibly Americans. At least a dozen people known to exist in Mexican towns in the middle of the last century continued to conceal their Apache origins to outsiders, as the enmity between cultures often produced ferocious reactions. Even today, revulsion and fear remain among people residing along both borders when the name Apache is spoken. A personal conversation in the late 1980s with an octogenarian descendant of *Cochise* County pioneer ranchers revealed an almost hysterical fear of Apache, and drove me into more research to better understand why. Clearly, for some the experiences are still entirely too recent.

LYNN GALVIN
Summer 2024, Phoenix, Arizona

The Number Four

Fall, *Mescalero* Apache Reservation, New Mexico

SAM CHARLEY AWOKE WITH a start, heart pounding, moistness beading along his upper lip and the hairline on his forehead.

He raised onto his elbows in the bed, peered into the dark of early morning gloom, and willed the dream to fade away. Instead, his dream continued, and a shape stopped at the edge of a mountain trail. Sam tried to wake up. The form moved closer, stared boldly into his eyes. "*Yushdé*" *(*Come), the shadow form commanded. The figure turned, looked back along the steep trail as more dim shapes moved behind it. "*Náhikah*," the voice said (We are coming back).

Sam Charley's dry throat constricted and his heartbeat increased. He shook his shoulders, unsure if sleep still held him, and the hazy forms with their mountain background dispersed like smoke.

He sat up from his pillows, looked about the small bedroom, shook his shoulders again, a kind of shudder. He thought, "Why would I dream such a rude thing? Why would someone look so hard, especially into the eyes of an elder? Of a medicine person?" He pinched his nose, rubbed between his eyes. Perhaps, he thought, a voice had come from outside and awakened him.

Marine training learned in his youth kicked in. Sam cocked one ear toward an open window, assessed the predawn noises, heard the sleepy churring of birds, sensed nothing amiss, no threat; breathed deep, willed himself back to calm.

For the fourth time he'd dreamed the same puzzling sequence of events. He'd dismissed the strange dream the first time, over a month ago. He knew that this, the fourth time, made it impossible to ignore. All of his people knew four was a number that required a reckoning.

He sat up and swung his bare feet onto the smooth, worn planks, shuffled to the front door and opened it. He stretched his neck toward the stars, saw that light would soon line the edge of the eastern horizon. Sam breathed in the sharp tang of fall's beginning, gulped the brisk air into his throat and chest.

The dream face and its luminous eyes suddenly rose before him out of the darkness, and he stepped back involuntarily, almost tripping, sucking in his breath. He heard the voice tone change, this time pleading. "*Náhikah le'*" (May it be so, we are coming back). Then the form faded into nothing.

Wide awake now, he realized he could not deny the summons. His people called him.

SEEKING A WAY HOME

CHAPTER 1

Nick's Country

Dog Mountain, *Cochise* County, Arizona

NICK KNEW HE COULD restore himself once he could reclaim his mountain.

A bright sky arced above the southern Arizona canyons in the *Chiricahua* Mountains of *Cochise* County. He relaxed, stretched out against the moss-covered ground. The speckled shade of a mountain conifer laced patterns across his form. Fifty feet away the chuckle of water bubbled at the edge of a natural rock basin creating a harmony with the rustle of pines in the afternoon breeze. He breathed deep, felt whole for the first time since he'd returned. And safe.

Nick Diaz was where he wanted to be. Memories of days in Afghanistan dimmed as he considered the lack of danger. No incoming missiles, no rocket propelled grenades. Most of all, no IEDs waiting silently beneath the shallow dust of roads. The nearby chock-chock-chock of a woodpecker mixed with a songbird's piping as he drifted toward sleep, head pillowed on a small backpack.

His eyes fluttered open at the slightest of sounds: the tiny music when pebble meets pebble, a tone hardly a noise at all. From the corner of his eye, Nick caught a buff-colored movement, stealthy. Muscles tensed, he waited for the materialization of whatever crept toward the mountain spring. A silhouette flattened itself at the rock pool, slipped its face into the water. No gentle lapping, but gulps Nick could hear like the soundtrack in a movie. The possibilities of a javelina, a deer, maybe even a mountain lion, flashed across his mind.

The drinking stopped and the head turned slowly to study the shadows. Water dripped from a wet mouth, spattering in tiny drops into the rock pool. Nick tried not to blink, not to breathe, knew tree shade camouflaged his outline. The head bent back to the water. Nick shifted one leg to inch himself forward for a better view. Astonished at what he saw, he did the wrong thing and raised up on one arm. The form's eyes instantly landed on the movement. Dark pupils drilled into his. A shock like electricity thrilled through his body.

Moments before he'd relished the solitude on Dog Mountain. For the past several years all he could think about was this exact sylvan ledge. In the hospital recovering, in the gym rebuilding limp muscles, he'd dreamed of his return.

In Afghanistan, he'd regained consciousness in a helicopter, already airborne. Confused to find his head propped against his Marine buddy's shoulder, Nick realized he couldn't feel his legs. His buddy kept repeating, "We're not gonna die. Not today, Nick. We're not gonna die." Nick cinched his own brain down right then on returning home. He'd decided he wanted his life back and he'd find it on Dog Mountain. Right here.

Finally, Nick had returned. Stretched out in the shade he'd watched the spring fill until it reached the granite lip and spilled over the brim of the rock bowl, slid easily into a rivulet wending down, paving the mountain stone with a green edge of life that clung to rock and earth. He'd drifted toward sleep, leaving memories of Afghanistan behind, until that small noise.

When he moved, the figure glided out of its kneeling crouch, back flat against the rock wall, eyes focused on Nick. Better than a mountain lion, he thought, and briefly smiled.

A girl dressed in a ragged-edged buckskin skirt wearing boots that wrapped around her calves stared back. An odd, silver-dollar-sized disc of leather decorated the toe of each boot. Her figure blended into the fall foliage, her once dark shirt faded to a no color, held at the waist by a woven leather belt with small dangling pouches. She wore a blanket folded across one shoulder, tied in a knot at her opposing hip. The girl's eyes held his as she slid down from the rock pool, disappearing into the ravine below, lips and chin still dripping wet.

By the time Nick gained his feet, mind racing, he could only consider the last thing he saw: a hand pointing a large knife in his direction. He'd flicked his eyes between any motion in her knife hand and her face, saw only himself reflected in the tautness around her mouth. Her expression, calm and intent, indicated not fear, but recognition of peril. Her countenance presented a level look of confidence, and he had not moved toward her.

Who would be hiking way out here alone? An illegal border crosser? Nah, she didn't look right. And yet, she sure wasn't local. His memory ticked up stories from the past about wild people, but he let it fly away. Pretty much seemed impossible. Somebody from a hiking club, he wondered. He even briefly contemplated various scientist types who came to study the insects or the birds or . . . He ran out of ideas.

"Where did you come from?" he asked out loud, filling the space and silence she left behind. He moved cautiously to where the water fell into the ravine. Hearing no splashing, no rocks falling, he stretched his neck forward and peered down to where the water flowed.

No one there. Especially, he thought, not the girl. He returned and placed his back against the canyon wall and stood quietly, hands on hips, for a good quarter of an hour, but nothing changed. "What the hell are you doing on my mountain?" he asked the silence. "And who the hell are you?"

CHAPTER 2

La Niña Bronco (The Wild Girl)

Chiricahua Apache Homeland

BIYOO', HER BEADS, HAD been on the move much of the night before. The trick of holding a smooth pebble under her tongue to ward off thirst worked only so long, and she had stopped to drink. Still, if the *Indah ch'iidn* (the enemy ghost) had not moved, she might not have seen him. She heard in her mind the hiss of Grandmother's warning that she must keep her senses alive. What good would she be to her people if captured or killed?

She knew how to approach water, always with caution. Following the trail to the spot she recognized in her mind map as Water Flows across Flat Rocks, she confirmed this was the path of Grandmother's youth. Grandmother taught the children the place names with the stories that guided their way; required each child to recite their knowledge before they were allowed to train as raiders. The girl knew water provided the one location where all life met, a source of sustenance and danger. She ran her fingers across the markings carved in the rock by the old ones, exactly as Grandmother described them.

She'd studied the shadows under the tree, saw nothing. The enemy must be a great warrior to hide so well. Perhaps he had a special power. She recognized him as a warrior when he stood. He took the stance of those who are ready. For the seconds it took her to slip over the edge of the rocks she saw his eyes move back and forth between her face and her knife.

Her Beads slid down from the pool where the enemy ghost seemed to have been as surprised as she, to the next pool below, scrambled into a crack at the bottom to wait, then into a patch of tangled mesquite, weapon ready. The sun's shadow lengthened. After a time she heard the voice of the man above; she waited longer, heard the sound of rocks crunching beneath his feet, and readied herself. Next, silence.

She knew better than to think him gone, thought of Grandmother's instructions. "Make yourself into something else when you must hide. Stay patient. Look like what you are not." She waited until long after she heard no more sounds to crawl from the mesquite. The warrior did not reappear, for which she thanked *Ussen*, the Giver of Life and her Protector. She crouched silent, knife in hand, alert, watching.

Her Beads thought of what she'd seen. The enemy ghost stood tall, black hair cut short, his eyes lively, as dark as her own. When he stood, he moved stiffly, but without wasted movement. "What kind of enemy was he?" she asked herself, considered if he might be *Nakaiyé*, one of Those Who Walk, the Mexicans. She feared them more than any other. Every *Nakaiyé* she'd ever encountered tried to kill her. No, he could not be *Nakaiyé*, she thought, as the enemy ghost had drawn no knife.

After the sun had moved into patterns of shade along the rim of the canyon's rocks, she crept out from cover and climbed up a steep gulley to a spot high on the ledges. There she settled in the shadow of a rocky overhang and scanned the country below. A hawk circled in the late afternoon sky. She watched a doe with a fawn drink from the same spring where she'd drawn her knife. She listened to the sounds around her, felt reassured at their normal patterns. Far below at the base of the mountain a plume of dust moved away and she realized it must be the warrior. She knew little of what such travel involved, but she recognized the track of a *béshnagháí* (a metal wagon), and that it could run faster than horses or men. She knew when she saw one she must travel another way.

Her Beads waited for dark, planning to descend, fill her gourd, and drink again, then find a place to rest for the night. She mentally embraced this perspective where the maze of canyons below spread out like misshapen fingers before her, a good location from which to watch. A small hash mark caught her eye on the low cliff wall and she smiled, certain some ancestor once sat exactly here, and carved the mark. Her eyes followed the metal wagon as it moved away and disappeared behind a bend in a canyon, a dissipating puff of dust rising behind it. She studied the lands below, watched the dust spread into nothing, then leaned back against the wall of the overhang with her legs straight out, and fell asleep sitting up.

CHAPTER 3

Who Was That?

Dog Mountain, *Cochise* County, Arizona

NICK MADE NO EFFORT to follow the girl, waiting to be sure she'd moved on, then scraped his feet to make noise, coughed, gathered his backpack. His curiosity piqued, he stepped over to the rock pool, shaking first one leg, then the other. He adjusted the left leg where his jeans had wrinkled up, rubbed his tingling right knee. A few smudges ruffled the earth like waves where the girl had stopped to drink. Her toes had pointed into the sand from which a narrow mark extended, unrecognizable as footprints. Standing back, he tried to work out what he'd observed.

"Oddly dressed hiker?" he asked himself. He thought of the attachment on each boot toe. What were those? The boots reached up her legs and over her knees, had folds in them. Worn and dusty leather indicated travel. He thought of the knife and how she'd drawn it from one of those boot folds. He considered she must have carried the knife against her leg. He played with that image for a moment; a shining blade against the curve of a trim calf. Too focused on legs, he admonished himself with a quick shake of his shoulders. Get a grip.

Nick peered past the shelf of the rock pool and the water that poured into the next basin.

From there water dribbled down a flat rock cascade from pool to pool, hollowed out over time. One curved wet mark at the edge of the pool below showed the only sign that anything had passed, already drying into nothingness.

He looked around at his mountain, reassured himself. This is home.

His left leg cramped and he automatically massaged his thigh. Didn't mean to scare her, he thought, as he felt the muscle relax. He shrugged his backpack onto his shoulders and turned to look again at the mountain glen. "What do you think," he said aloud to himself, "she's going to magically reappear?" He shook his head, as if to dislodge the girl's image. "Pretty though," he said and wistfully wondered where she'd come from and where she was headed.

He drew his cell phone from his chest pocket, swiped it on, thinking maybe someone at the ranch could identify a knife-in-hand woman roaming the mountain. No signal. The *Chiricahua* Mountains, famous for poor cell reception, included too many narrow ridges, deep canyons, and valleys.

He strapped the waist belt of the backpack tight, looked over the ravine thinking he'd given the girl enough time. He turned to go down the mountain, balancing his weight against the steep decline of the granite shelves. Take it slow, he reminded himself. No reason to hurry. Don't want to run into her and her knife again. He grinned, as a thought ran across his mind, thinking he wouldn't mind running into her some other time and place. Then laughed, thinking further, without her knife.

Nick carefully descended from the mountain ledge following the steep granite shelves of a game trail. His left thigh cramped twice, a reoccurring annoyance. He massaged it and moved on, his walking stick helping ease the strain. His legs carried him well, but he remained vigilant anytime he moved up or down a steep hillside.

At the bottom of the canyon, he laid his walking stick in his truck bed and leaned against the vehicle's door. He rolled up both pant legs, revealing gleaming metal prosthetics. He inspected his left leg, a below-the-knee amputation, and his right that reached mid-thigh. He checked both silicone sockets, titanium pylons, his one artificial knee joint, and found nothing troublesome beyond a little dust; wiped both legs with the bandanna from around his throat. He knew that luck had let him keep one stump below the knee, and he felt grateful to be one of the Afghan vets with the latest model of computerized knee. He used the auto drop-down step to help himself into the truck and slid behind the wheel, an expert now at operating hand controls.

He took the cell phone from his pocket, tried again to call the ranch. Still nothing.

That was a problem in the *Chiricahua* Mountains, beautiful to see but challenging to penetrate technologically, let alone by foot, horse, or vehicle. Rough country. "Nothing that can't wait," he said aloud, enjoying the comforting sound of the engine as it started up.

The girl's face and threatening knife circled in his mind. What was she doing here? His reflection came a full 360 degrees to . . . nothing. He could think of no satisfactory explanation for her presence. The dirt road twisted around boulders in the bottom of the canyon, across a dry stream bed, bumped between thick clumps of mesquite and cactus.

At one point he saw a tarantula, his first since he'd arrived, and he stopped to observe its eight-legged lumbering passage.

"Where you think you're going?" Nick addressed the tarantula. His voice did not affect the invertebrate, which continued picking its way across the road. A light breeze ruffled the dark hair on its legs as it stilted on. Nick scowled as he saw the arachnid reach the shadow of the truck and rare back on its legs, testing the air for danger. "No problem to squish you," he said, but knew he wouldn't.

Small burrow holes likely dug by tarantulas spotted the side of the road. Mating season, he reminded himself. Need to watch where I put my hands. The tarantula lowered his legs and seemed to shift its position to a hole, where Nick could see another tarantula emerging. The first tarantula moved steadily forward. "Must be a hot date," he laughed, unable to imagine approaching any eight-legged creature with the idea of mating.

The pretty girl's face returned to his thoughts. "I wonder how she deals with tarantulas." He didn't expect she'd be the kind to scream and run away.

By the time he'd made it down the mountain, he realized that the tugging heaviness around his heart had lifted. Should have shown up here earlier, he thought. Should have known it would be better here.

Pretty girl with a knife in her boot. Couldn't even dream that one up.

CHAPTER 4

Following in the Ancestor's Tracks

Chiricahua Apache Homeland

SHIWÓYÉ (GRANDMOTHER) HAD TALKED so many times about the paths, the mountains, water sources, and following the marks of the old ones scraped into the rocks, that *Biyoo'*, Her Beads, could recite them word for word. She saw the paths in her own mind, knew their names and the stories of each landscape, for she also knew that wisdom sits in places. Grandmother's stories created mind maps of the routes to the homeland, of the locations and seasons to find water and food, of the sites that offered protection and respite. *Her Beads* also knew that every place carried potential threats because the world was filled with enemies. Her encounter with the enemy ghost left her resolved to find an alternate route. The enemy ghost did not follow, a good thing. But knowing he'd seen her at all alarmed her. Her Beads knew it would bring scorn from Grandmother if she learned of it.

In fact, it would have brought scorn from all three grandmothers *Her Beads* had known in her life. Each one had led the children throughout the Blue Mountains, intent on keeping them well. But one had disappeared in a landslide of rocks over a cliff edge as she sought a safe path for the children. The second had been mauled by a bear and died from the wounds (although the children had not been harmed). The third grandmother had stayed the longest. That grandmother now cared for the children and had sent *Her Beads* on this journey. At the last council fire, after a visit by a wounded runner from the warrior's group, the old woman had called the children together. She spoke, saying, "We are the invisible people of the Blue Mountains. Our power is to be the rocks and the earth. Our warriors protect us but they have suffered many deaths and wounds in a big fight in the villages below. The messenger that came returns to fight to his death with the last few others. We've been told all of them have been injured one way or another." The old woman looked around the fire, worked her mouth back and forth as she gathered her words. "Listen closely. They can no longer protect or feed us. We must decide for ourselves how to stay alive and how to kill our enemies."

The children sat silent. Some exchanged questioning glances, but no one spoke. The fire snapped and threw out sparks. Its flames crackled in the quiet and the light danced around the gathering and lit their faces.

Her Beads's gaze cast around the circle of children, weighed their strengths and weaknesses. Of course, the oldest were the strongest and more experienced. She counted them using her fingers and toes to remember. After herself, at seventeen and the eldest, came *Naadiktaz,* It Wiggles, age twelve. He already showed leadership with the younger children, who instinctively followed his directions and advice. Her Beads knew he would probably be her husband in the future, as eldest of the boys. She sighed deeply, partly because he was still just twelve, and partly because, as a maiden who had completed her ceremonies, she dreamed of a warrior husband.

Next were two eleven-year-olds: *Zhonne,* Pretty One, whose job was to organize the children and care for the youngest (although all were expected to help one another) and *Jeeh,* Piñon Pitch, a girl so good at hunting that she taught all the others her skills. Ten-year-old *Bikécho,* His Big Toe, was It Wiggles's lieutenant. In spite of his wall-eye which sometimes made his vision untrustworthy, *His Big Toe* added practical common sense to the mix. If in doubt, the other children always sought his advice. The other ten-year-old, *In'łt'áni,* Cricket, was a girl with a voice that sounded like an enemy's metal saw in the woods. Three nine-year-olds (two boys and one girl) *Baishan,* Knife, and *Bee eshgané,* Left Hand, and *Dahsts'aa',* Strawberry, were all skilled trackers, always ready to challenge one another. Strawberry was also especially good at working with horses. *Izee,* Medicine, a girl of eight, gathered herbs, tree bark, special stones, and leaves as the group walked. She collected and carried what she found, for it seemed that in a camp of so many children, someone always had a small injury that must be tended. Two boys, *Na'iłt'oolé,* Tarantula, and *Ch'anáidił'įį,* He Hides It; and two girls, *Łichii,* Red One, and *Ch'a banné,* Big Ears, were all aged seven. The last three children were *Yaa',* Louse, age six; *Binat'izh,* Eyebrows, age five; and finally, *Gidi,* Cat, age four, youngest of the Blue Mountain People.

In spite of their tender ages, the children received Grandmother's message quietly and without complaint. No one wept, not even the youngest, at learning most of the warriors, men and women, were gone or injured. They understood that fighting to protect their homeland was what the adults were supposed to do and that sometimes they died doing it. They had all been trained to silence, courage, and patience.

The elder children understood their roll was changing.

The younger knew they were being prepared to eventually fight. Each had been placed under the tutelage of an older child who taught them the fine points of surviving high up in the mountains with Grandmother.

The old woman, her face deeply lined, stared into the fire, then raised her head and looked all around the circle of children. "It is time we leave the mountains and return to the homelands. We no longer have protection and we must go and find our place with our people."

A small murmur passed like a breeze through the group. The children otherwise kept silent.

"*Biyoo'* will be our leader and take us to the home of the ancestors."

Throughout her trip north, Her Beads practiced invisibility and walked at night. She rested concealed during the days. She felt discomfort in the darkness when she could not see, but feared the light of day even more. The *Indah*, the Living, the ones with pale eyes, and the *Nakaiyé*, Those Who Walk, the Mexicans, her people's greatest enemies, must be avoided. She herself had seen how they chose to kill her kind, the *Ndee*, the Dead, the Real People, and most especially the *Ndee Nnaahi*, the Nameless, the Invisible, who lived in the Blue Mountains. The Nameless, now reduced to a remnant, could no longer expect to make their living without the protection of the men and women warriors who'd given their lives to protect them. Now, all of those others, all, were gone.

Her Beads first felt pride when Grandmother selected her to go north. Then the reality of such a journey overwhelmed her. "Grandmother," she said respectfully, "I do not know the journey's way."

The long-ago last contact accomplished between those who still lived north in the land of the ancestors, and the Nameless Ones, resulted in bringing back one old man, a healer who knew the chants for the Sunrise ceremony to celebrate the coming of age of girls. The healer lived several years with them, long enough to oversee several girls' ceremonies in the Blue Mountains, and taught some of the chants to a younger man, before he died. Alas, the younger man was killed soon after in a raid.

Her Beads felt fortunate to have completed the ceremonies that recognized her entrance into womanhood. She was the only one among the children allowed to wear her hair in a *nah-leen* (*a* maiden's knot).

"When we find our own people," Grandmother explained,

"We will all be blessed in full ceremonies, but for now, we use what we know."

Her Beads, who'd reached the signs of womanhood, had swayed on her knees to the chant, a piece of white shell dangling on her forehead. The customs had been kept, the blessings and harmony of life protected. Yet Grandmother described the beauty of full ceremonies and the proper way of life so well that Her Beads and all the children longed to link with their own kind, to become a part of the Real People, to find their relatives. They knew only the dangers of living, the heart thumping pain of scrabbling up mountains to hide, the fear and anger against those who would steal the smallest children and kill all others.

In her youth, Grandmother told them, she had raided in the land of the ancestors with others, all now dead. On their journey to the homeland they'd found everything changed. Springs and streams had been difficult to use, sometimes enclosed within enemy *kih* (fences). Enemy houses dotted once favorite glens and canyons of the *Ndee*, the Real People. No safe place remained for raiders to conceal themselves, to rest their horses, and feast on stolen goods. The raiding party turned back toward the mountains of the Mexicans. The Nameless Ones, those who began to call themselves *Dzilthdaklizhéndé*, the Blue Mountain People, gave up the idea of locating their relatives, separate in their own future.

Thus, the girl who grew up to become the last Grandmother returned from the failed mission, and along with the other people living in the Blue Mountains, pushed farther into the Sierra Madre, forced into a final and difficult craggy retreat. One by one the warriors, men and women, gave their lives defending the children by keeping a separate existence. Some warriors died in raids. Some in accidents.

No one died of old age.

Eventually, only children and the last woman called Grandmother survived.

"This is the rule," Grandmother told the band of children many times. "One protects all. You live to honor your people."

When she repeated it and assigned Her Beads the desperate task of trying to do what the raiding party fifty years before had failed to accomplish, the girl suddenly saw the old woman as frail, weakened by her years. Grandmother, the backbone of the group, the one authority that ensured survival for those who learned well, neared the end of her life. Her Beads and a few of the older children understood that other grandmothers had come and gone before this grandmother. They never lasted long in *Her Beads's* experience, but they all taught the same way. Either a child learned the way of the people and lived, or the child did not.

"Hundreds of your people lived here," Grandmother taught the children around winter fires. "*Ussen*, the Creator, provided. There were deer. There were acorns. There were always cattle and horses to take. These are our Blue Mountains." Grandmother's lined face, calm, resolved, reflected the glow of the fire. "Now, look at one another. You are the last of the Blue Mountain People, of the Nameless Ones. When you are gone, there will be no others."

Her Beads and the others examined one another's faces. She knew each one; each one knew her. "You are the children of a great people. Your task is to praise those who bore you by surviving."

Grandmother gave instructions to *Her Beads* on four consecutive nights, the same instructions each time at the evening fire and before the group, so that all might learn the route home.

"Hear and remember: Protect your own life, in order to preserve one another." The old woman had looked around the group of children and returned to Her Beads's face. "Follow the ancestors' marks and the stories that cross the land. Wisdom sits in places. When you know the stories on the land, you know where you are and that your ancestors were there before you. It is our land and our right. Find our relatives. Deliver the message that we live and wish to grow old with our people."

Grandmother insisted they chant together the names and stories of the four most important places to gauge their journey. All four offered safe shelter. All had water. The ancestors had traveled between the places, knowing each as a safe haven, offering each child a chance for a future. Four. Her Beads and the children understood the number held magic. Every good thing came in four to the Real People. She and the others memorized the four goals, the four places, remembered the wisdom and stories on the land.

As the children sat by the home fire, Grandmother told them the time had come to leave the Blue Mountains. All carried the mind maps in their heads, brought to life when Grandmother drew the mountains, the springs, the trails, in the smoothed dirt. Grandmother called it: "Following your ancestors' tracks."

A host of dangers waited along all paths. The children listened respectfully each winter night, digested the stories whole. They listened to the last hope. When the time came that Grandmother no longer led them (and all knew life began and ended) there would be no one else to guide them.

"My time is coming," she told them. "There is no one else to help you."

Her Beads understood there would be no more grandmothers. No other adults had been seen for a circle of seasons. They all knew none survived.

The youngest children stared at Grandmother. They could not think of life without her.

"The last thing to remember," Grandmother instructed, "is places have not changed, but everything around them may have. Follow what you have learned; remember the names on the land. The *Ndee,* the Real People, are there, waiting to greet you. Our relatives, are waiting to find you."

Her Beads had left at the end of summer and walked beyond

one moon cycle. She carried extra moccasin soles as walking ate up the leather on her feet. She avoided sign left by other humans, walked great circles around places where people lived, slept away from trails. When she heard voices, she hid. She shrugged off bad memories when surprise encounters forced life and death actions. She did not like to think of those hard decisions.

Her Beads carried a buckskin bag with dried meat and ground mesquite flour hanging from her waist, but she tried not to eat from it. She made small traps from sticks and strings woven of cactus threads and her own long hair and produced a series of meals of rabbit and squirrel. No *Ndee* willingly considered eating raw meat, but when fire must not be lit, she dried meat strips on rocks. She watched for piñon trees as she walked in the high altitudes. She gathered so many piñon nuts in one place near the Canyon of Caves that she cached bags made from pieced rabbit skins, using four lines pecked in a row on a rock to mark the hidden locations for later collection. She shelled the surplus and carried it in a belt pouch as additional trail food. She knew how to live.

Grandmother warned her not to take a horse until she entered the country of the *Indah*, the Living, The Ones with Pale Eyes. The Blue Mountain People had continued to live in the mountains only because they seemed to not really be there. The *Nakaiyé*, the Mexicans, now believed all *Ndee* gone. Wiped out. Experienced in maintaining invisibility she felt shock at her discovery by the *Indah ch'iidn* (an enemy ghost). She'd instantly made her heart strong, ready to kill.

"Life is hard," Grandmother told them, "in the past for your ancestors, and now for you, the last of your people." Their ancestors had run into the Blue Mountains in order to escape the enemies, lands claimed by the Mexicans; wrongfully, of course. The Real People had been there long before them. Everyone knew the Blue Mountains, valleys, and rivers belonged to the Real People.

Eventually the ancestors of their fathers' fathers had been tracked down by their own relatives, those who led the soldiers to their secret places. The *Ndee,* low in numbers and supplies, led by Geronimo, surrendered to their brothers and uncles and cousins, knowing their relatives had chosen lives with the *Indah*, the Living, the ones with pale eyes. It was the end of most of the *Ndee* in the Blue Mountains, except for the very few who somehow managed to hide, to run, to make a living by raiding. And to remain invisible.

Her Beads's mission on behalf of the others was a supremely important task. Grandmother, last of the wise ones, the only one who knew the way home, cautioned them. "All I once knew, my family and clan, my age mates, all who chose to live free, all of them are gone." Grandmother had looked into the night sky when she said this. "You are the last," she told them, "from the smallest that must be protected and taught how to make a living, to those who know the trails, the places, and their names."

Grandmother poked a stick into the fire as the children listened; sparks spun up toward the night sky. She bent toward *Her Beads.* "Eldest Sister, you will go north. You will be our 'talk carrier' and take a white cloth to meet with those others we don't know. You will find our relatives and they will welcome you. If you do not return before first *zas* (snow)," and Grandmother paused, indicated Oldest Brother by pointing with her lips. "He will decide to follow or send another."

It Wiggles, at twelve next in line after *Her Beads* to lead, had cast his eyes respectfully down. He looked up without making eye contact, and agreed. *"Ha'ah."*

Her Beads suddenly understood that Grandmother prepared for her own demise, and created a chain of leadership order, in case *Her Beads* did not return. Only a few years before, It Wiggles had ridden on Her Beads's back, but now he was next in years to herself. Her Beads's throat tightened, aware of the weight of duty entrusted to her. She saw a flash of pride cross

It Wiggles's face that almost immediately turned into a worry line across his forehead.

Grandmother's words replayed in Her Beads's thoughts as she recognized the canyon with the beautiful rock pools as one of her memory places. She knew she drew near to the hidden canyon now, perhaps only two days. She knew that soon she would find the safe cave of the ancestors. Perhaps there would be stored things she could use to help her journey. She carefully left sign at each resting place to guide It Wiggles should she not return to lead the children herself.

She thought through her actions again in meeting the enemy ghost. She'd escaped him, shown herself a threat. His eyes had widened in surprise and narrowed with interest, rather than fear. One thing kept turning over in her mind. She didn't understand the enemy ghost's reaction as she held out her knife. She'd wanted him to know she stood ready to use it, that she would not allow herself to be overcome without a fight. Certainly, he understood that as he did not threaten her further. But something else had happened. A smile had played across his face.

Her Beads's mind had turned over and over one question since that meeting: Why would an enemy ghost smile?

CHAPTER 5

The Dream Demands

Ruidoso, New Mexico

ALBERT SILENTMAN GULPED DOWN the last swallow of coffee and picked up the phone on its fifth ring, just before it flipped over to the answering machine.

"All Clans Apache Museum. Albert Silentman speaking."

Albert, founder of the museum just outside of Ruidoso, New Mexico, occupied multiple jobs, including director, tour leader, publicist, cashier, and custodian. It also gave him a community seat on the *Mescalero* Tribal Council representing native business.

"*Dagot'é!*" (Hello!) a clear voice said in Apache, "What the heck took you so long?" Sam Charley, tribal council elder and fellow Marine vet sounded annoyed.

"*Dagot'é*! It's early! Hardly had my first cup of java."

Sam Charley's voice rattled. "I had a dream."

Albert knew all about Sam's dreams. He'd been listening to Sam's dreams all of his life. Sam's power was to dream, and through the dreams, to protect. Sam had even dreamed Albert safely through his time as a Marine in Iran.

"Alright *shiłt'ii* (my friend). You want to wait a minute more? I just opened and somebody's coming in."

"*Ha'ah*" (Yes). Sam heard voices as Albert's receiver clunked lightly to rest on a countertop. He listened to Albert's tinny voice welcome customers.

"*Dagot'é*! Welcome to the *Mescalero* Apache All Clans Apache Museum!"

Sam listened further, picturing Albert as he swiped a credit card, issued tickets, and provided a small map of museum displays, chatting as he worked. He heard Albert direct the family into the small room identified with a homemade sign: Theatre (Occupancy: 15). The swell of drums and a lone ceremonial singer's voice indicated someone had pushed the button that began the video.

"Okay. I'm back. Nice family from Ohio." Albert lowered his voice. "They wanted to know, looking straight at me, where they could see a real Apache Indian."

Sam couldn't help but snort.

"I told them they were looking at an original, red-blooded, all-American Apache. I even turned sideways so they could see my profile."

Sam began to laugh.

"The guy says: 'It's fine to tease the tourists, buddy, but you look more like a Marine than an Apache.' I couldn't believe it! I told him: 'I AM a Marine!'"

At this Sam laughed so hard he wheezed. "*Da'izháa'!*" (Stop right there!). Aww, Lima Charlie," Loud and Clear. "You make me laugh. I'm wiping tears from my eyes."

Albert took a deep breath, said in a firm voice, "Nobody's allowed to insult the Corps or the *Chiricahua.*"

"Semper Fi and *dá'áiyee* (correct), my friend." The rustle of a folded paper whispered through the telephone. "I got something to read to you," Sam repeated.

"Damn right it's correct." Albert shifted his weight on his stool. "You know, I could probably read it for myself and actually still take care of my job."

"It's short," Sam said, dismissing Albert's complaint. The rustling newspaper sound came again. "Lorraine found this article in last Sunday's *New Mexico Review*. Pull up your stool against the wall and listen."

Albert, already leaning against the wall, said, "Ready when you are."

"O.K. Jarhead. The headline reads: 'Vigilantes ready to fight wild Apaches believed vanished in Mexico.' Quite a title, eh? Came out of a newspaper in Chihuahua City, Mexico. Pretty good translation, too." Sam sniffed.

"Ah, the City of Mules, as our ancestors would say." Albert's voice remained unimpressed.

"Not so many mules now as in the good old days!" Sam paused while Albert laughed.

"Those ancient ones really knew how to make a living."

"That they did," Sam agreed. "Maybe still do. Listen," and he read aloud without waiting for Albert's agreement.

"'Dateline Chihuahua City, State of Chihuahua, Mexico. Sierra Madre ranchers, miners, and farming colonies in two of Mexico's northern states are threatening to organize bands of vigilantes and track a group of Bronco Apaches previously believed to have vanished early in the last century. The threat follows efforts by law enforcement agencies to investigate a string of raids at remote locations scattered across the Sierra Madre in the states of Chihuahua and Sonora. Blas Lopez, owner of the Rio de Almas ranch in Sonora, said, 'If the police are going to ignore this, we have to take matters into our own hands.'"

"Sounds angry." Albert said. He bent his head to one side and his neck popped.

"Steam coming out of his ears, friend," Sam cleared his throat, continued.

"'According to police, property owners on both sides of the mountains have reported losses of livestock, food, and other supplies in past years. Previous losses were locally attributed to an increase in mountain lion and bear populations. However, law enforcement officials stated thefts in the isolated region are more likely due to drug traffickers.'"

"Sounds like everybody's got an idea," Albert crossed one leg and leaned an elbow onto a knee.

Sam's voice went up an octave. "There's more!"

"'There are no Bronco Apaches left,' Officer Yolanda Gutierrez, spokesperson for the Regional Provincial Police in Chihuahua, stated. 'Most renegade Apaches surrendered with Geronimo before 1900. A few were left behind, but haven't been reported since the Second World War. Vigilantes risk prosecution themselves, and must not interfere with official investigations.'"

"Like she'd know!" Albert cleared his throat. "She's got her finger out there shaking it in everybody's faces." Albert assumed a haughty look and waved a finger as if Sam could see him.

A note of disgust crept into Sam's reading voice. "Listen to this! Believe it or not this is a Mexican talking! Dr. Pedro Fierro, director of the Chihuahua Native People's Assistance Association. Never heard of him or the group, have you?"

"*Dah*" (No).

"This Dr. Fierro says, 'No one believes there are any wild Apache in the mountains today.'" Sam inhaled deeply and stopped reading. "'Course he didn't ask us! They never talk to us. Why talk to Apache?'"

"*Ha'ah*," Albert agreed.

Sam read on: "He says, 'People of the Sierra Madre are bound to cause problems if they use firearms. Who knows who they'll kill? We still haven't learned from the past. We're not living in the 1930s now. We're not following Francisco Fimbres into the mountains to kill off every Apache ghost left. If these vigilantes persist, a modern retaliatory bloodbath could be imminent.'"

"Then it says: 'See pg. 11 for a history timeline.' But I think we know enough about that; about Fimbres chasing the Broncos after they killed his wife and took his kid, and the expeditions scouting with airplanes, and stealing kids."

Albert's attention broke as he sucked in a chest full of air. He hadn't realized he was holding his breath. "Uncle Sam's Misguided Children, for sure, *shiłt'ii (my friend)*! Do you think some of *Ndee Nnaahi'*, those 'Nameless Ones', could still be there?"

"I've always wondered about them. My father told stories of the way they lived. He used to call them the Invisible People."

"Remember those so-called 'wolf children' in the Sonoran villages? What year was that?" Albert paused, tracing his memory back. "I remember I was still in high school."

"Yeah, I was just back from 'Nam when it happened, so it was about '69. The Mexican villagers tried to capture a bear and left food out. They trapped two little kids instead. Maybe six or seven years old, crazy wild and hungry, all scratched up and dirty."

"What happened to those kids?"

"My Dad used to say we did wrong that nobody from *Mescalero* traveled to Mexico to see if they were our kids, our people. There I was fighting on the other side of the world and here my own people might still have been fighting to survive in our own backyard." Sam sighed again.

"Nobody went down to find out?"

"Dad said by the time people thought about going down, the kids were gone. They were taken to different villages, and later disappeared. The Mexicans looked for 'em, but couldn't find 'em. Poof! Gone."

"Invisible people." Albert chewed on his lip and watched the tourist family as they left the little homemade theater. In the doorway the big brother pinched the back of his little brother's neck. Neither parent seemed to notice the pinch nor the ensuing yelp. "What are you thinking, my friend?"

"I'm thinking it's time to teach the grandkids about the ancestors, maybe take a look down there and see what turns up. Want to come, Jarhead?"

Albert considered the proposal, leaned back in his chair,

and watched as the two boys wrestled their way out of the film room. The bigger boy flipped the smaller one onto his stomach and sat on him.

"Hold on, Sam." He laid the phone down, stepped over to the struggling boys, glared at them each in turn with an icy eye. Meanwhile the father returned, grabbed the boys by their collars, and marched them out the front door.

Back at the counter Albert retrieved the receiver. "You still there, Gyrene?" he asked.

"Where else would I be? You want to go to the Land of the Ancestors after the week-end?"

"To Mexico?"

"Nope. You gotta have passports now to get into the Sierra Madre. Too much trouble. Just back to the Stronghold and the Land of Standing Up Rocks; back to the homeland. I want to see if anyone's left a message."

"Like who would leave a message?" Albert asked.

Sam sounded thoughtful. "Well, that's kind of the point. You know what the old people say."

Albert chuckled. "Man, Devil Dog, you ARE the old people now. What do YOU say?"

Sam sniffed. "The old ones said: 'Never go back.' But that was when the ranchers and miners were still saying they'd kill every Apache who showed up in *Cochise* County." His voice took on intensity. "You know how nasty the fighting got down there."

Albert's eyes flicked past the counter and onto a black-and-white photo display on the entry wall. Several of old Tombstone, Arizona's, most famous photographs taken by C. S. Fly showed historic Apaches squinting without expression into cameras from over a century before. "You think the news article is real? Maybe some of those Broncos are still in the Blue Mountains in Mexico? It's an awful long time."

He stood and walked around the counter to study the photos. Apache faces stared flatly back without expression. The men wore moccasins that came up to the knee with leather discs at the toes, bare thighs beneath looped lengths of cloth between the legs. All held weapons. The women's skirts were long, their hair shoulder length cut uneven. One's nose had been cut off (an indication of infidelity), and Albert rubbed his own nose as he looked at the picture. The people in the photos all stared piercingly, directly back at the viewer. Albert felt like they were studying him. "How could they be there anymore?" he asked Sam.

"You're looking at their photos right now, aren't you! 'Course they could stay alive. Couldn't you?"

Albert thought of his time in Marine survival training, his assignments in the Middle East. "I expect I could, but the question is, would I want to?"

"Think of it this way," Sam said. "When you don't know anything else, why wouldn't you? In a way, those Nameless Ones were just the same as Marines, trained by our own people. The first Devil Dogs."

"I agree with you on that," Albert said. "Any of those old-time warriors would make the best Marines ever."

"Well, they're who we came from. Why wouldn't they still be there, knowing what they know about survival?" Sam cleared his throat. "There is a place in *Cochise* County, not so far from Tombstone, a place every Apache used to know they could leave sign. If we go check we should be able to tell if anyone's left a message in the old homeland."

Albert stretched his neck and shoulders, returned to his seat behind the counter. "That would be something, wouldn't it?"

"It would." Sam Charley's voice softened. "I did have a dream, and I am thinking maybe it's real." He paused. "Then again, maybe not. When I read the news article, my friend, it matched my dream."

"Tell me."

"I saw riders and walkers in my dream. I saw *dikohe*

(apprentice warriors) who wiped out tracks. I saw a group of warriors moving north in a faraway place with sharp mountains and deep canyons. It seemed like I knew it. They had a leader, young." Sam's voice continued steady, calm. "I know this sounds strange; I stood right there in my dream on the side of a trail." Sam swallowed and his voice thinned. "They passed by me wearing old time clothes, carrying food in pouches on their belts, blankets tied across their chests, braided rawhide ropes around their waists. The leader looked right at me and I had to look down and give respect. In my dream I saw I wore moccasins and deerskin leggings, too, dressed for the raiding trail, just like them. When I looked up the leader beckoned me to follow." Sam's voice stopped. He swallowed hard. "She said, 'Yushdé (Come). Náhikah (We are coming back).'"

Albert's head snapped back in surprise. "She? A woman?" Albert asked, and his mouth hung open. In *Chiricahua* tradition, women looked down in respect to men. Not the other way around.

"I know. I know." Sam sighed. "A warrior woman." He was silent for several moments. "Now, I am saying to you, *shiłt'ii*, what she said to me. '*Yushdé*' (Come)."

CHAPTER 6

Back to a Future

Zig Zag Trail, Blue Mountains— *Chiricahua* Apache Homeland

WHEN *NAADIKTAZ*, IT WIGGLES, returned from hunting to the shelters above the Zig Zag Trail at *Juh's*, Long Neck's, Stronghold, the first thing he noted was the worry in the faces of the two young scouts. The boys waited, hidden in the shadows just below where the trail peaked on top, already skilled at avoiding a silhouette. One of them bounded up and ran to the shelter. He returned immediately with *Zhonne*, Pretty One, following.

Pretty One reached his side quickly. "It's Grandmother. She fell on the rocks and cannot rise."

"Where is she hurt?"

"We had to carry her to the shelter. Her hips and legs seem broken."

"Can she speak?"

"*Ha-ah* (Yes). She wants to see you. She's very tired, brother. She has pain." Pretty One watched as It Wiggles stepped up to the pine flat from the trail. "Also, brother, there were the sounds of men and dogs all day at the bottom of the hills. We could hear them making wood." It Wiggles nodded and started toward the shelter. Pretty One held out her hands for the three rabbits that dangled at his waist and carried them away.

"Is there more meat?" he asked her retreating back.

29

"Ground Squirrels. The hunters have all returned." She stopped and looked back at him. "Except for our two younger sisters, all are here."

It Wiggles nodded. Two girls had left the day before on a raiding mission. Pitch, age nine, tasked with training seven-year-old Big Ears, aimed to collect supplies while practicing raiding skills. He hoped the girls would bring back something good to eat, but raiding consisted of as much training as plundering. The Blue Mountain People must be careful to maintain invisibility, their destiny relied on it. Even when they found something good, it must seem like either nothing was taken, or if gone, taken by an obvious culprit, forest creatures such as mountain lions, bears, or badgers.

It Wiggles entered the shelter, pushed aside the tanned hide used as a door, announced softly, "Grandmother, I am here."

Grandmother's small form, covered in blankets, stirred on the ground. The old woman groaned, then asked in a low, breathy voice, *"Shizhaazhé* (my son), is there meat for my children?" She called all the children of the Blue Mountain People her own.

"Ha-ah, Grandmother. My sister prepares it now." He squatted beside her pallet, asked, "Where are you injured?"

"I fell too far, too hard, my son. My legs are smashed." Her words slurred into a groan. "Now you must save the little ones. Follow Eldest Sister." Her voice rasped with strain.

It Wiggles settled on the rush strewn floor, knowing Grandmother's reference to Eldest Sister meant Her Beads. The group used kinship terms for daily face-to-face interactions, even though most did not necessarily share blood relationships. Otherwise, a nickname served if a name must be used. Real names, spoken aloud only in ceremonies, lost spiritual power each time spoken, and also might invite attention from the dead or witches. It Wiggles had never heard Grandmother's real name. He studied Grandmother's age-worn face. "When, Grandmother?"

"K'adi" (Right now). She raised one trembling hand in

emphasis, her face damp with fever. "You are no longer *dikohe*. You are a warrior."

The boy's eyes gleamed. In the world of the ancestors, boys of twelve worked as *dikohe*, apprentices, until sixteen or seventeen, sometimes older. It Wiggles kept his eyes on the ground out of respect, but his heart surged, pleased; then receded. He wanted to be ready, but at twelve, he did not feel ready. He did not want Grandmother to travel to the Happy Place, and touched her hand, gulped. "Grandmother, we cannot live without you."

She attempted to speak. "The children ..." but the pain overcame her, interfered with her words. Pretty One pushed inside the deerskin used as a door and entered the shelter. She carried a small gourd dipper with water. "*Ná*" (Here), she said to Grandmother, as if to a small child, and held the gourd to the old woman's mouth.

It Wiggles and Pretty One remained silent as Grandmother swallowed.

The old woman rested, ran her tongue over her lips. "The little ones need not mourn me." She stopped and took a few deep breaths. "The journey is everything. You will be safe as long as you stay invisible." She blinked once, "*Dołkáh! K'adi!*" (You go! Right now!) Then closed her eyes and slept.

The two young people watched Grandmother's chest rise and fall in shallow waves, glanced at one another, understood she'd given them a final instruction. None of the children clearly remembered other adults that once occupied their world, except for Her Beads, the eldest. Pretty One sometimes dreamed of a smiling face that she could not quite recall when awake. It Wiggles remembered the day someone had left him alone, afraid and hungry, threatened with death if he made a sound. He remembered the sound of someone slowly parting the bushes around him, to reveal the lined face of Grandmother. He could remember no other adult face. That was all either of them knew of their lives before. Grandmother, purposefully isolated with the children by the warrior men and women, had eventually become the only remaining adult. Grandmother raised and trained each one, used the older children to help with the younger ones. Grandmother had saved them all.

Pretty One raised her eyes to It Wiggles, her forehead lined. "We will do as Grandmother says." It Wiggles's words confirmed Pretty One's unspoken question.

"*Ha'ah.*" Like all of the children, Pretty One understood Grandmother's wisdom. Of course, they would do as she bade them.

It Wiggles left the shelter, taking note of the sun's failing light. He beckoned several children to follow and moved across the flat mesa to where a corral stood. No horses mingled there, all lost or eaten. He instructed the helpers to assist him in removing the poles and rails. The children moved all of the wood to the side where it could be concealed in brush.

Pretty One sent a child about the camp to quietly call in the others. Youngest sister, tiny *Gidi,* Cat, delivered the message in a quick loop around the camp, voice low. All of the children, even a four-year-old, knew to keep voices soft, whether at play or work. The big iron kettle, which had been brought on the back of a mule to the top of the mesa by their ancestors, bubbled with a mixture of rabbit and ground squirrel stew, wild potatoes, and roots. As each child arrived at the firepit one of the older girls issued a portion, along with a flat bread made from stolen corn and collected grass seeds, baked on a griddle stone. Only a half dozen gourd bowls existed and the children shared the bowls.

Darkness descended. A faint light flickered from the cook fire deep in its pit. As the children finished their food, they waited patiently. No games began. No voices called out or laughed in happy play. Grandmother had taught them all the value of a noiseless existence.

When It Wiggles stood, the others sat, eyes on the ground, respectful.

"Brothers and sisters, today the *Nakaiyé* were heard in the valley below. When we hear them near, we move. Tomorrow we travel north." He looked at the group, all younger than his own twelve years, and counted them. Only fourteen children in camp plus the two girls, Pitch and Big Ears, away raiding, plus Her Beads gone two weeks ahead to lay the trail north. He counted them carefully on his hands. Three hands plus two. Seventeen children in all watched over by Grandmother. Once there had been hundreds of people, *Ndee Nnaahi*, the Nameless Ones, the last of the free.

"We will leave before the sun rises. Everyone must have their food bags tied at the waist, blankets on their shoulders. All will carry a water gourd. Older Sister will lead the group." All eyes turned toward Pretty One. "Elder Brother will scout ahead." He exchanged a nod with his first lieutenant, *Bikécho*, His Big Toe. "You two," and he looked at the two young boys who'd stood watch at the top of the Zig Zag Trail, "will be my *dikohe*." Both boys, *Baishan,* Knife, and *Bee eshgané*, Left Hand, sat a little taller. "You will follow the others with me and wipe out the tracks."

The two boys stared at the ground respectfully and agreed together, "*Ha-ah.*"

The fire crackled. The sharp points of stars in the black sky stared down at the small group. "We are the last of the true *Ndee*, the Dead. But we know there are others in the north. Grandmother has taught us well and we'll find them."

A smaller child snuffled and leaned into the big girl next to her. It Wiggles looked carefully to ensure the child did not cry, for that had been forbidden. "If we follow the rules of Grandmother and the will of *Ussen*, we'll live. We'll find our relatives." It Wiggles looked around the circle of children and his eyes stopped at *Yaa'*, Louse. "Little Sister, tell us how the ancestors moved across the land to make their living."

At age six Louse had two black spaces where her front teeth

had been. Her pink tongue probed the space between her teeth before she spoke. Her hair reached her shoulders and created a frowsy halo in the firelight. "They moved high on the mountains like a *shash (bear)*. When the enemy didn't see them, the enemy couldn't hunt them. They slept ready to fight. They left no tracks."

The Nameless Ones respected the way *shash* moved and fought and the way they lived often illustrated clever ways to survive.

"*Enjuh*" (Good). It Wiggles stepped closer to Louse and rested an approving hand on her shoulder for a few seconds. Louse's face displayed no outward expression, but her eyes beamed.

It Wiggles looked around the circle of children. "Everyone knows the Blue Mountain trails and where to hide. If there's trouble we'll meet at the first safe place, in the Canyon of Caves."

His gaze landed on His Big Toe. "Where's the second safe place at the end of the Blue Mountains?"

His Big Toe, ten years old with a lazy eye that looked sideways, flashed up his good eye at It Wiggles. "The second safe place is at White Rocks. It's a good place to hide horses."

"Perhaps we'll be riding by the time we get to that safe place," It Wiggles said. "We'll need horses to travel fast like the ancestors. Otherwise, we'll be walking a long time."

The circle of children agreed softly, "*Ha'ah*." All knew to keep their voices from bouncing against mountains and rocks.

"Older Brother will plan a way to get horses after the White Rocks."

His Big Toe's good eye snapped up with a pleased expression, understanding his assignment.

"Only Grandmother and Eldest Sister have traveled farther north and we must all know the path." It Wiggles let his eyes roam about the circle, stopping on the faces of the group's youngest members. "You small ones will memorize the way at our night fires and we will tell the stories many times." He paused, saw the faces of the children showed a studied intent. It Wiggles felt his heart swell with pride at their focus. "Because no one must ever be lost. If you know the way, you can always find us."

Gidi, Cat, sat, teeth clenched in concentration. *Binat'izh,* Eyebrows, a year older and seated next to *Cat,* patted her knee just once. *Cat* relaxed, looked up at It Wiggles. He cleared his throat and continued.

"The ancestors knew every spring, every rock. That's why we know the path. We'll make our living from the land. Beyond White Rocks we cross a plain to the Spring That Always Flows, where the canyon beyond is called It Hides the Way, and is marked by four big stones. Follow it to the valley and cross west at night into The Land of Standing Up Rocks, the third safe place. After the Two Tails Mountains are seen, the paths all go to Water Standing. The water is good, and it is a place where the ancestors left messages for one another. We will search for messages, but it is near where the soldiers live, so we will stop in the valley beyond at the fourth safe place Where They Ground Seeds. You will know it by the many grinding rocks."

Cat, her eyes growing heavy, had leaned against Eyebrows's shoulder. Others already blinked their own eyes to keep them open.

"That's enough tonight," It Wiggles decided. "*Enjuh,*" and the group echoed in soft voices, "Good!" and stood up, then dispersed to find their sleeping places.

Pretty One woke It Wiggles before dawn by tossing a pebble softly on his chest. He leapt up quickly, hand on his knife. He saw her face was wet. "Grandmother is gone."

He looked into the starry night, and bit the inside of his lip. "That's the way things are."

"Will we delay our journey?"

"*Dah* (No). We must begin the journey." He thought of Grandmother's words a few hours before. "We'll leave her bones where others will not find her. Bring some digging sticks."

He and Pretty One walked out to the area of the horse corral. They both knew they would not follow the custom of finding a rock cleft and covering the burial with stones. They did not want to upset the smaller children, and they had no time. It Wiggles and Pretty One used their sticks to scrape a shallow grave in the loose, trampled earth.

Pretty One went back to the shelter to complete the things necessary at death. It Wiggles heard her quietly singing a prayer song, and knew she would soon wash Grandmother's face and tie the best of their blankets about the body with hide rope.

Meanwhile It Wiggles opened a hole in the north side of the shelter. He broke the dried mud away and pulled the dead branches and fibers from the frame, widening the opening with his arms and pushing the bottom of the frame down with his feet. Spirits of the dead always released themselves toward the north.

"Are you ready?" It Wiggles asked.

Neither wished to touch a dead body, even of someone well loved. The spirits of the dead, always angry at being sent away from the living, meant no one knew what those spirits might do. But Grandmother herself had told them the rules of the old times had changed to help them in the new times. No one of the *Ndee*, the Dead, feared death as much as they feared the *Indah*, the Living, and the *Nakaiyé*, Those Who Walk.

"She will not harm us," It Wiggles pronounced in a confident tone.

"*Ha'ah*. Still, it is difficult to do." Pretty One's voice rose in a soft blessing chant for protection.

At the end of her singing they hesitated before lifting the slight body through the rough opening. It Wiggles went first through the hole, then pulled as Pretty One pushed. They carried the wrapped body to the corral area and placed it in the earth, scooped dirt over it, patting it down with hands and feet. Pretty One took a pinch of *hoddentin* (cattail pollen), from a pouch hanging on a leather cord about her neck, and made a faint line between the living and the dead. She chanted a prayer four times, facing a different direction with each repetition, then lightly tossed a pinch to the worlds above and below.

Grandmother, do not linger here.

Grandmother, travel quickly to the Happy Place.

Grandmother, we'll follow your teachings.

Grandmother, we'll find the way to our relatives.

When Pretty One finished, It Wiggles used a branch to brush away all evidence of the shallow grave, and the yellow pollen disappeared as it mixed with earth.

"Grandmother," he added in a whisper, "Do not be angry you are gone."

Hearing the whisper Pretty One smiled. "Hear us, Grandmother."

It Wiggles had already sent His Big Toe at dawn to scout ahead. It wasn't until the group stood ready to leave that the smallest child, Cat, asked, "Where is Grandmother?"

It Wiggles's voice floated out calmly. "She travels before us, preparing the way."

Cat's head turned in confusion to Pretty One. All knew that Grandmother had been sick.

Pretty One smiled at Cat reassuringly, answered her question by using the age-old phrase that gave them all a sense of routine. "May it soon be usefully so."

"What about the raiders?" Left Hand piped. "They will not be back for many days. Should someone stay to help them follow?"

It Wiggles cast his eyes at the early morning sun and thought of Pitch and Big Ears. "They will follow our trail sign. If they don't know how to find us, they are not Real People."

The first group stepped away from the Zig Zag Trail and down a slope into one of the many canyons that had protected them for so long. Each older child was responsible for a younger child. Each younger child followed their protector carefully. Those who had not learned the rules of life did not live long among the *Ndee Nnaahi*, the Nameless Ones. And they all wanted to live.

It Wiggles waited until the group, Pretty One leading, set off from the plateau and began their descent into the first canyon before he set the two *dikohe*, Knife and Left Hand, to the business of creating invisibility for anyone who might come after. As they dragged away the remains of their shelters, the two boys used dried branches to erase footprints. It Wiggles carefully selected a few live coals and placed them in a small woven container, lined with dried mud. He then finished scattering the cooking fire, burying the blackened, dead embers, ready to assist the boys with destroying the last shelter, the one where Grandmother had lived and slept.

Distress appeared on the faces of the two *dikohe* as they approached. "Eldest brother, are we to tear down the last shelter?" The voice of Left Hand, sounded stricken.

It Wiggles looked up, repeated what all three boys knew. "Our task is to be invisible."

Left Hand's voice squeezed into a high pitch. "*Ha'ah*, but there is a hole torn in the north side."

It Wiggles turned toward the ruined shelter's side. All knew a hole in the north side of a shelter meant a dead body had been removed, delivered to the gods on its journey away from life.

"*Ha-ah*. That one is gone." It Wiggles did not name her, for that might invite a lurking spirit to return. He passed the coals in the woven container to the boys. "Burn the shelter. That should send any spirit away."

Neither boy moved.

"How will we cleanse ourselves?" Knife asked, his eyes wide.

"It cannot be helped," It Wiggles stated flatly, though he knew the lack of cleansing might bring illness or madness. Or death. "That one taught us the ways of the ancestors and that sometimes we cannot follow the old rules. Whatever happens to you will happen to me first." His face and manner stayed steady. "It has been ordered and it will be so."

The dry hut blazed up quickly in the predawn. It outlined itself brightly against the backdrop of the mountains, where peaks reached up like teeth to bite a chunk of dark sky. The three stood back, and the two younger boys nervously watched the flames consume the hut. When the fire burned down, they used branches to brush the charred remains away. They walked across the small plateau checking one last time for evidence of any sort left behind.

"*Enjuh*," It Wiggles said, and thought to himself that Grandmother would find no fault in their work. He beckoned the boys toward the trail. There he left a trail sign message at one side of the path for the two raiders, an irregular line of stones and a small clutch of woven grasses that meant: "This way."

The three boys took turns at the last place in line, brushing out their own footprints.

Pretty One must be setting a fast pace, It Wiggles thought, as the three moved quickly along the trail without catching up to the group. He followed, pleased, when Knife, noting an uneven cluster of four pine cones, turned into a side canyon moving east.

No words passed between the three boys. They kept silent when moving, constantly aware of trail sign, watchful for food sources, aware of trail markings where animals or humans had passed, wiping out their own passage, leaving a blank trail.

Invisible.

CHAPTER 7

Rancho What?

Diaz Ranch (alias Republic of Dog Mountain Ranch), *Cochise* County, Arizona

THE DAY NICK RETURNED home he'd driven south from the I-10 through Hidalgo County from Lordsburg, New Mexico, to the south border of the Animas Valley. His excitement had grown as he neared the landmarks that defined his youth. Released from the hospital only a few weeks ago, it seemed already like years in the past. All Nick thought of was returning home. He knew he'd feel better on the ranch than anywhere else. He'd felt certain he'd find his purpose, figure out why he'd survived.

Nick's brand-new diesel truck, a three-quarter ton, four-wheel drive, factory built to his exact needs, ran smoothly down the highway. The browns and yellows of natural valley grasses mixed with green shoots creating a soft palette of color against the blue and gray of the Peloncillo Mountains that divided southeast Arizona from southwest New Mexico. He rolled a window down and deeply inhaled the native scents of his childhood.

He passed the turn off to Skeleton Canyon, the not-so-secret historic shortcut of choice used by Apache resistors, outlaws, cowboys, and posses that cut through the mountain range into Arizona. He thought of the monument commemorating Geronimo's final surrender at the head of the canyon on the mountains' other side, and of how the territory remained physically unchanged, filled with a jagged jumble of peaks and cliffs. He'd drunk in the mountains' familiar silhouettes, felt a calmness settle around him and a returning sense of joy. At the bottom of the range he'd cut onto an unpaved road that skimmed along beside the border with Mexico. He'd noted the border fence had been built higher and that metal units on folding stilts looking much like wild game stands now provided heightened views into Mexico.

A government truck with U.S. Border Patrol insignia came up fast behind him, trailing a plume of dust from where it left the paved highway. The red lights on its cab revolved and sparked into the pulse that indicated, "Pull over."

Nick watched in his rearview mirror as a uniformed man stepped from the truck and approached his vehicle. In the quiet of the high desert he heard the man's footfalls tramp softly. He saw a second officer waited in the truck.

"Good morning," the officer said, "Driver's license, please," and Nick handed him his identification. "Well," the officer said, looking up after studying the card, "I guess you've forgotten your old friends."

Nick looked up into the dark glasses, puzzled.

"Beneficio Cortez, Nick." And he grinned a wide, bright smile, at the same time removing the glasses.

"Benny?" Nick could not contain his elation. He opened his door, but Benny leaned hard against it. Nick pushed, still smiling. "What's up, man?"

"Let's not give my partner a heart attack. We got procedures. Hold on." He stepped back from the truck and signaled to his own vehicle. A moment later a second officer stood smiling. "This is Juan Fuentes, not from around here."

"Actually, hate to admit it," Fuentes said, sticking his hand up to window level, "Phoenix, born and raised."

Nick extended his hand, shook, and asked, "Now can I get out?"

Standing beside the truck, Benny and Nick shared an abrazo, pounded one another on the back.

"So how long you been back?" Benny asked.

"This is it, man. I'm just coming in."

"Okay. We're going to clear you through, but these unpaved roads can be trouble to drive. Mostly only two kinds of traffic. Us," and he jerked a thumb toward himself and his partner, "and them," and he threw an extended arm out that took in the entire area beyond the border fence into Mexico. "We're running the line right now, on duty, so we'll have to get together later. I want to hear everything about what happened. You know you made the hometown paper!"

Nick nodded his head. "Yup. Tia Elena sent me the issue." Jeez, he thought to himself. I hope that's not going to be all anybody wants to hear about.

Benny wrote something on a slip of paper and handed it to Nick. "Cell number. Doesn't work out here. You leave a message and I'll get back, okay?"

The radio in the Border Patrol truck crackled with static, followed by words.

Fuentes reached into the truck, listened, then lifted out the mike, and called to his partner. "Benny, possible problem in C sector."

"Man, I hate C sector. Full of cholla. Got to go, buddy. Damn, I'm glad to see you."

The Border Patrol truck pulled away, looped on back toward the paved road, and sped off.

Nick continued without further interruption, returned to pavement outside of the small town of San Enebro, New Mexico, named for the juniper scrubs that peppered the area. When he stopped by his aunt's neatly painted yellow-and-white house no one answered his knock. He scrawled a note saying he'd stopped and would see her at the ranch, ended the note with "Good to be home!"

He felt a kind of triumph. His world was finally coming back together. He'd get past the hometown pity and life would begin to make sense again.

A half hour after crossing into Arizona and the San Bernadino Valley he turned the truck onto a well-used dirt road at the base of the *Chiricahua* Mountains. Five minutes farther Nick rolled to a stop, trailing a plume of dust, at the Diaz ranch's main entrance. He leaned his chest against the driver's wheel, peered at the gate through his windshield and shook his head, perplexed.

A collection of mostly handwritten signs had accumulated along a shiny new steel tube cattle gate. A black wrought iron arch stretched high, with a decorative cut-out shield containing the letters RDM superimposed on the outline of a mountain. The same design in black on a yellow and red flag snapped in the breeze at the side of the gate.

The biggest sign in the middle of the gate presented the name: Republic of Dog Mountain. Below it a smaller sign declared: "This Republic is an independent nation, with a ratified constitution and elected leader. Long live the Republic! Proclaimed by Vicente Diaz Jr., President for Life."

Across the gate an assortment of various sized signs announced: "Absolutely No Trespassing," "Patrolled and protected by Smith & Wesson," "Rattlesnakes Abound Here," "Entrance by Permission of the President Only," and "Attack Dogs Loose on Property. Stay Out!"

Nick snorted at the last one. There'd always been dogs at the ranch, a collection of strays, friendly and happy to find food waiting daily in the stables. He was unaware any of them had ever attacked anything except their food dishes.

All the signs, Nick thought, seemed like the kind of thing a real nut might put up. Maybe a survivalist. A padlock joined a chain around the gate and gatepost and Nick drew his cell phone out. "What the hell?" he asked the voice that answered. "This is Nick at the gate. What's going on with all these signs out here?"

Tomás had arrived in a funnel of dust a quarter of an hour later. "Oh man, Nicky, I never been so happy to see nobody!" Barely sixteen, he flashed a brilliant smile, ear to ear. Born ten years behind his brothers, Tomás had eagerly attached himself to his cousin Nick from toddlerhood. Ignored by the two older cousins, Nick and Tomás grew up together, pursuing adventures.

They shared a powerful and warm abrazo. Nick pounded him on the back, and Tomás punched Nick on both shoulders. "I been waiting for you!" Tomás almost danced in delight, as he threw jabs at Nick.

Nick backed against the gate for balance, part of his recent physical therapy strategy to protect his equilibrium. Happy to see his young cousin, he stood grinning ear to ear, gestured toward the signs. "What is this? Do I need a passport?"

Tomás's fancy cowboy–booted feet shuffled in the dust of the road, and he shrugged. *"Quién sabe, primo?"* (Who knows?) "I'm just glad you're back."

"C'mon Tomás. What's this about?" Nick lifted an arm that gestured toward the fence.

"Ah, Nicky, I don't know. Vicente did this. I think it's loco, but don't make fun of it. He gets mad." Tomás stood, one hip cocked, one hand on the opposite hip.

Nick recognized the stance of his father and uncle from childhood. He thought to himself, I'm really home with my own people. He nodded his head, listening as Tomás continued. "Wait. Say that again."

Tomás changed his stance to the other hip. "He says we're the country between Mexico and the United States now. I didn't even know what a republic is. That's next year. Civics is for seniors."

Tomás's earnest explanation made Nick smile.

"No, don't laugh. He says it's our own country. He says he can do what he wants because he's the president. I don't know, what do you think?"

Nick scanned each sign again, shaking his head, wondering

if Vicente had gone crazy. Vicente, the middle brother, had always been the least predictable of his cousins, the most prone to practical jokes. But a republic? "Who's in his republic?" Nick swung his gaze from sign-reading to Tomás. "If he's president, who elected him?"

Tomás raised his arms in exasperation. "That's what I'm talking about! Who's he president of?"

Nick stared at Tomás. "You?"

The younger cousin's face fell. "I didn't vote for no republic."

"So, when did he put all these signs up?"

"I been in San Enebro since school started, staying with Tia Elena. Except Vicente called her last week, said I had to come help him this week, that he couldn't do it alone." Tomás rubbed his bottom lip. "Man, I wish Mom and Dad were here."

Nick reached one hand out to his cousin's shoulder and gripped it. "We can't change that."

Nick thought of his uncle and aunt, the two people who'd raised him with his cousins after his own parents died in a car accident when he was barely nine. Ten years later in Afghanistan he'd been appalled to learn of his aunt and uncle's deaths in a fiery airplane crash, repeating the same fate. On family leave he'd joined his cousins as pallbearers and mourned the passing of their parents. The four young men attended the reading of the will, its results a surprise to no one. They'd all grown up knowing Roberto, as eldest, inherited the working cattle ranch. Roberto, in turn, made it clear to his brothers and cousin that each had a lifetime place on the property, should they want to live and work there. When Nick returned to Afghanistan, he'd left his three cousins feeling confident the family ranch was under their care. And then, Nick had stepped on the I.E.D., his legs and his whole life blown apart.

Tomás tilted his head. "You know, he said the old name was bad luck."

Nick snorted. "Right. The family name is bad luck? I don't

think so. Did he decide to change his name, too? What the hell?"

Tomás let go with a loud "Aoooww!" in a shout that bounced against the canyon walls. "I knew it! But Nicky, don' laugh at him. He really gets mad."

Nick flashed a wide grin at Tomás in pure enjoyment. His cousin's accent, a combination of Spanish lilt and Texas drawl, made him feel right at home. "Tomás, I've missed you. And don't call me Nicky, man. Haven't heard that since about seventh grade."

"Oh, okay." Tomás, embarrassed, cast about for a change of topic. "They got you back in shape, right? Can you ride a horse?"

"I haven't tried yet, but I don't know why not. I can do most everything; not the same exactly as before. Sometimes I'm not too graceful." Nick moved his lips in a grimace to the side of his mouth, shrugged. "They fixed me up about as well as I can be fixed."

"*Que chido*" (How cool). "We all wanted you back in one piece, Nicky … I mean Nick."

"Yeah. And I'm mostly still in one piece, just using parts replacements now."

Tomás's face fell before he decided Nick had just made another joke. "You bring some gear? Let me give you a hand."

"Sure, though I could use a leg more." Tomás's face blanched. "I don't think that's funny," he protested.

"Well, primo, you've got to laugh, and there are times when I joke about my legs."

"No, hombre, don't do it. That's serious shit."

More of the same, Nick thought, then took pity on his cousin's youth and good intentions. Nick hated when people tiptoed around the subject. He'd lost his legs. That's what happened and what he dealt with every single day. Depressing enough to face the idea of being legless for life without the ego crunching pity of others. He had to remind himself to welcome each day. Whether it hurt or not. Whether it made sense or not. Whether he'd ever be able to establish a real life again gnawed at his inner core. People asked questions or made unthinking remarks or offered to help; useless.

"Look," Nick said, "I'll try to hold in my sense of humor about missing legs, and you try to forget to notice I haven't got any." For a moment he almost laughed, but replaced the urge with a friendly smile. "Okay?"

Abashed, Tomás swung the gate wide open. "Well okay. I'll try. Welcome home, Nick. You know that." He cocked his head, looked up at the surrounding cliffs of the canyon beyond the gate. "You know it's the same place, but it ain't the same."

"Nothing stays the same, man. Things change."

Tomás, obviously flattered by Nick's treatment of him as an equal, said, "Yeah, except Vicente left me here, and he keeps sending people to stay overnight, and I don't know what they all do." Tomás looked away. "Since Dad died and Roberto took over the ranch, nothing's been the same, and now Vicente's running things, and he put up these signs, and what was wrong with the old ranch name anyway? Diaz Ranch. Has a solid ring, you know? Dad would be so pissed."

"But why's Vicente running things? Where's Roberto?"

"Roberto," Tomás's face went bleak; he swallowed hard before finishing his sentence, "took off. I thought you knew."

"Not a word." Nick raised his eyebrows. "What happened?"

"He just wasn't there one day, you know?" The fancy boots toed into the dust. "Remember how he liked the girls in high school? Maybe he went off with one of them. Well, that's what Vicente says."

Nick frowned. Roberto married young, had a family, and kept a house in San Enebro so his three great kids could go to school. "What's his wife say?"

"She don't know." Tomás looked down at his feet. "I never thought Roberto would run off and leave his family like that, but Vicente says it happens all the time." Tomás squinted. "I know I seen it on TV."

"Have the police been involved?"

"Yeah, but they don't know where he went."

"Things work out. That's what your dad used to say. Is somebody watching out for Roberto's family?"

"*Claro que si* (Of course). We all are, but I wish Dad was here."

They stood looking at the gate and all the signs. "That's wild stuff," Nick said.

Tomás shook his head. "And we got to keep it locked all the time now."

He'd dug in a pocket and brought out a key. "This is for you. When Vicente heard you were coming he said you need a key."

"And why is it locked all the time?"

Tomás looked strangled. "He says he's tired of tourists running down our road and interrupting our work."

"Tourists? What tourists?"

Tomás shrugged. "Ask Vicente, primo."

"So, he's up at the house?"

"He went to Tucson. He should be back in a day or two."

"Clue me in, Tomás, how come you're not at school?"

"Well, that's it, man. When he goes away, he wants me to be here so everything's ready when he gets back. Just a week this time." Tomás shifted his weight. "I'm no student, you know? But I been missing an awful lot."

Nick looked off, made no comment.

The buildings, the mountains, valleys, even the wide-open sky occupied memories from his childhood like no others. Away from home, Nick would have sworn the ranch and its surroundings were the most perfect places on earth. Today, he wasn't so sure.

• ● •

Returning from Dog Mountain, Nick's mind kept rattling as he reached the ranch gate. He shook his head again at the crazy accumulation of signs, slid from the driver's seat, and unlocked the padlock with the key Tomás had given him. He swung the gate open, re-entered the truck, and drove it forward. His left leg was slower to bend itself in climbing out. He pushed on the computerized joint, felt it close properly, and stepped out of the truck again, closed and locked the gate, stepped back up again. Man, this up and down stuff gets old, he thought.

He drove slowly to avoid raising dust. The canyon walls, a half mile apart, soared a thousand feet above the road, a streambed that sometimes ran with water. He saw tarantulas again moving in the brush. His open truck window carried the smell of sage to his nose, sharp and familiar.

He stopped the truck at the low rise above the old home place and looked down on the buildings. The ranch nestled among scattered oak trees in the head of a box canyon that widened into a protected glen. Pines climbed up layers of natural shelves on the sides of the canyon, and bent in the winds on the rim. The house, a low, long building of faded pink adobe, squatted in a squared U that created an inner courtyard. The adobe looked like it'd been there before the rocks. Vigas, massive log beams, extended out into a Spanish colonial porch in front. The old wrecked buckboard still slanted against a gnarly cottonwood. Outbuildings included a log barn, corrals, and the incongruous blue eye of a hot tub winking in the sunlight.

He thought it looked the same, more or less, except for the addition of the hot tub. Nick decided that looked pretty good.

A battered four-wheel-drive pickup truck and a late model Chevy sedan, both layered in dust, nuzzled the gate of the fence that surrounded the house, looking like a modern hitching post for vehicles. Dust boiled up in one of the corrals, and Nick saw Tomás working a young gelding.

Nick pulled up next to the sedan, cut the engine, and listened to the quiet. The sounds of rustling trees had always brought him a sense of peace. Stepping out of the truck he walked around to the corrals. Nick stepped onto the bottom rung of the corral and folded his arms over the top rung. Tomás nodded at him, continued to work the horse another quarter hour before riding to the fence where Nick watched. He dismounted and began to remove the saddle.

"Nice workout." Nick leaned over the top rail and stroked the horse's neck. "He reminds me of your dad's range rider."

Tomás slid the saddle off and put it over the fence, removed the bridle, slapped the gray gelding on the rump. The horse kicked out its back legs and trotted around the corral. "This one's from Fargo, Dad's stallion. I think it's the horse makes me look good. He got a little fire, this one, but he's a buddy boy. We just call him 'The Gray'. You want to ride him?"

"Thanks, primo. I'd like that. Maybe tomorrow."

"*Chido* (Cool). Let me just stow this stuff, give The Gray a quick curry, and we'll go eat."

Tomás disappeared into the barn and Nick looked around the corral, stretched his shoulders, peered up into the surrounding cliffs. Late afternoon sun streamed into the ranch yard. It occurred to Nick he heard none of the usual working ranch sounds; no muffled voices from barn workers; no nickering of horses. Even the birds had stopped their conversations.

Tomás reappeared in the open barn door with a bucket, shook its contents, and whistled to the horse. The Gray trotted over.

"Pretty quiet. You the only one around?"

"Yeah, Vicente took Chapo with him. Tia Elena comes out from town every week and cooks for us. She leaves different stuff for dinner. I'm hoping she left my favorite for tonight."

"Chile rellenos, right?"

Tomás opened his eyes wide. "Wow, primo, you remember that?"

The Gray stuck his nose in the bucket, found oats, and whickered softly.

"Still a favorite of mine, too."

Tomás led the horse inside the barn, shaking the bucket to keep the
animal's interest. Nick followed. "Chapo's the only hand? What happened to everybody else?"

"Vicente let 'em go. Sometimes Tia brings Lucy. Mostly it's just me, Vicente, and Chapo. 'Course he brings different hands and sometimes work crews. They come and go." Tomás frowned, looked off. "Never see the same ones twice. Makes me wonder where they go."

Nick wondered what kind of work crews never returned, but said, "Lucy must be getting big." He thought of the last time he'd seen Roberto's oldest daughter. A freckled face with a mouth missing teeth formed in his mind. "What is she, seven? ... eight?"

Tomás hooted. "You been gone too long, primo. Lucy's eleven, going on forty-two. She's a good hand, too, but Tia don't let her come to the barn when there's workers here. 'Too rough,' she says."

"I saw a girl today, up on the ridge of Dog Mountain, by those springs that drop into rock pools. Couldn't have been much older than you."

Tomás set the empty bucket aside and led The Gray into a stall. He hooked the halter to a short line, began to curry the horse's neck and front legs. He stopped, one hand flat on The Gray's neck, and straightened up to look at his cousin. "I'm sixteen." He smiled, added, "But I like older women. How old you think she was?"

"I don't know. She didn't look like anyone I remember from around San Enebro."

"Did you talk to her?"

"No. I'm sure she thought she was alone; at least at first. When she saw me, she pulled a knife."

Tomás's chin came up in surprise. "¿Qué pasó?" (What happened?)

"She left. I didn't follow."

"Could you tell where she was headed?"

"No idea. She dressed kind of funny. Wearing a leather skirt."

"Oh man, primo. I LOVE girls in leather. That's hot!"

Nick laughed. "She reminded me of . . . this sounds lame. She reminded me of something like a deer, something wild. I thought of the stories your dad used to tell about the old days on the ranch. Rustlers and outlaws and wandering Indians."

"I always liked those stories." Tomás stroked The Gray's nose. "But all those people, the outlaws and the Indians, are long gone, even before Dad's time." Tomás looked up at the ridge that surrounded the box canyon. "We see hikers sometimes. Had some scientists a few years ago studying tarantulas. Forest rangers come and go; lately a lot of Border Patrol." His mouth curled up in a jesting twist and his eyes slid sideways toward Nick, "But no girls in leather skirts."

Nick swatted at Tomás who successfully ducked and continued to brush down The Gray's legs. Dust motes flickered in the streams of light falling inside the barn.

Nick leaned both arms on top of the stall, rested his chin on his hands, and enjoyed the rustic perfume of hay and horse. He inhaled a deep breath.

Tomás smiled. "I like the smell, too."

"Remember the story about Don Luis when he found a bunch of Apache cooking a steer over a campfire?"

Tomás looked up, eager. "I love hearing all that old stuff from the 1800s when Geronimo and his group still went back and forth between Mexico and here."

"Your Dad said his grandfather, the one that only spoke Spanish, found a group of women and children one time roasting a ranch steer. He said they were so skinny he could almost see through 'em." Nick shook his head. "Don Luis just rode away. Said they needed it more than he did."

"Yeah. Dad said Don Luis never had problems with Indians

like a lot of the ranchers talk about." Tomás left the stall and put away the curry brush, carried a bridle to its place on a wall peg. "Why did that girl make you think of that?"

"She looked . . . hunted or like she was escaping something. Kind of wild. I mean, she didn't look like a girl from San Enebro or from a ranch. And it was the way she was dressed. At first, I thought she must be Mexican, but . . ." Nick's voice trailed off.

Tomás nodded, and he looked around the stall making sure everything was put away.

Nick finished his thought. "This girl was wearing a kind of homemade boot that wrapped around her leg. Thick. I never saw that before. And something different with the boot toes. They had round ends that stuck up like discs." He leaned forward, teasing. "And the leather skirt you like so much was buckskin, with the edges the shape of the animal, like she lived in the woods. She looked really surprised to see me. And her eyes . . ." He tried to think how to describe them, gave up. "They were different."

"What? You mean the color?"

"No, not the color. I guess she had dark eyes, but that's not it. She didn't so much look *at* me as all around me. It was like . . ." Nick reached for words again. "Like . . . some of those Afghan hill people. They run scared all the time. The only people they trust are relatives, and they don't always trust them. The rest of their world is made up of enemies. I could tell she'd do whatever she thought she needed to do with her knife." He stared away through the open barn door. "Desperate. Really . . . wary."

"She sounds afraid. We got signs up and down the roads about watching out for border crossers. If she got separated from a group, she's probably scared." Tomás hauled some hay into the trough and shut the stall door behind The Gray. "Nobody goes up on Dog Mountain except us. I don't think even hikers go there. Too far. Steep. You're sure she wasn't Mexican, huh?"

"I don't think so. I thought it was a strange place to run into such a pretty girl."

Tomás studied Nick's face. "Now you tell me she's a pretty girl. She's not hot, but she's pretty. She dresses funny, you said, and it turns out to be in a leather skirt. Right." Tomás grabbed Nick around the shoulder good humoredly and started moving toward the barn door. "Keeping her to your own self, primo?"

Nick, caught unaware, stumbled and almost fell.

Tomás's face turned white. He grabbed Nick with one arm and steadied him. "Oh man. I forgot. You okay?"

"Sure." Nick leaned one shoulder against an empty stall. He looked over his shoulder down the row of a dozen stalls. Only a few others held horses. "Tomás, where's the rest of the horses?"

"Changing the subject from pretty girls in leather. I get it."

"No, I'm serious. Where are they? There used to be a whole remuda in here."

"*Pues* (Well). Vicente takes them sometimes. Other times he loans them out."

"Has he joined the rodeo circuit?" They both laughed. Everybody in cow country had a try at rodeo riding, but in a phase they all went through at about Tomás's age. Vicente was over thirty.

"I don' know what he does, but it ain't no rodeo." Tomás rested his eyes on Nick's face. "Pretty sure he sold 'em."

"Why?" Nick demanded.

"*Quién sabe?*" (Who knows?) Tomás looked unhappily down the row of stalls. "He don't like me asking questions."

They left the barn. "How many cattle you running?" Nick asked.

"We had a couple hundred head last year, but . . . maybe half that many now and they're all split up in the canyons so I can't even say for sure."

"Really?" Nick stopped so suddenly Tomás, right behind him, ran into his back. Nick turned to face his cousin. "So, when did Roberto take off?"

"Umm, I guess about a year ago this time."

"And you didn't let me know?"

Tomás answered in an injured tone. "You were in the hospital, Nick. Vicente said we should leave you alone and let you get better."

Nick, thinking of their shared family history, started to sputter. "You'd think somebody would have told me something!"

The ranch had always been a cattle operation. The Diaz family had lived on the original Spanish land grant since the 1700s, which included parts of the southern *Chiricahua* Mountains of Arizona and much of the New Mexico Animas Valley. Each generation had clung to the land through Apache troubles, rustler raids, changes in borders and nationality (Apache, Spanish, French, Mexican, United States—both Arizona and New Mexico), drought, and disease. When they entered the early 1900s the size of the acreage had become burdensome and parcels were sold off. But always the family ran a cattle herd, supplying first the Spanish military and the Catholic missions, trading meat to the Indians, selling to the Mexican provincial capitals, and providing steaks to the mining camps of the Arizona Territory. The Diaz ranch, famous as a place of hospitality, respite, sometimes hardship, but always a place of cattle, held title both to longevity and history. Their brand, the DXX was recognized throughout the greater southwest, and mail in the pioneer era could reach them with that simple address: DXX, Arizona Territory.

"Man, talk to Vicente. It's not the way it used to be. Government's changed the grazing permits and rules. 'Makes it impossible,' Vicente says. You been gone a long time. I was just a little kid when you joined the Marines."

"Only three years is all. Three years ago I joined the Marines, came home when we lost your mom and dad. I got my legs blown off in Afghanistan, spent a year in the hospital, came home to find Roberto disappeared, the cattle herd's gone, and what else do you know you haven't told me?"

Tomás looked up to the mountains, thinking hard. "I don't

know. You should come with me tomorrow morning. I got to cake the little herd of cattle we still got for sure at the bottom of Dog Mountain."

"I saw some today. That's where I was when I ran into the girl."

"Good, I'll ride The Gray over and you can drive your truck and bring the cake. Maybe we'll see that hot girl. We'll take an extra saddle and pick up Larry and go riding."

"You're kidding me! Larry's still around?" Nick's joy resurfaced at the thought of riding Larry, a mule that he and his cousins had all staked a claim to use. At least some things were just like old times.

The following morning Nick drove his truck around the ridge to the next canyon, several bags of cattle cake bouncing in the truck bed. Tomás rode over the ridge on The Gray and was already there, walking at the edge of the tree line as Nick drove up. Tomás hopped in the truck bed and told Nick to take a wide swing around the pasture. He held one bag at a time over the tailgate, allowing the cake to dribble out in a big circle. The cattle eagerly distributed themselves along the dribble line, lipping up the pellets. When they'd emptied the bags, Nick drove over to where The Gray contentedly cropped at the natural grasses and Tomás jumped from the truck bed.

"Usually Larry's out in front for cake. Damn mule."

They waited a bit, watching the cattle and hoping for the mule to emerge from the tree line. But Larry did not appear.

CHAPTER 8

Finding Dog Mountain

The Raiding Path, *Chiricahua* Apache Homeland

Biyoo', Her Beads, made good time riding the mule.
A familiar noise had awakened her at dawn, a distant braying.
She emerged from her sleeping place at the back of the overhang.
She felt at home, as if in her own territory in the Blue Mountains.
Pine trees swayed in a morning breeze on top of a large flat area
that formed a ridge separating two canyons. She walked along
the top of the ridge, keeping in the tree line by habit, pleased to
find a little brook where she drank her fill, smoothed her hair
with water, and washed her face. Renewed, she chewed on roasted
rabbit strips, leftovers from a kill the day before.

She stopped and faced the rising sun to the east, as it climbed
along the side of the large, cone-shaped mountain where she'd seen
the enemy ghost the day before. She recognized the mountain's
shape, a cone with a notch on the side, as the one Grandmother
called *Dzil Nii'łeezhé Bigowa*, Prairie Dogs' Home Mountain.

She knew the story of this mountain place well. Here the
siladáá (soldiers), of the *Indah*, the Living, the Pale Eyes, had
ridden hard in pursuit of the *Ndee*, the Dead, the Real People.
The soldiers traveled so fast they did not see the ground squirrels'
holes and their horses tripped and foundered as hooves pounded
behind fleeing Apache. And her ancestors got away.

Her Beads sang her morning prayer to *Ussen* with her palms

faced out and up, a song of welcome to the new day and of gratitude for the warmth of the sun, the bounty of the land, and the protection of the Creator.

Across the valley and north she saw movement, identified a string of men humpbacked with packs, moving slowly up a trail. They traveled ahead of her own route and she resolved to get soon past them and remain undiscovered. She'd seen such human pack trains before in the Blue Mountains. When Grandmother received reports of those groups, she ordered the Blue Mountain People to move. "Never," she counseled the children, "allow yourselves to be seen by them. Never steal from them. Their packs are useless to us. There is no food or cloth."

Five-year-old *Binat'izh*, Eyebrows, asked Grandmother, "What is in those packs?"

"*Izee' déncho'i*" (harmful medicine). Grandmother explained how the medicine made people go crazy. "It's something the *Indah*, the Pale Eye people, like. There's no understanding it."

For their entire lives Her Beads and the other children had learned to run and hide from both the *Indah* and the *Nakaiyé*, whether they ate bad medicine or not. How could anyone understand why they hunted and killed the Blue Mountain People?

Her Beads's goal: a dwelling of those who once lived high on the sides of cliffs that held supplies left by the ancestors. She hoped for at least a metal knife or hatchet, knowing anything once edible would have become unusable decades before her own life. Such caches had existed long ago as part of her ancestors' survival tricks and Grandmother instructed her to stop at several points to see what might still be useful.

Her Beads began to walk. When she reached the edge of the ridge she sat down with her back against a pine. She listened, thinking of what Grandmother would say. "Take no chances. Safety exists only when no one sees you." The ridges marched over and up to the cone-shaped mountain. Presently, *dzaneezi* (the one with ears long and slender, a mule) brayed.

I think the mule is talking to me, she thought. A steer below in the meadow made a whuffing sound, a challenge to another steer. Too much meat, she determined. I cannot take a beef today. But I think the mule might like to come with me. She unwound the hide and agave cord quadrupled around her waist and prepared a small noose at one end, then slung it over her shoulder.

She made her way down the side of the canyon and toward a meadow she'd seen from the ridge. She plucked an armful of long, green grass as she walked. By the time she slowly approached the mule, stopping often, she looked like a walking mound of grass. She halted and let the mule come to her. As it nibbled at the grass and became accustomed to her smell, she moved slowly to one side.

"Mule, I think you are used to people."

She dropped the grass gently. The animal lowered its head to continue eating and she looped the small noose around its bottom jaw, pulled it tight, placed her arms around its neck and mounted in one graceful jump. She held on tight, waiting for it to buck, but it didn't.

"Come Mule," and she tightened the noose tugging its long nose up, "we must follow the tracks of the ancestors." She veered westward to avoid the bad medicine walkers.

By late afternoon she'd selected a new trail to follow, a route that brought her to clumps of pines on the edge of a box canyon, and a choice of two trails. She tied the mule to a tree and approached the canyon rim carefully, tracking one path on top of the canyon and visible from below, and one that led downward where she saw a huddle of large enemy houses and empty corrals. A beautiful horse, the color of Grandmother's hair, grazed off at one side, tied by a long rope to a tree. A small circle of blue drew her attention. A hot spring? Two men sat in the water, resting their arms on a surrounding circle of wood high above the ground, odd to her eyes. Their voices and laughter bounced against the canyon walls.

Details on the canyon floor below began to fade as light dimmed. She saw no one else around the shelters and considered the idea of taking the beautiful horse when the men left. She saw an old dog limp toward the blue spring and lie down at its base; tucked the memory away in case it might be useful.

As the light waned further one of the people climbed from the spring, a short person, with wide shoulders and very short legs. She squeezed her eyes, straining to see better, but the dusk made it difficult. The figure boosted itself by its arms into what she knew the enemy used to sit upon. The Blue Mountain People had no such things but sat on their Mother Earth. Watching, Her Beads sucked air into her mouth in surprise and thought the *Indah* world a place of great wonder. She watched as the figure pushed against the round legs of the thing to sit upon and rolled it toward one of the houses. When both figures went inside, she saw lights brighten from within. She'd seen such lights in villages near the Blue Mountains, but did not understand how they burned without fire.

Her Beads decided to return to the mule, but heard the growling sounds of *béshnaghái* (metal wagons) approaching the shelters. In the dusk two metal wagons with eyes, yellow and bright as *ndolkah* (the cougar), approached the shelters. She shuddered involuntarily, thinking such things came from a different world. They must have some kind of enemy ghost power. Pulling her medicine bag from under her shirt, she grasped it tight. Her lips moved as she recited her power song silently, praying for protection. She saw the two metal wagons stop and go to sleep, yellow eyes closed, near the blue spring.

Retreating from the bushes she hastened to the mule, tied to a low pine, that cropped grass near the rim. The animal nuzzled her hand as she untied the rope. "*Dah* (No), I have nothing for you but to travel this night." She broke off a small branch, stripped it clean, then laid it across the path leading downward, the larger butt end pointing to the other path that circled the canyon rim. The Blue Mountain People, if they followed her route, would understand not to take the descending path, but to follow the rim. Then she collected a handful of small pine cones and chose four that she arranged in a careful scatter where the two trails diverged. She placed her pine cone sign beside the rim trail so that any of the Blue Mountain People who might follow could be certain of her route.

She gathered a handful of coarse mane, leaped onto the mule's back. It turned toward the trail that led down, but she yanked its nose away and directed her mount to follow the curve of the back of the box canyon, looping above the valley, trusting its senses to help them keep away from the edge. By the time the moon came up they had reached the other side and found a steep enclosed gorge in the folds of the hills. She made a dry camp and used her filled gourd sparingly. Before retreating to sleep among a tumble of boulders she made sure the mule's front legs were closely hobbled.

Her Beads awoke a few hours later to the sound of the mule cropping grass nearby. Pleased the animal had stayed near, she considered it with friendly regard. It browsed closer toward her, lifting its head when she stood up. The sun, only a promise edging the horizon, gave no warmth and her stomach growled. She examined the small collection of bags tied at her waist, found a single piece of prairie dog jerky. She drew it out and ripped a mouthful off the stick's end, then placed the remainder back in her pouch. Still sucking bits of jerky from her teeth she decided she must stop to gather food later.

She removed the hobbles from the mule and swung up on his back. More than one moon had passed since she'd spoken to any living thing beyond herself or the mule. Her voice croaked a little in her throat. "Let's find a drink for you, and maybe a nice, fat rabbit for me. Then maybe I won't have to eat you after all, mule."

CHAPTER 9

Vicente's Country

Tucson, Pima County, Arizona

VICENTE BATHED IN THE afterglow of his own physical satiation, filled with a sense of righteous power. This is how a man is supposed to feel, he thought, and stroked the girl's body possessively down her hip with an open palm.

"Maybe you'd like to come to my country," Vicente murmured in the girl's ear, his warm breath moving the wisps of hair that curled at her cheek.

But the girl, procured from a Tucson barrio corner, moved ever so slightly away, and examined her blue painted fingertips. She allowed his caresses, then lay back provocatively, hopeful for a generous tip. She'd already demonstrated a mastery of her trade and now nuzzled his earlobe, as he ran his hands over the flatness of her belly.

"What country?" she answered without curiosity, moving her lips down his neck, gliding her wet tongue across his chest and toward his navel.

"Vicente's country," he bragged. "Maybe you'd like to come with me?" At least for a while, he thought to himself. It's my country. I can do what I want.

The girl's tongue flicked farther down his torso. Her red hair slid brightly across his skin. His older brother, Roberto, always said, "Red hair brings troubles." Always nagging at me,

Vicente thought. He suddenly pushed the girl's head away with a sour feeling.

"*Estupido Roberto!*" The words exploded from his throat. Just the thought of Roberto brought a poisonous taste to his tongue, a kind of venom that launched him toward a headache.

The girl pursed her lips, considered his change of interest, switched to a new approach. Pressing herself against him she began sliding along the length of his body. For a moment he thought of nothing but the smoothness of her skin; but suddenly, Roberto reappeared in his head, talking, always talking: "You'll be dead before you're ever rich. You'll never get anywhere if you don't work hard. You've got a lot to learn." Roberto always ruined things for him. And all because Roberto, the first born, could claim the fruits of the eldest. It wasn't fair!

The girl nibbled delicately at his thigh and he could feel his body responding, groaned aloud as he gave into the movement of her lips. He turned his hip toward her and the warmth of her breath excited him. With one hand wound into her red hair he urged her onward. Compliantly she opened her lips when again Roberto's face swam into his head. *Chingado* (Screw) Roberto! What good was all the power if Roberto wouldn't leave him alone?

"Stay away!" he erupted at the vision of his brother, even as he pulled the girl's head forward by the hair. Roberto's imagined face grew shocked, wavered in his memory.

The girl struggled away leaving him grasping a handful of her hair. "*Pendejo!* (Fool!) That hurt me!" She held one hand to her head.

"I hurt you?" he roared. "Look at what you did!" The strands of red hair in his hand disgusted him; he wiped them from his fingers on the bed covers, stood up naked beside the bed, shaking with rage that a *puta* (a whore) could cause him so much anger. He grabbed her arm, pulled her roughly off the bed and flung her to the floor. "You're just a Red Dog!" he yelled, and kicked at her.

Screaming, she rolled toward a side table, scrambled up and grabbed her clothing, raced through the door and slammed it behind her.

Seconds after, he threw the same door open, and yelled, "Red Dog!" at her bare back as she fled around a corner at the end of the corridor. Chest heaving, he thought to himself that once more he'd been wronged. "She'll be sorry," he said aloud to the empty corridor, then yelled, "Get back here! You'll learn exactly WHO you've mistreated!"

He returned inside the room and helped himself to a shot of tequila from the bottle beside the bed, stood breathing heavily as the heat of the liquor fanned warmth into his body. He poured a second shot, tossed it down, and calm descended. "That's the way," he told himself gently.

An hour later he'd picked up Chapo, his *segundo* (second-in-command), and they started the drive home to the ranch, HIS ranch now, HIS own country. He smiled to himself. They could not ignore his importance anymore. As the president of Republic of Dog Mountain, they'd have to deal with him.

Even as he contemplated his status and a rosy future of wealth and respect, the kind that becomes fear and dissolves other men's bellies into water, his stomach rumbled. "Chapo," he said as his helper climbed into the truck, "You drive. I got to think." And they switched seats.

All he could think of, though, was the Red Dog and how she'd tried to injure his dignity. Past the edge of Tucson, Vicente began to describe his encounter with the girl. Chapo flinched when Vicente finally barked, "Let's get something to eat. Ay, that little Red Dog left me with an appetite!"

In Benson they stopped for hamburgers and pie at the Lariat Café, a regular watering hole for I-10 travelers. A neon cowboy whirling a giant lasso, yellow/blue/yellow/blue, flashed at the off ramp. Vicente still complained about the Red Dog, as they pushed past the "Howdy Folks, C'mon In!" sign looped across the doors. The smell of hot, fragrant coffee pulled them toward round stools at a busy counter. A waitress approached them. "Coffee?"

"Please," Vicente's smile gleamed when he decided to charm. He threw one leg over the stool as the waitress turned to a gurgling urn and picked up cups and a glass pot of steaming coffee. Her black skirt molded across the roundness of her buttocks as she leaned forward for the cups. *"Ay caramba!"* Vicente shook one hand loosely in front of him. "Give me some of that," he said clearly to Chapo.

Chapo kept silent. He'd been with Vicente a long time and knew to respond carefully, if at all, to his boss's moods and appetites.

The waitress poured the coffee, and kept her distance. "What can I get you?"

Vicente smiled lazily. "What do you recommend?"

She pulled two menus from behind the napkin holder, placed them in front of the men, gestured to a sign. "Special's on the wall." She moved away with the coffee pot to refill other cups.

"Ayyy," Vicente elbowed Chapo. "She knows how to wear a tight blouse, eh?" His voice carried easily to her retreating back. She turned to look at him with a frown, and he lifted his two hands, palms facing the front of his chest. "Coconuts," he said, exaggerating the word.

When she returned, she stood back from the counter to take their orders. Vicente pouted. "You don' like our business, darlin'?"

"We're always happy for your business," she responded, straight faced, and took their orders.

"I'd like to give her the business," Vicente said to Chapo, loud enough again for her to hear as she walked away. "Hey, come back!"

"Ah, leave it alone. She probably hasn't had a tip today." Chapo said.

"Yeah. Women." Vicente wanted to spit. "I'd like to find me that Red Dog and finish my business with her, too."

Chapo swallowed his food whole when their meal came, and stood up.

"What's your hurry, hombre?" Vicente chewed deliberately and watched the waitress as she wiped a table on the opposite side of the room, and Chapo moved toward a door marked Cowboys.

By the time Chapo returned, Vicente had eaten. He fished in his wallet and laid a tip down.

As he walked to the cash register, the waitress whisked the used dishes into a bin under the counter, then picked up the tip, a $20 bill. She turned it over once in her hand and waited until Vicente finished paying. She held the bill shoulder level and waved it limply. It was enough motion to catch his attention. The smirk on his face slid as he saw her tear it in half, then half again, and drop it on the floor.

Vicente's face reddened. *"Puta"* (whore), and the word lengthened out in a streamer that seemed to snap in a banner around the room. Inquiring faces in the cafe turned toward him. He pushed against the door and flung back his final opinion: *"Pendejos!"* Chapo, head down, followed his boss outside.

Vicente began to vent his frustration. Once started he couldn't stop. His lips flecked with spit as he berated the waitress, other customers, the restaurant, the Red Dog, people in general, his father and brothers, all of mankind, until he finally ran out of names for his list. "I'd like to see what they'd say if they knew. Then I'd show them."

Chapo managed to keep him moving toward the parked truck. Vicente, consumed by his rage, seemed surprised when Chapo opened the rider's side door.

Vicente's breathing, heavy with emotion, quieted and he addressed his companion. "Except for you, Chapo. You're the only one I can trust."

Chapo had heard it all before, said nothing, just tipped his head to the side in a reassuring way.

Vicente looked hard at him, bit out the words. "And that's the way it must be. I don't know why you're so quiet, but you make me feel quiet, too." Vicente placed a hand on Chapo's shoulder. "Always so quiet. I wonder what would happen if you weren't so quiet?"

Without comment Chapo raised one hand and settled his hat farther down, stepped back, and closed the passenger door. He walked around to the driver's side and slid behind the wheel, started up the engine.

"One more stop to pick up the men," Vicente reminded him. "Same place as last time." He leaned his head back against the seat and slept.

CHAPTER 10

Intruders

Rancho Garcia, West Side Sierra Madre Range, Sonora, Mexico

ESTEBAN GARCIA AWOKE HEARING a dog bark just one sharp note. He lay at attention, listening. He arose, pulled on jeans and huaraches. His son continued to breathe deeply, undisturbed. Esteban hefted a shotgun from beside the door, racked a round into the chamber, pulled back the door brace, and slipped outside. The mountain cabin, tucked into a fold in a cliff wall, boasted protection on three sides. He stepped to the corner expecting one of the dogs to appear. A muffled sound reached him from the horse corrals and he peered blindly into the darkness of a night with no moon. He looked up at the stars and saw at least a few hours remained before morning light.

He stepped back inside, rested a hand lightly on his son's shoulder. "Ignacio, there's a *tigre* (a mountain lion) after the horses."

Ignacio woke at his father's touch, silently pulled on jeans and shirt and armed himself. The two men moved quickly into the ranch yard. They followed a routine well established over the years. Ignacio crept into the trees that surrounded the homestead, disappeared west toward the corrals. Esteban, with less distance to cover, waited until certain his son had reached a point of equal distance. He blended into the darkness, running from the cover of the house to the woodpile and then against the tack shed. The entire time, soft thudding sounds and nervous muted horse snorts issued from the corrals.

Why? Esteban asked himself, are my horses so quiet? If a tigre is near, surely they would be loud.

Then, a horse nickered. Esteban heard the slight jangle of the chain loop that held the corral gate closed and the creak of the gate as it opened.

It flashed across his brain—not a tigre at all!

The thwack of a hand or stick against the croup of a horse cut the night air. Suddenly, the horses hurtled out of the corral, and Esteban bounded forward, yelling. As he sprang forward he tripped on something soft, fell and skidded forward on his stomach. A gun blasted from across the corral. The horses swept past the yard and Esteban rolled to one side to avoid being trampled. The noise of their hooves swiftly disappeared into the trees on the far side of the clearing.

Esteban picked himself up, ran back to where he'd tripped. A furry form lay there, impossible to see clearly in the dark. He knelt down and ran his hands over the still form. "Aii, Negrito."

Ignacio called out to his father as he ran across the clearing. "You okay? I took a shot but I don't think it hit any of 'em."

"Negrito's dead."

"Where's Negrito Dos?"

"Don't know." The two dogs were from the same litter, both black, one large, one small.

Father and son moved toward the corral through the wide-open gate. They breathed in the pungent sharp smell of churned soil and horse.

"*Cuidado*" (Be careful), Esteban warned his son in a low voice.

They both walked once around the corral. All six horses ... gone.

"Did you see anyone?" Esteban asked Ignacio.

"Too dark," Ignacio said. "People for sure. I could see they rode without saddles."

Esteban's throat tightened as he realized all of their horses were gone; the horses that they used to farm and ride to the fields; the horses that he knew he could never replace. Without the horses, they could not live. He swallowed hard, breathed deep, and said to his son, "We have got to get our horses back."

Ignacio said, "*Aii Papi*. We'll go after them; catch them in the jeep. Nobody knows their way around here better than us." He turned and tripped as his boot slid through something that tangled around his heel in the loose corral dust. He bent down, unwrapped the impediment from his boot, strained his eyes to see what it was, but could not see in the darkness. Ignacio jammed the snarl into a shirt pocket. "Let's go!" he urged his father.

"Can't track 'til light," Esteban said, "and we don't know what we're up against."

Once in the house they pulled the curtains tightly closed before lighting a kerosene lamp. There'd never been electricity this far up the mountain, and now they didn't want to risk the noise of starting up and running the generator. Ignacio sat away from the lamp and the windows and drew out his find to examine it.

"I thought it was a rope," Ignacio said, "but it's something else." He looked at the article, rubbed his hand against the hem of his shirt, reluctant to touch it again, and dropped it on the table. He grabbed a pencil and poked at it. "Is it a necklace?"

"I don't know." Esteban reached for it and ran the cord between thumb and fingers, a loop of four twists of rawhide. "Bumpy." Woven into the cord was a yellow stone, a blackened piece of wood, a natural crystal, and a small blue seashell. A little bag hung at the bottom of the cord along with a flat tweezer of metal. Esteban opened the bag and found a smooth powdery substance. "Drugs? Maybe the narcos have finally found us."

Ignacio sucked in air through his teeth. "LM? Why would they come up here?"

"Who else would dare steal so many horses?" Esteban's head swirled again around the loss of the horses and what it would mean. "We've got to find the horses."

Rancho Garcia had never been the target of *narcotraficantes* (drug growers and dealers). It was a hard scrabble rancho, with only one road in and out. The cartels wanted everything easy, which Rancho Garcia's location did not offer.

The LM, short for *Los Muchachos* (The Young Ones), a cartel of recent bloody history, preyed in the canyons of the mountains. In the valley far below, along the highway north and south, they raced their shiny pickup trucks and Suburbans, corridos wailing from their open windows. The Garcia men, aware of the rude finality with which the cartel claimed territory and property, worked to keep a safe distance. Neighbors had warned them their time would come.

"I can take the cell phone and climb up the mountain to get a signal," Ignacio offered.

Esteban peered blankly into the dark morning. "Wait for dawn. Someone might still be watching." He gulped hard, hoping it was not true. "Or waiting." He laid the strange cord on the table, rubbed one hand over his face, thinking of those others, Los Broncos, (the wild ones), long gone since before his father's time. Surely not, he comforted himself. We've heard nothing of them for so long. He turned to his son. "And we cannot see to track yet."

"*Claro*, but we need to do something!"

Esteban laid his rifle flat on the table, close at hand. He began to load a knapsack with food, jacket, and water bottle. Ignacio watched his father for a moment, then did the same.

In the pearly light of morning they again circled the house and corral, looking for anything to help interpret what had happened in the dark. They found the shed door standing open, the shelves swept clean of bags of beans and flour, of coffee and canned goods.

"Why take our horses? The LM can get better horses anytime," said the son. He looked around and added, "They took the ropes and buckets, too, but left the saddles. At least that's something."

"*Más se fue en el diluvio.*" Esteban always had a *dicho* (a saying).

"It could have been worse," Ignacio agreed. "But why strip our supplies? Just weighs them down."

"They took what they wanted, maybe figured they left us helpless. Without horses, food, we'd be done. But no. They must not have seen the jeep." Indeed, leaving the jeep away from the house under a tarp in a grove of trees had been a sound idea.

Esteban dragged Negrito's body to the shed. While Ignacio kept watch, Esteban hefted the black dog onto the work table, and examined the still form. Negrito, slashed from throat to hind legs, had bled out.

"No tigre. But why, if it's LM, why not just shoot him?" Esteban wrapped feed sacks around Negrito's body. "We'll bury him later."

Ignacio found faint footprints, revealing no arches and rounded at the toe, in the dirt under the bedroom window. Something had been dragged over the prints, just enough to smudge them.

"That is odd, also." Esteban said, the worrying idea from the past beginning to bother him. "Not cowboy boots."

The jeep growled into life on the second try. Esteban drove, felt naked in the open vehicle, an easy target, as he followed the horse tracks down the dirt road toward the valley pass below. He stopped the jeep several times and examined side routes for marks of horses or men. Each halt brought a shiver of apprehension across his neck. "They're staying together. No split ups."

When they reached their own property line the gate stood open. Horse tracks moved off in a northerly direction across the open vale. Ignacio closed the gate after the jeep went through, examining the ground at the same time.

"Papa, there are no tire tracks coming in. Where did they come from?"

Esteban shook his head, shifted down, and edged off the road over the lip of an arroyo and back up again toward a line of oak and pine trees that ran along a low ridge. The whine of the engine seemed loud in the quiet of the mountains. At the trees both men got out of the jeep and cast around for tracks. Ignacio squatted on his haunches and studied the crumpled earth. A thick layer of pine needles had been disturbed by the movement of hooves. Esteban saw places on the trees where reins had been tied and the movement of horses had peeled off the bark. He picked up a short piece of rawhide, no thicker than a shoelace. He held out the strip, thumbing the ends. "Cut. They put covers on the horses' hooves. Harder to track them."

Esteban circled the edge of the area, looking for tracks away. Ignacio moved in the opposite direction and the two looped one another as they examined the forest floor.

"Here." Ignacio found the faintest of hoofmarks, leading toward the slope of the mountains. They looked north, studied the canyon fissures, the tree line. "What do you think?"

"They know the country. They came prepared with covers for the horses' feet. They'll reach Copper Spring before we can get there. After that they'll go toward Bonito Creek or Oak Tanks. The Tanks are dry, and I think they may know it, so Bonito."

"How would they know?" Ignacio asked.

Esteban tapped his head without explaining.

At the tree line something dark lay across the path that led into the mountains.

"Papa." Ignacio pointed. They moved forward, intent on the area around the trail and behind the low oak growth. The father disappeared into the trees, while Ignacio stepped closer.

Negrito Dos, smallest of their two dogs, stretched dead across the path. Though Esteban was unsentimental about working ranch animals, he valued the loyalty of their faithful companions. He knew his son felt the same and as he came out of the trees he watched his son bend over the dog's body, placing a hand on its flank.

"Still warm, Papa."

Esteban swept his eyes northward. "They left a message." Esteban slid one hand slowly over the dog's head in a farewell pat. "They tell us they will do the same to us if we follow. But how can we live and work without our horses? Not possible." His worn hand worked itself down the dog's neck. "Strangled." He spat into the dirt. "*Brutos.*"

Bonito Creek was on the far side of the sierra in Chihuahua, within forty miles as the crow flies, but over rough terrain that crossed mountain trails and peaks, with rivers at the bottom of deep canyons. They were separated from Bonito Creek by more than a hundred miles around the north end of the range by car, on dirt roads that could chip teeth and flatten tires.

Esteban stood. "I'm going around to Bonito Creek. I've got to get the horses."

"*Si, Papi.* I'm coming, too."

Nacori Chico, the closest Sonoran town, lay on the road in the valley below, its buildings scattered along the potholed highway. In less than an hour Esteban stopped the jeep outside an adobe building with a vandalized sign. Faded letters splashed with black paint erased some of the words: *D par miento de Pol cia.*

Esteban entered and returned in a few minutes. Teeth gritted, he shook his head negatively. He regarded Ignacio's anxious face and reseated himself in the vehicle, said just two words: "Colonia Suiza."

The son understood there would be no help from the police.

At the edge of the north side of town they stopped to fill

the gas tank. Ignacio climbed out, checked the oil and tires in readiness for a long drive. The *colonia* could not be reached by car directly across the mountains as there was no road suitable for modern vehicles.

Esteban placed the nozzle back on the gas pump, twisted the cap onto the jeep's tank. "The police are useless," he told his son. "They say, 'Drugs and juvenile delinquents.' Some cowboys on the Chihuahua side reported a problem about stolen supplies." His right nostril quivered in protest. "*Estúpidos.* We will go to Don Rafael and his people. They will help. They know who these robbers are, just as we do."

Ignacio nodded. He'd only heard the stories about the times before his own life. He had never seen evidence of their existence. Never dreamed they might still exist. He looked at his father's strained face.

Ignacio's voice quavered ever so slightly. "Are they back?"

Esteban engaged the gears of the vehicle, and looked straight ahead as they pulled away to follow the road around the north end of the Sierra Madre.

"*Si*, my son," he confirmed, "Los Broncos (the wild ones) have returned."

CHAPTER 11

Storyteller

Mescalero Apache Reservation, New Mexico

SAM CHARLEY'S SHIRT HAD been washed so many times the chambray cloth stretched almost transparent across his shoulders. He stood outside the doorway of his home, watching as his daughter maneuvered her SUV across bare ground to the pile of equipment he'd stacked on the porch. The morning autumn sun slanted long beams of golden light across the land and warmed his face.

Around his neck hung a war cord, a twist of four rawhide loops with a flat tweezer cut from tin as a pendant. Some Apache people said Sam challenged the spirit world by wearing a thing that once belonged to the dead. Invariably Sam responded, "My grandfather put the war cord around my neck when I joined the Marines and went to Vietnam. It belongs to me, not to the one who's gone."

Still, there were rumors, and Sam remained vigilant in defending his right to wear it. His life rested on his skill in remembering. It formed the basis of his placement on the tribal council of elders. Whether the cord presented a necklace of strong medicine or a curse, the people had to respect it. As a storyteller he told tales around winter fires. As a council member he reminded others of what had come before. The stories of the ancestors related history, the names of the places where their people lived and died, incidents that described the choices between good and evil, loyalty and betrayal, life and death.

At seventy years old he still carried the standard for those who knew his true name: *Doo yidah da,* He Does Not Forget. Of course, no one who knew it would ever speak it aloud unnecessarily. That would be a waste of his name. But still, when Sam wore the cord outside his shirt, it was the same to the people around him as if he'd donned a uniform, a visual announcement of his official Apache self.

Sam hugged his daughter.

Lorraine said, "So it's an official trip, huh?" and smiled.

Sam smiled back and clasped each of his identical six-year-old twin granddaughters, Susie and Elsie. "Everything's ready to load up and go," he told the girls. "Don't wander off. We want to be in the homeland before dinner."

The twins giggled, promised not to wander. Living only twenty miles away in Ruidoso, New Mexico, they visited their grandfather frequently on the *Mescalero* Apache Reservation. As Sam carried camping equipment to the vehicle, Lorraine took charge of stowing each article. She'd already prepared food supplies and an ice chest which sat in the back of the SUV.

"Time to leave," Lorraine called out and she walked around to the driver's side. The two girls came scrambling from the house, excited at the prospect of a camping trip. Sam followed behind them, stopped to turn a key in the lock.

"An exercise before we get in the car," Sam called out. He presented a bottle of water to each and told the girls they would practice like the ancestors. "Fill your mouth with water but do not drink. We will run a race and spit the water out at the end of the race. This is how the ancestors taught children to be mindful." Sam watched the girls fill their mouths, then asked Lorraine to determine if the running girls kept themselves from drinking the water.

"Run!" he called out to the twins. "Run to the big pine to

the east! Who can make the fastest return?" He took a swig of water, holding it in his mouth, and followed behind.

Both girls ran full out, their cheeks bulging with water, trying not to laugh as they raced to the largest pine tree. Even so water leaked from their mouths, wetting their chins and T-shirts. At the big pine each girl ran around the trunk and raced back, tried to spit their mouthfuls of water at Lorraine's feet. Although Lorraine scooted back to avoid the splatter, only a little water landed, and both girls raised surprised eyes to their mother. Sam loped in behind them and spit his mouthful on the ground.

"*Enjuh*!" (Good!), Lorraine said.

Sam nodded, still catching his breath. "It is the way of the ancestors. We will have to race these girls a little farther each day and make them strong." He looked out and over the forested hills toward the west to the *Chiricahua* homeland. "Tomorrow we race where the ancestors ran." The twins quieted. "But for now, it's time to travel." He spoke a phrase translated from his native Apache language quietly in English. "Don't let the sun step over you."

"The sun's barely up!" Lorraine replied. "Is Albert still coming?"

"He should have been here by now, but let's go. We'll stop at the All Clans Museum on our way out and see."

Twenty minutes later at the museum they found Albert ready to depart, but not for the homeland.

"Sorry," Albert told Sam, "it's my job." He'd already placed a closed sign on the museum's door. "*Dichoshé*, Old Shaggy, needs a "mini exhibit" that highlights 'the Apache experience' for a Southwest trade conference in Albuquerque." Albert's expression brightened. "Going to be a lot of news coverage, even somebody from *National Geographic* magazine. *Dichoshé* says it's bound to get the tribe some good press."

"Did you forget about going to the *Chiricahua* Mountains to check the message spring?"

"*Dah*, course not. If this finishes fast, I'll join up with you in a day or two. I want to check out that crazy news story from Sonora, plus ..." Albert didn't mention Sam's dream, not sure if he'd shared it with Lorraine.

Sam understood Albert's hesitation. "Lorraine knows," he said.

Sam turned away, aware that when the tribal president asked for help, any council member would do what they could. *Dichoshé* worked hard on behalf of the Apache people, and if Sam's presence had been requested, he'd have changed his plans, too. "You tell *Dichoshé* to get a haircut before he goes. He looked like a buffalo last time I saw him."

"You're right. Give me a call if you find anything."

Sam stepped in closer to Albert. "Had another one last night."

"We may have to change your name to *Nahiyeel.*"

"'He Dreamed It,' huh? I can live with it. Be sure to put on your noble look, and let Old Shaggy know I've gone south to check on messages . . . and dreams."

"Sure. Does he already know about the newspaper story?"

"Yeah, he should, unless all that hair interferes with his brain working." Sam cleared his throat. "There's something pulling me hard, old friend," and he swallowed, repeated, "hard."

Albert heard the emphasis. "Call if you need me. I'm not liking the way it's starting to feel down there in the homeland."

"I love the way it feels down there, Devil Dog. It's the land of the ancestors."

More like the land of ghosts, Albert thought, but didn't say it, because the old people said that saying the words aloud might invite a spirit's attention. "Well maybe it's thinking about the past makes me nervous."

Sam knew Albert referred to the centuries of violence and struggle between his ancestors and the different newcomers who took turns fighting the various Apache bands in New Mexico and southern Arizona: the Spanish, the Mexicans, fur traders and miners, settlers, finally the U.S. military. Both men, aware that unofficial bounties on Apache scalps lapped over well into the twentieth century in *Cochise* County, Arizona, also knew that local vigilantes had continued an on-going war declaration against Apache even after Geronimo's final surrender in 1886. Returning to the homeland had been publicly forbidden at that time under threat of death for the *Chiricahua* people. No official return visit to *Cochise* County by any Apache was recorded until the 1980s in the centennial celebrations since the end of the Apache wars. *Cochise* County held a "no go" status even into the present in the minds of most Apache people.

The reassurance of backup from a fellow Marine placed Sam's travel mood in the proper perspective. "Let's go, Daughter." The twins took their seats. Sam raised a hand in farewell as he placed one leg into the SUV.

"What are you going to do if you find something?" Albert asked, and the question stopped Sam.

He finished sitting down, brought his second leg in. Good question, he thought. He pursed his lips together, looked at Albert. "I suppose whatever feels right, Jarhead."

"Right, Gyrene." Albert formed his right hand into an approximation of a telephone, placed his thumb by his ear and his little finger near his lips. "Call me," he mouthed, in imitation of an overly repeated television ad.

As the car moved away from the forests and hills of the reservation the twins begged to listen to KNGP, a Navajo station that bounced over the mountains from Gallup.

Sam, scandalized, protested. "A Navajo station? Why?"

Lorraine laughed. "They like traditional Native American music and KNGP plays those kinds of songs. For me, I like country western."

"No," Sam said. "This is a journey to the *Chiricahua* homeland. If it isn't Apache, we don't listen." When heavy sighs sounded from the back seat, Sam turned and looked at his granddaughters. "We must put our minds in the right place." Then he began an Apache chant.

Soon the repeating stanza included Lorraine and the girls. The counterpoint of Lorraine's wavering soprano, his own gravelly bass, the twins' clear piping, swelled. "I learned that traveling song from my father who learned it from his father." Sam translated the Apache words for the twins:

With the favor of the sun, we are traveling.
With the favor of the sun, we are protected.
With the favor of the sun, we travel safely.
With the favor of the sun, we are blessed.

A few hours into the drive they'd reached a river canyon, and Sam asked Lorraine to pull into a picnic area by a great bridge. He opened his knapsack and selected a leather-wrapped packet, unfolded the deerskin revealing a suede pouch. He dipped two fingers inside that came out dusted in *hoddentin* (cattail pollen), a pale powder the color of platinum that gleamed across his fingernails. Sam tossed a dash of the soft dust toward the sun, then placed a pollen-laden finger on the crown of each of the twins' heads, his daughter's, and finally his own. He put a pinch into each open mouth, then into his own. The gritty taste of the holy grains settled on his tongue. "Now we are ready to ask for safe passage over the river."

When they stood on the bank of the tumbling river, he lifted a second packet from his knapsack. The children hung at his elbows as he unrolled the deerskin. There, nestled in folds of leather, lay natural turquoise stones.

"Take one."

Each child carefully selected a stone, and they moved down the bank as close as possible to the water's edge.

"Throw it into the middle. Thank the river and Sun for crossing."

The swift river, frothing white plumes like horsetails, raced below. Susie threw her turquoise first. The rushing noise of the river's flow concealed the sound of Susie's stone as it hit the water. Elsie's stone skipped into the flow, not quite as far as her sister's and slid under without a whisper. The girls looked at their grandfather.

"It is well. The river and the Sun have accepted your gifts."

Lorraine drove on, passing from the mountains onto the plains of lower New Mexico and Sam napped. He awakened in Lordsburg at a fuel stop, unfolded himself from the car, and stretched. The high desert reached away on all sides. A few horses grazed off to the south on land barely tufted with natural grasses that ruffled in a mild breeze.

As the car passed into Arizona on the I-10 freeway, Sam began to recognize mountains and passes on both sides of the road he could easily name. He called out the place names in Apache, where old trails once connected, battles had been fought, hunts had fed the people. He felt himself grow stronger, more vital, as the mountains to the south grew closer.

"There," he exclaimed, pointing with his lips, "there's something you've never seen! Those mountains are named for us, our homeland!"

Before them a jagged range of peaks loomed. The *Chiricahua* Mountain range looked gray and bare, with rocky clefts and spires that hid the high pine forests and grassy valleys within their folds.

The twins leaned forward. "How do you know, Grandfather?" Susie asked.

"They're in my mind map." He shook his head, remembering. "Given to me by my grandfather." He looked forward to the end of the range, topped by the distinctive configuration of two immense nodules of rock, clearly outlined against the sky. "Now I give them to you to place in your mind maps, and now that you know them, you can never be lost in the homeland."

Lorraine pulled the car to the side of the road and slid a AAA map from a door pocket, opening it over the driver's wheel. She ran a finger down the I-10 as it crossed between New Mexico and Arizona and held her finger on the map. "Here it is girls. See how the map says *Chiricahua* Mountains running all the way down toward the border with Mexico. And look. See those two bumps on the mountain. They're called Dos Cabezas: two heads in Spanish."

The girls craned their necks to see the two bumps that were heads, then laughed that a mountain could have heads. Susie placed a hand on Sam's shoulder. "Is that the way the ancestors really called them?"

"*Dah*" (No), Sam said in a sad voice. "The Apache name is the Two Tails. They mark the *Chiricahua* homeland. Maybe that name is all we have left now of our people's life here."

"No there's more," Elsie said, beaming, and laid one small hand on her own chest. "We're here."

Sam turned, smiled broadly at his granddaughters. "Yes, you are."

Lorraine pulled back out on the freeway. "And why do they not teach the mind maps today, Father?"

Sam sat back in his seat. "Didn't seem to be much of a point to knowing it after the Bronco survivors returned from the east. They believed no one could ever go home again. The people here promised any returning Apache only one thing: death. And with you, Daughter, I waited to teach it until now."

"You can't blame them for protecting their descendants after all they went through," Lorraine said bitterly, thinking of the stories she'd heard aging relatives relate. The removal and isolation of her family's ancestors to the American south for almost thirty years still brought tears to her eyes.

Susie bent forward, laid her head sideways on the back of the front seat so she could look into her grandfather's eyes. "But it's okay now?"

"Right." Sam looked at his daughter's hands held tight on

the steering wheel. He understood the helpless feeling of being unable to fix troubles from the past. "That's old trouble. Nobody thinks of it today." Sam's eyes shifted to the *Chiricahua* Mountains south and he looked up at the Two Tails, sighed. "Now we're just tourists."

"More than that, Dad," Lorraine objected. "We have the stories that live on the land."

Sam agreed. "This is the home of our people. The land will remember us. We don't expect a welcoming committee," and he turned his head to smile at the twins in the back seat, "but nobody should be running us off, either."

DIFFERENT JOURNEYS

CHAPTER 12

Following Biyoo'

The Raiding Trail, *Chiricahua* Apache Homeland

NAADIKTAZ, IT WIGGLES, BLINKED awake when a pebble dropped on his chest. His head pillowed against a slanted rock had kept his sleep light. He looked uphill to an area littered with boulders. He saw the children still slept, laying against the canyon rocks on the uphill side so they would not roll down the steep hill. The strategy protected the children from surprise and often fooled enemies who always seemed to expect their quarry to camp on flat land. No one stirred.

It Wiggles saw that *Łichíí*, Red One, left to guard the sleeping group, stood nearby watching downhill.

"The raiders bring horses," she murmured.

Grandmother taught them to think ahead of nature when they could, and always ahead of their enemies. He knew the moment Red One saw movement in the dry canyon below; she had leaned forward into the night, straining her eyes to pierce the darkness. He heard the quiet chuckle of a quail, the raiders' signal, and understood the raiders let them know of their approach.

It Wiggles moved silently and stood by the trail. A line of six horses padded silently up the canyon toward him and his heart swelled with joy.

The successful raid meant food and mounts to help them quicken the group's pace. Surely *Ussen* watched over them with great favor. Rawhide covered hooves muffled the sound of horseshoes on rock. Four riders passed by and continued upward. The last two horses moved heavily, loaded with packs. It Wiggles moved to the head of the line to help with the horses, as Red One hunkered down and watched for signs of pursuers. It Wiggles smiled as he examined the horses, sent the raiders to *Zhonne,* Pretty One, for a quick breakfast. He touched each on the shoulder as they passed in recognition of their success.

Pretty One handed sticks of dried rabbit to the raiders, then turned to rouse the sleeping camp. The children came alert easily and each faced east to meet the new day with individual prayers. At some point each noticed the smells or noises of the captured horses. And all had to race to investigate the mounts that *Ussen* had provided. Soon the band grouped and moved up toward the saddle of the pass, then down the other side into a canyon where a stream wended its way under a canopy of cottonwoods. The two *dikohe,* Left Hand and Knife, followed at the end of the group, sweeping sprays of tumbleweed across the travel marks of people and horses.

As the dawning light grew the children reached the ridge of the next hill. Beyond the valley the mountains faded into a wide stretch of plains. It Wiggles expected bumps on the horizon would grow into hills as they approached. A thin river flowed between the hills and the upland on which they stood. Grandmother had used a Spanish word for the distant place below them on the flatlands. "Enmedios" (In the Middle), It Wiggles breathed out.

Next to him Pretty One surveyed the distances. "Almost half way to the ancestors' homeland," and he dipped his chin in agreement.

By late afternoon they came to a river. First the children filled their water containers, then drank deeply, all trained well in the discipline of travel. A grin spread across It Wiggles's face as he watched the children help the raiders unload the pack frames beside the shallow river, allowing the horses to drink and rest.

Na'iłt'oolé, Spider, tried unsuccessfully to shift a pack alone. A small girl, *Binat'izh*, Eyebrows, ducked under his arms and braced against his chest to help. *Dahsts'aa'*, Strawberry, the group's foremost horse handler, splashed water on the horses in the river, then wiped them down with bunches of dry grass. The smallest children, excited at having horses, eagerly helped rub the horses dry.

It Wiggles gathered the four raiders and asked if any enemies had followed. "*Dah*" (No). *Bikécho*, His Big Toe, leader of the raiders, gave the report. "We used the path called 'There is no water.' We took all their horses." His wandering eye wavered one way while the other gazed forward.

It Wiggles put one hand out and briefly squeezed His Big Toe's shoulder. "*Nłt'éégo áłzaa*" (Well done). "The ancestors would be proud."

He patted two fifty-pound bags of beans balanced in one pack frame like old friends. He saw another held containers with flour, salt, and coffee. A third clanked as buckles opened and the children saw cans of tomatoes and peaches. It Wiggles yipped happily and the group converged around him.

In the old days they would have stopped here for a celebration, to honor those who'd made a successful raid. He looked around the group. "Our raiders have brought us a feast! We'll walk to the tip of this range today and cross to Enmedios after dark. The smallest will be placed on the horses so we can move quickly. We'll eat these good things when we stop to rest at the Spring That Always Flows. What do we know about that spring, *Yaa'*?"

All eyes focused on *Yaa'*, Louse. "There's always water to drink." The little girl's shoulder-length hair, wind-blown, uncombed, stood out in scraggly strands from her head.

It Wiggles waited patiently, looking across the plain.

Louse gulped and added, "There may be thirsty enemies, too."

"*Ha'ah.*" It Wiggles patted Louse on the shoulder. "We'll

take care our enemies never know we're there." He looked out at the plain again. "What will we have with our water, *Gidi?*"

Four-year-old *Gidi,* Cat, youngest of the group, entwined her fingers anxiously and pushed her arms out stiff before her, rocking back and forth. "A feast!"

All eyes measured the plain before them, considered the prospect of their empty bellies. Flat, open spaces must be crossed at night. Pursuers rarely observed *Ndee* in the mountains among rocks and trees, but on the desert or plains, motion drew the eye. There, all movement put them at their most vulnerable. No one asked how long the journey would be to travel the distance. Even the smallest could see the space would take the rest of the day and into the night.

And already their stomachs rumbled.

CHAPTER 13

The New Nation

Republic of Dog Mountain Ranch, *Cochise* County, Arizona

AFTER A DAY OF caking cattle and mending tack, Nick and Tomás relaxed in the hot tub. The heat did wonders for Nick's thigh muscles. Tomás sat down to take off his sandals so as not to stand over Nick's shortened body and tried not to watch Nick get into the tub on his stumps.

"It's okay to look. It is what it is, primo." A grin worked its way to the corners of Nick's mouth. "You always wanted to be taller than me when we were kids." And Nick rolled a small wave toward his cousin.

"I know." Tomás could not help feeling embarrassed, used his palm to smooth the wave. "I just got to get used to it."

"Hey, I'm glad to be alive." Nick's upper body, trim and well-muscled, evidenced his excellent physical condition.

Tomás tried to find the right words. "I want to have muscles like you. I want to have all the hot girls coming after me!" He looked at his older cousin, his face naked in its expression of longing. "Do you think I could be a Marine?"

Nick laughed and splashed Tomás. "Primo, I bet the girls are already running after you." His words reassured the teenager. "And yes, you're what the Marines want."

Tomás grinned. "One of the brave, one of the few."

"Hell, yes."

Dusk gathered as Nick maneuvered himself to exit the hot tub, dismounted the stairs on his stumps, and reached for a towel. He dried off, hoisted himself into his wheelchair and wheeled along the concrete walk to the kitchen's back door.

Tomás wrapped a towel around his waist before following. "Nick, I just wish it hadn't happened. It's not fair."

Nick swung the kitchen door open. "Nope. Not fair at all. Just like life." He used momentum and the strength of his arms to pull himself across the threshold. "I may be shorter but I'm just fine. Don't worry about me, Tomás. Marines don't need legs. We're all about heart."

And I hope I can remember that, Nick thought to himself as he heard the door slam behind Tomás. Nick wheeled himself to his room, began the tedious process of dressing for the second time that day.

At the kitchen table for dinner Nick savored the taste of Tia Elena's chile rellenos. A pot full of frijoles and stacks of fresh flour tortillas waited on the counter for a second course. As they began to enjoy their meal, they heard the sound of a diesel engine grinding up the canyon toward the ranch.

Tomás looked up from his plate. "Vicente." A second engine sound followed the first. "Yup, probably got some people with him."

Nick swallowed hard. "Just in time to eat," he joked. Privately he wondered how Vicente would interpret his presence. His childhood memories left him with conflicting memories. Vicente had always seemed to be the cousin who somehow provoked childhood quarrels but who also failed to receive blame or punishment. Nick remembered he'd wondered as a kid how Vicente squeaked out of blame range.

"Eat fast. You never know how many there are with him." Tomás scooped another serving of rellenos onto both of their plates.

"We can always make more beans," Nick remarked.

Tomás looked up, his face honest and open. "That taste like Tia Elena's?"

"I see what you mean." Nick followed Tomás to the counter. They both laid out two tortillas, added dollops of beans and cheese, and rolled them into burritos. Nick wrapped his into a paper napkin and thrust the bundle into his Levi jacket pocket, while Tomás made fast work of finishing both rellenos and burritos.

The sound of the engines in the quiet of the evening moved around the house toward the corrals and stopped. A metal creak and crunch and the jingling of a chain preceded the falling thud of a truck ramp. Soon they could hear the hollow sound of horses' hooves on metal and the voices of men urging animals toward the corral.

"Yup," Tomás confirmed, swallowing his last bite, "Vicente's baaack."

Vicente surged in, blinking in the bright light of indoors. "Is there anything to eat around here?" He stopped short when he saw Nick. "Hey! Nick!"

Nick stood up, turned, almost fell over as his cousin wrapped him in a bear hug, then pounded him on the back. "I didn't know when you'd be coming." Vicente pulled back. His smile seemed genuine.

"Me either." Nick looked out toward the corrals. He could see men moving in the lights from the stable. "Who you got out there? They need some food?"

A lazy smile formed at the corner of Vicente's mouth. "Just some cowboys. And if you ever meet a cowboy who isn't hungry, let me know. Tomás, bunkhouse ready?"

"Yeah, *claro*. Always."

Nick watched as Vicente grabbed the relleno pan, stacked the tortillas on top, and placed the pot of beans square in the middle for balance.

"Let me give you a hand." Nick reached for the doorknob, stopped short of opening it.

Vicente's eyes flashed in annoyance, then went flat. "What?" He shifted his arms full of food closer to his chest.

"Wait a second. Why's Tomás holding down the ranch alone when he should be in school?" Nick watched as Vicente's face clouded. "Your dad always said, 'School first.'" Nick paused. "And Vicente, we need to talk about Roberto."

"You stop me for a conversation with my arms full and a hungry crew waiting outside? Move it, primo."

The two cousins locked eyes. Long seconds ticked by.

"I tell you what," Vicente broke, smiled, "I know you want to catch up, so let me get them settled out there and I'll be back in a flash."

Nick nodded slowly. "Sure," turned the knob, and opened the door outward.

Vicente pushed his way past. His boot steps crunched across the yard toward the barn. Nick watched until Vicente's receding back turned the corner to the bunkhouse. Tomás shrugged, lips clamped, scraped at his plate as he finished eating.

They took care of the dishes, an agreement of long standing with Tia Elena that she'd cook, but she expected a clean kitchen on her return. Tomás led the way in silence into the living room where he lit a fire.

Nick followed, settled on a sofa, and raised his legs onto a scarred oak coffee table. His prosthetics clunked against the wood. Resting his neck against the back of the sofa he looked up at the great vigas of oak that held up the roof, and thought of how many Diaz ancestors had gazed up at the same ceiling before him.

The fire caught and was snapping before Vicente returned, bringing a smell of horse and sweat. He threw himself into an armchair, hunched forward and studied Nick intently. "Does it hurt?"

Nick drew his legs back from the low table and sat up. Shrugged.

Vicente rubbed his palms together toward the fire. "Just glad to see you, man. You wouldn't believe how often we talk about you, especially from when you got hit."

"Thanks. I dreamed about sitting right here on the ranch every single day. Just like old times."

"Yeah, feels good, primo." Vicente unhooked one boot from under the other. The fire crackled and Tomás punched a poker into a log.

Nick watched his two cousins as the fire danced, thinking how much the two resembled one another, both long legged and square shouldered.

"Tomás says you guys didn't want to bother me in the hospital with ranch problems. But I wish you'd let me know about Roberto. Then I get here and find Tomás working alone." Nick searched Vicente's face. "You guys got me worried."

Vicente shifted forward, forearms resting on his knees, watched sparks fly up the chimney. "One day Roberto was just gone. Phfft!" He pressed his lips together in disapproval. "Never said a word to nobody."

"His wife and kids?"

"Marta knows Roberto always liked the ladies." Vicente's mouth curled into a thin smile. "I guess we all know that, eh?"

Nick sat back. "I can't picture him taking off from his family. What does the sheriff say?"

"Open investigation. No one's seen hide or hair of him for the past six months." Vicente stood and moved to the fireplace. "Give it."

Tomás handed the poker to his brother and Vicente jabbed at the wood sending sparks like fireflies flying onto the hearth and beyond.

"Damn, bro'!" Tomás stood and pulled his chair away from the fireplace, brushing his legs and the seat of the chair.

Vicente snorted. "Few sparks ain't gonna hurt you."

"So, what's up with changing the ranch's name?" Nick said.

Vicente turned to warm his backside. "Figured, 'What the

hell!' Roberto's gone, so I guess he don't care." Firelight played across Vicente's face, illuminating one side and leaving the other dark. "I changed it and made it a republic." Vicente's tone was defiant. "It's like our own country now."

"Hmm. I never thought of it as anything but the Diaz Ranch. I don't understand what you mean, 'like our own country.'" Nick stretched his arms, held them behind his head, elbows out. "Who's in your republic?"

"OUR republic. OUR country." Vicente walked across the room, ran one finger along the line of books on the top shelf. "Maybe it should be called something different. I mean I believe in democracy and all that, but we could call it like one of those countries in Europe." Vicente's face lightened, then glowed.

Nick hoped it was the firelight, and listened as his cousin continued speaking.

"When Roberto disappeared, I had to do something to keep us going. Somebody had to protect the family fortunes." Vicente reached a hand toward the bookshelf and pulled a volume out, placed it next to Nick on the sofa.

The book's cover of natural leather felt rough when Nick reached for it. The title, picked out in dim gold, gleamed softly. Nick read out loud:

"*Reino Perdido*. 'Lost Kingdom'. I remember this book." He looked directly into Vicente's eyes. "Your folks always said we were never supposed to touch it."

Vicente ignored his last sentence. "Kingdom. I thought of that." He leaned against the bookcase. "But I can't be president of a kingdom. I'd have to be a king, right? And I ain't no king." Vicente laughed softly.

Nick studied his cousin's face. "Suppose not. Kings go with kingdoms by right of birth, and presidents go with republics when they're elected." Nick lowered his gaze, and watched Vicente carefully. "So, when did you hold the election, Vicente?"

Vicente's expression shifted and his eyes flashed red, reflecting the fire. "You know Mom and Dad never let us touch that book."

"Well, yeah. That's what I just said, Vicente. They didn't want kids messing with it. What do you think they'd say about it now?"

Vicente blinked. "You're just like Roberto and Tomás. Jealous that I was the favorite. I can't help it if they loved me the most. They always liked what I did."

Nick sat back, amazed at Vicente's statement.

"You know I loved my mom and dad more than my brothers ever did. Mom always said I was the one who got things done, and now I'm doing those things."

Vicente held his hands out to Nick, who returned the book to him. Vicente opened the book and flipped gently through a few middle pages. "Well, we're not kids now. After Dad died, Roberto wanted to leave it on the shelf behind glass. But you know what it is, primo? What it really is? It's a way to organize our new country. It's a national treasure."

"How do you figure?"

"It's the beginning papers that establish the nation of the Republic of Dog Mountain." He stared into the fire, as if for inspiration. "Just like the U.S. Constitution."

Nick leaned back on the sofa. "I don't know, Vicente. It's kind of hard to compare the two. And isn't the ranch already part of another country?"

"C'mon. These things take time. You know, it's been part of different countries before now. First the ranch was owned by Indians, including the Apache. They sure thought it was theirs! Along came Spain, then Mexico. Somewhere in there France claimed it, too. Finally, Mexico sold it to the United States." Vicente placed the book back into the cabinet. "I keep it on the shelf, but it's always available to look at." He patted the book spine. I notified the government, state and federal. I sent them official letters and a declaration of separation."

"Really!" Nick smiled, a little taken aback. "And what did

the government say?" Nick felt warm. He wished he could think it was the fire.

"I never got nothing back." Vicente's voice held a note of triumph. A sheen of perspiration glistened across his cheeks and nose. "I raised our flag, posted our new name and signs, and here we are." He lifted his head higher, gazing down his nose into the fire. "Wouldn't Mom and Dad be proud? I did it for them! I even put it on the internet as a new nation! It really wasn't that big of a deal. Nobody ever cared that much about the border area, except maybe the Indians and the cavalry." He shrugged. "Nobody else cares about it now."

Nick shifted in his seat, sat up straighter. "Tomás and me care about the ranch. The other ranchers care about their spreads. The people in San Enebro and in Douglas care. Think about what happens every so often in *Cochise* County with Benson and Wilcox. Somebody gets a wild hair about taxes and threatens to secede from the county and the state!" Nick brought his legs off the table, leaned forward with an elbow on his one knee, and looked at his cousin. "It might be no one took your announcement seriously."

Vicente's face grew dark; his voice thickened. "More likely those old boys just don't get it." He leaned the poker against the native stone of the fireplace and stepped over to the chair where he'd left his jacket. "The Republic of Dog Mountain ain't no joke and neither am I. They better take me seriously 'cause I'm not messing around." Vicente turned on his heel and left. His words hung over the room like a dark cloud. The fire snapped, threw a spark onto the outer hearth.

Tomás let out a long breath, breathed out softly to Nick, "Now you see what I mean?"

"Yeah, I get it. Does anybody know what he's doing?"

The tips of Tomás's boots silhouetted against the flames created what looked like two mountain peaks. "I think Roberto might know." He paused. "Wherever he is." His lips puckered sideways.

"And Chapo, he might know, but I don't think he'll say anything."

"Chapo?"

"Vicente's foreman."

"I thought you were his foreman."

Tomás rested his head on one hand, elbow on the arm of the chair. "Just for the ranch. I don't know Vicente anymore. I'm scared of whatever it is he's doing."

"Vicente may be in charge, but we're here, too. And if we could just find Roberto...."

"We need to be careful." Tomás cast his gaze away. "When Vicente's mad . . . well, it's no telling what he'll do. Hardly anyone comes out anymore from San Enebro, just Tia Elena and once in a while Lucy." Tomás unfolded his knees, and stood facing the fireplace. "I just try to stay out of the way."

"We've got to trust one another, Tomás."

Tomás nodded.

"You know what a recon patrol is?"

Tomás nodded again. "Like in the movies when soldiers check out what's going on somewhere, so they can figure out what to do next?"

"You got it." Nick stood, stretched his back. "That's what we're going to do. You and me are on recon. We're going to gather information and decide what to do. Meantime, we keep it just between us."

Tomás's face brightened. "So, I'm like a Marine, Nick?"

"My first recruit. Think of it like a practice run to join up."

Tomás squared his shoulders and grinned. "Reporting for duty." His forehead creased. "Okay if I miss another day or two of school?"

Nick laughed out loud, stood up, and clapped him on the back. "Going to have to be."

CHAPTER 14

Looking for Tarantulas

Republic of Dog Mountain Ranch, *Cochise* County, Arizona

THE AROMA OF FRYING bacon tugged Nick awake as dawn lightened his window. He heard a woman's voice and remembered Tomás saying to expect Tia Elena in the morning.

At the same time, Nick reached down to scratch an annoying prickle on his foot. Mosquito bite, maybe. His hand moved down his thigh and past his right knee to ... nothingness.

"Damn!"

It was incredible how his body continued to feel something that wasn't there. Doctors told him he'd eventually reach a point where such brain stimuli would cease, but meanwhile the phantom itching continued. And it still surprised him. He threw his arms up above his pillow and settled into a ferocious concentration to will the tickling gone. He didn't want to get up.

He lay listening to the sounds of the ranch coming alive. The cheerful blue-and-white checked curtains of his childhood still hung at the bedroom window. An empty blue eggshell dangled from a ceiling viga, where he and his cousins had tacked it during shared childhood summers, along with some miniature pinecones, rattles from several snakes, and a pair of old-fashioned Spanish spurs, complete with pointed rowels, they'd found in a cave.

He still didn't want to get up. "I know, I know," he mumbled under his breath. "I MUST get up."

He didn't like putting on his legs, a tedious job that brought back bad memories every single day. The doctors and therapists at Walter Reed had taught him it was a normal reaction. His rehabilitation doctor had himself lost two legs in a ski accident. None of the amputees could BS another amputee, especially a medically trained one. "First thing you do every day is make the decision to get up immediately. It's what we do." The Doc eyeballed him and it made Nick squirm. Now he pushed away the desire to burrow into his pillow; threw the covers back, sat up. Incredibly, the phantom itching of legs that were no longer attached to his body stopped.

"Damn!"

Both prosthetics lay against a chair beside the bed, the left one plugged into an outlet. Nick began by unplugging it and turning it on. Next, he sprayed a mix of rubbing alcohol and water lightly into a silicone sleeve and slid the sleeve over his left residual limb. He checked to ensure the sleeve was flat against his thigh and pulled it tight over the stump. He sprayed the same lubricant lightly into the space-age prosthetic with a microprocessor "smart" knee, and pulled it up, using the button on the prosthetic to suction out the air and tighten the bionic leg to his body.

"One on," he said out loud, and groaned as he reached a little farther out and grabbed at the other prosthetic, "and one to go."

His right leg, with his own knee intact, was less of a nuisance, and always easier to arrange. A few spritzes into the sleeve and prosthetic and he pulled and secured his right leg on below the knee, no electronics needed. He tugged on his jeans, never easy, as his manmade foot invariably caught all the way down through long pant legs. It helped that he'd had his pants tailored with zippers along the seam of each leg. Next began the laborious process of adding his boots. Balancing himself carefully on the chair, he used the bed as a failsafe. He preferred to wear shorts, as shoes could be added to his legs easily before dressing. But at the ranch he needed jeans and boots, and there was no way he could put a prosthetic foot into a boot and then through the leg of a jeans.

In the bathroom he swiped a wet comb through his hair, finished snapping his brown plaid shirt, moving slowly to keep from a walk that began with a "hitch." Once in motion he barely limped, but he occasionally forgot to start slow, and had ended up more than once in a tangle on the floor. Not the most graceful, or safe, method of beginning a day. His legs smoothed into an easy walk without a limp as he entered the kitchen.

Tia Elena, his mother's younger sister, stood at the stove stirring potatoes and onions as bacon fried in an adjacent pan. She looked up, smiled at Nick. "Good morning, *sobrino*" (nephew).

Nick's hand released the door behind him and he moved toward his aunt. "Tia, now I know I'm home." He watched her smile widen and admired the familiar face.

Something rattled in the pantry and his aunt looked away. A blurred figure threw itself in a tornado from the pantry doorway, almost pushing him over.

"Niiick!" Eleven-year-old Lucy pounced on him, wrapped her arms tightly around his waist, burrowed her head into his chest.

Nick laughed out loud. "Who is this? What happened to my sidekick?"

Lucy drew back, her face electric. "It's me!" She laughed with delight. "I've got so much to show you. Let's go saddle the horses for a ride. We'll go down canyon and count how many tarantulas we see. Tomás said you can ride, right? Lemme' see your legs. Oh, is that rude? Never mind, let's go. Do they hurt?" Lucy had grabbed one of his hands and was pulling him toward the kitchen door.

"Not so fast, Miss Lucy. Give your uncle a chance to sit

down and eat his breakfast." Tia Elena set a steaming pot on the long ranch table. "And don't I get a hug, Nick?" She opened her arms wide and embraced her nephew, placing a big kiss on his cheek. "There. That's better."

She turned to Lucy. "And maybe your Uncle Nick has some plans this morning. And yes, that was rude. *A Dios mio.*" She held out a cup to Nick. "Here's your coffee, *nieto.* You've got to understand Lucy's kept her fingernails chewed to the quick since you ended up in the hospital."

"I loved your letters," Nick squeezed Lucy's shoulder. "They really helped." He grabbed one of her hands and held it up to the light. "You can stop chomping your nails now."

She grabbed her hand away. The offending appendage disappeared behind her back. "I wanted to remind you of everything here so you'd come back." Suddenly shy, she jammed her hands into her jeans' pockets.

Nick remembered the trials of being eleven. "I could see the ranch and the mountains, the horses and the trails, when you described them."

Lucy beamed. She moved to the stove, heaped eggs, potatoes, and crisp bacon onto a plate and delivered them to Nick. She passed him two biscuits from a basket on the table, and sat down. "Eat. We have a lot to do."

The kitchen door opened and a brisk waft of air swept into the room. Vicente stuck his head in the kitchen door. "Where's Tomás?"

Tia Elena stepped back from the stove; her spatula held as if she might take a swat at him. She eyed him with disapproval. "No 'good morning'? *Falta, sobrino*" (Forgot something, nephew).

He breathed in deeply, ignoring her criticism of his rudeness. "Oh, it smells good in here. I hope you have a plate ready for me, Tia."

"Good morning, Vicente," she pursued. "How many people you feeding this morning besides yourself?"

Vicente's eyes flattened. "Not too many. Tortillas and beans are good." Something clicked and he finally greeted his aunt. "Good morning, Tia."

"Give me a couple of minutes and I'll have eggs and potatoes ready."

"Okay. Where's Tomás?"

"He already ate and rode out. He said you wanted a pack horse waiting at the trail head." Tia Elena moved sizzling strips of bacon onto a plate, added some eggs and potatoes, and handed the plate to Vicente. "Sit. It's easier to eat at the table."

Vicente sniffed the plate appreciatively, took a seat across from Nick and Lucy.

"I told Tomás I'd help him. He should've woken me up." Nick broke a warm, homemade biscuit in two and Lucy passed him butter, then honey.

"He came through here before light. I'm not even sure he ate anything. I was just starting up with cooking." Tia Elena shifted a pan off the stove.

"I'm sorry I missed him." Nick turned to his cousin. "But in that case, anything I can help you with this morning, primo?"

Vicente swallowed his mouthful of egg. "Nothing really to help with. Chapo and the boys know what they're doing."

"Well, good." Nick wondered why Vicente turned him down. Extra hands were always a bonus in ranch work. "I can ride, you know."

Vicente frowned. "Sure, Nick. It's just there's no need. You should be doing something here for fun. The crew's got it under control."

A thought wafted across Nick's mind. What does he not want me to see? He turned to Tia Elena, held up the last bite of his biscuit. "I missed your biscuits, Tia."

His aunt flushed, pleased. Lucy whisked his empty plate away and refilled both his and Vicente's coffee cups. Nick gave her a smile and a wink.

"So, Vicente, how many hands you taking to Old Man Loreto?"

Vicente looked up, his tone mild. "Just me and Tomás and the crew. Loreto's doing the end of fall round up, bringing in the last of their cattle from the canyons. It'll just be a lot of canyon riding."

Nick raised his eyebrows, noticed his cousin had not included the number of hands. "Things must have really changed. We used to take every rider we could get for that."

"Yeah, you're right. Things have changed." Vicente's mouth opened. He scooped up a mouthful of potatoes, chewed.

"How is Old Man Loreto anyway?" In their youth the Loreto ranch had been an often-visited neighbor. Four Loreto daughters, all of them pretty, had ensured a constant stream of young male visitors for week-end rides, picnics, and parties. Some of Nick's best summer memories revolved around the Loreto Ranch and those girls.

"Same as ever. Always thinks he knows everything best." Vicente stood up, still chewing, and made his way toward the door. "See you later. Got stuff to do."

"Hey, Cuz, okay if Lucy and I go riding?"

Vicente straightened. "Sure, why not. There's a couple of horses out there."

"Alright man."

Vicente saw that Tia Elena had placed a big pan of eggs, bacon, and potatoes with a stack of fresh tortillas, all covered with a clean tea towel, on the counter. He grabbed the pan, paper plates and napkins, and plastic forks she'd set beside it. With his arms full, Vicente nodded and tipped his head at Tia Elena to open and hold the door. She pursed her lips, but pushed the kitchen door outward and he quickly stepped past her.

"*Falta*," she said critically again. "I always wonder if anyone out there is left hungry." Tia Elena grabbed a sponge and swiped at the counter.

"I guess they'd ask for more," Nick responded.

Tia Elena sighed. "I wonder." She folded the dishcloth and laid it across the sink.

Nick swallowed his last gulp of coffee. "What do you say, Lucy? Looks like you and me are released from all duties." Plus, he thought, I want to get out and see what's going on.

"Let's go!" Lucy said and pushed back her chair. The scraping sound brought Tia Elena's attention.

"Watch out for this speed demon, Nick!"

Nick made his way across the kitchen, stopped to give his tia a peck on the cheek, and jammed his hat on his head. He laughed at Lucy's receding back as she raced to the barn, and he followed more sedately. Home, he thought, jamming his hat on his head. So good to be home.

Twenty minutes later saw Nick mounted and moving down the dirt road toward the ranch entrance gate, Lucy riding ahead and chattering in high spirits. They saw their first tarantula just before they reached the gate.

"Look!" Lucy called, startling her mount, a young red roan, who side-stepped.

"Whoa." She turned the roan around and put him into a series of figure 8s. "I ride this one all the time, but he never gets used to tarantulas. He sure is nervous."

"He's just young." Nick watched Lucy reassure the pony of who was in charge. She urged the roan into a short spurt back up the road so it could settle.

Nick's horse, a bony buckskin, plodded forward undaunted. Nick pulled up on the opposite side of the road to wait, tried to swallow his own revulsion at seeing the big spider. Morning sun warmed his back and he shook his shoulders and straightened his posture.

He inhaled the tangy smell of sage, put his attention on the tarantula's progress. It continued to make its eight-legged way in a businesslike manner, scrabbling over pebbles. Nick's buckskin shook its halter, jingling, as Lucy wheeled the roan in beside him.

Lucy stared down at the tarantula. "Makes me think of some horror movie. What if it was big as my horse?" The roan blew out and Lucy laughed.

"I don't even want to go there," Nick said. "I always think of that old joke: 'Why does a tarantula cross the road?'"

"I think that's a chicken joke." Lucy said. "I've been around tarantulas all my life. They don't worry me. Look!" She handed Nick her reins, stepped down from the roan, picked up the tarantula and held it upside down toward the horses. As the eight legs thrashed the air, both horses shuffled backward, stirring up dust. "See?"

"Just don't complain if it bites you." Nick held both horses at short rein and tried hard to hide his discomfort.

"Nah. He won't do that. I know how to hold 'em. I'm just moving him out of the road." She placed the large arachnid several yards onto the high desert floor, headed in the same direction. "There you go." She watched as the tarantula walked around a large chunk of stone and continued relentlessly toward the source of the aroma that beguiled him.

"We could try following him to the female's den, but they're so slow. Let's go up on top of the cliff. Last week I saw a whole bunch there."

Nick nodded. "I'd like to ride that ridge, look at all the places I missed for so long."

Lucy reached for her horse's reins and Nick held them high. "First, wash your hands, tarantula lover."

Lucy wrinkled her nose in protest. But she took a moment to pour water from her canteen over her hands and wash away any bothersome tarantula hairs which could cause rashes and itching.

"Alright, totally no hairs," Lucy said. She remounted, dug her heels in the roan's sides and went into a trot. She ignored the gate with all the signs and led Nick on his buckskin back into the rocks where a narrow deer trail climbed up the slope of the box canyon. Once on top they gave the horses a chance to blow while they surveyed the ranch from the west side of the canyon.

"Looks like the ranch is asleep." Lucy shifted in the saddle. She saw no movement below. No horses or vehicles moved. No one appeared outside. Even the dogs had disappeared.

"I've seen it look like this in other places." Nick's voice went soft. He thought of Afghanistan and the mud villages that slept, sun drenched at the base of mountains, in the middle of plains, or by the side of thin rivers. They looked asleep, but it was a lie. There was always something about to happen.

"Like where?" Lucy's question hung in the air a moment.

He had to shake himself away from memory. "Oh, I dunno. Maybe it's just me daydreaming. Let's head over to the canyon with the cliff dwelling caves, you know the ones."

"Not so many tarantulas there."

"Maybe not, but it's a pretty ride."

"Okay! But I get to lead." Lucy grinned.

Nick returned the grin, suddenly buoyant with life, free of worries for the moment. He encouraged the horse forward with light heel pressure.

Back home.

CHAPTER 15

Rocks in the Road

Enmedios (In the Middle)
Chiricahua Apache Homeland

NAADIKTAZ, IT WIGGLES, PUZZLED over the first reports the scouts brought. They had reached the Spring That Always Flows at the place called Enmedios, In the Middle. The water bubbled fresh and cold from deep within the earth. Animal sign around the water indicated its use by area wildlife. A few boot tracks smudged by wind and overlaid by animals showed a recent human presence of just a day or two past. The entire group of tired children separated into two parts: those who hobbled the horses for grazing on scanty desert shrubs and those who began a concealed fire and set pots of beans to soak in preparation for cooking.

It Wiggles sent two girls on a search for signs left by *Biyoo'*, Her Beads. They returned and reported to It Wiggles who followed them eagerly to where a dry bush struggled to keep its hold against the rocks near the spring. Hidden under the bush's branches he saw a broken stick with one end pointing west, the other severed part lay under the first pointing north. Up against the rock leaned a woven cloverleaf where the wind could not dislodge it; in front of the cloverleaf a handful of small pebbles lay in the sand.

"What does it mean?" It Wiggles looked at the two girls.

"The way is broken." *Binat'izh*, Eyebrows, pantomimed breaking a stick with both hands. "We must go west, then north." She closed one eye at It Wiggles. He waited. "It broke our way and we cannot go straight north."

"*Ha'ah*," It Wiggles approved. "What are the pebbles?" This time he looked at ten-year-old *In'łt'áni*, Cricket.

Cricket picked up several of the small stones and rolled them between her fingers, her raspy voice almost a song. "Many people. Or maybe many animals." She stared at the pebbles in her hand. "Umm, they are between the spring and the way north." She smiled shyly, flashed a quick look at It Wiggles. " 'Watch out for them,' our eldest sister says."

"*Enjuh*." It Wiggles complimented the girls, and asked them to pass the word to the other children.

He assigned two of the boys, *Bee eshgané,* Left Hand, and *Ch'anáidił'įį,* He Hides It, to investigate what might have broken the way and to watch while the others rested as evening descended. He made sure the scouts received food before they melted into the dusk climbing upward onto the slope of the big rocks.

Left Hand returned in under an hour and reported lights at the north end of the rocky ridges that made up Enmedios. He described lines of yellow and red eyes in the dusk, moving above the lights of what he thought must be a village. "The eyes follow a path. They curve in long loops, always on the same trail," he reported. "Yellow eyes go all one way; red the other."

It Wiggles, perplexed by the details, followed Left Hand to where He Hides It lay concealed, watching the valley. He Hides It beckoned his leader forward. Flattening himself beside the scout, It Wiggles looked into the dark space below and peered at lights in rows that outlined a large number of square-shaped houses at the north end of Enmedios, a place that should have no village. He picked out figures in the fading light that moved from one square house to the next. He caught his breath as he saw a set of yellow eyes crawl toward the edge of what the boys had described as a village. Farther out, a line of yellow eyes moved one way and red eyes moved opposite.

"Ah! The yellow eyes come toward us, brothers, and the red travel away. They are the eyes of metal wagons."

The boys sucked in their breath.

"And houses made of cloth," It Wiggles said softly. "How many people do you think?"

The boys exchanged a quick look. Left Hand whispered. "Many times our number, but they have guards," and nodded with his chin at the perimeters of the settlement.

"And guns," added He Hides It.

"Soldiers." It Wiggles said quietly, and described the signs *Her Beads* had left them at the spring. "We must take another path."

The boys drew back from the stone ledges and It Wiggles crawled behind them to the western side of the rocky ridges. Left Hand whispered. "We saw a dry streambed to the west, perhaps a half day's travel. Eldest Sister must have chosen that way."

It Wiggles gazed long into the low desert, willing himself to see through the gathering darkness. He realized they would not be able to see ahead before they must travel. "Be ready," he told the boys. "We will move later tonight."

He turned back to the camp, found the children already sleeping, a guard overlooking the south end of the desert. He gave instructions to the guard to awaken him when the moon reached the middle of the night. In a few hours the guard roused him and the two boys moved about the sleeping children, dropping pebbles on chests.

When It Wiggles found Pretty One she came awake at once. "We must move now in the early dark," he told her.

"The children have slept so little," she told him, "but the beans should be ready."

It Wiggles nodded and Pretty One moved to the hidden fire. She scraped the coals from around the cooking vessels, filled bowls with the cooked beans as children came forward, and the entire camp ate quickly, silently, passing the bowls on to others.

Horses, kept calm with handfuls of dry grasses, drank their fill at the spring, stood steady as loads were tied on their backs. No human voice disturbed the night. It Wiggles sent a child to bring in the scouts, and when they arrived, he held a quiet council.

"It is as Grandmother told us here at The Spring That Always Flows." The children grouped noiselessly, the scouts finishing the last of the beans from their bowls. "Our ancestor *Ndee* have found water here from before the lives of our grandfathers' grandfathers."

The children followed his every word, still licking at the corners of their mouths.

It Wiggles used his lips to point north. "There's the path we want to follow. But it's blocked by people in cloth houses, soldiers. We know where to find water on that path. We know it leads to the canyon called It Hides the Way and that a raiding trail crosses the desert to the mountains of the *Mescalero* people." He looked off into the west. "Eldest Sister has gone before us. She marks our path, and we follow her sign. Our younger sisters have found her message here, and we move now in the dark to avoid those soldiers. She tells us to go west."

It Wiggles's face didn't register the trepidation he felt. "Everyone has eaten? All must drink, as we do not know the path we follow, across the desert west to the first deep riverbed. There we will sleep through the day and travel again tomorrow night. We are close to the land of the ancestors and *Ussen* will protect us if we follow the chosen path." It Wiggles waited as a small rustle moved around and through the children.

"Now we will disappear. Our older brother," and he indicated His Big Toe with a push of his lips, "will choose two others to move the horses. Little Ones, you will help move everything else; the rest will find grass for the horses and clean away our tracks and firepit." He looked about the small group. "Fill your water containers. Drink deeply again before we leave."

The children quickly and silently filled their gourd canteens and drank from the spring, then went about their tasks, burying all evidence of their fire, sweeping away foot- and horse prints as they moved out to the edge of the desert. Four of the older children bent close to the ground, made a final sweep of the area around the spring, remembering to use their knuckles and palms to form some tracks of lizards, coyotes, a few birds near the lip of the water. They melted into the dark, brushing away the marks of their own travel a good quarter of a mile into the desert.

• • •

When a military jeep pulled up on the desert floor midmorning below Enmedios spring, no indications remained to show any human visitors had rested there earlier. Four men in Mexican camouflage uniforms carrying AR-15s scanned the area with binoculars before climbing up the gradual incline to the spring.

"The usual," the leader reported on the jeep radio. "Nada, nothing. A few animal tracks. No sign of anything else."

CHAPTER 16

Return to Fear

Colonia Suiza, East Side Sierra Madre Range, *Chihuahua*, Mexico

ESTEBAN AND IGNACIO RECEIVED a warm welcome when they arrived at the Colonia Suiza big house right at the dinner hour. The *colonia* made Ignacio dizzy. So many blue- and green- and grey-eyed women, some even blonde and redheaded, in a country where dark hair and eyes were the standard.

Rafael Ellsworth, hair as red as the grandfather who'd settled his group of Swiss immigrants in the foothills of the Sierra Madre a century before, greeted his neighbors. "You'll stay the night?"

Ellsworth, born and raised in the *Chihuahua colonia*, followed a modernized version of what his ancestor established with three wives and numerous children in a religious commune. What had begun with a family of twenty was now a thriving settlement of two hundred. It would have been larger except twice in the last century the group had split, needing more farming and ranching space. Children turned out to be the largest crop of all.

Ellsworth, a large man whose deep-set eyes and broad jaw were reflected in many of the faces of the children around the main dining room, ushered Esteban and Ignacio to sit at his table. Unaccustomed to the presence of so many at table for a meal, Ignacio shyly took the seat indicated, next to an attractive young woman about his own age of eighteen.

"Will you try the beef chili, señor?" Her eyes were very green above the bowl of beans and meat.

"*Si, gracias,*" Ignacio said, his tongue clinging to the roof of his mouth, making him lisp.

He saw his father bite a smile back and Ignacio's polite turmoil increased. Indeed, the woman was very pretty. And women, pretty or not, were a scarce commodity at Rancho Garcia.

"And will you try some fresh corn? We picked it only today."

Ignacio smiled. "*Si, por favor.*" He could not stop staring at the woman's lips of palest pink.

The woman offered no conversation, but passed tortillas. At one point she asked Esteban, across the table, if he would care for a second helping, and then turned again to Ignacio, and asked the same. He reached forward clumsily, bumped the dish and all the tortillas scattered onto the table. As the woman recovered the tortillas, Ignacio sat back with a blazing red face. Several other women moved quietly around the table offering coffee and cuts of a quince cobbler.

"*Dulce?*" (Dessert?), the women asked.

"*Si,*" Ignacio answered, biting back his discomfort, thinking who could dare refuse homemade sweet pastry?

He accepted a dish and the green-eyed woman immediately asked, "*Helado?*" (Ice cream?)

Small wisps of raven hair curled around her temples, dark halos that framed her green eyes.

"*Si, gracias señorita,*" he responded again, utterly entranced by her charm and the table tittered. Ignacio looked around, puzzled that his best manners would draw laughter.

The young woman smiled. "*Señora,*" she corrected. "Señora Ellsworth."

Ignacio's ears and face burned. He now saw the ring on her slender hand and realized his mistake. Father and son exchanged a glance of understanding that they'd momentarily forgotten the *colonia* custom of plural wives.

"Perdóneme, Señora Ellsworth." Ignacio looked to the head of the table, *"Y Señor Ellsworth."*

A second titter traveled softly around the table and Ignacio looked up to see his host's eyes examining him with what appeared to be pity.

As dinner ended Ellsworth invited the father and son to retire into the big house's study where the purpose of their visit could be discussed. The two Garcia men settled into soft armchairs while their host took the chair behind the desk. "Now gentlemen, what brings you to our side of the sierra?"

"We are here, Don Rafael, for help." Esteban addressed him in the way of the mountain people, as an equal.

Esteban described the theft of horses and supplies from their property, footprints under the bedroom window, the two dead dogs, the route taken by the thieves into the sierra, the finding of the odd leather necklace.

Ignacio pulled the necklace from an inside jacket pocket. He laid it on the desktop, spreading it out so the peculiar piece of metal folded over with a hand-worked scalloped edge and the things woven into the four strands could be examined.

Ellsworth poked at it with the end of a meaty pinky finger, and looked at his visitors. "Hold on. We need somebody else here." He left the room and returned a few minutes later, followed by a grizzled, older man. "This is Lucero Gonzales. He's from down the Sierra Madre, born and raised near Creel. He asked the man, *"¿Qué le parece,* Lucero?" (What do you think?)

Lucero reached a tentative hand toward the necklace, but withdrew it quickly without touching it, exactly as if it could bite. With eyes wide he peered at Ellsworth, then the others. Lucero backed away from the cord. At the same time, he drew a cross from under his shirt and held it tight in a closed fist. *"Es muy malo, patron"* (It's very bad, boss).

The others all looked up, questioning.

"*¿Brujería?*" Esteban's hushed voice slightly quivered.

"*Peor que brujería*" (Worse than witchcraft), Lucero replied. Esteban drew in a breath. "I knew it." His face blanched and a frisson shivered across his shoulders. "I was afraid to know it," he said quietly. His head wagged back and forth in alarm, and he stated aloud words no one wanted to hear. "Los Apaches."

Ignacio, as the youngest present had not spoken. Confused, he looked at both his father and Lucero. "*¿Qué dices?* (What are you saying?) That's all done with now."

Lucero's voice, tight with fear, asked, "Perhaps it is old? Found in a cave?"

"Thieves dropped it in my corral as they stole my horses last night," Esteban said firmly. "It is not something old."

"Perhaps someone found it and left it to mix you up?" Lucero's face seemed hopeful.

"No," Esteban said, shaking his head. "We did not see them, but we know they came on foot. There were no tire prints and no other horse tracks besides our own. Anywhere. And they headed back into the sierra with our horses."

Lucero moved several steps backward toward the door, his expression distraught. He looked at each face in the room. "Then it can only be the Broncos. Where did this happen?"

"Across the sierra about forty miles south, near Nacori Chico."

Fear flooded his face. "They could be anywhere in the sierra by now."

Esteban stood, looked around the room. "News of this can do us no good. The Broncos will go places they know, places we know. We must take care of this ourselves, before outsiders come."

Ignacio's voice thinned, one leg jigging with nerves. "But father, the Nacori Chico police thought it might be drug runners, or maybe juvenile delinquents. It can't be the Broncos," he argued, although no one argued back. "They've been gone for all my life. How could I never see one?" He glared at his father and raised his voice. "You told me they were gone!"

"They should be gone." Esteban said in a flat tone, stared in revulsion at the cord as if looking at a ghost.

"*¿Quien sabes?*" (Who knows?) Ellsworth interrupted, rubbed his fingertips in small circles at both temples. "We all miss a cow or a goat or a horse once in a while. We always think it's a bear or coyote. We see no one."

Lucero turned his hat in his hands. "Don Rafael, the vaqueros today sent someone down for more supplies. They said a bear got into their camp."

Ellsworth stared at his foreman. "Where in the mountains?"

"The canyon called Pinos Altos, Tall Pines."

Esteban shook his head. "No, Tall Pines Canyon is too far from our ranch. It can't be the same ones who stole our horses."

Ignacio turned in his seat, eagerly agreed with his father. "It's just a bear," he said, "don't you think?"

"Unless they are moving in different groups." Ellsworth frowned. "They do that, you know."

Lucero's rough hands trembled as he turned the brim of his hat round and round between his fingers. His eyes slipped back to the cord that lay across the desk. "*Patrón. Los demonios están de vuelta*" (The devils are back).

CHAPTER 17

Crossroads

Chiricahua Mountains, *Cochise* County, Arizona

VICENTE RODE A QUARTER mile in advance of the porters, whose measured pace annoyed him. The sky, a clean blue, stretched above the aspens turning yellow and red along the trail; a perfect fall day, exactly the kind Vicente remembered from childhood. Seated on the roan, a horse once reserved for Roberto, he filled his lungs with the crisp morning air. The day was proceeding just as he'd planned. An early telephone call had alerted him that the semitruck waited ahead. He'd sent Tomás to bring in a pack animal and shoved Nick out of the way. The trail was wide open, and soon, he congratulated himself, he would be very rich.

At the trailhead Vicente found The Gray nibbling grass at the base of a stand of aspens. Tomás sat on his haunches, his back propped against a tree, watching some birds that fluttered in and about the canopy of fall leaves. The mule Vicente had sent him to collect and bring was nowhere in sight.

"No Larry?" Vicente had expected to use the mule to carry water and food, and as a back-up if any of the porters gave out. Maybe, it briefly occurred to him, he shouldn't have sold most of the horses.

"Nope. Probably find him in a canyon along with some maverick steers."

"The porters are right behind me." Vicente looked around. "Do you know how long Nick is planning to stay?"

"Well, I think he's come home."

Vicente scowled. "Ride over to Loreto's. You only need The Gray. When you get there, find out if they've seen Larry. Do whatever they need you to do. I'll see you back at the ranch in a couple of days."

Tomás studied his older brother. "I thought we were doing the usual. I thought you and Chapo and the others were going to help at Loreto's."

Fall roundups were the same every year: bring in cattle, separate calves, count them,

brand calves, run them through a tick dip, reunite them with their mothers, herd them back into valley pockets to find cover for the winter months.

"Not this year. You, little brother, are the official family representative. Chapo and I are busy."

Tomás opened his mouth to respond, then shut it, as Vicente turned away.

The line of men approached. Vicente shook his head impatiently at Chapo who led the column onto the path toward Hackberry Canyon and the Crest Trail, once used by the Apache to cover their approach and withdrawal from raiding. It especially annoyed him that Chapo seemed to be enjoying a leisurely jaunt, and continued to whistle an old Mexican cowboy tune about roping a devil steer. "What took you so long, Chapo?"

Chapo looked behind him at the walking line of men. Each carried an empty pack frame on his back. "They're just getting used to the packs, boss, and it's all uphill." He glanced at Tomás, raised an eyebrow, and moved past.

Tomás rose from sitting on his heels, asked his older brother, "What are you doing with these guys? What are the packs for?"

Vicente narrowed his eyes. "You really want to know my business, *joven*?"

Tomás bit back a protest at the inferred insult of being called a youth too young to comprehend his brother's business. "What do you want me to tell the Loretos? They're expecting more help."

Vicente's face darkened. "Don't worry about it. Tell 'em there's no one else to help, except a cripple who'd just be in the way. Tell 'em they're welcome very much for your help."

Tomás rolled his lips, frustrated, said nothing. Suddenly thought, so why did I have to meet you so early? But didn't voice it. He placed one hand on The Gray's pommel, swung into the saddle. He nodded at his brother and turned onto the path leading toward Loreto Ranch.

"Good answer," Vicente said, watching his little brother ride away. "And stay out of the way," he muttered to himself, pleased he'd succeeded in getting Tomás out of his hair. No complications. Just the way he wanted it.

Vicente jabbed his own mount in the sides with the heels of his boots and went into a canter after the file of porters. Took care of that, he thought smugly as he pushed his mount past the porters. For a quick moment he felt bad at having called Nick a cripple. Ah well, let him babysit Lucy. The kid was always underfoot asking about her Daddy. Now Nick wanting to know, "Where's Roberto?". Those two could have a great time whining at each other. Pretty inconvenient Nick had to turn up at the ranch at this moment. And Tomás could just grow up. Time for him to take on some responsibility and recognize the Republic was about to become something really big. Vicente took a deep breath. It's all coming together, he thought.

At the trailhead he decided to ride on alone on the high trail, a shorter route to their destination, but steeper. Let Chapo play nursemaid on the flat route. Vicente watched his *segundo* lead the line of men away, some of them already limping.

"Pah!" he spat on the ground. Not even a mile from the ranch, without a load, and already their feet hurt. He'd paid for this crew and he wanted his money's worth. Of course, once this deal was over, he'd be in the big money. His lips curved into a smile. And in his own country.

CHAPTER 18

Biyoo's Path

Chiricahua Mountains, Chiricahua Apache Homeland, *Cochise* County, Arizona

BIYOO', HER BEADS, SAW the enemy warrior with a young girl, both on horseback, approaching uphill from the south. The mule brayed once before she hauled his reins in tight. She already knew a few of the mule's bad habits: the first, to avoid moving fast; the second, to make too much noise.

She leaped from his back, muffled his nose, pulled him down a rocky slope into a cluster of pines, knowing she left a thick slide mark behind under settling dust, trusting the riders were slow enough coming uphill the dust would settle and they would not notice it. She remained shadowed in the pines, confident the line of their forms became indistinguishable in tree trunks and shadows. She waited, hand tight across the mule's nose, watching the dust settle just a handful of seconds before hearing the riders pass above her.

"Mule, you are too much trouble," she said quietly, at the same time she scratched her mount between his ears. "I could still eat you."

The mule bent his head left so her fingers could reach a little farther. *Her Beads* obliged him, watched his eyes close in bliss. She would have laughed aloud at his expression, but instead pulled the animal behind her farther down the slope toward the creek below. She knew she couldn't return to the trail for a while, and she wanted nothing to do with the enemy warrior. She thought of his ready posture by the spring. He must surely be a warrior of strength and cunning. She knew her own skills likely to be challenged by such a man. Still, she thought, he had smiled in a way that showed no evil intent. Stop, she thought, brushing a loose strand of hair away from her face. Grandmother would not find these thoughts helpful. And yet, she could not dismiss the interest in his eyes. The enemy warrior did not seem to match what she'd been taught to expect.

At the creek's edge she tied the mule to a tree so it could drink and feed on grasses by the water. She drank there, filled her gourd, sat and thought. She was off the trail of Grandmother's memory. She knew the path was the most direct, but she could not follow it with so many other travelers. Her stomach rumbled. She patted her food bag, found it flat, and looked around. Rocks jumbled along the stream and scattered into a small meadow where rabbit droppings caught her eye. *Ussen* provided.

Her Beads unloosed a six-foot piece of handmade agave fiber rope from around her waist. Picking up a few rabbit droppings, she rubbed them in her palms, hiding her human odor, then ran the cord through her hands. She bound the cord around a sapling, and positioned a slipknot noose to hang over a rabbit path about two inches off the ground, held in place by a stick driven into the earth. Along the creek Her Beads found and pulled out clumps of watercress, arranged them under the noose. Her trap was ready.

At the creek she washed her hands, rolling pebbles through her fingers. The water was cold and refreshing, and she drank to fill her empty belly. The mule had already cleared the area around its tree of forage. Following along the waterway, Her Beads gathered grasses at the water's edge, carried them back to the mule, noting deer tracks. A salamander splashed among the rocks. Her Beads settled into the shelter of a low thicket and slept.

She awoke with a start at the high-pitched scream of a rabbit. Scrambling out of the brambles, she ran toward the sound. The shrill cries would bring in predators, and she couldn't afford to lose her meal. The rabbit's wail, strident, piercing, filled the little meadow so that all other noises ceased. She raced to her snare and found a fat rabbit dangling pitifully by one hind leg. No dewlap, a male. The thrashing of its body had quickly worn a bald spot on the ground. She unsheathed her knife, grabbed the rabbit by its ears, and slashed its throat. She held the animal in her hands, thanked *Ussen* for providing. Resetting the snare, she placed more watercress as bait, hoping she might catch another.

At the edge of the creek *Her Beads* attempted to remove the skin in one long inside out pull. The knife nicked the skin in two places that she'd have to mend later. She scraped the major bits of muscle and flesh away and laid the pelt underwater, held down by stones.

Her Beads arranged the carcass on a rock and removed the intestines. She retained the solid two pounds of meat and moved to the hillside where large rocks would conceal her from above. An overhanging tree helped dispel smoke. After building a fire, she passed a hardwood stick through the rabbit carcass and placed it to roast over the small fire. The liver and heart would be baked separately, favorite tidbits that cooked fast.

Light slanted west as she began her meal, eating half, wrapping the remainder in long grasses. She swallowed each bite of the seared sweetmeats with special enjoyment. She delayed leaving, but no other rabbit took her bait. She collected her snare cord, brushed the ground with a branch, returned to the creek to wash the watercress from the trap and ate it, enjoying the fresh green taste. She recovered the rabbit skin from the water, laid it across a boulder to drip, extinguished the fire, brushed it into oblivion. Nothing remained to indicate her brief presence other than rabbit's entrails. Those would be gone before morning, a gift to small animals.

Her Beads tucked the damp rabbit skin under her skirt's waist at the small of her back, and jumped onto the mule. She'd seen a low place in the valley wall that would make an easy climb back up to the path, and she hoped to shelter near the house of the old ones, if she could find it. She wanted to parallel the way described by Grandmother, until she could resume her journey on the main mind map trail.

And she didn't want to see the enemy warrior again. His power was strong, or how would he have come to ride the same trail she now followed? Her hand went automatically to the power bag around her neck, seeking its reassuring protection. She let out a deep breath and urged the mule up the cut of the steep valley wall. "Help me, *Ussen*," she prayed, "to see the enemy ahead."

DANGEROUS TRAILS

CHAPTER 19

Searching for the Good Old Times

Hackberry Canyon, *Chiricahua* Mountains, *Cochise* County, Arizona

LUCY TURNED HER HEAD to look at Nick. The midafternoon sun angled across the mountains and valleys, and caught Nick and his mount in a slant of light. "You look like an old-time cowboy."

Nick grinned. He felt like a cowboy riding out of the past. He knew the canyon and the trail from his boyhood, part of the connecting trails that wound through the *Chiricahua* Mountains all the way north to Ft. Bowie. A cavalry trail, no doubt imposed over an Indian one, ran the ridges of the mountain range.

He eyed Lucy's boots in the stirrups. "If we were back in the old days though, you wouldn't be riding in pants. You'd be riding side saddle!"

"No way!" Lucy's lip stuck out. "I can out ride, out rope, out shoot ..."

Nick cut her off. "What do you mean out shoot? You better not be messing with guns on your own."

"Dad used to take us all out to the gun range to practice. Since he's been gone Tomás takes me along when he target shoots. He's always careful, and me, too. In fact, I can out careful any old boy. I can out ... "

"Okay, okay, I got the picture Annie Oakley." He stretched

his arms and shoulders, regarded his niece's back ahead on the trail. "What do you know about your dad being gone?"

Lucy pulled her horse up to let Nick come alongside. "I don't know anything. He kissed us kids goodnight and that was the last time I saw him." Her horse shifted weight and cocked a hip.

Above, a pair of circling hawks sailed with the wind. Nick watched the birds of prey soar upward and his eyes drifted down the back of the ridge they'd just crossed, to the path they continued on. He noted fresh hoofprints ahead that could only be Larry's by their size. Silently he wondered how Larry had managed to get so far away from the grazing meadow. "What do you think happened to your dad?"

Lucy's chin dropped for just one moment; she bit her lower lip that had begun to tremble. "I don't know. Mom sat around and cried for days."

"Where did she think he went?"

"Mom said he told her he was driving out to the ranch, but . . .," Lucy's voice quivered, "but Vicente told us he never got there. And Tomás didn't see him, but he said he saw my dad's truck go by on the highway that day."

"Any news since?"

Lucy shook her head no.

"Where else do you think he might go?"

"Vicente said he has girlfriends. That's what he told my mom." Lucy looked defiantly into Nick's eyes. "I don't think it's true. Do you think it's true, Nick?"

"I don't know, Lucy, but I'd never think your dad would leave your mom and you kids. It just doesn't make sense to me. I know he loves all of you more than anything."

"That's what I told my mom." Lucy frowned. "She says she thinks something bad happened, but I don't know what's worse than him just disappearing. Do you?"

"Did his truck show up again?"

Lucy shook her head no.

"Not knowing at all is the worst, more than knowing even a little." Nick paused, crinkled his forehead, considered if it might be too harsh for an eleven-year-old to hear, went ahead and said it anyway. "Even if it's bad." The horses, still side by side on the trail, made it easy for Nick to reach over and pat her shoulder. "I can't promise we'll find out what happened to your dad, Lucy. But I'll promise to try. You stay strong for your mom, and tell me anything, ANYTHING, that you learn."

"I knew you'd help us. I was so worried about you, Nick. But now I see how well you are, and I'm not so worried."

Nick stopped his mount, stood in his stirrups to stretch his hips and look ahead.

"You don't need to worry about me, Lucy. We're going to see if we can find out where your dad went."

At the same time, he thought to himself: wish I could stop worrying. The girl at the spring reappeared in his brain. Now there's someone to worry about. He mused on how quickly she'd disappeared. Where, he wondered, would she be going?

Nick found himself staring at the ground. "What do you make of those hoofprints, Lucy?"

She imitated his motions and peered forward. "Looks like Larry's." She cast her eyes across the landscape. "How'd he get over here?"

"No idea, but maybe we can bring him back. Keep an eye out."

Ahead the trail looped between a mesquite-covered hill and a rocky bluff that folded in on itself creating dips and shadows in the sunlight. "There's the ridge with the cliff dwelling."

Lucy squinted. "Yeah, but I don't see the wall." She urged her mount forward to find a better vantage point. "There's a deep shadow up high, Nick." She pointed ahead.

"I think this is the place. The trail curled along and into the next canyon. We used to climb up there and play at ambushing one another. Let's get up farther. Maybe there was a rock slide." He clicked his tongue to his mount and took the lead.

The two horses continued along the rocky side of the bluff. A few stunted trees clung to the sides of the slope, interspersed with large boulders and brush that had already turned brown in readiness for the harsher climate of winter. Nick refocused his attention back to the cliffs rising before them and searched the mountain face for the ancient wall across the dark shadow of a cave. He puzzled at the difference between his memory and the rocky bluff's appearance. "Am I wrong? I thought it was right above us here." As far as he could see there was no opening on the face of the rock. Disorienting. He looked around, felt sure this should be the right place.

"I don't see anything up there that looks right." Nick reined in his mount. "Maybe we should go back for today, find out if we got on the wrong trail."

"Nick, there goes Larry's tracks off the path. Looks like he slid down."

Nick looked downslope, saw where the prints turned into a series of gravel ridges that bared the soil beneath. The slide marks led toward a copse of trees above what he surmised must be a hidden brook, as the slender valley seemed painted with various shades of green.

"Good eyes," Nick said. "Must be looking for water. Let me check if he's down there."

As he turned his horse's head to follow Larry's tracks, he looked down the trail they'd just ascended. Surprised at what he saw, he pulled in his reins. A line of men with heads bent down, plodded toward them several curls of the trail below. One man on a horse followed behind. A few men on horseback would not be unusual, but a group of walkers? Nick counted fifteen, plus the rider. Sixteen, Nick thought, and here in the middle of nowhere. The walkers had backpack frames, wore dark clothing.

The lead walker carried a weapon at the front of the line. Don't like the look of this at all, he thought.

Lucy stopped and looked back the same way. "Who are they?"

"Don't know." Nick swiveled his head north. "Let's forget about Larry for the moment and move on up canyon. See if we can cut around behind the mountain to the loop trail."

They urged their horses into a fast walk. When they rounded a curve on the trail that closed off their view of the walkers, Nick led off at a trot. They'd covered at least a quarter mile before they hooked around the bluff ahead and came to a sudden halt. A horse and rider blocked the way.

"Isn't that your dad's blue roan?" Nick asked Lucy.

"My dad?" she said eagerly, urged her horse forward into a gallop, came to a halt in a spray of dust where the rider sat.

Nick arrived swiftly behind her. "I saw the horse and thought for a moment . . .," and his voice trailed away. "Aren't you supposed to be at Loreto's?" he said.

"What the hell are you two doing here?" Vicente demanded.

CHAPTER 20

Headless Horses

Chiricahua Apache Homeland, *Chihuahuan* Desert, Mexico

THE CHILDREN WALKED ON and on toward the edges of their mind maps. They followed *Naadiktaz*, It Wiggles, away from In the Middle after only a few hours of sleep and a short council of the older children. Finding *Biyoo's*, Her Beads's, trail sign and seeing the military camp so close, convinced them they could not risk spending more time by the spring.

The forward scout's report into the western unknown desert revealed the existence of a high fence, as tall as trees, patrolled by many *Indah*, the Living, the Pale Eyes. Their path toward the next known water in a *tseebitu'* (water held in natural rock tanks), appeared blocked. When It Wiggles finished describing their choices, he paused and looked around the tired faces.

Zhonne, Pretty One, tensed. "Can we go around the fences?"

Bikécho, His Big Toe, did not usually provide opinions. His voice cracked. "We must travel where no one expects us." He blinked his wandering eye at the others. "Go where there is no water."

It Wiggles took a deep breath. "Yes, we must stay invisible with only the water we carry."

Unsure of how long the small children could continue without water, both His Big Toe and Pretty One fell silent. During preparations to leave the camp they'd ensured each child had drunk and drunk at the spring and that every child's gourd brimmed with water.

"We'll do this as the ancestors did it before us." It Wiggles tightened his headband, motioned all to keep moving.

Dikohe (scouts) roamed ahead guarding the safety of the route, while those in the rear covered the marks of their passing. Only one horse now carried supplies, for the children had eaten into their largesse quickly. It meant two more children could ride, which made their travel even swifter. The little ones slept as they rode, exhausted from the efforts of their flight out of the mountains and their short rest at In the Middle.

Striking rapidly into the dark across the desert meant they had nothing against which to check their route or distance. The quarter moon waited and supplied no real light to judge their progress. The stars had not yet wheeled into their patterns. Without the guidance of the stars, even a slight miscalculation could throw them off their intended path. Yet they must put distance between themselves and In the Middle. It Wiggles prayed as he walked, asking for protection.

As they pressed on It Wiggles watched as *Yaa'*, Louse, raised the water gourd that hung from her waist, licked the edge, and heard her soft complaint, "My water's all gone."

"You drank too fast." Pretty One held her own gourd to the smaller one's mouth. "Sip slowly." She allowed several gulps and then admonished Louse to wait until they stopped again.

The little girl rolled her lips together and licked them, black hair straggling around a smudged face.

Pretty One hugged the child. "Soon there'll be more."

Eventually the dark sky became a blizzard of stars, familiar. As It Wiggles took in the brilliant night sky, he clasped the small leather bag, his power, which hung around his neck, and held it while he prayed for his people. "*Ussen* guide us," he repeated to himself, hoping, wanting to believe it. "Protect the invisible people."

The scouts had pushed the group toward a system of dry gullies that would allow them to drop below eye level, find shade in daylight and rest. As they hurried west, then north, the scouts hunt for sign left by Her Beads for the detour. But they found no further markers.

The travelers reached a crisscross of gullies and dips, sand and stone. The *dikohe*, led by *Bee Eshgané*, Left Hand, sought easy passage for both the horses and those on foot. Children and horses stumbled and bumped their way across the dark land.

Pretty One stayed close behind the horses, and jumped forward when she saw a child slip silently off into the loose, deep sand. *Gidi*, Cat, had fallen asleep and slid softly from the horse. The little girl, exhausted by their progress, had curled up on the desert floor, not awakened even when Pretty One transferred her to It Wiggles's back.

It Wiggles chewed on his lip. "Put one older child on each horse to hold the little ones on. That will give everyone a chance to rest."

He trudged on as Pretty One rearranged the smallest children with the older ones. The group continued forward the entire time.

Sometime before dawn, they came to another wide, hard path; easy to cross, no metal wagons within sight. It Wiggles saw that light would soon flood the desert and they must find cover for the coming day. Lights winked on the far horizon to the north and It Wiggles chose a deep, dry gully where the children could rest.

The scouts returned after sunrise. The children already slept, clustered together, arms and legs akimbo. The horses, staked in the shade of the gully wall, nuzzled the bare ground.

Left Hand searched for words to describe to It Wiggles what they'd seen. "There's a *bidahtenistł'ooni* (that which goes around them, a fence). It's very tall except through the center. There's a place where we can get through but there are guards and men riding along the fence." Left Hand straightened his shoulders. He swallowed, unsure of how It Wiggles would accept his next words. "They ride horses that have no heads."

It Wiggles could not imagine a headless horse, but he tried to make sense of it. "Grandmother told us tales of our people and how they fought monsters. Perhaps these are monsters."

Left Hand compressed his lips and his voice narrowed in the quiet. "They growl and scratch up dust. They make tracks. When we watched during the night, only two guards stayed behind to protect the open space going north."

"Show me."

It Wiggles and Left Hand left the group and followed the bed of the dry water course north, bending below the rim when needed to keep out of sight. The desert stretched off, devoid of all but occasional rocks and cactus, thin clumps of dry grasses. Bent metal containers, blowing papers, and other things left behind by *Nakaiyé,* Those Who Walk, the Mexicans, impeded any unwary step. At the rim of the gulch they checked their surroundings, ensuring their position. When Left Hand signaled, It Wiggles followed on his belly over the rim of the gully, and both boys slithered carefully to a point behind several small boulders. The fence, higher than any they'd seen previously, straggled in a line broken by an opening in the distance where a group of men stood. Strange sounds rolled across to the boys, and they saw Left Hand's headless horses move off along the fence.

It Wiggles sucked in his breath. "Show me those creatures' tracks."

When he studied the tracks, it seemed more like a bird, It Wiggles thought, than a horse or beast, a bird that flies across the land instead of the air. When a metal wagon passed and left a puff of dust behind at the break in the fence, a new idea came. "Look at that, brother! Those others are neither monsters nor horses without heads. They are the children of the metal wagons."

The boys watched as two of the metal wagons' children moved rapidly away in both directions along the fence lines. "It's good they're not monsters," Left Hand said.

"*Ha'ah.* We don't know how to trick monsters, but we can trick men."

Left Hand examined the land that fell away behind the fences into a muddle of hills and mountain tops. "Is that the home of the ancestors?"

It Wiggles looked beyond the fence at the spread of the yellow grasses rolling uphill turning into pale and then darker green, and finally into white snowcaps on top of a jagged range of mountains stretching ahead. He felt his eyes water, and a pull on his heart as strong as his yearning to be a great warrior. Our people's mountains, he thought. Home.

The two boys lay the entire day, only a quarter mile south of the fence, unmoving and silent. They took turns sleeping, just behind the lip of a small rise concealed by rocks. One curious hawk coasted overhead. They took turns on watch to study, analyze, and try to understand the purpose of everything these enemies did. The day turned toward dusk before It Wiggles gestured to withdraw and they crawled back through the series of gullies and hollows that hid their movement.

It Wiggles felt certain that with a diversion most of the older children had a chance of getting through and beyond the gate without being seen, but he worried about the youngest ones. And they needed to get the horses across, too. His day-long reconnaissance left him with two ideas. They could follow the fence until they found a better place to cross which meant more travel without water. Or, if they gained entry through the gate, they needed to create a distraction and clear a path.

He'd counted the number of metal wagons passing through the opening during the day, less than twice the number of his fingers. Even so, men continuously guarded the open crossing. At dusk lights came on, and they closed one side of the opening. It seemed no easy place existed to enter the homeland.

Reaching the arroyo where the rest of the band waited, they heard no voices, no human sounds. The children sat or lay listlessly in the shadows of the gully, hard to see, even within a hundred feet, until they moved.

It Wiggles approached Pretty One. "Water?"

"*Dah*. Gone since morning."

It Wiggles turned to His Big Toe. "Where is the next water?"

His Big Toe's one eye that never looked straight roamed somewhere off to the left and canted into the sky. "Homeland. Grandmother told us there are *tseebitu'* (rock tanks) in the little hills beyond the fence, but none on this side." His wandering eye roved back to It Wiggles's chin. "No water."

It Wiggles ground his teeth. If only Grandmother still lived, she would have a solution. Here they waited, without water, blocked by a giant fence.

As leader he must decide, a lonesome feeling. It Wiggles thought hard. It would be of no use to wait, conserve the last liquids, and grow weak. Better to use them now, he decided. Give them all a chance for immediate strength and the ability to successfully cross before they lost energy.

"We will eat the last of the big red berries." He'd been saving the round, metal containers with pictures of large red fruit taken in the ranch raid for their liquid. He'd held them for an emergency and this was the time. "His Big Toe, Pretty One" he said, "open these cans with your knives or a sharp stone. We will share them, two of us to each round, metal container."

As the sky grew into darkness he spoke quietly with His Big Toe and Left Hand. "We will travel tonight and use surprise in our favor." The boys listened intently to the plan, then helped Pretty One open the last of the big red berry cans and provide the final liquid, a half can, to each member of the group. The older children ensured each younger child finished their portion. They gathered the cans together and dug a hole in the sand to hide them.

Seven-year-old *Łichíí*, Red One, nicknamed for her love of the color red, helped push the empty cans with pictures of tomatoes, under the sand. "Will we find more?" she asked Pretty One. "I like those big red berries."

As Pretty One tamped the sand down she said, "When we reach the homeland, we will ask our relatives for more."

The night was still when the boys each led three horses up the gully as far forward toward the fence as they could without risking being observed by the men at the gate. The two smallest girls, Louse and Cat followed on foot.

It Wiggles chose the youngest girls for their size; easiest to hide their small frames against the line of the horses' backs, and no one would have to carry them. "Little sisters," he told them, "you must become the horses' necks. Remember to stretch out long."

The girls, wide-eyed, listened earnestly. When placed on the horses' backs, each arranged herself along the mounts' withers and backs, arms stretched along the horses' necks.

It Wiggles moved between them, encouraging each to lace their fingers into their horses' manes. "You must not fall off," he instructed fiercely. "The others depend on you. Hold on tight."

"*Ha'ah*, older brother," and Cat laid along the horse's backbone as instructed.

It Wiggles watched, approving, as His Big Toe and Left Hand checked the girls and their mounts.

"Remember," His Big Toe reminded the girls, "when we hear the call of the night bird, we ride together fast to the open place in the fence. They'll be surprised and we invisible riders will draw their attention away. The other two horses will run beside us and the *Indah* will think we are just a herd of frightened horses, running. They will look at us, but they will not see us."

"*Ha'ah,*" both girls responded, preparing themselves.

"Little sisters, you will keep in the middle of the horses." It Wiggles's eyes reinforced his words. "If something happens and we get separated, what will you do?"

Louse was quick with her reply. "Go to Grandmother's *tseebitu'*" (rock pools).

"*Ha'ah.* If no one is there, what will you do?"

It Wiggles looked at Cat. She swallowed. "Look for markers?" Her hair straggled about her neck, ruffling in the evening breeze. "Go forward to the Standing Water if there is no marker?"

"*Enjuh*" (Good). "And what sign marker will you look for?" Left Hand, twitched his fingers nervously.

Cat blinked. "Pebbles in a row. Or maybe sticks."

It Wiggles nodded, satisfied the girls knew what to do. He clasped the hand of the girls and of the two boys. "May it all be usefully so."

He turned as the six horses and their four riders moved north under the line of the arroyo, silent and hidden. Seeing the horses and children in place he returned back down the gully to where the rest of the children waited. It Wiggles's eyes roamed the sky, identified the blackest part of the night to begin their passage; then moved the remaining children swiftly toward the lights on the horizon.

When the soft churring of the night bird came to the group of four riders on horseback, Cat caught her breath and clenched her teeth together.

"*K'ad!*" (Now!), His Big Toe said low, and urged his horse up and over the dark rim of the gully.

They found themselves several hundred yards from the tall fence. They could see the hard, black path and the gate with one side open.

Left Hand urged the girls' ponies into the middle of the huddle of horses. "Stay flat!"

The horses picked up speed, the rumble of their hooves on

the earth loud in the night. The two girls crushed themselves along their mounts' backs, blending into the lines of the horses. The boys clung to the hidden sides of the horses by the horses' manes and their own determination. His Big Toe pressed against the pony's ribs, peered with his good eye under the jaw of the horse. He saw the shocked and startled faces of two men dressed alike, one yelling, and one running toward them. Good, good, he thought. Look this way. At the edge of the light he caught movement and saw It Wiggles lead the others in a dash around the fence. He knew they needed only a few seconds to run into the shadows along the inside second fence, away from the building.

In less than a half minute the riders rushed onto the black path. The six horses cornered through the gate, careened away onto the earth on the other side of the fence. The horses plunged forward, flinging themselves in a mad hurtle through the lighted area toward the edge of darkness, eyes rolling, hooves pummeling, tails and manes streaming, a stampede of six runaways.

Elated, the two *dikohe* didn't slow the horses until they'd raced up into the foothills, leaving the lights and shouting behind them. They rode hard before cutting uphill toward the mountain base where they knew Grandmother's *tseebitu'* waited. Within a half hour they slowed to a stop as they reached an area of giant boulders and the glint of water waiting in rock depressions among the boulders. The boys dismounted, grinned at one another, held the excited horses' heads, and walked them to slow their pounding hearts before drinking. His Big Toe handed off his reins to Left Hand and moved through the still blowing horses. He found Louse still clinging to her mount's back, and helped her down. He had to uncurl her fingers one by one from her pony's mane.

Tucked in a fold of hills, away from the black path, on the slopes leading into the mountains, the horses calmed. The stars stretched across the night sky like sparks from a fire. His Big Toe glided silently between the horses looking for Cat.

No Cat.

"I've looked, but she isn't on the horse." His Big Toe's voice trembled. "I thought maybe she got down alone, but she's not here."

Louse stepped forward. "Did she fall?" She stepped a few paces away from the animals, listening. She knew she could not call out and instead made a sound like the whirring of a mourning dove. No answer.

His Big Toe bounded onto his horse's back. "Take the horses and drink at the rock pools," he instructed Left Hand. "Find the others, but do not wait for me."

He turned his mount around and started down the hill, eyes scrambling at the earth, squinting in the dark, seeking Cat. It was well known that survival of the group outweighed the individual, but always, if at all possible, the young must be protected.

CHAPTER 21

The Message of the Birds

Loreto Ranch, West Side *Chiricahua*
Mountains, *Cochise* County, Arizona

TOMÁS REACHED THE LORETO ranch by way of the back trail out of the mountains. As always, a cloud of whirling birds brashly announced the arrival of anyone by road or trail who visited the remote ranch. A flurry of aviary sound and movement brought the rancher Manuel Loreto out to the gate.

"I'm getting the full treatment today," Tomás said, grinning, throwing out one arm that indicated the wheeling, chattering birds above.

"I figured it must be you." Manuel's family had depended on the birds announcing human presence for several centuries, a natural early warning system in the days of wild Apache and outlaws. "But you just missed Border Patrol. Birds didn't even settle down yet."

Tomás dismounted, let Manuel take the reins and lead his horse toward the corral.

"What's Border Patrol up to?" Tomás followed Manuel into the corral. He began to strip the tack from his mount, flung his saddle over the top corral bar.

"Usual. Drug traffic and illegals. Saw Benny Cortez in town last week and he said they're trying some new strategies, tracked some into this part of the Cheery-cows." Manuel raised his eyes to the rough crags of the *Chiricahua* Mountains, where a few circles of birds still fluttered. "Said they might be using the old Apache raiding route. You see anything on your way over?" Manuel turned and looked at Tomás.

Tomás thought of Vicente's work crew, dismissed the thought. "No." He thought again of where exactly Vicente said he was headed; thought of the path they'd taken. Wrong direction to climb directly to the Crest Trail. Shook his head. "No," he said again. "Did Border Patrol check out the split trail up on the other side of the range? The one Apaches used to avoid the birds? Did they try there?"

"Don't know. Whew! That trail! Too skinny to stand still on." Manuel rubbed along his jawline. "I only been up there a few times. Dad took us when we were kids to keep us scared away. Worked for me! Big rock slides where the trail's given way. Lots of bones below where cattle and horses fell off. People, too, I suppose." He shook his head. "Nobody in their right mind would use that trail."

Manuel brought the halter over the nose and ears of the pack horse, turned him nose in to the corral and smacked a palm on his hind quarter. He watched the horse canter into the center and shake his head, happy to be free of straps and burden. "But I guess they wouldn't run into anyone else."

Again, the line of men led by Chapo occurred to Tomás. "Not likely," he agreed, but wondered silently what the heck Vicente was doing with those men? As Tomás queried himself silently he realized simultaneously he didn't want to know, because it couldn't be a good thing, could it?

"So, where's Vicente?" Manuel asked. "I thought you guys had a crew."

"He took some hands up the canyons this morning." Tomás felt uncomfortable in what felt like a white lie, but loyalty to his own family prompted him to add, "Trying to find where the last of our cattle found range, I guess."

Manuel noted his stress, placed a hand on his shoulder. "That's always the problem, Tomás. Everybody needs to do the same thing at the same time. No worries. Let him know I said thanks, and appreciate his sending you over." He checked the water trough. "Hungry?"

"I could eat," Tomás admitted.

They crossed the space between the house and corral. As Manuel opened the back door to the kitchen, he asked, "Got any other news at Diaz & Family?" His eyes sparked. "Or should I say over at the Republic?"

Tomás blushed. "I don't know why he did it, Manuel. Changed the name, I mean."

Manuel nodded. "What about news of Roberto?"

Tomás shook his head. "Nothing." His head dropped, then raised. "One good thing though is Nick's back."

Manuel's face split into a grin. "How is he? Why didn't he come with you?" Manuel saw his daughter Belen setting food on the table. "One more for lunch," he called ahead to her.

Tomás ducked his head inside the kitchen. "He said he'd come, but then Vicente told him no. Told him he needed to take it easy for a while." He shrugged. He automatically removed his hat and wiped his feet on the mat by the door. "Hi Belen!" He grinned as the smell of fresh pie wafted across the kitchen. "Something sure smells good!"

Manuel's face registered empathy. "You tell Nick we want to see him just as soon as he feels good enough to be around people. Right Belen?"

Tomás bit his tongue not to stutter. Realized Manuel had the wrong idea; decided not to correct him. "I'll sure let him know."

Belen greeted Tomás with a quick hug. "Of course, we're so excited to see him." She set a fresh pie in the middle of the table with a knife and spatula. "Fresh peach today, but let's see, what was Nick's favorite?"

Together Manuel and Tomás answered. "Rhubarb," then laughed.

"You tell him I just happen to have some rhubarb saved for him in the freezer!"

After supper Tomás excused himself to see to his animals. He'd sat in the ranch house with Manuel and a few ranch hands trading conversation for a while, before the hands left for the bunkhouse. They planned to rise early in the morning and take advantage of first light in collecting cattle. Tomás had barely sunk into slumber in his guestroom bed when the landline began to ring. He heard the sound of Manuel's feet creak cross the wooden planks of the old house's floor. He checked the clock beside his bed and saw: 11:30. Knew it must mean some kind of trouble.

Tomás heard the door open.

Manuel called softly. "Tomás, it's for you. It's Tia Elena."

Tomás came wide awake and bounded from the bed, walked barefoot swiftly across the cold floor.

"*Diga me*, Tia" (Talk to me). He listened, eyes flat, face blank. Lucy and Nick had not returned from their ride. Did he know where they planned to ride?

"*Si*, Tia, they were aimed for the old cliff dwelling." He thought hard. Obviously, something had kept them from returning. "I'll go looking at first light. No point to head out in the dark before then." He listened. "I'll check in as soon as I know something. Border Patrol was here at Loreto's today. I'll check with them, too."

"Could be almost anything, Tia. Maybe they lost a horse. Maybe they're on foot. Or something happened so they're waiting for daybreak. I know Lucy never leaves her cell phone behind. She'll call when she finds a cell tower. It'll be okay."

When Tomás hung up, Manuel had his head in the refrigerator. "You know, Lucy's with Nick, Tomás, so she'll be safe."

He passed some food from the refrigerator to Tomás. "You'll be too early for breakfast so I'm fixing some sandwiches. Go on to bed."

Tomás lay down again, tossing until the urgent ring of the alarm he'd set for 4:00 a.m. roused him. He got his horse ready first, then returned inside the house, picked up the paper bag from the counter and a stainless-steel thermos of coffee left by Manuel.

Manuel's note said: "Let us know soon as you can when you find them."

It was those birds, Tomás thought. Manuel's worried, too.

He mounted his horse, opened the bag, and ate all three sandwiches before he'd gone a half-mile. Didn't even think Manuel might have intended two of them for Nick and Lucy.

CHAPTER 22

Enemies All Around

Hackberry Canyon, *Cochise* County, Arizona

THE MOUNTAINS TAPERED INTO the upward trail of a narrow valley, lined in dense brush and scattered with stones settled beneath crags and outcroppings. Vicente shifted his seat as Nick guided his horse next to his cousin, so that both faced the downhill path. Lucy drew up behind them and continued to scan the hillsides beyond.

"*Tio*" (Uncle), Lucy asked, "Where's the cliff dwelling? I thought this was the right canyon, but I don't see it."

Vicente's face, already flushed, darkened to a deeper shade.

"Yeah, I thought this was the place, too," Nick said, puzzled, and craned his neck.

"Tricks of memory," Vicente said between his teeth. His displeasure at their interruption came at the same time movement below caught their attention. A single man appeared on the trail from behind the curve of one mountain, then disappeared again as he continued to loop behind the bend of another ridge.

"Oh yeah," Lucy said. "There's a line of people carrying packs coming up. We just saw them and...."

Vicente cut her off, growled, "We don't own the trail. People can hike."

Nick looked at his cousin. "Kind of unusual for here, though."

Vicente stared hard at Nick, who returned the look without expression.

Vicente placed fingers at his mouth and whistled a long, piercing note. A moment later a figure trudged upward.

Nick saw a bulge on the man's leg, knew it for a weapon. Lowered his voice, said to his cousin, "Right leg."

"Got it," Vicente reached one hand down to the stock of his shotgun, rested his hand on the butt of the weapon.

From about three hundred feet away the stranger stopped and called out, *"Hola!"*

"Hola," Vicente responded, stretching his neck toward the single walker. "I know this guy, no problem," and he smiled at Nick and Lucy. Then he called down the trail, *"Sobre el tiempo! Creía que era una siesta"* (About time! I thought you were napping).

"What the...?" Nick started to say.

The man swiped one forearm across his forehead. *"Caminata larga, patrón"* (A long walk, boss). He kept moving forward.

"Boss?" Nick asked Vicente with raised eyebrows and a studied calm.

"Umm." Vicente's eyes followed the man on the path. "I'll take care of it."

As the walker came close, obviously carrying a weapon, Lucy's eyes widened. "I'm scared."

Vicente hissed, demanding silence, but Nick reached over and patted Lucy's knee. Peering directly into her eyes he said in a low voice, "Move behind us. If anything happens you take off and keep going. Do NOT turn back for anything. Got it?"

Lucy nodded, but her face had drained of color.

The man halted ten steps away. "It's good to see you, patrón. We feared we'd missed the meeting place."

"Tell Chapo to have the others rest, eat something. They'll be walking late tonight."

The man tipped a hand to his forehead and began to turn back.

Nick glared at Vicente, "Walking late tonight? What is this, Vicente?"

Vicente wavered, then called to the armed man's back, gestured east up the slope beside them. "Remember the ruin?"

Vicente pointed uphill. Nick followed Vicente's finger, saw nothing there but a mountainside of rocks.

The man stared up at the same mountain side. *"Si, patrón."*

"Bring a few men to remove the tarps. Then we'll bring the load down."

The man walked back the way he'd come and reached the curve.

Vicente watched Nick's face harden, turned away from his cousin, but he still heard Nick's voice. "Time to explain, Vicente. What load? What tarps?"

Vicente glanced back. "Nothing to worry about." He saw that Nick's expression registered deep concern.

Nick spoke, ice in his tone. "Good, we'll leave it to you then. Lucy and I are heading back to the ranch. Tia's waiting."

Vicente's lips compressed. "Nobody going anywhere. Got to finish this business."

"Your business, Vicente," Nick emphasized. The leather in his saddle creaked as he turned to look north up the trail. "We'll be at the ranch when you come in."

Vicente's face suffused into a dark crimson. The shotgun shifted toward Nick, who found himself looking down double barrels.

"Think again."

"Tio Vicente, I have to get back." Lucy's voice hung thin in the air.

Vicente studied his cousin and niece, felt compelled to confirm his previous statement. "I told you, nobody's going."

Several things happened at once. The armed man disappeared as he walked behind the trail's curve. Nick looked at Lucy, said: "Ready?" Vicente's neck snapped around in surprise as Nick suddenly dug heels into his horse, wheeled its backside into Vicente's mount. "Lucy, go!" Her face registered determination as she whirled her horse and galloped north on the trail.

Nick rammed heels into his mount's flanks to push hard against the other horse, reached out to grab for Vicente's shotgun.

Missed it.

Vicente expelled a surprised groan of air as Nick elbowed him in the ribs. As he gasped for a breath, he fought off his cousin, brought the butt of his rifle down on Nick's head and a distinctive crack rent the air. He looped an arm around his cousin's neck and dragged him backward off his mount, dropping Nick's unconscious body to the ground.

Vicente looked up to find Lucy and horse vanishing as they rounded a bend of the mountain, heading north. Only a low cloud of settling dust remained to show anyone had passed.

"Great," he snarled, "Now I got to go get her."

• ● ○

Nick didn't know how long he'd been out when he returned to consciousness. His head throbbed at the back of his skull. He tried to rise, but nothing happened. He found himself in the dip at the side of the trail, his body trussed. Light hurt his eyes when he tried to open them as a wave of nausea rocked his stomach. He finally squinted painfully through his eyelashes down his body. He saw only his trunk; his legs had been unattached from the stumps. He braved several undulating swells of queasiness before a second look confirmed not a trace of either leg within his vision range. No sign of his horse.

He heard movement nearby and kept his body motionless. Voices moved around him, some on the trail and some up the slope on a deer path climbing the hill to the east. Several men had gathered on the slope of the rocky cliff wall. He thought he must be dreaming as the men pulled at the cliff and the mountainside came slithering down. Nick shut his eyes, then opened them to see that is exactly what they'd done. Immense camouflage tarps slid down the mountain and two men began to roll them and pull them toward the trail.

The sun still hung bright in the afternoon sky and he figured he couldn't have been knocked out too long, maybe a quarter of an hour.

He could now see the old cliff dwelling exposed. His head pounded as he tried to think his way through Vicente's behavior, the act of disguising a cliff dwelling with camouflage tarps, of meeting up with packers in the backcountry of the *Chiricahua* range.

Men shuffled by his head, raising dust and Nick fought off a cough, kept his eyes closed. Definitely the group he'd seen climbing the trail. A short time later, raising more dust, he saw the same men descend slowly on the shale, loaded with heavy packs. Really, he thought, hating to name it. He knew it could only be drug smuggling.

The crunch of boots sounded on the ground near Nick. He heard Vicente's voice. "Did he come to yet?"

Nick kept his eyes closed, didn't move.

Hands prodded his chest, tested the ropes around his arms. "He's out cold. Or dead."

Chapo, Nick thought.

"*Pendejo* (fool), he's not dead." Vicente poked him in the ribs with a boot toe. "Look, he's breathing. Finish up the loading. We need to leave."

"This is bad. Your own cousin. A war hero."

"He attacked me. Now I gotta go find Lucy."

Chapo's voice moved away. "Lucy's not a problem. And Nick's like your brother."

Nick heard the creak of leather as a rider mounted a horse. Vicente's voice, sharp as a knife: "Brother, hah. Nothing but trouble, my brothers.

Again, Chapo's voice, "Just leave me out of it," and then the sound of a horse's hooves trotting away.

Nick risked squinting through his eyelashes, saw Vicente turned toward the packers, rifle in hand, watching the men form up behind Chapo. His mind raced, ignoring his throbbing head, trying to think what he could possibly do to save himself. How much time did he have, Nick wondered, before Vicente decided to kill him?

CHAPTER 23

Hog Crossing Surprise

Hog Crossing, U.S. Border Checkpoint, Cochise County, Arizona

HOG CROSSING, ONE OF the quietest crossings along the Mexican border, rarely experienced night traffic. Benny Cortez, pleased his Douglas assignment had changed from the lurid happenings of a major city to the valued quiet of this rural border crossing, silently congratulated himself. No more tunnel crawls. No pathetic cars with undercarriages molded out of marijuana, no groups of teenagers trying the same tricks, over and over, to get across. Here, local ranchers and occasional authorities from either side crossed on business. No place for migrants to find easy food or water or help. In fact, when he and Fuentes had started the shift, the most excitement of the week had been a fence cutting about a mile east into New Mexico. The four-wheel ATV patrol had found the fence hole, expertly severed and concealed. They repaired it, tracked down a small group of a half dozen unhappy wanderers, the coyote guide long gone. Their big week. And Benny could not be happier.

When he first heard a rumbling noise Cortez thought it must signal the approach of an older truck. His eyes went quickly to the camera monitors that fed into the computers and also noted the time as approaching midnight. The first set of cameras, placed a mile out from the crossing, recorded all highway traffic.

He saw nothing on those screens. Lights along the highway displayed an empty road.

Benny saw his partner Juan Fuentes had just completed walking the inside fence of the station, a requirement every hour; watched him stiffen and draw his gun, alerted by the low rumble.

The noise increased and out of the dark horses streaked through the crossing onto the pavement and spun past Fuentes. He stood swinging his weapon in a circle, but found nothing to take a bead on.

Cortez, already on the radio, reported the incident. "Herd of horses just ran through the gate." He listened, answered "Guess something spooked 'em. No traffic, no people."

The horses raised a roll of dust still settling under the bright lights of the station when Cortez caught a tiny movement at the corner of his screen, and Fuentes entered the station door. Cortez looked along the road where the stampede had happened only moments before. Off to the side of the blacktop, at the edge of the light, a small shape formed a hump.

"Fuentes," he called out, "I'm checking next to the road at two o'clock."

"What is it?"

"Something moved." Cortez hooked his radio on his belt, drew out his own weapon. "Cover me."

Fuentes edged sideways to keep his firing lane open, and watched as his partner ran bent over, weapon held in two hands, barrel down. After Cortez reached and circled the target, he glanced quickly around, then lowered and holstered his weapon. He crouched over the small dark hump, picked it up gingerly and brought it against his chest. He walked in a measured, careful way back.

"What you got there, Cortez?"

No answer. Benny returned with his arms in a forklift position. When he reached the building, he called out to Fuentes. "It's a kid."

"What? What the hell?"

"He's got a broken leg. Look. Bone's sticking out."

Cortez could see the child's eyes open, conscious. In spite of the fact he must be in terrible pain, no tears and no noise. "*Tiene dolor, pequeño?*" (Does it hurt, little one?) Dark eyes bored into his own.

Fuentes rushed ahead to the radio.

"Hog Springs Crossing check in. Fuentes here. Request help STAT with an injured child, not sure of age, maybe three or four? Broken leg. Lot of blood. I think he's in shock." Fuentes listened. "Kid's alone, no adults. Haven't seen anything but a running group of horses ten minutes ago." Static interrupted. "What's that?" He listened and responded with annoyance. "How should I know? Dressed kind of funny. Odd shoes. Not talking. Not crying." He listened. "Cortez's getting blankets on him now. Right," and ended the connection.

The partners took turns watching the child and the gate over the next forty minutes. At one point Cortez left Fuentes and loped around the inner fence. He thought it possible the child might have fallen off one of the runaway horses, but the kid was so small it didn't seem likely.

"You know what gets me?" Cortez returned from his hourly sprint around the enclosed area. "There must be some people missing this kid. Where are they?"

Fuentes found some ice in the office refrigerator, wrapped it in a towel and placed it against the tiny broken leg. He'd also found a Popsicle which he offered to the child who'd turned his head away.

"That's a funny kid," Cortez said to Fuentes, "doesn't want a red Popsicle."

Cortez studied the child's face, the fierce eyes, the straggly hair that didn't look like it had ever been combed. "I don't know, pal. I never knew a kid to pass up a Popsicle of any color." He reached a hand out. "But I'll take one."

Replacement border guards appeared at the same time as the ambulance and relieved the partners. Ordered to accompany the child to the San Enebro Regional Hospital, the nearest emergency services, the two men sat in the back with the paramedic and the child who did not utter a sound, even when the leg jostled in crossing road bumps or swaying around curves.

The paramedic attempted to administer a painkiller by mouth with no success. He finally belted the small form down in order to start an IV line and used the two border guards to hold the patient steady. As soon as he'd placed the IV and turned away to grab an ampule, the little arm flexed and left the needle dangling in air.

"I thought you guys were gonna hold the kid down," the paramedic complained and started over. It took two more tries, but as soon as he ran the medications into the line, the small patient relaxed under sedation and the paramedic moved to stabilize the leg and complete his examination. "She sure is grimy," he pronounced.

The two border guards looked at one another in surprise. Benny said, "How do you know it's a girl?"

"I sneaked a peek."

"Oh." Cortez watched the paramedic pull off the child's shoes and wrappings, preparing to wash her feet. "What do you make of those shoes?" Cortez asked.

The paramedic set the shoes and wrappings on the bench, examined an odd disc decoration at the toe. "All made of leather. Can't say I've seen anything like them before. Usually illegals wear huarache sandals."

Cortez picked up one of the shoes and ran a finger along the inner shoe wall. "Soft inside."

The paramedic shrugged his shoulders and checked her blood pressure. "Looks like a moccasin. Maybe she's Tarahumara?"

"They wear huaraches, too. Or go barefoot." Cortez had seen a lot of immigrants when he worked as a border guard in Douglas. But he'd never seen a child dressed like this one. When they arrived at the hospital, he put the child's odd shoes on his mental back burner and followed the gurney into the emergency entrance.

CHAPTER 24

Hot on the Trail

Colonia Suiza, East Side Sierra Madre Range, Chihuahua, Mexico

ESTEBAN OBSERVED RAFAEL ELLSWORTH as he organized the posse overnight, mostly recruited from his own *colonia* and the village nearby.

The recruits trickled in at first light, rifles in scabbards on horses, or in the back windows of pickup trucks. Ellsworth invited all to eat breakfast as the group grew. Esteban counted twenty men assembled as dawn edged the horizon, ready to solve problems. Filled with tortillas, eggs, and coffee they met in the staging area before the *colonia*'s big house.

Experienced at surviving disagreements in the Sierra Madre, Esteban listened carefully as Ellsworth explained the mission.

"*Bienvenidos caballeros,*" (Welcome Gentlmen) Ellsworth's voice rang out authoritatively. "*Tenemos un gran problema.*" (We have a big problem.) Men shuffled in the dust or squatted on their haunches, a few smoking, all intent on the Elder's words. "Here are Esteban and Ignacio Garcia from the other side of the sierra who bring us bad news. It's not their fault. They are right to come here quickly so we can solve this problem together. Tell them, Don Esteban," and Ellsworth stepped back.

Esteban, almost breathless at being singled out, looked down at his feet then back up at the group. "The Broncos, the wild ones, have returned."

A buzz rippled through the group. "How do we know?" a man in scuffed boots asked.

Garcia father and son retraced the events that led to their arrival at Colonia Suiza. Esteban pulled the curious necklace from his pocket and held it up for all to see. A groan welled up from the crowd. The older men shook their heads in dismay, while the younger crowded forward to see it better. No one reached to touch it.

One small wiry cowboy dressed in leather chaps crossed himself as he stepped backward, distancing himself from the necklace. "I am Domingo Mendez." He looked around at other faces, blinked. "I have heard of these evil things, worn by Apache warriors." He looked at the necklace that dangled from Esteban's hand. "I've lived here all my life but have never seen an Apache." He swallowed hard. "But my family lost two children to them, and many cattle and sheep."

The group waited for him to continue, but he looked mournfully down at his feet, twisted his wide brimmed hat in his hands, and said no more.

Esteban ran one hand across the stubble of his chin and sighed. "My son and I wish we'd never seen them."

The men laughed nervously, looked around to see how everyone else registered the information.

Ellsworth moved next to Esteban. "With luck, today you'll see them from a distance." His eyes rose and traveled across the group. "Today we search only for sign of the Broncos. Do not go against them alone. Take turns leading. Watch behind you as much as in front of you. Be careful where someone can jump from above." Ellsworth cast intent eyes around the men, came back to Esteban. "Today we find where they may be. Tomorrow we go to find them. Anything else?"

Esteban's cheek twitched. "You're hunting *tigres*. Human *tigres*," and his eyes flicked back to his host.

Domingo crossed himself. "As God wills. We know from our own families the Apache take what they want and kill without pity."

"Now," Esteban confirmed grimly, "we must return the favor."

Ellsworth, hands on hips, face somber, nodded to the men around him. "Remember, we do nothing that will bring the *federales* or the *policia*. If pressed by them, we must all give the same response."

The men nodded back, thinking each in his own way of how the far apart Sierra Madre communities resented and refused the unwanted involvement of outsiders. Known for clannish villages, fundamentalist religious groups, hidden marijuana fields, and a dislike of the prying outside world, the region formed a life philosophy of its own. The group of men hummed in agreement.

"Officially, we are looking for the Garcias' stolen horses. Nothing more. Of course," Ellsworth finished, "if Broncos are found, then . . .," and he tipped his head and raised his shoulders.

The group stirred, some with eagerness, some with discomfort.

"Be sure you're ready." He cast a stony eye around at the men. "Only one thing that can be done to solve this problem." No one looked away. "If anyone needs a weapon, see Lucero," and Ellsworth nodded toward his foreman.

Ellsworth and Esteban directed and divided the men into small groups, sending them out of the compound in four-wheel-drive vehicles or on horseback. Ellsworth chose Lucero and Domingo as trail riders on the high ridge paths and sent them to the barn to saddle up. When the riders returned, Esteban checked them for the metal bits on their gear so no jingling might signal their presence.

Meanwhile several jeeps and pickup trucks exited the *colonia*. All agreed to return before dark to share reports.

At the gate Lucero swept off his hat to Ellsworth, followed by Domingo. "*A sus ordenes*" (at your service), Lucero said. Both riders dipped their chins to chests.

Ellsworth gave them their assignment. "Scout *La Sartén* (the skillet)."

Both men's eyes widened. "To the gates of Hell, then," Domingo said.

"*D'acuerdo*" (That's right). "Search where the 'handle' of the skillet connects the fry pan to the mountains."

The men waited, thinking of why no one went to the skillet even now, though more than a half century had passed since a verified Apache was seen there. It was a place of ghosts and danger. As if in tandem, both men moved a hand to check the security of rifles in scabbards on their saddles.

"Plenty of ammunition?"

The men stared back, their expressions hard. Lucero mounted his horse, bundled the reins in one hand, clicked his tongue. Domingo finished tying a jacket down with saddle strings and followed. The two riders headed out of the ranch yard through the gates and broke into a canter along the base of the hills, trotting silently away, apparitions seeking other spirits returning into the past.

CHAPTER 25

Stranded

Cliff Dwelling, Hackberry Canyon, *Chiricahua* Mountains, *Cochise* County, Arizona

THE AFTERNOON LIGHT DIMMED as Nick lay trussed beside the trail. He felt the beginning chill of evening and wished he had his jacket. He remembered he'd tied it under the cantle of the saddle on his horse. He thought even more wistfully of his legs; without them, he was as good as done for out here. He listened as Vicente gave orders as the line of porters passed, each carrying heavy loads in packs.

Two of the workers slung his body between them and carried him up the slope to the cliff dwelling where he and his cousins once played as boys. As the men struggled across the scree, Nick saw the cliff dwelling had been well disguised by desert camouflage tarps, now pulled off and piled against the centuries old man-made wall. He recalled he'd seen such concealment gear employed by *mujahedeen* in Afghanistan. Both men hauling him were breathing hard by the time they reached the barrier. The two men laid him on top of the wall as they prepared to push him over and into the cliff dwelling. As they pushed, Nick came suddenly alive kicking out with his bound thighs. The men jumped to the side and shoved Nick head first like a sack of potatoes onto the sandy floor of the prehistoric room. He rolled across the small entry area and righted himself into a seated position, before demanding, "¿Dónde están mis piernas?" (Where are my legs?)

No answer. The two men joined him over the barrier and lugged him roughly to where they propped him against the inside of the outer wall. Nick saw multiples of marks in the sand where some kind of containers had rested, understood something had been stored there.

The men checked and tightened the ropes that bound his arms behind his back. Then one of them caught each end of Nick's two empty jeans' legs and tied them together in double knots. "*Eso lo aguantará*" (That should hold him).

The other bent low to step through the doorway into the adobe-bricked rooms.

"Stay out of there. Patrón won't like it."

The man backed out. "Just empty rooms."

"Not important to us. Let's go." The two scrambled over the entrance wall without a backward glance.

Nick sat listening until the sounds of their steps slipping down the shale path faded. He could hear other faint sounds, the jingle of a bridle, a horse's snort. At one point, Vicente's voice rose and trickled away. Then, quiet.

At full dark Nick could see nothing except a dim outline of the wall against the outside night sky. He was a little surprised to find himself alive. Still, he expected he had only so much time before someone returned. He remembered pottery shards strewn along the wall when they played in the cave as children, and a few *metates* for grinding corn in bedrock boulders. Surely, he thought, he could find a shard or an uneven surface to work at cutting his bindings. He just needed to figure out how to move.

He used his one knee to prop himself up, and discovered he'd been effectively hog-tied. Carefully, he shifted his shorter leg forward, put his weight on it, and slammed flat on his face. A sift of powdered dust coated his head, settled down his shirt. He rolled onto one side and sat up again. A warm trickle ran down his lips and chin. He twisted forward to see if he could reach the double knot in his jeans with his teeth. Impossible. He worked his legs apart minutely stretching the jeans fabric with each push of his thighs, gained a tiny loosening, and used his one knee to prop himself up. This time when he shifted to his knee-less left leg, he aimed to move under an inch. Slowly, he shuffled peg-legged (peg-knee'd, he thought) across the sandy floor to the cave wall, the knots digging into his stumps, raising more dust that made him cough.

He waited for the dust to settle, then turned his back to the wall and scooched himself along its surface in the dark, using his tied hands to sift sand along the join line of the wall and floor, seeking anything with an edge. The knots dug deeper into his stumps causing excruciating pain, and he finally sat down with his back against the wall and slid, running his fingers into the loose surface sand, using his arms and elbows to help scoot his torso along more quickly. Slow work. He tried to visualize where the shards had accumulated, remembering boyhood searches for pieces decorated in glyphs and symbols. He found a small shard with a broken edge and began to saw slowly at his bindings. Although difficult to make headway, he rested against the low wall every few minutes, stretching his wrists. Eventually, exhausted by his efforts and the day's events, he slumped against the wall and nodded off into a half sleep.

Nick came fully conscious in the quiet dark before dawn. Disoriented, he peered into the blackness around him. A low scraping noise he recognized as shale sliding downhill made his skin prickle. Something approached the mouth of the cave across the scree of the steep hillside trail. He clenched his teeth, took a deep breath, and resolved that if Vicente came to kill him, it would not be without a fight.

CHAPTER 26

Cat, the Invisible

Medicine House, *Chiricahua* Apache Homeland

GIDI, CAT, FELT SNUG and drowsy, surrounded by a white cloud of soft warmth. Her eyes fluttered, hesitant to open wide in the brightness around her. The sun beamed down upon her face without heat. She tried to raise her hand to shield her eyes and found she couldn't move. A second unsuccessful try, and she understood she couldn't raise her arms at all which rested across her chest, strapped down. She blinked at the sun again and saw the light was not the sun, but smaller; the place not outside at all.

An enemy dressed in white stood over her looking rudely into her face. She lowered her eyes, baffled to see herself lying supine inside what appeared to be a low metal fence in a world of shiny metal and whiteness.

She moved her head trying to see if she might be dead and in the Happy Place. But she saw none of her people in this shining surrounding; just this staring *Indah*, a pale-eyed man, one of the Living. Her heart pounded in fear.

Her right leg rested on several pillows. She tried to move her leg off the pillows but the enemy beside her bed reached out an arm, said "Oh no you don't!" Utter gibberish to *Cat*. She couldn't move it anyway, she realized, because they'd placed something heavy around her leg to hold it down. She stared a moment at her leg and a white stone that seemed to grow around it.

What was this stone on her leg? she silently asked herself. If they did this to children, what chance would she have for escape? *Cat* thrust her bottom lip out and tears welled in her eyes, but she maintained silence. She swallowed hard and kept the tears at bay. If this was torture, she would do as she'd been taught. She realized she needed to make her rescue call, so some of her people could hear her and find her. Where was she? Where were her people? How could she fight this evil?

The *Indah* enemy who stood beside her had what looked like a small, yellow snake around his neck. She saw his hands up close, spotted with brown. She thought he might be a witch. He held a piece of metal attached to the yellow snake and bent to place it on her chest.

"*Dah!*" she screamed in utter horror. She fought against the ties, rattled the fence with her movements, and the man quickly stepped back.

Slender and balding, he removed the snake and held it behind him. She saw the same brown spots sprinkled across his face. She wondered if those spots might be a sickness. *Cat's* eyes flew about the room, seeking any help.

Digging in his pocket the enemy brought out a slim, metal stick the width of a finger and held it before her face. She heard a quiet click like stepping on a twig and light poured as if water into her eyes.

Frightened into complete stillness, she clenched her eyes shut. The man lifted one eyelid to look into her soul. She smelled his too sweet body odor and her upper lip twitched in revulsion. His breath tickled against her cheek. She opened her eyes, and looked directly at him in a blaze of rage.

He immediately withdrew, casting a few quiet words softly behind him. Cat had no idea what he might be saying.

When the *Indah* left, a woman enemy stepped forward. Her

skin, hair, and eyes, all different shades of brown, showed dark against the pale blue of her clothes. She smiled at Cat, who turned her head to the side and closed her eyes. The Brown Woman left, and Cat lay listening. Voices filtered through the doorway. She thought the enemies' language sounded like insects buzzing.

Cat lay supine, a prisoner within her fence, and thought of Grandmother's stories about the enemy world.

"Those enemy ghosts, both the *Indah*, the Living, and *Nakaiyé*, Those Who Walk, hate our people." The old woman's eyes had swept over the children by the fire. "Never trust one. If they offer you food, it will be poisoned. If they seem kind, they're thinking how to kill you or make you a slave. If they give you something, it will hurt you. They've been killing our people from the beginning of time." She shrugged. "Naturally we have killed them back." The children had made low sounds of agreement. "There is only one thing to do if you're ever taken captive."

They'd all waited, tense with wanting to know how to survive captivity. They knew that Grandmother had been captured long before any of them lived; before the rule of their own lifetimes, the rule of *Doo dat'įį dahi,* That Which Can't Be Seen, the Invisible.

"You must play the Invisible Game." Grandmother's eyes reflected pinpoints of light from the fire. "What does the tortoise do when attacked?"

The children's shoulders all rose, their necks scrunched down, and they pulled their legs and arms close to their bodies.

"He pulls in his legs and his head." The high, croaky voice, came from ten-year-old *In'lt'áni,* named Cricket because of the rasp of her voice.

"*Ha'ah*" (Yes), Grandmother said. "What else?"

"He becomes a stone," offered *Łichíí,* Red One, and she scrunched her seven-year-old self to the size of a human boulder.

"*Enjuh*" (Good). "Tortoise waits for enemies to pass. Waits for enemies to think he's asleep. Or to think he's a rock."

Grandmother's hair wisped around her face in the heat draft of the fire. "When the enemy is not looking, the tortoise escapes, even slowly. The tortoise knows if he waits too long, he will forget how to live, where to live. When I was taken captive, I was no older than Slender Sister," and she poked her chin toward Red One. It took me many months to escape. My people did not want me back. 'You are changed now,' they said. 'You are *Nakaiyé*,' they said." She paused and spat into the fire.

Her capture supplied the source of what they all knew about the language of the *Nakaiyé,* for Grandmother had been a prisoner an entire circle of seasons.

"Our people hid from me when I came to their fire, afraid I'd become the enemy. I was the last child they ever took back." Grandmother raised one weathered hand to the stars. "*Ussen* knew, and gave us protection. Our Blue Mountain People disappeared, became invisible. We stopped making a living from the villages. If we raided, we made sure it was in secret. If we took animals, we left sign showing it was bear or coyotes, not *Ndee*, the Dead, the Real People. Everything we do keeps us hidden. The *Nakaiyé* no longer believe we live. We are *Ndee* and we are invisible."

Cat remembered. It was her time to play the Game.

Cat lay with her face to the wall, closed her eyes whenever anyone entered the room. She did not seem to hear words spoken to her, or to be aware that others stood next to her. Inquiries in English and Spanish received the same result: nothing.

By early evening of her first full day with her leg propped up on the bed, the Brown Woman had released her arms and Cat had stretched her elbows out and opened her hands with great relief. Cat continued to refuse all food and drink by ignoring it. Of course, she reasoned, it would be poisoned. When the woman offered evil smelling food that made Cat's nose wrinkle, Cat knocked it on the floor. Seeing the white curved lumps in a yellow sauce, she closed her eyes, nauseated. But the smell had permeated the room and caused Cat to sneeze and sneeze. The smell of the food was loathsome. She could not imagine from what kind of poison it came. She was grateful when the woman cleaned the mess and took it away.

Later she heard the rustle of Brown Woman as she reentered the room and turned her eyes to the blank, white wall. Cat felt the pressure of something laid next to her foot. After a moment a light weight nudged against her toes. Cat lowered her chin so she could see what the weight meant. A many-colored kitten, black and brown and tan, with white chest and white paws, trembled against Cat's ankle.

"Kitty!" Brown Woman touched one finger under the kitten's chin.

Cat looked at the woman and kitten with a start. She thought to herself: How does the enemy know my name, *Gidi*? Why does she say it aloud? It's only my nickname, but if spirits are near in this white place, they may wish me harm.

The kitten began to investigate its environment, mewing softly as it roamed upward straddling Cat's leg. Cat, restrained, could only move her head and neck and arms. She slanted her eyes down to the right in an attempt to see what the kitten might do.

Brown Woman moved the little ball of fluff closer toward the child's pillowed head. "She's a little, bitty, kitty, isn't she?" Brown Woman smiled at Cat. "She wants her Ma."

Cat recognized Brown Woman had said her name again. She wanted to pet the kitten, for her people always had cats around their living places. Grandmother liked them because they kept mice and other things away. That's how Cat got her nickname. She loved to hold and pet them, and so the other children called her by the same name, *Gidi*.

Brown Woman left the room and returned with a flat saucer of white fluid. Cat's small hand met with the kitten's soft fur, and she stroked the kitten's head, then moved her hand away when she saw the woman.

Cat swallowed. The liquid trembling in the dish reminded her of her thirst.

"C'mon, Kitty, Kitty," Brown Woman crooned and lifted the kitten to the side table.

The table was even with Cat's head, and her eyes followed the kitten's progress as it

wobbled its way slowly toward the saucer. The kitten placed a paw on the edge of the dish, tipping it and wetting her entire leg, eliciting a sound of surprise from Cat. *"Eiyah!"*

The kitten shook the wet paw, groomed it, and then did exactly the same thing again.

Cat giggled, then clamped her lips together as she remembered Brown Woman was in the room.

Brown Woman stepped out through the door, and Cat twisted sideways to get a better view of the kitten. She thought to herself—the kitten drank and was not poisoned. Her stomach growled and she strained her body away from her pillowed leg, turned it sideways, and managed to get her face up next to the kitten on the table. "Little *gidi*," Cat said softly, "Do you like the drink? Because I am very thirsty."

It was only for a few seconds, but there, companionably side by side, together the kitten and child lapped at the milk.

CHAPTER 27

The Dead Rise to Help the Living

Where They Left Cloth, *Chiricahua* Apache Homeland

Biyoo', Her Beads, picked her way slowly over the trail. The end of the afternoon sun slanted beams of light across the mountains. The mule traveled quietly along the path, its hooves wrapped in buckskin covers she'd fashioned, leaving no hoofprints. She kept her eyes moving from the path to the distance ahead, as the enemy ghost and young girl had earlier gone this way, their mounts' tracks clear to see.

Another trail wended its way from one hillside into the trail she traveled. When she stopped to examine signs of traffic where the trails met, she blinked in alarm to see the marks of many feet had churned the dust. The footprints continued in the same direction as she traveled, and trod on top of the horse tracks of the man and girl. Her Beads dismounted the mule and bent over the new impressions in the trail. Only one horse. She studied the length of stride, and the depth of individual prints. Maybe 15 people; one ahead on horseback and one behind the others. She knew that meant *dikohe* protected the line of men.

"*Nakaiyé,*" she hissed.

A hundred feet up the trail something fluttered on the path. Her Beads progressed slowly toward it, studying the landscape beyond the trail for threats. She stooped to pick up the object, held it in her hand. She smelled it cautiously while continuing to scan all about her. The rich, sweet smell caused a sudden saliva to flood involuntarily into her mouth. She folded back the shiny, dark brown paper and the aroma increased; inside she saw a flat, glossy cake, with teeth marks etched into one end.

Her Beads sucked in her breath as the smell intensified. I know this trick, she thought. It is as Grandmother said. They will poison us if they can. And yet, the fragrance appealed so strongly that she did not throw it away, but slipped it into a pouch.

She decided to follow the trail farther and then cut over into woods where she could leave the mule. The dust had not settled into the tracks of the group before her, and she didn't want to surprise them. Or even worse, be surprised by them.

The afternoon had drained away when Her Beads tied the mule to a tree. On foot she reached a point midway up the hillside, where she could see the trail as it meandered north. She crept along the side of the path to a rock where, concealed, she could observe the path. She immediately ducked her head. The walkers had stopped a hundred yards ahead of her, and strewn themselves along the path, resting in shadows. One man at the head of the line had dismounted from a horse and studied the trail ahead, while another man had gone forward on foot and just turned the corner of the hill out of sight of the others. She saw he appeared a few minutes later and hailed three people on horseback. She sucked in her breath, recognized the enemy ghost from the mountain. Behind the enemy ghost a young girl on horseback stared forward at a third mounted man and the one who approached walking.

The people seemed to know one another and the walking man soon descended back toward those resting. But suddenly she heard shouts and the girl whirled her horse around and raced away, slapping her pony's flanks with the ends of her reins.

Her Beads watched the stranger on horseback club the enemy

ghost, knocking him off his mount. When the dust cleared, she perceived the unhorsed enemy warrior now lay spread-eagled on the ground. The man on foot had turned back running toward the two fighting men and the girl had ridden away and out of sight.

The victor dismounted, examined the supine figure, and directed the returned walker to do something. She watched as the walker sliced a knife up the pant legs of the victim. Her Beads had seen cruel behaviors and unexplainable things, but she peered now in disbelief at what she witnessed. Within minutes the two men had taken the enemy ghost's legs. She thought he must be dead.

The light waned as she saw one man take the legs and look around him. He walked up

the trail the way the girl had ridden, pushed the legs into a manzanita thicket, and returned empty handed.

Ussen, she prayed silently, protect me from this evil.

All of her life she'd accepted Grandmother's tales of the ugly and bizarre ways of the enemies. Now, her stomach lurched as she thought of anyone who would cut off the legs of another. And how did they do it, she puzzled. No disjointing, no bone breaking that she could see or hear. The enemy warrior must be dead where he fell. The girl on horseback must be his sister, for he'd sacrificed himself to help her get away.

Meanwhile, the line of men proceeded past the motionless warrior on the ground, climbed a slender trail, knocking shale off the path in noisy passage. Her Beads watched, wondering why they climbed there. They stopped and several men seemed to put their hands against the mountain at the same time. Her mouth dropped open as it seemed they next pulled the side of the mountain away and began to roll it up, revealing a waist-high wall. The very cliff dwelling she sought from her mind map revealed itself beyond the waist-high barrier. She knew the place in her memory map as "Where They Left Cloth." Her

Beads had hoped to find something of use there, and a place to rest. Why, she asked herself, would anyone hide the side of a mountain with ancient houses? Truly, the ways of the enemy people could not be understood.

Within minutes the men had all pushed themselves over the wall and moved about purposefully. Dust rose up and drifted away with the breeze. After a while the men descended, their packs filled, obviously with something heavy. The last two stopped at the order of the man on horseback who had killed the enemy warrior. The two men dropped their loads, picked up the enemy from the ground, and carried him up the faint trail. They slipped and slid along the loose footing; their burden slung like a dead deer between them.

Her vision, almost eclipsed by the murk of oncoming night, followed their forms as they lifted the body into the cliff house. Just as they rested their burden on top of the wall, the body wrenched sideways causing one carrier to fall back and slide down the slope. Her Beads could hear an angry shout echo against the hills. She felt her heart leap with gladness as she realized the enemy ghost still lived. She watched as the warrior, pummeled by both porters, was dropped inside the wall. After the men regained control, she saw their heads bobbing from inside the wall and wondered if they beat the man with no legs. Then, only the rattle of shale disturbed the mountain as the two men slipped and slid back down to their loads waiting on the trail.

Her Beads could close her eyes and see Grandmother instructing the children in the ways to survive as one of the *Ndee*, the Real People, the Dead. She knew Grandmother would advise any *Ndee* to make a large circle away from the violence of the enemy. But she also remembered the warrior had helped her on her way by not interfering. He didn't trick her. He didn't lie. She'd thought him dead, but then he fought. She pondered her next step as she waited for the men with loaded packs to leave.

Leaning her head on her arms against the boulder the hours of darkness crawled forward and she dozed and dreamed of Grandmother's words: "Avoid the ones we call *Nakaiyé*, Those Who Walk; and the others, *Indah*, the Living. They are the enemy. They will always lie. They will always trick you."

In the early hours of darkness, she awoke, checked the mule's hobbles, listened for a time, and finally approached the trail. She walked the canyon trail edges carefully and silently before reaching the path leading up to the house of the old ones.

I want to know if he is dead, she thought. I cannot stop there to rest, but I can check to see what has been done there, and I can honor a warrior.

The loose rock, difficult to walk upon, slowed her progress as she strove to climb it noiselessly. She finally found herself beside the wall that closed off the front of the cave. Boulders littered the hillside on either side of the entrance and she reaffirmed the location match. She breathed out a silent prayer of supplication to any spirits that might linger inside, then waited several minutes to ensure no otherworld response came. She reached the wall, miscalculated in the dark, slipped downhill, causing a small slide of shale to rattle down the cliff slope.

Stunned at her error, Her Beads leaned against the hillside and caught her breath. She listened to the silence that settled for several minutes before scrambling back up to the wall, dislodging other small falls of rock. Above her all remained silent. Slowly she crept forward again, placed each foot sideways on the slope to maintain her balance, leaned her body inward before solidly grasping the wall edge. Light barely trimmed the eastern horizon, but when she peeked over the wall into the house of the old ones the blackness made it impossible to see inside.

An arm punched out of the darkness, encircled her neck and chest, and dragged her roughly over the barrier. She landed flat on the hard earth, breath knocked out of her lungs, powerless to claim the use of her hands and draw her knife. As she struggled for breath the arm closed hard across her throat and she realized she had failed her mission. The blackness around her squeezed upward from her throat and into her head, cutting off her last thought.

CHAPTER 28

Man, Woman, or Beast?

Cliff Dwelling, Hackberry Canyon, *Chiricahua* Mountains, *Cochise* County, Arizona

NICK HAD LEANED INTO the corner where the native rock met the manmade wall when he heard shale rolling down the hill. He pushed himself up on his stumps balancing dangerously on top of the knots in his jeans to renew his sawing of the rough-edged stone back and forth across the ropes. He heard the "plink" of one strand separating. He renewed his efforts and pressed harder. Strand by strand, the remaining rope parted.

Nick heard a larger sliding of rock that took someone or something farther down the slope. He bore down on the last strands with all of his strength and weight, sawed through; lost his balance once again. This time he caught himself with his freed hands. He lay for a moment, flexed his wrists; untied the knots in his jeans' legs. Swiftly, he positioned himself to wait.

Too dark yet to make out a profile. Nick waited to hear movement and in the dark felt the tiniest swish of air enter his space. He brought the rock back to strike. Stopped. Against the night sky an even darker shadow crawled across the ledge. It could not be Vicente. Way too small. Young mountain lion? He thrust out an arm and caught it around the throat. He pressed down and held. The body flailed under the pressure of his arm lock; then went quiet. Must be one of those Mexican smugglers?

He kept one hand over the mouth, placed his ear on the form's chest, felt the shallow but distinct heartbeat. The faint rise beneath his cheek and ear suddenly resolved into recognition of an unexpected shape. Breasts? Startled, he moved away for a moment, but softly prodded the inert form beside him. No question. Breasts. He collected the rope he'd discarded from his own bindings, returned to hog-tie the woman's hands to her feet. Then he sat back, waiting for light.

CHAPTER 29

Keep Your Enemies Close

Where They Left Cloth, *Chiricahua* Apache Homeland, Arizona

HER BEADS CAME AWAKE to the sound of birds greeting the new day. Her throat hurt. She started to sit up but was stopped by a hand on her shoulder. She lay on the floor of the house of the old ones, looking up at the owner of the hand. The enemy warrior sat with his back against the wall of the ancients, or, she thought, at least the top half of him.

Her Beads tried to think of how the enemy warrior could still be alive, even without legs. Perhaps she saw his ghost? She began to move the arm farthest from him toward her boot legging and found herself sturdily tied. She closed her eyes, decided to begin again, but when she opened her eyelids he still sat there and her hands tied to her legs made movement impossible. The worst of possible outcomes, and yet, somewhere in the back of her memory, Grandmother's voice counseled: Patience. Wait your enemies out.

The enemy warrior held something up above his head. Her knife.

He raised his eyebrows. "Is this what you want?"

She could understand none of his words, but she watched his expression, seeking a clue to his next move. Blood had dried on his forehead and cheek, and stained his clothes. She gasped, unprepared when he leaned forward and pulled her up into a sitting position. He is strong, she realized, even without legs. She wriggled a bit hoping the ropes might loosen, but the knots held tight.

He reached one hand to her throat, gently moved aside her necklace of black and white beads, and examined the bruised area where he'd earlier attempted to strangle her.

"I really am sorry about that," he said, speaking the gibberish words of The Living, the Pale Eyes. She had no understanding of what he said, but his light touch and soft tone surprised her.

She weighed the probable meaning of his words, but the idea of an apology did not occur. She strained away from his hands.

"I've got some water. Want a drink?" More gibberish, she thought. His hands rested against her necklace and she strained away. He looked directly into her eyes.

She didn't like his hands on her mother's necklace, nor his eyes on her face. She swiped her teeth hard against his wrist.

"Damn!" He raised his hand to strike her, but drew it back. She saw her teeth had drawn blood. "I shouldn't have touched you." She did not know what he said, but heard his voice held no anger. "I don't want to hurt you, don't want you to hurt me." She leaned back as he stared long into her face. Still more words. "No more of that." It sounded like an order and she drew her own eyes into slits, disturbed.

He held the container out toward her lips.

It must be poison, she thought. She turned her face away. When she looked back, she saw he studied her. She noted the same deep brown color of his eyes as those of her own people.

He drank from the container himself, then held it forward. "Water?" Then in Spanish. "*Agua?*" She knew that word from Grandmother. He drank again while she sat silent.

It's not poison, she decided, or he wouldn't drink it. She watched his throat move as the water passed into his body. Something about his taut neck gulping below the stubble of dark beard on his chin impressed her as being vulnerable. The level in the container stopped at half and he held it forward one more time.

She surprised herself and spoke. "*Ha'ah. Tú. Agua.*" She watched the enemy. His eyes startled, but eagerness also formed there, the same benign, unfathomable smile as at the spring. "*Agua, Tú.*" she repeated. "*Agua.*"

"*Agua,*" he confirmed. He held the container to her mouth and she swallowed it in one long draft. She saw, as she drank, he considered her necklace, the black and white beads double-looped around her neck. Had he never seen such a decoration before?

"*T – Twoh.* Is that how you say it?"

She tilted her head up, understood he tried to say her word. "*Tú,*" she carefully enunciated.

He held her knife in his hand, gesturing that he could cut her bonds.

She stared back. "*Ha'ah,*" she said. "*Si,*" her voice low, throaty.

"*Si,*" he said back to her, swiping the knife through the air.

"*Si,*" she agreed, understanding only that he'd made some kind of threat.

He placed the knife to one side, and began to untie the ropes. She saw he noticed her eyes on the knife before he reached over and placed it behind him. She looked away.

Hands free, she sat still, waiting. The enemy warrior wound one of the rope pieces twice around his middle, and secured the knife in the loops. He then reached into his jacket and brought out something, handed her half.

Food wrapped in flat bread. Her mouth watered, but she made no move to accept it.

He brought it back to his own mouth and bit off a chunk. "You don't like burritos?" Again, his nonsense talk, although she recognized the Spanish word "burrito." He ate half and offered the remainder.

This time she took it. If he ate it, it must be edible. Pleased to find the stuffing made of beans, she took three huge bites before the flavor of the same stinking food *Nakaiyé* ate attacked her taste buds. Her mouth turned into a grimace and the enemy warrior peered closely.

She spit out what she hadn't swallowed. Yellow bits of cheese dotted what she'd rejected.

"You don't like cheese?" For a moment she wondered what his words meant, noticed he ended them with a rise in tone, just like a *Nakaiyé*. He rewrapped the second burrito and returned it to his jacket pocket.

"*Doo łikąą golįh da,*" she said, emphasizing the last syllable, mouth turned down.

"I get it. You don't like it. *No le gusta.* Okay."

She rubbed her hand across her mouth. She mimicked his last word softly. "O kay."

Surprised, he looked at her and smiled. "Well, okay then."

She opened a pouch from her belt and brought forth the sweet-smelling piece of food wrapped in brown paper. "*Ná,*" she said, and handed it to him.

Nick unwrapped the paper. Immediately the aroma of chocolate wafted around them.

"For me?" He brought it up to his mouth as she watched, hesitated, then offered it back.

She peeled a bit of the silver foil inside the dark brown wrapper and nibbled a corner off. Her face lightened as she savored the morsel on her tongue. She nibbled at it again. "*Łikąą golįh!*" She handed the chocolate bar to Nick again. "O kay," she pronounced carefully.

He nodded his head, broke off a piece of the chocolate and popped it in his mouth. "Ummm."

She watched his expression, copied his sound. "Ummm."

Her Beads wrapped the remainder carefully and tucked it back in her pouch.

He put one hand on the low wall that fronted the cave, beckoned her forward. She saw it would be easy to get away, but she did as he indicated and peered down the hill to the trail.

He raised himself to sit on top of the wall, swung his torso over the edge, and almost immediately swung himself back in again. "*Baje!* Down," he said, and placed his hand on her shoulder, forcing her down beside him.

A hot fear raced through her body. Maybe he was going to kill her! But she heard the sound of a horse nicker and relaxed. Someone had arrived below on the trail. They lay silently and could clearly hear the horse blow out and its hooves clomp against rock. Saddle leather creaked when someone dismounted. The enemy warrior placed a finger over his lips. Her Beads understood.

Nick stretched his neck warily up and peeped down through the grayness of early morning to see the familiar silhouette of his cousin's wide shoulders. He watched as the figure below dismounted, looked about to find a place to tether his horse next to the trail.

"He's back," Nick said softly.

She did not understand but knew he saw something he didn't like.

He motioned her to move to the back of the dwelling. This moment she could easily escape, she thought. Still, she didn't know what enemy trouble might be waiting. She followed his direction.

He prodded the girl into the deeper darkness of the cliff dwelling's second room. He patted his hand in the dimness along a ledge at the back until he found a narrow space. There, between the wall and the rock, he recalled disappearing during childhood games of hide and seek. He prepared to tuck the girl in it, not sure of her cooperation, but felt a drive to protect her. As his hand dropped into the space it came into contact with cloth.

"What's this?" he said in a low whisper. He moved his hand

over the cloth, collapsing what lay below it. The quiet sigh of dried sticks deteriorating into dust, rather than a crunch of breaking, confused him.

Her Beads could see nothing; but the earthy smell of the cave floors released some bubble of scent she caught; automatically she shifted her movement backward. Nick held her in place, while his left hand continued exploring behind the ledge. "*Dah!*" (No!) she whispered, then urgently, "*Dah!*"

Nick could not see her face, but understood something caused her to fight against him. At the same moment his hand landed in the darkness on a dry, round shape with two depressions above a dip in the middle.

The girl struggled, certain of the smell now, trying hard to pull away. Nick held tighter.

She tried to warn him, "*Ch'iin. Ch'iin. Gocho'*" Ghost. It's a bad place.

But he didn't know the meaning of her words.

At that moment the crunch of feet on rock reached the cave entrance.

"*Silencio.*" Nick grasped her arm hard, pushed her to the side of the ledge.

She understood and lay still. He could feel the tenseness in her body, silently thought: she thinks the same as I do. He took a deep breath. He knew what the smell was.

FRIENDS AND ENEMIES

CHAPTER 30

Lucy's Wild Ride

Chiricahua Mountains, Cochise County, Arizona

LUCY BENT OVER HER horse's neck, clamped her legs to the saddle and flew along the trail away from Nick and Vicente. She didn't understand exactly what happened between the two men, but she trusted Nick. Why would Vicente hold a gun on us? she thought. She must get to the home ranch and get help.

By the time she had curved around a loop in the trail that placed both distance and the view from anyone who followed, she slowed her horse to a canter, saving the young roan's energy for the several miles home. Lucy needed to find safety quickly, but realized she must reserve the horse's strength for when she needed major speed. She slowed to a trot as they crossed a small brook and had just dug her heels into the horse's side to move back into a canter when she saw movement on the trail ahead.

"Did he get ahead of me?" she wondered. "No, that's impossible," she silently reassured herself. She reigned the horse back a little, watching the movement ahead. Late afternoon shadows made it difficult to make out who or what crossed the trail in the distance. A string of figures seemed to lope across the path. "Oh," she thought, "it must be deer." But the distant figures became clearer as she neared them and she saw the figures were not deer at all, but people. Some of them quite small and wearing brown clothing, top to bottom, that looked like no clothing she'd ever seen before. She peered harder as the line of moving people cleared the trail. By the time she reached their crossing place they had all disappeared. "Like ghosts," she thought and shivered.

She stopped a moment to study their tracks, but saw that basically there were no tracks. "How can that be?" she puzzled, and scanned the forest for any sign of what she now was beginning to think might not have been. Her horse put its nose up and nickered nervously. "There, there," she said and reigned in, patting its shoulder. But the roan could smell something she couldn't. Its eyes rolled and it whinnied, then it suddenly burst away onto the trail and ran full out.

It took Lucy a good quarter mile before she regained control of the spooked roan. Once it calmed, it seemed to forget its experience. Mystified at the horse's reaction she rode on, looking backward to see if Vicente or anyone followed, and came to a trail divide. She knew Vicente would expect her to return to the home ranch, which meant that doing something he didn't expect would be the best way to escape him. She decided to take the path that led to their neighbors' place. She knew the Loretos would help her, and their ranch was closer, although she would have to cross a mountain spur.

"You up for a climb?" she asked the red roan, who snorted in answer, tossed its head, and began to ascend the path as she pointed it upward. After a few minutes, she stopped, dismounted and carefully tied the roan to a tree trunk. She stripped several branches from a leafy bush and descended to the path they'd just left. She quickly dragged the branches across the horse's hoofprints, effectively erasing them, and walked back up the trail to the roan, brushing all the way. She tied the branches together with a hank of rope from her saddle bag, remounted and dragged it behind, and continued up the trail to Loreto's. She watched below, but saw no one, especially not Vicente.

The path snaked upward and she frantically tried to remember the most direct route to Loreto's. Dozens of game trails, old lumber and mining roads, and hiker paths crisscrossed, paralleled, angled high and low. If he followed her this far, how to select one that Vicente would not expect?

Lucy's memory pulled her toward an old road closed long ago after the crash of local mining interests. She knew it intersected farther on with two fallen-down huts and a mine shaft obstructed by rocks. She also knew a trail ran above the huts, used now only by whitetail deer, smugglers, and the occasional hiker. The Crest Trail, sometimes called the old Apache Trail, clung to the sides of the highest cliffs, always just below the ridge line. Apache had used it in the old days to pass from one end of the 150-mile mountain range to the other without being seen. In places it shrank to no more than a two-foot width along the edge of high crags and precipices.

When she reached the mining road, she crossed it and continued into a shallow creek. Staying in the water, she urged her horse north into the middle of the creek, exiting the shallow stream only after reaching an area of granite outcrops. She moved onto the dry, rocky slabs, and aimed for a thick copse of pines, where she paused to listen. She heard nothing but the soughing of branches in the mountain breeze and the friendly chirrups of birds. She watched the wet marks of her horse's hoofprints dry into nothingness on the rock. To the distant northwest the jagged escarpments along the edge of the *Chiricahua* National Monument stood dark against shades of lemon and peach colors cast by the fading sun.

"If we cut through the edge of the Monument, we can angle toward Loreto's. They'll help us." She watched her pony's pinna flick back and forth listening to her voice. The route, a dangerous trail she'd never used, indeed been warned to never use, and of course, never alone or in the dark. For a moment Lucy felt overcome. Fear made her mouth dry.

Something bad is happening back there to Nick, she thought

to herself. His voice replayed in her head, over and over, "Lucy, go!" She was his only hope.

"What would Nick do?" she asked the horse.

Lucy leaned forward and patted the pony's withers. Its skin rolled in a tremble beneath her hand. It cocked one hind hoof on its toe, allowing its hindquarters to shift, blowing out companionably. "I think you're right. Sometimes you just have to cowgirl up." She dug her heels into her mount's flanks and headed toward the jagged skyline, bad trails in the dark and all.

CHAPTER 31

Vicente's Quandary

Cliff Dwelling, Hackberry Canyon, *Chiricahua* Mountains, *Cochise* County, Arizona

WHAT TO DO ABOUT Lucy? Why did these things happen just when he could see everything coming together? Vicente considered his options as he watched the two porters carry his legless cousin up the path to the little cliff dwelling. Right now, getting the bundles to the drop point prioritized his actions. He'd have to come back later to deal with Nick. No witnesses.

Keep it low key, he reminded himself silently. Even Chapo had made a comment. Not good. Chapo took his money and kept his mouth shut. Vicente didn't want to start worrying about Chapo. And now Lucy. It would take another couple of hours to get the group across the ridges of the old Apache raiding trail, down into the inner range, through the pass, then out to where the truck waited. And to his money.

When the two porters returned, he hurried them to take up their packs, herding them from behind to catch up with the rest of the group. The two packers sweated profusely in the next hour before they saw the backs of the other carriers ahead, and another quarter hour to become the tag end of the line. Both porters, red faced and panting, turned rebellious faces away when Vicente forced them to the side. He hailed the others ahead to

193

stop. Trotting his mount along the path, the whole line of men shuffled to the side, eyes to the ground.

Far ahead Chapo rode sentinel to clear the trail. When he saw Vicente approaching, he pulled up and waited.

"*Pendejo!* (Fool!) I know I told you to get over the mountain as fast as you could, but you might have lost me."

Chapo tipped his cowboy hat up with a blunt thumb. "I been watching for you, boss."

Vicente changed his complaint. "The way these guys walk, the Crest Trail may be too tough for 'em. They move like old men. I don't want to lose the payload down the side of a mountain."

Chapo shrugged his shoulders, studied the pommel of his saddle. He bit back what he wanted to say. Too fast? Too slow? Stared at the ground before answering. "Up to you, boss."

Light had faded down to the final dimness at day's end. Vicente leaned forward in his saddle, stretched his legs in the stirrups. "It could ruin me, you know. If the loads get to the truck by tomorrow night, no worries. But if we don't make it . . . well . . . you can't disappoint these people." His voice strained thin and trailed off.

The packers had all taken advantage of the riders' stop, and settled on the edge of the trail, ready to rest in the full dark. They leaned back against their packs at the side of the path, legs sprawled out.

Vicente raised an arm and swept it toward the mountain ridge. "Take them to the old mining camp and tell them to sleep for a few hours. I'll meet you there by early morning. You're the only one I can depend on, Chapo."

Vicente didn't wait for a response but wheeled his horse to the end of the line of packers. "*Ándaleti!*" (Come on!) He totally missed the determined expression that formed on Chapo's face.

"*Vamenos!*" (Let's go!) Chapo ordered the resting men, and amidst a low chorus of groans, the men stood and shouldered packs. "Maybe just one hour and you can sleep."

Vicente stopped at the end of the line, satisfied to see the men moving again, clicked his tongue and urged his horse back on the trail to where he'd just come from. Let's get this business finished, he thought to himself. No witnesses, now. I can handle Lucy. Take care of Nick and everything else falls into place.

CHAPTER 32

The Posse Returns

Colonia Suiza, East Side Sierra Madre, Chihuahua, Mexico

AT COLONIA SUIZA TORTILLAS and beans waited for returning searchers. Each tired man took a plate into the courtyard, sat on garden walls or on their heels as if at a branding, and ate. But Esteban and Ignacio swept right through, ignoring the hot dinner smells and the too quiet resonance of failure, and went straight to Ellsworth's office. Ignacio snatched a tortilla from a platter carried by one of the women and chewed on it as he followed his father. Within minutes the jingle of spurs announced the entrance of Lucero and Domingo, their faces grimy from their day in the saddle.

Ellsworth looked at their faces, could see they'd found something.

Esteban began. "We followed the old logging trails north in the jeep to check out different springs and *tinajas* (rock pools). Stopped at three places before we tried Bonito Springs." He looked around him. "Horse sign there and Ignacio and I knew them."

"You saw your horses?" Ellsworth asked, misunderstanding.

"No, Don Rafael. Tracks. Definitely our horses."

Ignacio nodded in agreement, swallowed the last bite of tortilla, and added, *"Segura que sí!"* (Absolutely). "I'd recognize the tracks anywhere. I shoed those horses myself."

"When we looked around in the nearby hills, we found a *cañón oculto* (a hidden canyon) in a fold in the cliffs, about a mile from the spring." Ignacio's eyes sparked with excitement. "Some old corrals made of branches, torn down brush houses, and mescal pits."

Esteban nodded grimly. "Oh, it's them, *cierto* (for sure)," Esteban said. "Nothing to see until we were right on top of it. Just javelina and coyote tracks. But from above the spring, a lookout can see the whole world to the north."

Ellsworth listened, revisited the place in his head: the snarled hills and slopes braided themselves into canyons that climbed into the mountain ranges and plunged straight down onto the immense valley floor that led to the international border. "It's a perfect place to watch for danger; to hide if trouble is coming."

"*Sí.* We split and looked every way, but found no more tracks. Just one other thing."

Esteban motioned with his chin to Ignacio who dug into a pocket, brought out a flattened can with a picture of bright red tomatoes on its label, handed it to Ellsworth.

Ellsworth turned it over, looked up at Esteban quizzically.

"No rust. Same brand as what we had in our shed. Put's them maybe one day ahead, no more."

Lucero looked closely at the can. "It's them."

"Hold on." Ellsworth rummaged in a drawer for a map. "Where's the closest water north from Bonito?"

Esteban shrugged. "Just *tinajas* (water held in rock depressions), 'til they get across the desert to the border."

"*Con su permiso,*" Lucero interjected. "No water except for the springs at Enmedios."

"*Ah, si compadre,*" Esteban agreed, "But the *federales* got a permanent camp on the north end. Why would Broncos go there?"

"Perhaps not . . ." Lucero sucked his teeth, thinking, "IF they knew about the *federales.*"

The room fell quiet.

"Maybe there's water at the Nuevo River?" Ellsworth said. "It rained up high yesterday."

The others nodded. The men knew the arroyo bed did not provide a route for crossing the desert. Usually, the New River simply did not exist. It took rain to flood the arroyo, which then seemed to be a river, but never for more than a day or two at a time.

Lucero slid one boot forward. "There is also what we found at *La Sartén* (the skillet). No people; well, no living people. A burned place, maybe a hut. And a buried body, not too deep, not there very long." Lucero shook his head. "It was the *Vieja* (the old lady). I've only seen her twice before; last time was twenty years ago. Who could think she'd live so long?"

"And no tracks anywhere," Domingo added, "Swept clean, which means they're on the move. Bad business."

Ellsworth summed up the information. "No one checked at Enmedios today because of the *federales* camp at the north end?"

Esteban nodded yes. "If the *federales* get involved it's a whole different thing."

The others agreed, shifted their stances, balancing their discomfort with knowledge.

Lucero shuffled more mud onto the floor, stated fiercely: "We don't want them back. Ever. Killers, every one of them."

Ellsworth considered the map. "It looks like they're headed blind to Enmedios. Maybe we can get there ahead and make sure to keep the *federales* out of it." Ellsworth locked eyes with Esteban.

"*D'accuerdo*," Esteban agreed. "This problem must end."

Ellsworth shifted his eyes to Lucero.

"Once and for all, Don Rafael."

The men solemnly extended their arms and one by one Ellsworth shook their hands.

CHAPTER 33

Surprises Are Not Always Good

Cliff Dwelling, Hackberry Canyon, *Chiricahua* Mountains, Cochise County, Arizona

THE MAN SCRAMBLED TOWARD the lip of the ancient low wall across the cliff dwelling and noted the rocks where none had been before. He'd seen a lot of tracks mostly leading up the path. He carried a .22 Remington in his right hand and balanced with his left against the steepness of the trail. His cowboy boots, so useful in stirrups, slipped on the upward grade. It seemed like he slid back one step for every two steps forward.

"Damn shale."

The sun, only just up, pearled the morning sky. He shouldn't have to sweat already. He'd ridden too far and had too much to do to be stopped now. He puffed hard as he swung his legs over and dropped onto the cliff dwelling floor. He saw a discarded water bottle, some blurry marks in the sand as if something had been dragged, and folded tarps against one wall.

Wariness settled between his shoulder blades as he scanned the small area. The overhang and its two rooms had occupied entire summers of his childhood, but now he couldn't remember the exact layout. How many places where his cousin could hide? He reached into a corner of the area behind the wall and found a pebble in the dust. He aimed it through the doorway, tossed it through the portal into the loose sand of the room's floor.

No other sounds.

"Nick?" he called softly and entered, his .22 raised in his right hand, a flashlight in the other. As his eyes settled into the gloom, he saw the cave was empty and advanced to the second low doorway. He took a deep breath, ducked his head before entering the doorway, flicked on the flashlight, and in one surprised second realized he should not have entered so swiftly.

* * *

Nick could hear someone moving quietly in the outer cave. Vicente is back to kill me, he thought.

He placed his palm gently over the girl's hand and gave four noiseless pats. The number of pats, done only to give comfort, meant nothing to him. He felt none of the spiritual power of the number four that immediately communicated to the girl as sacred protection.

Keenly aware of his loss of height without his legs, feeling his vulnerability, Nick made an instant decision, pressed her knife into her hand. At least she'd have a chance this way if he went down. He'd begun to back away when her hand on his shoulder halted him. He first thought she wanted to stop him. Then realized her hand held him back, a warning.

As boots thumped across the floor in the first room, he slid toward the doorway and prepared himself. Standing on his uneven stumps in the dark, his drill sergeant's voice echoed in his mind: "Throw your strength against the enemy's weaknesses." He went down on his one knee and waited.

Only a rim of reflected grayness around the low doorway broke the darkness. Into that frame of dimness, the broad shoulders of a human form materialized. A flashlight flicked on, slicing through the dark to the opposing wall. Nick hurled himself forward, propelling his body into the other's. He leapt on top of the intruder's body, worked an arm around the neck, clutching his thighs around his adversary's legs, pinning him.

The lack of his lower legs and feet to wind about the attacker hampered Nick's hold, but he got his opponent's face down in the sand. The light from the front room disappeared under clouds of loose dust. Nick choked and hacked as grit blocked his nose and stung his eyes. The flashlight rolled across the ground, its beam skewed onto the ceiling of the first room, lighting the dust. His opponent threw his weight to one side and lunged across the dirt floor; dust everywhere increased to a blinding fog. Nick braced his arm on the wall and bore down on the other's Adam's apple, thinking of how much he hated Vicente.

The young woman picked up the flashlight and whirled its light over their heads, her voice strident. *"Doo ts'iziłhee da!"* (Don't kill him!) When he didn't stop, she called out louder. *"Dah!"*

Nick saw she had the knife in her other hand. He understood only her last word, urgent and clear. The body under him had gone limp, and gurgled on the floor. Nick rolled away and rose on his stumps above the billowing dust, gasping for a clear breath. He leaned down and twisted the shoulders of the inert figure to flip him face up.

"Hadín láhi díí?" (Who can this be?) She lowered her knife. *"Ła'ihíí,"* she insisted (The Other).

Confounded, Nick saw the man was not Vicente.

Nick grabbed the legs and clumsily dragged the inert body into the outer cave, where dust did not clog the air. *"Agua,"* he directed the girl.

She looked around and picked up the bottle. Empty. *"Dah,"* she said.

He pointed over the edge of the wall. *"Agua,"* he demanded again, then *"T'wohh."*

She vaulted over the wall, plastic bottle in one hand, and disappeared sliding down the shale.

He realized he might just have messed up everything. Given the girl her knife and freedom. Killed a man not an enemy. What a fool he was. Not a chance he'd ever see her again. Nick fanned the dust away from the face that had lain downward on the floor, dragged him out in the open area by the wall and opened the mouth with his fingers, jabbing dirt from the tongue.

"I am so sorry," he said to the still figure.

Then he pinched the nose with one hand and began to give mouth to mouth resuscitation to his younger cousin, Tomás.

CHAPTER 34

Fighting the Odds

Cliff Dwelling, Hackberry Canyon, *Chiricahua* Mountains, *Cochise* County, Arizona

NICK POSED ABOVE TOMÁS, who'd begun to sputter. "C'mon, Tomás," he begged, "Come back. Breathe." He almost wept for joy when Tomás's eyes flew open, registered shock, fear, relief at seeing Nick. Nick placed one hand behind his cousin's head, tried to help him sit up. A hand thrust a full water bottle between the two cousins, and Nick snapped his head left in surprise to see the girl.

"You came back!" he said, a smile of relief on his lips. "Thank you," and he took the water bottle from her hands.

The girl regarded Nick with no expression, moved her gaze to Tomás.

Tomás blinked, stared at her, as Nick dribbled water between his lips. His attention on the girl, Tomás took in too much water too fast and his choking renewed.

The girl sat back on her heels, waited.

"Take it easy, primo." Nick held the water bottle aside until the choking stopped and he saw his cousin's eyes refocused, then handed it to him. "We thought you were Vicente."

Tomás wheezed. "Tia called . . . at Loreto's. Lucy, you . . . missing." His voice rasped as he tried to explain.

Nick nodded. "Don't talk. I remember you went to help at

Loreto's." He chewed on his lip. "Long story about Vicente, but Lucy got away. Then the girl turned up and was about to help me out of here."

"Girl?" Tomás tried, and went into a paroxysm of coughing.

"The one I saw on Dog Mountain at the spring."

Tomás's eyes went wide even as he coughed. "Hot chick?" he croaked. "Where?" and he looked wildly around. "Tia said . . . find Lucy and," he coughed, unable to finish.

"Lucy should be safe by now," Nick reassured him. He looked about him for the girl as he had not heard her leave. "The girl from the springs kind of comes and goes," he said.

"Illegal?"

"I don't know." Nick handed the water to his cousin for another drink. "She was trying to tell me something about the cliff dwelling, but I didn't know what she was saying." He picked up the flashlight the girl dropped when she left to get water. He shone the light about them, and stepped toward the darkness of the back room. "Let me see if she went back in there."

Tomás tried to stand. Dust formed a halo around his head, setting him coughing again, and he slid down with his back against the stone wall.

"Sit tight while I look. Breathe."

Nick beamed the light into the second room and moved clumsily to the back. He boosted himself onto the rock ledge, smelling a musty odor again as he crawled to the wide crack between the rock shelf and the wall. When the beam of light revealed what lay in the crack, he drew back quickly, turned away, and swallowed hard. He sat on the edge of the rock for a moment, then slid down to the sand floor and returned to the front of the cave.

Tomás watched Nick's awkward return as he moved, clumsy on his uneven stumps. "Where's your legs?"

Nick took a gulp of water, then several deep breaths. "Too much dust," he gasped.

"Where are they, man?" Tomás insisted.

Nick watched his younger cousin's face. "Vicente took them." Tomás stared hard back at him. "No." His voice was astonished.

"Afraid so. He acted crazy yesterday."

Tomás stuttered. "But . . . What? Why? No." He shook his head in misery. "Oh, man. That is so bad."

"Yup." Nick placed a hand on Tomás's shoulder. "Girl's not back there."

Tomás looked ready to cry. "What else could happen?"

"We need to get out of here before Vicente shows up. We need to find some help. We need to be sure Lucy got to safety."

Tomás leaned against the wall and pushed himself up to stand. He stepped over to look outside. "Nick, my horse is gone."

"Looks like I need a ride to the bottom of the hill and then we can see what to do."

Tomás gritted his teeth, even and white, through the wet streaks of dust across his face, coughed, asked again, "Girl?"

"She's used to taking care of herself." And I'm a lot more worried about Lucy, Nick thought.

Nick clambered from the wall onto his cousin's back. Tomás handed the water bottle to Nick, began to descend.

From the vantage point of Tomás's back and the height of the hill, Nick surveyed the terrain in case Vicente had just tossed his artificial legs aside. On the second sweep he caught a movement less than a hundred yards up the trail.

"Look, Tomás. Eleven o'clock."

Tomás stopped. "I see it."

A dense thicket of scrub oak and berry brambles trembled, shook, then erupted, leaves flying onto the ground. The girl emerged from the bush.

"Is that her?" Tomás asked eagerly.

The girl turned, held something in the air.

"She found my legs." Nick slapped his palm against Tomás's shoulder.

"Think she can find my horse?"

They reached the bottom of the hill, stepped onto the trail. The girl neared, both prosthetic legs held against her shoulder like a rifle. Tomás stopped and slid Nick off onto the main path.

The girl halted. She laid the artificial legs on the side of the path, gracefully motioned to Nick.

"*Diyééhinee béshbijád*" (These are your metal legs).

The two stared at her. She motioned toward the legs, repeated her words.

"I don't know. I think she's telling me to take them." Nick started to move toward her; she immediately moved backward. He stopped. He placed his right hand over his heart, said to her, "Thank you. Gracias."

She turned, began to walk away.

Nick quickly examined his prostheses. He'd already shrugged halfway out of his Levi's when Tomás turned and flushed red in embarrassment.

"Damn, Nick!"

"Can't put them on without taking off the pants."

The girl had stopped a second time, watched.

Nick flashed a grin at her as he worked at lining up the prostheses with his stumps. Keenly aware of her attention, he secured the sockets, raised an arm to Tomás for help in standing. She advanced a little closer as Tomás pulled Nick to his feet. She nodded when Nick pulled up his pants and stood.

Tomás looked around the girl, then Nick. "Where's your boots?"

Nick smiled, looked down at the metal frames of each leg he'd have to balance on. "I suppose on somebody else's feet. More important, where's the horse?" he asked.

The girl looked at him blankly.

"*Caballo*," Tomás said. "Horse." Then he threw his head back, snorted, imitated a horse's whinny, pawed the ground with one foot.

Until Tomás's foot slapped at the ground her face showed no expression. Then, she laughed, catching the cousins by surprise. "First time I've seen her smile," Nick approved. "I'll take more of that."

She'd rewound the string of black and white beads close around her neck. She now wore a thin blanket wrapped across one shoulder, bandolier style. Apparently, she'd left some things at the bottom of the trail. Her dark hair, gathered and bound in a rawhide knot at the nape of her neck, framed the warm, light brown skin of her face.

"She's beautiful," Tomás said. He took a step toward her. "I think I'm in love."

She repeated Tomás's first two words. "*Caballo*. Horse." She watched their faces. "*Łįį'*." She said the slurred, nasal word a second time. "*Łįį'*."

The cousins stared at her with raised eyebrows. Nick's face brightened. "That's her word for 'horse'."

Tomás tried to wrap his mouth around the slushy word and mustered "What language is that?" Then he tried to imitate her. "Cleee."

The girl turned, headed into the brush.

Tomás called out "Cleee" again.

She looked back. Her expression remained blank, but she began to talk in a soft rolling stream, filled with clicks and tones.

The two young men regarded her in fascination.

"What's she saying? What's that language?" Tomás leaned forward, trying to understand.

"Not a clue."

The girl peered at them intently. She pursed her lips toward the east and raised her chin. They both stared at her in bewilderment and she strode away. This time she did not stop.

"Go after her and I'll follow you. Don't know how long my battery charge will hold. And it's real work keeping from falling over without boots. Help me find a stick to walk."

Tomás broke into a trot to keep up with the girl's receding figure, at the same time looking for a bush or tree branch. Nick followed clumsily behind him, aware he walked on borrowed time. Once his bionic leg drained its stored energy he'd be crippled in his movement, not to mention the tough balance on his unprotected metal feet. He followed behind the other two, waiting for his one knee to seize up, hoping to catch himself before he fell. Just a matter of time, one way or the other.

CHAPTER 35

In the Land of the Ancestors
Chihuahuan Desert, *Chiricahua* Homeland

NAADIKTAZ, IT WIGGLES, WALKED away from the camp and found a rock against which to rest his back, next to the spreading branches of a blue spruce. The smell of the tree made him feel so homesick for the Blue Mountains that he leaned his head forward onto his folded arms and almost gave in to tears. The group had settled down to sleep the remaining few hours of the night, but he could not rest. Both the walkers and riders had arrived near the tanks within a short time of one another, excepting *Bikécho*, His Big Toe, who came in late, and *Gidi*, Cat, who did not.

No amount of tracking back to find Cat made a difference. He could not dream it true. Gone. The enemy had taken her.

It Wiggles knew he should be helping to arrange shelter for the children, make sure everyone got something to eat. But now he felt immobilized. He'd lost Cat. How could they ever get her back? He sat staring at his feet.

A quiet footfall in front of him caused him to look up. "My brother," Left Hand said. "You must come back and rest."

The *dikohe* held out a hand offering a flat portion of mescal paste.

"No, I'm not hungry."

"We are all hungry, brother."

"Then you eat it."

Left Hand returned the food to his pouch, walked past It Wiggles and sat down several strides behind him.

It Wiggles knew it didn't matter if he insisted the boy go away. *Dikohe* protected the warriors. Left Hand, as *dikohe*, would remain nearby no matter what. It Wiggles's feelings of inadequacy washed over him again. Grandmother told him he must lead the children to their relatives. But he felt so incapable. He wished powerfully that someone, any of the others, could make decisions for the Blue Mountain People. He thought of *Biyoo'*, Her Beads, and hoped they would find her soon.

Finally, It Wiggles rose, stretched his legs. He looked up into the star-filled sky and saw in a short time the blackness would begin to ebb as a new day began. *Ussen*, he prayed silently, guide us. Help me lead the children. Return Cat to us. He turned and saw Left Hand had fallen asleep. He looked down at the nine-year-old boy, too young to be a *dikohe*, just as he himself held too few years to be a warrior.

He picked up a twig, softly tossed it against Left Hand's chest. The boy sprang to his feet, immediately alert, hand on the upper part of his legging where he kept his knife.

Impressed, It Wiggles gripped the boy's shoulder. "*Enjuh*" (Good), he said, and thought perhaps the *Ndee*, the Dead, with *dikohe* like Left Hand, might survive this journey after all.

CHAPTER 36

Paradise Lost

Cochise Stronghold, Dragoon Mountains, *Cochise* County, Arizona

"DOES THIS FEEL RIGHT, Father?" Lorraine slowed for each gulley on the narrow road, her hands limp on the wheel. The afternoon sun had begun its slide across the sky.

Sam Charley, He Does Not Forget, knew they hadn't reached the break in the mountains yet, the place that allowed easy admittance into the protected center of the Dragoon Mountains. Two wrong turns in the last ten minutes.

"My memory is old, but we are near *Cochise* Stronghold entrance."

He searched the craggy line of mountains, watching for some sight to trigger his memory. His gnarled right hand held tight to the open window jam.

They'd left Wilcox an hour before, traveling south down the Sulfur Springs Valley between two rugged mountain ranges, to the east the lofty *Chiricahua* and to the west the Dragoons. Sparsely settled, with a vast dried lake bed stretching toward the Mexican border, wide valley views lay before them.

"Why do we have to go this way?" Susie pouted from the back seat.

Lorraine turned west where an arrow pointed, followed by the words Stronghold Road. The car rattled over potholes up and down the hills. Only one other vehicle, a beat-up farm truck, crossed their path. Scrub oak bristled along the side of the road with occasional green patches. Here and there the tires thu-thumped across culverts that led into acres of pecan groves.

Sam's eyes locked on a series of gigantic rocks jutting out from the Dragoons, forming a jagged outline. He smiled broadly and stretched his neck toward the children in the back seat. "Girls," he said, "Those yellow and white rocks are the entrance into the Stronghold. This is the way the ancestors came home."

The Suburban entered a pass into the rocky-walled canyon. Ahead, towering granite domes extended into the sky. Shade from low oak trees dappled the way as the twins sat forward and rested their chins on the back of the front seat. Shadows flickered over the family's faces as they drove forward, riding into a place from their ancestors' past.

A small herd of javelinas trotted nonchalantly across the lane in front of the car and Lorraine slowed for their passage. Sam watched them scuttle into the scrub. When the car reached an immense boulder sitting in the middle of the road, Sam remembered his father bringing him to the exact same place so long ago.

Lorraine rounded the giant boulder, drove farther into a spacious hollow encircled by high cliffs. She stopped at the campground entrance. Once, *Cochise* and his *Chokonen* band of *Chiricahua* people lived in this place. This sacred place.

Sam got out of the car and gazed across the grounds, appalled. He stood on a paved road that wound through the small valley, punctuated with paved campsites. Tents, travel trailers, and recreational vehicles stretched around the trimmed back trees and the protective canyon walls. An automated drink machine hummed next to a stone building with signs pointing to bathrooms and laundry. Sam felt his face stiffen as a man, munching from a bag of chips, exited a nearby RV and approached him.

Lorraine joined Sam, and the man settled a baseball cap on his head, smiling warmly. "Welcome to the Stronghold. I'm Carl, the campground host. You folks need a campsite for tonight? Just one left!"

Sam raised his shoulders slowly. "No," he said and looked at Lorraine. "No, we cannot stop here." He could hardly bear to look around, so offensive the changes. Ruined. "Is it always like this?"

"Usually!" the man confirmed cheerfully. "People just love it. You know this is where they fought the Indian Wars!" He swept one arm around the once pristine hollow. "Cavalry versus the 'Paches, you know. 'Paches planned their raids right here." He peered proudly around at the loops of RVs and tents. "Battles, fights, everything. Right here. The history's amazing!" He crumpled up the chip bag, rolled it into his pocket, pulled out a cigarette. He lit it, offered a smoke to Sam and Lorraine.

They stared at him, blank faced. Lorraine shook her head no, asked: "Where's a not so crowded campsite?"

The host pointed a finger back the way they came. "Just follow the loop around the Stronghold here, go back the same way you came in. Cross over to the Cheery Cows to the Wonderland of Rocks."

"Cheery Cows?" Sam asked.

"*Chiricahua* Mountains," Carl smiled. "Cheery Cows is what all the locals call them. You folks have a map?"

"Thank you," Lorraine said in a flat, cool voice. "We don't need one." She placed a hand lightly at Sam's elbow, opened the car door, and helped him get back in. Under her breath she muttered, "Cheery Cows, here we come."

Sam looked one last time at the man's face. "You may want to recheck your history."

The man tilted his head to one side, puzzled, blew a stream of smoke from his nose.

"There was no Indian War fighting in this place. This is where *Chokonen* lived, where they came to find safety."

"No, the 'Paches lived right here."

Sam looked him squarely in the eye. "*Chokonen* are Apache." He gestured toward himself and his daughter. "We are Apache."

The host blew out a smoke ring and squinted. "You're 'Paches?"

Sam nodded.

"But, the Buffalo Soldiers from Ft. Huachuca chased the 'Paches out of here. We find arrowheads and old cartridges all over the place."

Sam shook his head. "Not from a battle. Didn't happen here. The *Chokonen* Band always left before the soldiers came."

Sam turned away and left the man arguing on his own.

The car wended its way around the loop, passing all of the paved campsites. Sam began to sing a low song to himself. Elsie, sitting behind him, placed a hand on his right shoulder and Susie reached over to hold his left shoulder. When they neared the huge monolith that split the road, Sam broke his song.

"Daughter, halt here."

Lorraine parked on the edge of the road. Sam left the vehicle, and beckoned the twins to follow. He placed one hand on the enormous boulder, and touching the stone, walked around it, singing. With the other hand he scattered *hoddentin* (sacred pollen), taken from the leather bag around his neck. Elsie and Susie followed, each with a hand on the huge rock and Lorraine behind.

Sam stopped when he'd made a complete orbit and asked the twins, "How many times do we say a blessing?"

The girls answered together: "Four."

His eyes lifted to the side of the canyon wall, seemed to climb up through the strewn boulders. "Here my grandfather played as a child." The twins bobbed their necks up so their eyes landed on the very rim. "Let us finish." The old man led them three more times around the boulder, then returned to the car. He sat down stiffly and buckled his seat belt. "*Enjuh*. It's all I can do here."

Lorraine's eyes shone as she repeated, "*Enjuh*" (It is good).

An hour later across the valley, the night sky darkened the mostly empty campground they found at the *Chiricahua* National Monument. As the sun fell behind the canyon walls, delivering the first chill of evening, the family sat down at the picnic table to eat. Everyone tucked in quickly, focused on eating the hot dinner cooked on a Coleman camp stove. Lorraine set out a jar of honey to drizzle on the fry bread and her father beamed.

"This turns fry bread into a feast." He smiled happily as he licked honey off his fingers and ate several pieces of the round, crispy bread.

"This has been an interesting day, Father." Lorraine kept one hand on his left elbow as they strolled after dinner toward the sound of nearby water flowing, a creek. "I'm not sure what I feel about it."

Sam watched the twins skip ahead, their flashlights bouncing brilliantly off trees, then creek water, then one another. They will sleep well tonight, he thought, in their people's homeland.

"There's always a reason, Daughter. *Ussen* must have a plan."

CHAPTER 37

Mountains and Canyons and Mountains and ...Canyons and ...

Chiricahua Apache Homeland

NAADIKTAZ, IT WIGGLES, WATCHED the children as they removed all signs of their presence and spread mesquite branches about the clearing, returning the location to just another spot in the wild. He watched as Pretty One led the youngest children away on four of the horses, leaving the rest to clear up the camp area and wipe out the trail forward. She also led one horse used to carry food and goods. This day they must move to the edge of the first range and cross the valley after nightfall.

It Wiggles no longer cared how many days they'd been traveling. They'd not been able to follow the memory path of Grandmother because of where they'd crossed from the land of the *Nakaiyé*, the Mexicans, into the land of the *Indah*, the Living.

At the rock tank the night before, he'd left trail sign for *Gidi*, Cat, so she could follow if she managed to get away. He bent down now, and placed a second sign, four pebbles in a row, showing the direction taken by the Blue Mountain People.

Bee eshgané, Left Hand, approached. "Ready."

The remainder of the group, hands filled with bunches of grass and small branches

brushed the ground, erasing all marks from the camping

place. Two *dikohe* fell behind the group as they moved away, ensured no evidence of the group's passage remained.

Dahsts'aa', Strawberry, rode off on the sixth horse and ahead of the

group led by Pretty One. It Wiggles knew he could rely on Strawberry to keep off the path when possible, acting as scout, watching the trails and countryside for signs of enemies. Her knee-length hair, braided now and tucked under her belt, swung against her back. It Wiggles had earlier teased her that she might leave some hair behind. She had carefully used a brush made of pine needles to comb out loose hair and burned the strands in their small cook fire.

Grandmother had taught them the way through the Place of Bones, named after the bones of raided livestock that littered a protected pass through the Guadalupe Mountains. "We are too far west of that trail," It Wiggles told Strawberry that morning. "We need to cross safely tonight at a narrow place in the valley."

At midmorning Strawberry reported to It Wiggles that a wide trail led onto the valley plain. Square buildings and fences where enemies lived sat miles away in the valley along the mountain range. Strawberry hobbled her horse to crop at grasses and joined It Wiggles to creep forward to a rocky point to examine the valley below.

"You can see where the *Indah* travel below, not too many." She indicated a black wavy line running up the valley, by raising her chin and pushing out her lips. "No one will see us at night."

"What about the living places of the *Indah*?"

Strawberry wrinkled her nose. "We can follow that arroyo, see? It goes between them."

Several buildings that looked like toys, surrounded by miniature corrals, scattered far below across the land.

Satisfied with Strawberry's assessment, It Wiggles peered farther onto the next mountain range. As Grandmother had described, he visually searched along the crest line looking for the patterns he'd committed to memory. He could not see far enough north to the Two Tails, but he did see a change of color in the middle of the range. Forest interspersed with granite. He felt confident he knew their location.

Pretty One stepped to his side and joined in studying the land. "A road there on the other side leads into the mountains. There must be more *Indah* buildings."

"*Ha'ah*. It will bring us in below the Place of the Standing Up Rocks, and at night we will not be seen. We'll watch for *Indah*, but the raiding trail should belong to us alone." They both looked out at the center of the range at the gray area that must be granite. "We will climb down at the end of light and wait for full darkness to cross."

The younger children looked expectantly across the valley to the mountains. "Is that our home?" *Łichii*, Red One, peered longingly at the peaks and shadows still so far away.

"Once it belonged to our people; but not now." It Wiggles headband had loosened, and some of his shoulder length hair blew across his face. He drew the hair back, re-tied it under the band, and stared up the valley. "We must go past these mountains. We will find our people farther north."

Red One sighed. "It is such a long way."

"Yes," It Wiggles agreed, "but when we find our relatives, we will finally be home."

The two stared north, their faces closed, their eyes filled with longing.

CHAPTER 38

The Choices of Men

Cliff Dwelling, Hackberry Canyon, *Chiricahua* Mountains, *Cochise* County, Arizona

VICENTE LEFT THE BIG blue roan at the foot of the cliff dwelling and ascended the hill on the narrow path. When he climbed over the ancient low wall, he hardened his heart. He knew he must take care of the job inside quickly, and get on with his plan. He didn't want to do it, he consoled himself. It was what he must do, to save the ranch, to save the family name, to prosper. I am a man, he told himself, and I must make the choices of a man.

He entered the first room fast, ready to deal with an attack, but found nothing. He swallowed a lung full of air, and prepared himself to tackle the second room. It was enveloped in darkness, a place he did not want to enter.

"Ni-i-i-ck?" he called softly in a sing-song voice, "Where are you?" Nothing. "Nick, are you there?" He craned his neck left and right. "I know you're mad at me, but I had to do that. I had to take your legs. I had to make my point with them. Those people are killers." Vicente cursed the darkness. He dug in a chest pocket and located a half-used book of matches.

He struck one of the matches in the doorway and checked both sides of the small room. No sign of Nick. The flat boulder at the back: bare. Vicente inched forward with caution. His match went out, and he lit a second one, then squinted into the cleft behind the stone.

"Still there, *mi hermano*" (my brother). "*Durmiendo, ¿verdad?*" (You're sleeping, right?) His tone gentle, his mouth bent into a tender grin, he asked, "You didn't tell on me, did you?" The second match went out. "No, of course not. You're very fast asleep, brother." He lit the third match and shuffled through the dust back toward the dimness of the first room. "Where are you, Nick? What did you find?" A sound like a small rock falling startled him from behind. He spun around. "Don't you dare!" he growled into the blackness behind him. He backed away from the door and into the entrance area, saw no one. He breathed in, expanding his chest, and reassured himself. "Spooky place," but he kept watching all around, front and back.

He craned his neck forward over the low wall and looked into the valley. "Where are you, Nick?" he asked the emptiness. His eyes scrutinized up and down the canyon. "How far could you get?"

CHAPTER 39

Ridge Country

Chiricahua Mountains, *Cochise* County, Arizona

CHAPO RODE HIS FAVORITE horse from the remuda, the one they called Salsa. She carried her rider flawlessly; like dancing a soft rhumba. Chapo always had thoughts of women when he rode her. Maybe when this crazy journey ended and the load disappeared into the back of a truck, he could take his share of the pay and vanish toward Texas. As his mind roamed, the rhumba idea leading him further into how he would spend time and money on pretty girls in El Paso, his chin dropped to his chest, and he dozed off slumped in the saddle.

Chapo awoke with a shudder to find his rifle in hand, aimed into the frightened eyes of Cruz, the lead porter. Cruz's fingers dug into Chapo's knee, interrupting a dream sequence involving a woman rocking her hips ardently under his own, that changed into a massage, that became some poor little cockroach scrabbling across his leg. Chapo lifted his hat by the brim, wiped sweat from his forehead, resettled the cap, and shivered because the whole sequence gave him the willies.

"What the hell you doing?" he demanded of Cruz. Chapo could just make him out in the darkness. He looked up, estimated the time as a couple of hours before daybreak.

The porter's voice rang as if from a well. "Look. I think here's the cut-off to the place. An old mine, you said. There's no sign, but there used to be one. See the stake?" Cruz waited until Chapo craned his neck in the dark and saw the sign remains. "We got to stop, boss. Been on our feet since yesterday dawn." Cruz turned his head sideways, his right eye rolled at the gun barrel.

Chapo peered dully around at the night, easing the weapon away from the porter's head. Vicente would be back, expecting them to be at the mine. "Yeah, follow me," and he turned the horse onto the uphill split. It was another half-hour before the road entered a clearing. "Yeah, okay. Tell 'em to rest."

Chapo dismounted, slung Salsa's reins over and around a bush. The horse immediately began to nuzzle the leaves. Chapo rolled his shoulders and stretched his back, yawning, as the men shrugged out of their packs. He unfastened the folded canvas bucket he carried on his saddle and headed across the clearing, past the crude hand-timbered shack, toward the sound of a stream. When he returned with the filled bucket, the carriers had arranged themselves on the ground. Within minutes the area was quiet. A man mumbled in his sleep, another coughed, and Salsa blew out a quiet snort at the bottom of the bucket, jingling her halter. Although tired, Chapo moved the horse to the edge of the compound where she could graze, loosened the girth on the saddle, ate a food bar, and finally sat with his back against the ruined cabin wall. He had a view of the entire clearing. He let the men sleep, waiting for Vicente's arrival, trying to recall the rhumba dream which danced away.

Surprised to awake with the sun fully up, stiff and cold from sitting on the ground, Chapo wished only for the warmth of a thick blanket. Amid the packs men stirred. Someone roamed the edges of the mining area, collected wood, built a fire. The man moved as if old and brittle, working patiently at coaxing a small blaze inside a ring of stones.

Chapo checked Salsa first, took the bucket and again filled it at the stream, returned to water the horse before approaching the flickering warmth of the rock-rimmed flames. The men clustered around the fire, sharing the last of their food. Chapo had stuck the remainder of a stack of tortillas in his saddle bags before leaving the ranch. He grabbed several and stuffed them in his mouth, offering the rest to the others. The tortillas lasted about a half minute.

Chapo rubbed his palms together over the fire, ran his hands through his hair before settling his baseball cap back down solidly on his head. What had happened to Vicente? He knew they waited in the right place and he should have returned by now. What should he do? Every time he'd second guessed Vicente the blame came home to rest on Chapo's shoulders. Should he continue to wait here, or lead the packers onto the old Apache Trail and hightail it to the truck? Where was *La Migra* (the Border Patrol)? Too many dangers. So many worries. Still at least six hours of hard walking to the meet place. As usual, he thought sourly, if Vicente doesn't make the decision, it's bound to be me who is wrong.

He surveyed the abandoned mine, a blank hole into the mountain. His eyes swept over the falling apart shack, rusted cans, and other discarded trash, and the leaning corral poles that still jutted up from the earth. In the middle of nowhere, he thought, and all kinds of danger. He silently cursed Vicente.

The sound of the creek running behind the derelict house seemed to dim, as another sound intruded. Birds stopped singing as the sound grew: the high-pitched hum of a motor, maybe more than one, whined and cut into the clearing from the road below.

"Get out of here!" Chapo ordered Cruz and kicked sand wildly onto the fire.

The lead porter called out to the rest of the men to grab their packs and go. "¿Dónde vamos?" he asked Chapo.

"¡Todos fuera del vista!" (Out of sight!) Chapo killed the fire, grabbed the horse. He tightened the flank cinch on Salsa, who stepped on one of his boot toes. Chapo hopped painfully around for a moment looking for the canvas bucket, now flat on the ground underneath Salsa's rear hoof. Hooking it upward with one hand, he threw the handle around the horn, and mounted. He saw the porters skitter with their packs over the edge of the hill and disappear down the side of the mountain, saw their tracks peppered the clearing. Dust swirled in the air behind them.

Chapo spun Salsa, rode her across the clearing to the brook where he urged her back and forth across the clearing and the tracks, churning the soft dirt. He re-entered the clearing and encouraged her to crow-hop with a spur to her ribs. The motor sounds crashed into the clearing.

At the same moment the horse came down in a spine jarring buck that left Chapo's buttocks numb, three Border Patrol ATVs slid into the open space. By the time Salsa trotted around between the ruined house and the mine entrance, officers had leaped off the machines and dispersed. One crouched on his heels at the edge of the clearing, studied the earth. Another cast for sign around the walls of the house. The last stood watching Chapo, hands at his waist, fingers stretched close to the grip of a holstered revolver.

Chapo brought Salsa to within a few feet of the man, but did not dismount. "Mornin'! Got a few wrinkles to iron out here." He made the motions of calming the horse with a few pats, grinned and leaned forward, offering a hand. "Chapo Morales."

The man's elbows relaxed and he reached out to shake. "Sector Chief Gomez, Border Patrol, San Enebro office." He stepped back and looked the horse up and down. "She's a pretty little thing. Had one like that I used to have to ride down every morning." He tilted his head, squinted his eyes up at Chapo. "Is she like that?"

Salsa seemed to understand she was the focus of discussion and jerked her head up and down, harness jingling.

"I figure she's gonna start to behave one of these days." Skittish, the horse sidestepped, stirring the dust, while the newcomer watched.

"You stop here last night?" The Border Patrol agent eyed smoke curling skyward from the fire ring.

"Yeah." Chapo continued to walk the horse around the edge of the forest opening, intent on casually obliterating any of the porters' footprints he might have missed in his impromptu horseback rampage.

"Who you riding for?"

"Diaz family, down on the edge of the San Bernadino Valley."

The uniformed man squinted. "You mean Roberto?"

"Vicente."

The agent's mouth pulled down. "What's he got you doing up here?"

Chapo kept his voice steady, hoped he sounded bored to the bone.

"Oh, the usual. Picking up strays. Checking fences."

"Seen anybody else?"

"There's never anybody else. Can't figure how the guys that mined here could stand it." He swung down from Salsa and led her to where the other man waited.

Chapo planted one needle-toed boot forward, noted the whereabouts of the other patrol members, listened for telltale sounds of discovery, considered what he'd do. He raised his belt, nocked it up a hole, then settled his pants back on his hips.

"Got caught in the dark last night. Decided both me and the horse was too tired to ride blind." He pushed his hat up his forehead with a forefinger. "What brings you up so high?"

"Just the usual." The sector chief scanned the line of rim rocks that clustered above the mine. "You been on that trail up there?"

Chapo shook his head. "Not lately. You seen how skinny that trail is?"

The other man chuckled. "I hear you."

The other two agents returned to the clearing. The chief raised his eyebrows in inquiry.

"Some tracks over by the stream," one of the men said. He looked at Chapo's boots. "Likely candidate, right there."

Chapo threw his hands up in mock surrender.

"Time to mosey on." The chief turned away to his vehicle.

By the time the ATVs disappeared down the rough road, Chapo, mounted and moving, edged toward the spot he'd seen the last porter slide downhill through the crags and trees. Salsa balked at the sharp slant of the hill. Chapo respected a good horse's opinion. He turned Salsa back, waited until the din of ATV motors faded away to nothing, and then began to whistle his favorite vaquero tune about roping a devil steer again. After a few minutes various men began to show themselves, climbing up the hill back into the clearing.

CHAPTER 40

Kittens and Devils

Medicine House (Regional Hospital),
Chiricahua Apache Homeland

GIDI, CAT, HELD THE tiny kitten next to her face and rubbed her cheek against its fur. It felt as smooth as new doeskin, the kind that Grandmother chewed to soften before making it into a skirt or moccasin legging. She and the kitten finished the saucer of milk together. The drink had awakened Cat's stomach, and when it rumbled, the kitten squirmed as if it was hungry, too.

"Are you hungry, little *gidi*?" Cat said to the small, furry kitten, who responded with a kitten-sized mew. "I am hungry, but Grandmother said we must always be careful with enemy food." She planted her nose against the top of the kitten's head and nuzzled the soft fur between its tiny ears.

Cat was caught by surprise when the enemy Brown Woman entered the room. Cat held the kitten protectively against her chest, and turned away. She listened as the woman moved about. There was a noise of setting something down, and then a swish as the enemy turned and walked away, her shoes squeaking, back to the door.

Cat remained facing the wall as a smell drifted her way. She rubbed her nose deeper into the *gidi*'s neck, but finally turned around to see what the smell might be. There, next to her bed the enemy had left a steaming bowl. A fragrant cloud hung above the bowl and Cat breathed in deeply. The smell of the hot food, a seed mush, made her mouth water. The noses of both she and the kitten twitched and Cat poked a careful finger into the bowl, then held it to the kitten's mouth. A delicate pink tongue curled out and lapped at Cat's finger.

Cat murmured to the kitten, "*Ha'ah, łikąą golįh*" (Yes, it tastes good), encouraging it to eat.

She set the kitten down on the bed and again dipped her finger in the mush and licked it herself. Although a spoon lay next to the bowl, she ignored it. "Yes, kitten, it tastes very good." She lifted the bowl to her lips, allowing the mush to run into her mouth, then took turns with the kitten to lick the bowl clean.

The nurse watched the closed-circuit TV screen from her ward desk outside and smiled. She picked up the empty paper packet of maple flavored Cream of Wheat and crumpled it before dropping it in the waste can. "I thought you might have a sweet tooth. First kittens, milk, and then cream of wheat." She drummed her fingertips lightly against the desk top. "What can I tempt you with next?"

She listened to the child speak softly to the kitten, wondered again what language she heard. The child, found at the border and obviously lost, must be speaking one of the border Indian languages. "Ahh!" she said in soft discovery when she realized there might be someone on staff who could help.

When the aides appeared to change linens, the nurse button-holed a petite woman she remembered had once told her she came from a village in the Sierra Madre. "She's a lost child who's speaking a language none of us know," the nurse explained. She seated her new ally to watch the child and the kitten on the television screen, found a round tin of Danish cookies under the counter, heated a cup of water for tea.

The small woman blinked in surprise when food and drink were set before her, smiled shyly. "She is not speaking my village's language, Opata."

The nurse smiled philosophically. "Oh well. It was worth a try."

"These are very good," the aide said as she munched cookies and sipped tea, watching the screen as the child played with the kitten. She suddenly stopped with the cup half raised to her lips. "Ay!" She placed a hand on her chest, as if to keep her heart in place. "I may be wrong, but I have heard some of those words before."

"Yes?"

"When I was a child, an old woman lived alone at the edge of town. She worked for people, cleaning, caring for babies, but we children were afraid of her."

The nurse raised her eyebrows.

"The vaqueros brought her to the village when she was a child. The people she lived with died when she was a young woman and she lived in their house. I can see her now. She did not like visitors. We called her La Forastera, the outsider, because she didn't act the same as the people in the village."

"How did she act?"

"In my village, all cats were called 'Gato' or 'Gata'." The woman's face blanched, and her dark eyes stood out. "She spoke Spanish, but she also knew the language of 'los diablos'." The woman looked at the nurse. "The little girl is speaking that language. I heard her call the kitten 'gidi'."

"I thought she was saying 'kitty'," the nurse said.

The small woman gritted her teeth. "She's saying 'gidi'. It is a word from 'los diablos'."

The nurse studied the woman's fingers, wrapped around the tea mug. The fingers gripped tightly, but even so, faintly quivered.

"Who are 'los diablos'?" the nurse persisted. "Do they have another name?"

The small woman set her empty cup down, crossed herself. "Those 'diablos', they're all dead from before my birth, except those who came as children into the villages. Now, they should all be dead." She crossed herself again. "I hope they are all dead."

The woman, who had kept her eyes on the screen, watched as the child and kitten finished their meal. Her face suddenly flattened into a grimace. "Señora, forgive me for bringing bad news." The small woman's eyes widened in fear as she turned to the nurse, "She's speaking the language of the devils, the Apache."

CHAPTER 41

Invisible Trail

Colonia Suiza, East Side Sierra
Madre, Chihuahua, Mexico

HOURS BEFORE DAWN ON the morning after discovering the route of the rustlers Esteban placed a gentle hand on Ignacio's shoulder. *"¡Levántate!"* (Get up!) The son woke, dressed swiftly, and grabbed the packs they'd prepared before leaving home, containing trail food, canteens, and ammunition. They'd slept a half night in the bunkhouse at the *colonia*, and both shouldered rifles and moved quickly outside to the *colonia*'s waiting SUV.

Lucero met them and helped store their weapons in a concealed floor compartment of the SUV. Two women, one of them Senora Ellsworth of the green eyes and pleasant smiles, carried thermos cups of coffee and homemade burritos as they followed Rafael Ellsworth from the main house. He gave each woman a peck on the cheek, turned to the other three men and asked, *"¿Listo?"* (Ready?)

With the morning stars fading, they crossed the desert from the mountains to Enmedios, part of it by an old wagon trail, part of it by Esteban's sense of direction. "By my nose," he said, tapping one nostril, grinning.

They arrived at the base of the Enmedios hills as the light came up, the whole world a gray pearl in the dawn.

They left the vehicles behind mesquite bushes in a fold in the hills, crept quietly toward the spring, when a roar of engines brought two desert camo jeeps around the cliffs. The four men from the *colonia* raced for cover, watched as the jeeps surged up to the spring. *Federales.*

Uniformed men leaped from the jeeps, sped on foot in several directions out-of-sight for long minutes, then returned. One voice called "Nada," Nothing. Within fifteen minutes the soldiers regrouped and the jeeps sped away.

Esteban exchanged looks with the other three and everyone nodded. They approached the spring carefully, ready to fly if necessary. But the jeep engines whined into nothing.

Other than jeep tread marks and the footprints of the soldiers, the sand around the spring showed nothing more than a few bird prints and a lone javelina. The four men scattered to examine the entire area more thoroughly and quickly reassembled.

"*Federales, seguro,*" Esteban pronounced. "But I don't think they noticed the visitors that were there before them."

Esteban and Lucero agreed the devils they sought had visited, rested in a side canyon behind the spring.

"How can finding nothing mean anything?" Ellsworth asked.

Esteban's eyes roamed the folds in the hills with a practiced eye. "It means sometimes you can try too hard." Esteban continued to examine the floor of the desert. "They erased too much."

"But the birds, the javelina . . ." Ellsworth voice trailed out onto the surrounding unmarked desert.

"ONE javelina's prints," Esteban pointed out. "Pretty unusual to see a lone javelina."

"They travel in packs," Lucero said. "Plus, I did not smell them. That smell should still be here."

"*Claro,*" Ignacio agreed. "They always rub their scent glands on the rocks and bushes."

"I don't smell it," Ellsworth said, holding his nose into the morning breeze.

"¡*Exactemente!*"

Esteban asked his son to climb the rocks and scan the surrounding area. Ignacio scrambled up to a high point and lay on his belly, using binoculars to study the landscape. Lucero came after him, the two working their way around the edges of the rocks and cliffs, noted the *federales* camp, the highway with early traffic, the dips and creases of the desert. They returned and examined the land stretching west. No people. No horses. No wildlife. The two descended the rocks by the spring and reported their findings.

"There's an arroyo running north, looks deep, that might connect to the border." Lucero turned and pointed off to the west. "What do you think?" he asked Ignacio.

"No cover any other way if they want to stay out of sight."

Esteban returned from his scout. He cut a trail of horse and footprints about a half mile into the desert.

"Looks like maybe eight to ten people on foot with others riding," Esteban said. "Somebody wiped the desert behind them, but still, I know our horses." Esteban's confident tone left no question.

Ignacio swept his gaze west and north, turned to his father. "And there's something else." He looked back up at the Enmedios heights. "Come up here, just a little way."

They climbed up the initial layer of boulders and stopped under the cliff line.

"Look," Ignacio said. "Follow the road with your binoculars to where it runs close to the border. See where the arroyo ends?"

They all peered intently to where Ignacio pointed.

"Maybe a quarter mile out from the border station?" his father asked.

"Sí. Now look west along the border fence. Maybe a mile? See that patch of gray green?"

The men scanned silently.

Lucero swallowed a swift intake of breath. "Holy Mother. That's where the coyotes used to take their *pollos* when they smuggled drugs. That's the cholla patch Border Patrol usually bypasses, but there are trails through it." He chewed on his lip, decided to explain more. "I made two carries as a *pollo* because I needed the money, and that was enough for me. Never again."

The men stared grimly at the distant grey green color on the land.

"I don't blame you, man." Esteban began to descend from the rocks, and the others followed. "Any time in cholla is one time too many for me."

Back on the highway the SUV looped twenty miles before Ellsworth pulled over where the road met the east–west Mexican National Highway #2. They headed west, joined into the constant traffic flow of semitruck loads of produce and products, all aimed for Nogales warehouses. Within an hour Ellsworth spun the wheel toward a cutoff to a rural border crossing located on the Mexico/New Mexico border.

Esteban craned his neck, watched for a particular crease in the seared brown rock of the mountains he knew to be in the United States. "There's a canyon used in the old days to line up where to cross from Enmedios."

"*Claro que sí*" (Clearly). Lucero replied, "Behind the border crossing."

"Would they use such an obvious trail?" Ellsworth, a good hundred miles north of his area of expertise, swam adrift in unknown geography.

"Why not?" Esteban replied. "It was always the main route. The Enmedios route is the only one that makes sense because it has water. Too many people and towns everywhere else."

Esteban's binoculars brought the pile of hills before them into focus, leading into a purple mass of mountains beyond. Everywhere offered a desert view strewn with pebbles, cactus, and mesquite, broken by ravines. Paper trash blew everywhere—empty water bottles, crushed wrappers and plastic bags caught on bushes, aluminum soda cans, who knew what else, the detritus of illegal border crossing.

Two miles from the border Ellsworth stopped the vehicle at one side of the road, drove into a thicket of mesquite that blended the SUV's silhouette into nebulous shadows.

Here and there ocotillo cacti stretched spiny arms upward. No sign of farming or fields or houses. A place to get across, stretching for lonesome miles all around.

Esteban glassed the area, the distant border fence on the horizon, a low guardhouse and gate marked by national flags on each side. "They had to avoid the *federales*," Esteban noted, "and they had to avoid the border guards. How would they do that?"

Ignacio tapped his shoulder. "That big wash we saw is over there." He pointed into the distance. "And look, it has one branch that comes out close to the cholla grove."

All four men glassed the border area.

Esteban brought the binoculars down and studied the land with his naked eye. "Ignacio, see if you can find any tracks that they went that way."

Lucero got out, too. "I'll go with him," and the two set off on foot. The others continued to glass the territory.

When the two returned they reported finding some sign near the border. "Looks like they tried to cover their tracks," Ignacio said, looking at his father, "but it's our horses and they were moving too fast."

Lucero's voice thrilled in sharpness. "They're just one day ahead. We're closing in."

Ellsworth accepted the information, thought about it. "Don Esteban, that cholla may be of use. Lucero and I have passports so we can cross and find those devils. We'll have to leave you and Ignacio in Mexico. But two of us alone is not very good odds."

Esteban shrugged. "What do you suggest?"

"There are ways through cholla. You'd need to get through some place they'd never look."

Esteban saw his son's face close hard in resistance, said, "We have to wait until dark as it is, so think about it."

The men sipped the last of their coffee, ate what food remained. At dusk Ellsworth and Lucero prepared to leave. "You two crossing, or not?" he asked the Garcias. "No hard feelings." Ellsworth looked north into the ragged ranges beyond the border. "One way or the other we will finish this problem."

Esteban glanced at his son, said, "*Sí, a sus órdenes*" (At your service). Ignacio sighed heavily, shuffled his boots in the dust. Esteban threw an arm around his son. "We want our horses back."

The men shook hands, waited for the dark to drop Garcia father and son closer to the fence.

The faces of all four settled hard into silence.

CHAPTER 42

Life's Too Short

Cliff Dwelling, Hackberry Canyon, Chiricahua Mountains, *Cochise* County, Arizona

NICK AND TOMÁS FOLLOWED the girl off the trail and into a small grove of trees. She led them directly to the thick brush where she'd left the mule. Nick nodded when Tomás noted the mule was the missing Larry. Next to the mule Tomás's horse cropped at the nearby grasses. Nick watched the girl jump onto Larry, then wait quietly while Tomás held his hands under Nick's foot hoisting him onto the horse, before swinging himself up behind Nick. Nick saw her make just one motion with her hand signaling to follow, turned the mule's head, and plodded away. Tomás, looking off to the north, missed her hand sign.

"Where's she goin', primo?" Tomás's voice, too loud in the quiet of the morning, caused a roadrunner to break cover.

Both Nick and the girl hissed for quiet. Tomás clamped a hand across his mouth as Nick turned the horse into the hollow, following the mule directly into a tangle of scrub oak and mesquite a few hundred feet farther off the trail. Here the girl dismounted, tossed the mule's handmade halter line to Tomás. The horses and riders could no longer be seen from the trail. She held one palm up then down, indicating the men must stay, quickly disappeared into the brush on foot.

Tomás turned the braided halter line of yucca and willow

strips over in his hand. "Hey, do you think she made this herself?"

"Quiet." Nick dropped from one side of the horse to the ground, his left leg and automated knee shuddering across loose grit. He clenched his teeth in pain as the stump grated against the hard parts of his prosthetic. Nick caught himself from slipping, regained his posture, watched as the girl appeared on the ridge above the hollow and then melted into a thicket of dense low oak.

"What?" Tomás asked in a whisper.

"It's like the closer I get to her, the less I know where she is. How does she do that?"

Both men stood waiting, turned as a footstep fell behind them. The girl entered the hollow, one hand extended across her mouth, demanding silence. She beckoned them to follow. She wrapped the mule's reins around one hand and pulled it, maneuvering on foot north toward an arroyo.

Tomás sputtered ready to ask a question, and Nick placed his own index finger across his lips. Tomás lifted the horse's reins and fell in behind the girl, with Nick behind. The horse blew out and shook its head, jingling the metal connectors against the leather harness. The girl instantly stopped and looked back piercingly at Tomás. He shortened his hold on the hanging reins, pulled a bandanna from his hip pocket, and wrapped it around the metal pieces on the harness.

She turned, led them along through brush into the arroyo that hid them from the cliff bank above, heads below vision line. Red-barked manzanita bushes crowned both sides of the arroyo, covering their movement. A slight ascending gradient brought them to another dry gully that veered east. They stopped when the girl slid off the mule, passed its reins to Tomás to hold while she again disappeared and reconnoitered their surroundings.

Tomás observed Nick as he tinkered with his left knee. He leaned in close and spoke in a low tone. "Somethin' wrong, Nick?"

"Joint's dry. Don't know how long the charge will last. I usually plug it in overnight." Nick looked up at his cousin's concerned face. "Don't worry. We deal with it when it freezes." Tomás turned away, unsure how to react.

Nick reached to grasp Tomás by the shoulder, speaking barely above a whisper. "Don't go all worried, primo. It may get me all the way back to the ranch. You know what the Marines say."

Nick watched as the girl came into view, flattened her body out at the rim of the gully, and began to crawl into the shade of a low tangle of greasewood.

Tomás leaned in, ready to hear the answer to Nick's question, but kicked suddenly away in a motion that ended in his diving off the horse and onto the earth into a low crouch. The stinging crack of a long-range rifle shot whistled overhead. At the same time Nick slid off the horse's rump and rolled across the sand. Both men pressed themselves against the inside wall of the gully. The sound of drumming hooves faded into the distance and they realized both the mule and horse had broken away. Nick placed his hand at the base of Tomás's neck, urging him to remain flat down. "Wait!"

The birds had gone silent and the gully and surrounds pulsed in a dead quiet.

A second rifle shot pinged against the top of the arroyo wall, spitting up an explosion of dirt. A sliding sound began in a whisper and the cousins looked up just in time to move deeper into shadowed cover as the girl's body slithered down the embankment into the arroyo's dry bed. Her body flopped onto its side a hundred feet away, a line of fresh blood running down her cheek. And remained still.

CHAPTER 43

Prisoner

Dry Gully, *Chiricahua* Apache Homeland

BIYOO', HER BEADS, COULD hear the pound of the drum. She slid sideways in a circle of people. On the heavy beat her right foot came down and her left foot closed in a glide over to the right. Dun de Dun de Dun de ... She wanted to hear the singing, and stretched her neck out to hear better. Dun de Dun de Dun de ... but could only hear the beat, not the song. A small voice came from the distance and worked past the drum beat. She could almost make it out. The drums increased in volume, thrust their clamor behind her eyes, resonating with rhythms that created an exquisite searing pain along one side of her head.

She opened her eyes and realized no drums pounded, except in her head. Pain beat as if it could pound through her skin. The man who'd fought the warrior stood a step away from where she lay on the sand of a dry creek bed. Dark, wavy hair framed a pinched face with close-set, bloodshot eyes. The man kicked negligently at her foot and Her Beads tried to sit up. Dun de Dun de ... the kick jarred her body, and sent an arrow of pain into her head, knocking her back into blackness.

The second time she regained consciousness Her Beads heard the sound of horse hooves on earth. She saw the color red through her right eye, reached up and swiped it, then examined her hand. Viscous blood covered her fingers and palm. Her head pounded, and again, everything went dark.

She felt the solid strength of someone holding her around the waist, both of them crushed into one saddle. As soon as he spoke, she knew him for the man who'd taken away the legs of the warrior. His voice, like a magpie, grated, repeated, scolded. She couldn't understand his speech. The way he bit off his words and threw them forward made her understand he spoke in anger. Her hair had fallen out of its knot and hung in a curtain around her face, sticky with blood. Slowly she began to remember what happened when she thought she heard drums.

The warrior, *Béshbijád,* Metal Legs, and *Ła'ihíí,* The Other, had followed her away from the place that Grandmother called Where They Left Cloth. A man on horseback pursued them and shot at them. She remembered that Metal Legs watched her scramble up the gully bank before everything went dark. His face, a warrior's face, remained calm in the sudden attack. The memory of his calmness helped her endure the insult of the grip of the enemy's hands.

"I will fight you to the death," she said in her own language to the man holding her. "I promise I will kill you."

He gripped her tighter, his only response.

She cautiously wiggled her leg and felt the weight of the knife in her boot against her skin; thought: I must wait.

CHAPTER 44

War Spoils

Dry Gully, *Chiricahua* Mountains, *Cochise* County, Arizona

Vicente muttered as he rode, holding tight to the girl he'd shot. "What did you say, *querida*? There's a little blood, but I've seen worse." He listened but after her outburst she remained silent. "I'm glad I didn't aim any better. When I saw you in the brush, I thought you were Nick. You were so fast, you just ran around my bullet."

His hand moved up from her waist, passed lightly across her chest, and touched the side of her head. She made no response to his movements, but he felt an involuntary quiver run across the wound. "Good thing it just sort of pleated your hair. Might even start a new fashion." He took a deep breath, expanding his chest so that his body filled the space between them, liked the feel of her slender torso straining away from his.

Vicente had looked in vain for Tomás and Nick. They'd disappeared swiftly into mesquite thickets once he fired. He knew they'd lost their mounts, because the mule and horse galloped away at the sound of gunfire.

He'd called out, asking them to return, that he wouldn't hurt anyone. "I didn't know it was you," he hollered. "Just a big mistake."

But nobody answered, and he felt foolish to even try to trick them again. He could get Tomás straightened out alright, but after leaving Nick in the cave he figured he had only so much time to finish what he'd started.

"I can smell mule on you," he said to the girl he held in front of him, "but all in all I'm bringing home a nice little trophy for the living room." His eyes narrowed. "Or maybe the bedroom, eh *querida*? The Republic's first battle in the war of independence, that's what it is: the spoils of war."

He could feel her breathing in and out and tightened his arm farther around her waist. Her breaths became shallower. "Panting for me, are you?" Vicente enjoyed his one-sided game for the next few minutes, tightening and loosening pressure on the girl. She gave no indication that she noticed it at all. "I'd like to know who you are and what you're doing in my country, *querida*."

Her body warmed his chest. He moved his arm up to her bust and felt pleased to find the shape of each breast fit plump into his hand. "Nice." He gathered one breast at a time and squeezed hard. The girl did not react. He moved his hand to her throat, clamped hard enough that she stopped breathing. No response.

His mount, freed of all guidance, slowed and stopped at the side of the gully, began to nibble at sprouting grasses. "Hey!" he yelled at the horse, and brought the reins up, jerking his hands from the girl's body. The horse fought to continue eating, and Vicente wrestled with the reins, sawing the horse's head back and forth.

In one swift movement the girl lunged forward and twisted under the reins. Her foot bashed at the enemy's head as her leg cleared the pommel.

Ears ringing from her kick, Vicente saw her dive to the ground, rolling, grabbed for his rifle which rested in a scabbard attached to the saddle. Vicente clutched at the weapon, grappled with her while struggling to bring the horse under control. He let the reins go and wrenched the gun from her grasp.

Her fingers caught in the trigger housing and Vicente, a red mark painting his cheek from where her moccasin heel struck, looked straight down the barrel she held aimed at his head. She struggled to get her fingers solidly in front of the trigger, all the time pulling. Vicente shoved the barrel sideways, just before her fingers reached the right pressure. A blast rent the arroyo, erasing all other sounds. The girl fell backward into the sand and curled into a ball as the bucking horse spun. Vicente clamped his thighs around the thickness of the horse's barrel, held his boots in the stirrups, and gripped the saddle as his mount caromed violently, shying away from the still smoking gun he'd somehow managed to get back in his hands.

He heard voices on the arroyo banks. As the horse crow footed and bucked, it took a few seconds for him to focus and see Nick and Tomás untangling themselves from the brush along the creek bed, running toward him. He flailed the rein ends against the horse's neck, and the panicked animal wheeled and stumbled into a run. Both Nick and Tomás scrambled to get out of the way, while the girl regained her feet. The echo of the shot still seemed to hang in the dry stream bed as Vicente thundered around the bend of the arroyo.

●　●　●

The three stood for a moment as the hoofbeats thinned away into nothingness.

Nick turned to the girl, put out a hand, and touched her arm. "You okay?" Nick knew she couldn't understand the words, but saw she listened to his tone. "You did exactly the right thing."

She shrugged his hand away making it clear his touch was not needed, turned on her feet quickly and stumbled. He caught her before she fell, and when their hands touched, they shared a frisson, electric. Startled, they both took a step back.

"Let me look at your head," he said to her, touching his own forehead to indicate what he wanted to do, and she allowed it. Her hair, wet with blood, surrounded a wound, a long tear at the hairline, but not deep. He breathed the faint essence of campfire smoke that he thought of as the girl's perfume. "You are one lucky girl. We'll get you some first aid and no problem." She watched him silently, kept her attention on his face when he wasn't looking, then dropped her eyes when he looked at her.

Tomás stood nervously by, watching the dry streambed both ways and the banks above it. "Let's get out of here, Nick. He might come back."

Nick pointed northwest toward Loreto's, the closest ranch. He watched as the girl's eyes followed the direction of his hand. He turned and adjusted his legs which felt clumsy, heavy, and dug too deep without his boots on to make walking normal. He heard Tomás step in behind him. A moment or two passed before he looked back, words ready on his lips to reassure both the girl and his cousin. He saw a clump of greasewood on the edge of the arroyo quaking ever so lightly. As for the girl, no sign remained, like she'd never been there at all.

RESOLUTE COURAGE

CHAPTER 45

The Last Protector

Wide Valley, *Chiricahua* Apache Homeland

"THE HARD PART," *NAADIKTAZ,* It Wiggles, said looking out over the space they must cross in the night, "is we must be inside the canyons of the *Chiricahua* Mountains before light."

Dahsts'aa', Strawberry, craned her neck toward the dark mass of the *Chiricahua* Mountains, homeplace of the ancestors. She studied the land, marked its fall and rise, the pattern of the paths below, observed the occasional metal wagons of the enemies as they ran along the black rivers.

"The metal wagons look like rabbits," Strawberry noted.

"Except they do not leave the hard, black rivers. They do not fear what comes from behind them."

Strawberry's hands looped nervously around her long braid and untucked it from her belt. She brought the braid to her mouth and chewed on its end. "What if we cannot get across in one night?"

It Wiggles looked beyond the black path to some dark blotches next to a fold of hills on the other side of the valley. "If we do not pass that enemy place," and he pointed with his chin at the valley, "we will have to stop and wait for a second night. That dry streambed may or may not be big enough for all of us to hide. Too risky to spend the day there."

Strawberry chewed.

"Sister, we will soon call you Bald One."

Strawberry stopped chewing, wiped the end of her braid against her deerskin skirt, and tucked it back into her belt, all the while scrutinizing the valley.

"Brother, tell me what my mother looked like."

As second oldest in the group, It Wiggles's memories often supplied the other children's knowledge of their own histories. He regarded Strawberry thoughtfully. "She had very long hair … like you."

Strawberry's face brightened. "Did she travel across this valley?"

"Once our people owned this valley, those mountains, and the next valley and the next mountains."

"Yes, but did my mother see them before the people had to be invisible?"

It Wiggles thought. "Maybe not. She came from a village in the Blue Mountains. I remember she could speak the language of *Nakaiyé*, Those Who Walk.

"Where did she go?" Strawberry's wistful question floated quietly between them.

The question seared into It Wiggles's childhood memory and produced an image of a young woman, baby at her breast. The child must have been Strawberry, he thought. Where did that woman go? he wondered, tried to think of how old he'd been when she failed to return. The adults, he recalled, had moved in and out of wherever Grandmother led the children. Sometimes they brought food or clothing. Women lived with them for short times when they birthed babies, then left the babies with Grandmother and returned to . . . where did they go? His forehead crinkled as he pondered. He'd last seen Strawberry's mother perhaps seven winters before, when she stopped coming. Like all of the other adults, eventually she did not return.

"I remember your mother carrying you in a *ts'aał* on her

back. She hung the cradleboard in a tree while we all picked berries, and that's when you got your nickname."

Strawberry looked at It Wiggles eagerly. "Tell me."

It Wiggles had told the story many times but Strawberry never tired of repetitions. "It happened at the meadow below *'Ihi'na' Ha'itin* (Trail to Life Goes Up), in the Blue Mountains. A drought made it hard to find food and your mother led us to a place at the bottom of a bluff. Strawberries grew along the banks of a small creek. So many berries! Your mother hung you in your cradleboard from a tree branch and you fell asleep. One child watched the trail that climbed up the bluff, and suddenly made the call of a night bird, our signal to hide. We all disappeared, except for you. A line of *Nakaiyé* cowboys headed up the trail on horseback. You awoke at the sound of the horses, blinked your eyes, and watched them go past. You did not cry. You did not move. Even though you were in plain sight they did not look your way. Later, your mother ate a strawberry, and placed it on your lips. You liked the taste. That was how you got your nickname. It happened at the meadow below *'Ihi'na' Ha'itin* (Trail to Life Goes Up), in the Blue Mountains."

"I know where that meadow is." Strawberry's voice squeezed small. "Will we gather strawberries from that place again?"

It Wiggles pulled gently on her long braid. "No. We will find a new place. Perhaps across the valley in our people's mountains." He pointed with his lips across the space.

Strawberry gazed across at the shadows and colors of the *Chiricahua* Mountain range, tried to remember her mother's face, but could not.

It Wiggles's eyes stared long at the purple and gray mountains of his people's home range. The sun cast its golden light across the rolling lands, and clouds shadowed the peaks and valleys below. He thought of Strawberry's mother who most certainly walked now in the lands of the Happy Place, and of all the children's parents who must also have gone there. Grandmother, the last protector, had been the only adult they'd seen in a circle of seasons, a whole year.

It Wiggles knew *Her Beads* walked somewhere ahead of them; knew she was leaving sign to show them the way. But what if she disappeared, too? He would be the eldest of the Blue Mountain People, and he did not know enough to protect them. He brushed a hand across his eyes, suddenly afraid, scolded himself and fought his way away from tears. You are a warrior, he thought. Warriors do not cry. What if all the *Ndee*, all of their homeland people, had ceased to exist? What if the Blue Mountain People were the last of all *Ndee*, and no relatives lived at all?

Strawberry had another question but when she turned to ask It Wiggles, his face was so

strained and worried she clamped her teeth into silence. She looked again at the homeland and decided what words might help.

"Oldest brother, show me the canyon we will travel to where our Blue Mountain People will go swiftly across the valley tonight." It Wiggles stared across into the peaks and cliffs beyond the valley. He studied the colors below. "There, Sister. See the dark spots that are dwellings of the enemy. We will pass that place into the canyon that climbs to the ancestors' raiding trail. By the time we reach the Land of Standing Up Rocks we will find Eldest Sister." He stopped. Considered. "Or, she will find us."

He thought further and reminded himself silently. Or, she is no longer there to meet us and has followed Grandmother to the Happy Place. He turned his face away, not wanting to display his concerns or doubts, his lips white where he bit them.

CHAPTER 46

One More Mountain

Off the Raiding Path, *Chiricahua* Apache Homeland

Biyoo', Her Beads, headed west, away from where she'd wrested her freedom from the enemy, and away from *Béshbijád*, Metal Legs, and *Ła'ihíí*, The Other. She knew they meant her no harm but she needed to separate herself from their trouble and resume her journey.

She covered the land and gullies at a loping gait, adjusted her direction to move north again. She found cover on a hill slope, hunkered down in a thick cluster of brush and boulders, where she could observe anyone who might pursue her. Once certain no one followed, she checked herself over. One sleeve gone, ripped off by the enemy who'd tried to take her prisoner. She still had her dry food pouches, her gourd of water, her blanket tied around her waist, and her knife in her legging. She breathed a sigh of relief when she placed one hand on her neck, found her power bag unharmed, her mother's black and white beads safely looped around her throat. Surely, she thought, *Ussen* protects me. She wondered what the warrior Metal Legs did when he found her gone. She thought: he is not like other enemies.

Her head snapped up at a scrape of gravel behind her in the brush, and she slipped her knife free from her leg wrappings; breathed out in relief when she saw only a large tarantula feeling its way across the pebbled ground. Using her knife tip, she turned it aside gently. It resumed a crawl at a different angle, still heading east. She wiped her knife blade against her leg wrappings to dispel any of the little hairs that tarantulas left behind causing rashes and painful itching. It struggled over desert debris, around cactus, between rocks. She thought it likely to end its journey before she did.

Her head hurt where the enemy's bullet had skimmed across her brow. When she put one hand up to her temple her fingers found blood still seeping slowly, wet. Her hand came away bloodied and she searched in the brush, seeking a treatment, remembered seeing one cactus she knew would bring some relief. She spied a small aloe vera, broke away one spine and squeezed it into her hand, then spread it across her wound. The juice mixed with her blood that still dripped down onto her face. Carefully she collected spider webs from the grass and patted them on her injury, a remedy that Grandmother used to close wounds. Her lips moved in a silent prayer of thanks to the spiders for their gift, and to *Ussen* for the bounty of her world.

Her Beads drank from her gourd, mentally retracing her route. She stood, brushed her skirt, and shifted her blanket up over one shoulder. One hand patted her meat pouch, felt the bulk of the remaining dried rabbit. Enough food to travel for one more day if she found other trail food. She carefully selected a game trail that kept her away from passes and hill crests and moved over the slope until she reached a high point that looked north up the mountain chain.

Curving between the hills and along the bottom of the range, a wide black path bent along the valley. Two sparse lines of metal wagons streamed in opposite lines past one another. Like ants building a nest, she thought. She could feel as much as hear the peculiar throb of the metal wagons breathing, almost a bubbling like water churning over rocks. Some of the metal wagons had stopped beside the road and men moved around them. Their voices, tinny with the distance, spooled up to her. She saw her route must be changed once again, in order to remain invisible. She would have to wait for darkness, she decided.

She lay on her stomach, studied the mountains marching north, and suddenly gasped with delight. There, in the haze of distance, emerged the outline she had never before seen, but knew by heart. She found a stone, drew the memorized design in the dirt; two humps together on top of a mountain. Two Tails. Her eyes widened with wonder and one hand went to her heart. Grandmother, she thought, you have taught us well. I've found the homeland.

CHAPTER 47

In the Land of Standing Up Rocks

Chiricahua National Monument Wonderland of Rocks, *Cochise* County, Arizona

SAM LOOKED UP AS a ranger's truck pulled in next to the campsite. The motor rumbled in the morning quiet of the campground, where even the birds still slept. It would be several hours before the sun streamed down to light up the narrow canyon along the clear stream.

Lorraine worked at their camp stove using a cast iron pan. Hair tousled from sleep, the twins stood nearby drawn to the crisp smell of fry bread intermingled with the bitter aroma of fresh coffee.

At the picnic table opposite the twins, Sam sat and watched the uniformed man emerge from the truck. The ranger touched the brim of his hat in an informal greeting, smiling. "Good morning. Looks like you folks have the right idea."

The children looked to their grandfather for a response, but it was their mother who responded. "You're just in time for coffee."

"Smells good, but I'm on the clock." The ranger laid a form on the table. "Just need to ask you to fill out a camp permit. You can stop at the Ranger Station later and we'll finish up your registration. We have a nice little museum, too. Some neat things for the kids to see."

The girls scanned their mother's face eagerly.

The ranger's eyes picked up the SUV's New Mexico plates. "First time here? Happy to answer any questions about what to see and do."

Sam snorted.

At that the ranger tipped the brim of his hat, smiled awkwardly, and turned to go. "Enjoy your morning. See you later at the Station." The truck's tires crunched on gravel as it continued around the campground loop.

"First time!" Lorraine sniffed. "Like it never belonged to anyone else before."

Sam patted his daughter's shoulder. "No reason he should know."

Lorraine would not be comforted. "Girls, this was where our people lived." She looked off to the east where the standing rocks stood in jumbled piles. "Our people hunted here." There was a note of triumph in her voice, and also anger. "Father, when did you first see this place?"

"My father brought me and my sisters and brothers waaay back, all six of us. I was the oldest and I was about twelve." His gaze swept down the canyon to the valley floor, then west across to the Dragoon Mountains and *Cochise* Stronghold. The fall season had turned the valley plains into a platinum sea of grasses, lapping against gray and dusky purple mountains. The view tugged at his heart, and he took a deep breath. "My father prepared us to run. We knew what we must do. There was no park. No rangers." He turned and lifted one arm that took in all of the rocky lands above them. "Jus . . . this. He planned our visit for a moonlit night and told us he didn't want anyone to know we came here. *Ndee* people had been told to stay away from their old lands." He looked at the twins. "But this was the land our people knew."

Lorraine sputtered. "Tell them, Father. Tell them how our land was taken."

"They fought us and they won."

Susie looked from her grandfather to her mother.

Lorraine rolled her lips in and out, and spat, "They fought us, yes, and then they stole it."

Sam let the words roll across the table, remained silent. He raised his shoulders. "This is the way of men, Daughter. *Indah*, the Living, had more people and they needed more land. They had more horses, more guns. They had the Buffalo soldiers."

"So that makes it alright to just take it?" Lorraine's eyes flashed.

Sam Charley looked down to the lands at the base of the canyon, and across the valley to the Dragoon Mountains. "Daughter, who gave us this land?"

"*Ussen*," Lorraine answered.

"Yes, but who owned it before us?"

Lorraine's eyes dropped to the ground. "It was different." The anger leached from her voice. "Father, I know what you're doing. But it doesn't mean it makes me any happier about *Chiricahua* history, and how *Indah,* the Living, the Pale Eyes, drove our people out of these mountains, and how they treated us." She placed her attention on the pan, covered it. Anger settled in a shroud around her shoulders.

Sam finished his cup of coffee and unfolded himself from the picnic table. He walked around to the stove, gently took the spatula from Lorraine and indicated with his lips that she should sit down. He filled her cup, then his own, and nodded at his granddaughters to sit.

"Our people fought to keep what they knew was good. The *Indah,* too, saw the land was good and fought for it. But never forget there were others before us who also fought hard to keep what they knew was good, people who lived in villages along the rivers where we raided. And they lost those places to us." Sam stirred the sizzling contents of the fry pan. "This is history."

He looked at the girls. "Ready to eat?" They both looked up eagerly.

Sam began to dish food from the pan. "I thought you wanted to know about when I first saw the homeland."

The twins, mouths full of fry bread, each raised an arm skyward.

"Oh ho." He filled Lorraine's plate, then both of the girls' and one for himself, sat down and forked a mouthful of sausage and eggs into his mouth, smiled at the mingled flavors. "My father sent us to run, and the youngest was no older than you."

The girls grinned at one another, always ready to hear a story from their grandfather.

"It was the way of our people to challenge the children, so that they could learn to endure. My father gave us each a gulp of water with the warning to hold it without swallowing." He raised his eyes to the twins. "Just like what we practiced at home the other morning." The girls nodded and continued to eat. "He sent us running from the mouth of the canyon, along the curls of the hills to where he drove and waited." Sam's left arm gestured north. "Probably five miles." He took another bite of his breakfast, chewed, and swallowed. "Once there we had to spit out the mouthful of water to the ground to show we could run that far without giving in to drinking it, because …" He paused to confirm he had his audience's attention. "… only those *Ndee* survived who proved their minds controlled their bodies. Those were the ones ready to learn the way of the Real People."

Elsie turned a look of concern on her sister. "What happened if you swallowed the water?"

"Yes," Susie asked, forehead wrinkled in concern, "did you get spanked?"

The old man looked off above the tree tops. "Much, much worse."

Both girls stopped eating, faces solemn, eyebrows raised.

"If a child failed to endure, the child was not ready to grow up."

Elsie frowned and Susie's eyes grew large with alarm.

"They were babies." Grandfather paused. "What use would such a child be to the Real People?"

"What did they do to the kids?" Susie insisted.

"Those who did not endure brought shame to themselves, their families, and their clan."

A tremor warbled in Elsie's voice. "Did they give kids a second chance?"

Susie's forehead wrinkled into a paragraph of squiggly lines. "They had to."

The twins watched their grandfather's face whose expression stayed flat.

"They had to," Susie repeated, "because kids have to be taught to take care of themselves."

"*Enjuh.* Children are the future." Sam saw both children relax, studied the downhill view of the canyon onto the plains below. "Perhaps we can do some training here."

The girls' faces brightened.

Lorraine intervened. "Finish your breakfast. Then we'll go to the ranger's museum and your grandfather can show us places he remembers." She turned toward Sam. "And did you run the whole way, Father, without swallowing your mouthful of water?"

He smiled sideways. "Of course, we all tried hard to learn the ways of the ancestors. I can tell you it is a difficult thing to run, to be thirsty, and to not swallow water in your mouth." He stopped, arched an eyebrow. "Sometimes it took more than one run."

Lorraine bit one side of her lips to fight away a smile that threatened to emerge, swallowed her last question, then turned to pour herself another cup of coffee.

CHAPTER 48

Livin' Large

Albuquerque Conference Center,
Albuquerque, New Mexico

ALBERT STOOD NEXT TO Curly *Dichoshé*, president of the *Mescalero* Apache tribe, and sipped his coffee as he waited for Curly to end a telephone conversation. The Albuquerque Conference Center boasted a sheer wall of clear glass that seemed to bring Sandia Peak right into the room. Albert moved away to find a comfortable cushioned sofa where he could relax before the strain of a full day working the *Mescalero* Apache booth in the Exhibitor's Hall.

"Uh huh, uh huh."

Albert thought Curly sounded pretty agreeable. He savored each sip of the gourmet roast, enjoying the mountain view. Curly ended his call, slipped his cell phone into a pocket, refilled his cup from a shiny urn, and chose a chair next to Albert.

"Livin' large, my friend. Livin' large." Curly settled himself into the deep cushion, swallowed his double caramel latte and sighed, deeply content. "This whole exhibit is working out well. Suddenly Apache people matter to the world." He laughed softly. "Connections with museums and art dealers in New York City. Requests for sponsorships on behalf of the tribe." He laughed again. "Pretty perfect." The tribal president's cell phone buzzed in his pocket. "Never know," he addressed Albert, before answering. "This one might be the best one yet!"

Albert listened absent mindedly as Curly responded in an official mode. "This is Curly *Dichoshé.*" He took a gulp as he listened. "Uh huh. I see."

Albert could hear a woman's voice speaking fast and loud, excited. He finished his coffee and stood up to get a refill.

"I believe we can help you."

Albert smiled to himself and thought Curly was the right guy to be the tribal president. He really had a smooth way of talking. He heard the "we" and chuckled softly to himself. Some poor guy's gonna get saddled with something, he thought.

Curly's conversation continued as Albert surveyed the coffee choices. Hazelnut, he thought, and refilled his cup.

"In fact, I'm going to refer you to a council member," Albert heard. He reached for a dainty sweet roll, the kind with white frosting painted in swirls.

"He can speak for me, as well," Albert heard Curly finish.

Albert almost swallowed the sweet roll whole, loving the frosting texture on fresh bread. He sighed with pleasure, drank to the bottom of his coffee, thinking: Maybe just one more.

When he lowered his cup, he found Curly's cell phone thrust in front of his face.

"Lady needs a translation," Curly said helpfully.

Albert frowned at Curly, took the phone.

"Please get back to me when you've finished talking with the lady?" Curly returned to the coffee urns, filled his cup, and left the room.

Albert tried not to sound irritated. "This is Albert Silentman."

A long pause followed. "Silentman?" The woman's voice tone sounded curious and a bit unbelieving.

"Yes, ma'am."

Albert never got used to the non-Apache world and the way his last name stopped them. In the Marines he'd proved himself by challenging wiseass jarheads to repeat curses in Apache: *"Dooli bi'chąą"* (manure of the bull), complete with glottal stop and nasal tones that closed the nasal passages. The jokes withered, as non-Apache tongues spluttered and failed over attempts at making previously unheard sounds. Plus, such curses were an Apache joke within the words, since Apaches did not curse and had no curse words per se. But Marines loved colorful new ways of expressing profanities. He'd won a few bets that way, had to beat up one or two guys before he cleared the air. And all the time, he remembered fondly, the joke was on them. Now he waited for the woman's voice on the phone to adjust to his name.

"Oh. I called your tribe, and they told me to call the president."

"Yes, Ma'am. President *Dichoshé* just asked me to help you."

"Yes. Uh, Mr. Silentman, my name is Lydia Castillo." Her voice became professionally cheerful as she introduced herself. "I'm with social services in San Enebro, New Mexico. May I ask what you do?"

"Sure. I'm director of the All Apache Clans Museum on the *Mescalero* Apache Reservation, and I also serve as a member of the *Mescalero* Tribal Council."

"I see." A riffling of papers sounded. "I work at the Mercy Regional Hospital in San Enebro, New Mexico. I'm trying to find someone who speaks Apache."

"Ndee k'ehgo hasdziih." A long silence followed, and Albert translated his own words. "I
speak Apache."

"Oh." The social worker's voice startled. "Was that it? Apache?"

"Ha'ah. Yes, ma'am. That is Apache." Albert understood Curly's sliding away. The president had better things to do than translate their people's tongue. Albert's sense of humor rose and he decided to build his expertise. "I even have a degree!"

"I didn't know there were degrees in Apache." His timing impeccable, he had to hold his nose to keep from laughing. "Yep. I got me a Ph.D. in Life … and in talking Apache. I learned it at my mother's knee." He cleared his throat when no response came. "The English I got from Uncle Sam."

The woman's voice, unsure again, needed reassurance. "You are an Apache, yes?"

"Yes, ma'am, I am."

The voice came back in a rush. "I'm so relieved! I've been trying to find somebody to help us."

Albert Silentman had lived his fifty years both on and off the reservation. He recognized all the signals of an unknowing world about who or what an Apache might be or do. "Yes, ma'am. What kind of help do you need?"

The woman took a deep breath. "We have a small child, maybe three to four years old, who was found alone and injured. So far we have no idea who she is." The voice paused.

"And you called for Apache help because …?"

The woman's voice curled into a smile, and in a confidential tone said, "Oh, she has the cutest dimples, just darling. But wearing the strangest, ragged clothing and shoes with little, round discs on the toes."

She stopped, gathered herself, and Albert used the moment to ask a question. "By any chance are the discs about the same size as a silver dollar?"

He heard the woman's intake of breath. "Well, yes, so you do know what they look like?" She didn't wait for his answer, but continued. "I got your president's name off the internet. And when I called, they told me to call this number and . . ."

Albert, thinking about his gourmet roast coffee chilling beside him, hurried her along. "And you reached us. How can we help?" He almost giggled. Apache as a resource for assistance did not automatically equate with most non-Apache seeking help.

Long pause. "One of our employees recognized words she

thought she heard growing up in Mexico. We wrote it down, but nobody knows what it means."

"And you think it's Apache? Tell me the words." He shifted one cowboy-booted foot so that a worn heel rested on the thick carpet. He leaned back into the curve of the sofa.

"The first word is 'giddy'." She paused, but there was no response. "And the other words . . ." a rustling of paper interrupted. "I took notes. They sound something like 'no week dandy nock eye.'"

Albert Silentman clamped his jaw down hard. "Umm."

"Does the first word mean 'cat'? She's been given a kitten and pets it and talks to it."

"Yup, *'gidi'* means cat. You sure you need a translation?" Albert laughed. "Tell me the second part again, real slow." He pushed the button that brought up the speaker phone to hear more clearly.

"No week dandy nock eye." She cleared her throat. "She doesn't say it quite like that." The social worker's voice was strained but he heard her plainly.

"Now, that second phrase. Does it sound more like this?" Albert's voice slid, then clicked over a glottal stop, flowed into a downward nasal tone that rose up and sliced off an accented end. *"Nohwik'edandiihi Nakaiyé."*

Relief poured from the woman's voice. "Yes, I think that's it exactly."

"Are the people over there Mexican?"

"Some of us are, yes."

"That's what it means in Apache. 'Our enemies that walk around.' That's one term that's used to describe Mexicans." Albert waited for a comment. "Hello? You still there?"

"Why are Mexicans enemies?" the woman asked, her voice timid.

Albert breathed out and looked up with long suffering eyes as Curly returned for a coffee refill. Hopeless. No one in the outside world knew anything real about Apache people. Albert clicked off the speaker button, lowered the cell, spoke quietly to Curly in Apache: "You want to explain this?"

Curly shook his head no. "Bring me the phone when you're done," and left the room again, trying not to spill a too-full cup.

Albert raised the phone back to his ear. "The simple answer is it's a lot of history. Apache and Mexicans fought over land; you know, who had the best right to be there. Our people struggled for hundreds of years." He paused, decided any more would get too complicated and brutal. "Apache lost."

Lydia's voice was unsure. "I didn't realize. I mean I've seen things in the movies, on television, but ..."

Albert cleared his throat. "Hollywood's take hasn't always been very accurate."

Lydia sounded apologetic. "I guess I didn't think beyond that. How could a small child who speaks Apache show up on the border of Mexico? Is there a reservation near?"

"Not now. There used to be. Southern Arizona was the homeland of the *Chiricahua* Apache, over in the Dragoon and *Chiricahua* Mountains. *Cochise* County's named after their leader, *Cochise.*"

"But now?"

"No. Closest place to find *Chiricahua* people now is with the *Mescalero* Apache tribe in New Mexico."

"I suppose I should know that. Of course, San Enebro is in New Mexico right on the border of Arizona. I cut across *Cochise* County all the time to get to Tucson. I know where the *Chiricahua* Mountains are. Only we call them the Cheery Cows."

Albert winced. He took a deep breath. "Apache don't visit the old homeland much now. Pretty much they don't go to *Cochise* County at all or near the mountains there between southern New Mexico and Arizona."

"Oh, the Peloncillo Mountains," she said, "but why?" Her voice carried interest.

"In Apache we call those the Black Mountains. Apache haven't been welcome over there for a long time." Albert took a deep breath. His people's circumstances often made him sad. "And they're not sure yet that if they do visit, even now, they'll survive the experience."

"What?" Lydia Castillo sounded shocked.

Albert shook his head, in a "here we go again" gesture. "The war between the Apache and everybody else, the Mexicans, the Americans, other Native Americans, everybody else, was bloody. They were all fighting over the same territories. It was a war. You with me?"

"Yes."

"The U.S. Cavalry, with the Buffalo soldiers, tracked Geronimo and his group into Mexico in 1886 because those last Apache wouldn't give up. They kept raiding into the United States, *Cochise* County mostly, although Hidalgo County in New Mexico suffered, too."

"Umm, excuse me but what are Buffalo soldiers? I didn't know we had buffalo around here." Lydia Castillo's voice contained a note of confusion.

Albert cleared his throat as he tried to ignore a stab of pain behind his eyes. Don't these people know anything? he thought, but patiently answered her question. "Yes, actually buffalo used to be there, but not so much by the time the Europeans arrived. Buffalo soldiers were African-American troops. Native people named them that because they thought their hair looked curly and black like buffalo. Black troops worked after the Civil War all over the West, including at Ft. Huachuca and Ft. Bowie in Arizona. They're the ones who finally got Geronimo to surrender and brought him and his people back to old Ft. Bowie. You know where that is?"

"Ohhh," Lydia Castillo pondered. "Not really."

"It's in the *Chiricahua* Mountains at the north end of the range, not too far from the little dried-up town of Bowie on the

I-10." Albert waited a few beats, hoping that would be enough, thinking to himself he bet her ancestors in the San Enebro area knew where Ft. Bowie was, the closest help if Apache attacked in the old days.

"What happened?"

"Lot of killing on all sides. Lot of bad blood. When the cavalry brought in Geronimo's group the local ranchers threatened to come out as vigilantes and kill 'em all. The cavalry followed orders from the government and put the Apache prisoners on a train that took them to Florida."

"So far away?" asked Lydia, incredulous.

"Yes, ma'am. I believe that was the idea. Isolation. Get them far away."

"Did they give them a trial?"

Albert snorted just once. "Not the way things worked then. Didn't need a trial anyway. By then the Apache were prisoners of war. They kept them in Florida, later moved them to Alabama. Lot of 'em died from different diseases, 'specially the kids and the elders. Tuberculosis. Measles. You know, native people had no natural resistance to a lot of diseases that came with the Europeans. U.S. government finally returned anyone still alive to the West after close to thirty years. 1913, I think it was."

Lydia sighed deeply. "Then they came back here?"

"No ma'am. Turned out *Cochise* County ranchers had long memories, even after more than a quarter century. The ranchers organized themselves into vigilantes again, threatened to kill any Apache if they put a toe in the county. So they sent them to Oklahoma and eventually most of them ended up in New Mexico. Mostly our *Chiricahua* people live with the *Mescalero* people now, close to Ruidoso."

"It sounds like something in a television series." Her voice sounded disapproving.

"Yes ma'am. There's a reason it's called 'the Wild, Wild West'."

"For goodness sakes." Lydia seemed overwhelmed.

"No *Chiricahua* Apache officially returned to Arizona, and I do mean literally, as far as I know, until the centennial in 1986. That celebrated the end of one hundred years since the surrender of Geronimo and all Apache left *Cochise* County. 'Course we're talking about descendants of the original prisoners of war, by then. Their children were taught the threat and I can tell you, nobody at *Mescalero* thinks it's a good idea to go visit the old homeland on a whim. I've only been to *Cochise* County a few times, and felt pretty apprehensive about visiting." He thought of seeing Sam earlier in the week. "Although, having said that, I know of one Apache elder who happens to be in *Cochise* County right now, showing his family their ancestors' homeland."

"I had no idea."

"Yes ma'am. Sometimes history takes a while to clear itself up."

"No one here can figure out who this little girl is, where she belongs. We're just . . . clueless. Do you know, is anyone at *Mescalero* missing a small child?"

Albert chewed his lip. "I suppose you've been to the police, Border Patrol, whoever?"

"It was Border Patrol that found her. She was at a desert crossing in the middle of the night, all alone. It doesn't make sense. There's no town, just desert country there and the one road from Chihuahua. She's so little. If we can just get somebody who can talk to her, maybe ..." Lydia's voice trailed off.

"Yes, ma'am. Let me get in touch with a few people and see how we might be able to help, and I'll give you a call back." He stood up. "Do you know if the Border Patrol has contacted federal or tribal authorities?"

"No one can understand her. I don't think they've made contact with anyone. Our first goal was to try and find a way to talk with her."

"Yes, ma'am."

Albert ended the call promising to get back to her later in the day, then sat still for several minutes, thinking. Finally, he pushed himself up from the sofa, moved around a corner to relocate Curly. He handed the phone back. "Mr. President, we got us an interesting situation."

CHAPTER 49

The Smell of Meat

In the Land of Standing Up Rocks,
Chiricahua Homeland

WHEN *BIYOO'*, HER BEADS, sighted the Two Tails, she rested in a grassy hollow between boulders. She laid back and ran her eyes over the remaining length of the mountain range spread before her, thinking maybe just one or two more days of travel. She sat up suddenly, as an obvious detail revealed itself. If she followed the curve of the mountains at their base, her route would eliminate the difficult and tiring ridge climbing along the raiding trail. She moved to a different viewing point and watched the enemy *béshnagháí*, metal wagons, travel along the hard, black rivers that ran between the mountains, and enjoyed a moment of exultation. She saw how the metal wagons looped along the mountain edges and made their route shorter. I can do this on foot, she told herself and memorized the mountain folds. She devised several shortcuts between loops of hills, and considered how the hard, black river could be followed without exposing herself. When she returned to the grassy hollow, she fell asleep with a soft smile, pleased to have made her discovery.

Her Beads awakened as birds sang their evening calls, closing the day into dark. She listened carefully to the sounds of her people's lands and found nothing out of order. Crickets chirped. Birds nestled into quiet. A gentle evening breeze stirred the trees and carried the bawl of a far-away calf. She ate her final strip of rabbit jerky, a handful of pine nuts, and drank from her gourd. Strengthened by food and rest she exited the hollow cautiously and began to walk.

By the time Her Beads saw the sky lighten, she'd slipped past numerous enemy houses, avoided enemy dogs, and hid when metal wagons rolled along the black rivers with their night eyes that might see her. The light of the new day brought more dangers as she crossed open spaces, and headed east into her people's mountains, seeking a place to find food and rest.

Along the curve of the mountain range, she passed a large square twice her height with the talk marks of the enemy on it. She stayed out of sight as much as possible from the hard, black river, where metal wagons frequently passed. With no perspective of her exact location, she stopped in surprise when she reached a place she recognized from the teachings of Grandmother. Her heart pounded in excitement. Along the black river and beyond a large enemy house, tall rocks reached into the sky. Many of them. So many made it impossible not to identify the Land of Standing Up Rocks, one of the favored living places of the *Chokonen*, the Rising Sun band of the *Chiricahua* Apache.

She walked and hid and climbed from sunrise into midmorning, her stomach's rumble constant. She halted but once to drink from a small rivulet dripping down the cliffs. As the sun gleamed light into the shadows between rocks and canyons, she stopped to think good thoughts. Facing east she prayed for Grandmother and for the Blue Mountain People. The morning shadows in the narrow canyon dissolved and she marveled at *Ussen's* great gift in the rock spires that seemed to tumble upward, rising askew, in clumps, in columns, in unending multiples.

She finished her prayer at the same moment a scent tickled her nose. It swirled and pulled at her, causing a rush of saliva to fill her mouth. Face raised, she sniffed the air and cast for the aroma's direction. Meat, she thought, but waited to cross the black river between two metal wagons that rushed past. She scrambled down to a clear, rushing stream, refilled her gourd, and washed her face. When she stood the smell was stronger, closer. She saw the place clearly through Grandmother's description, easily recognized it as where *Chokonen* once built their shelters. She felt immediately comfortable. Home.

Her nose led her forward, but her feet moved with caution. She stopped in shadows behind pines bordering an open space. A small cloth shelter crouched there and a sleeping metal wagon rested with its eyes pointed in the opposite direction. A fire burned in a green box, the source of the meat smell. A gray-haired man wearing an enemy hat bent over the fire, and the sound of raindrops splashed. Surprised, Her Beads searched the sky. No clouds. No rain. She fast realized her mistake. The splash sound came not from above, but from the sputtering fat of cooking meat, the very smell that invited her interest.

She watched the family that sat at a stone table, heard their soft morning chatter. *Her Beads's* eyes flashed from her hiding place, shocked. She sucked in her breath, and held it.

A woman at the table drank from a cup. The man piled food on plates and passed them to the woman and two children. Her Beads automatically registered their ages, gender, clothing. But the front of her mind was jumping about, trying to grasp what she heard. It clawed at her consciousness like the talons of a hawk. The people who sat at the stone table before her, the meat sizzling on the fire, all looked toward the man. He passed the food one at a time to each person. "Fill your bellies," the man said. "There is more."

Her Beads listened and understood, her stomach clutching at her insides; her mind gnawing at what she heard.

The people spoke Apache.

CHAPTER 50

New Relatives

Chiricahua National Monument Wonderland of Rocks, *Cochise* County, Arizona

As the sun rose higher over the narrow canyon, drops of sunlight speckled the campground and the stream running through it. Sam sat comfortably at the picnic table sipping his fourth cup of coffee, his stomach full of sausage, eggs, and fry bread.

One of the children, her mouth full and already wriggling toward the end of the bench, asked, "Can we play some more?"

"Swallow first, then speak."

The girls stood up, chunks of fry bread still in hand, looked at their mother for permission.

"Don't go far," Lorraine said in Apache. "Your grandfather wants to show us some places."

Lorraine looked at her father as the girls trotted off toward the creek.

"You look tired, Father. Can you rest in the tent for a bit?"

"I dreamed, Daughter. This is a good place to hear our language." He looked approvingly around him at the home territory of the ancestors.

The children's voices echoed back and forth in a game across the campground. The morning breeze rendered a kind of music between the laughter of the children, the tumble of the brook, and the soft rustle of pine branches brushing against bark. Lorraine refilled her own cup and they sat companionably admiring their surroundings.

A pebble landed on the table with a clunk, skipped to the ground, startled them both as they sat. Sam swung one leg out and began to rise; stopped midway, staring with fascination, he slowly lowered himself back onto the picnic bench.

A teenage girl stood before them. No noise. Like she'd come out of the earth. Dressed in a rough leather skirt, a blanket around her shoulders, leg wrappings covered her calves, and each toe displayed a leather disc attached to the tip of her moccasins. Strands of black and white beads looped under her chin and she held a white cloth in her hand. Pouches hung at her belt along with a gourd to carry water. Everything old style. She seemed to step out of time; a ghost from the past.

The stranger's eyes flicked around the table. "*Hadínyaa?*" (Where are you going?) It was the old greeting of the *Chiricahua* to other Apache they did not know. She kept her eyes low as she spoke. "*Shíí Dzilthdaklizhéndé*" (I am Blue Mountain People).

Sam recovered first, spoke softly. "I have dreamed of you, Granddaughter."

The girl looked at him with flat eyes, then swept her gaze down in the respect given to an elder.

"In the dream you told me, 'Come.' " Sam made the approach sign, then swept a trembling hand at his daughter. "And we came."

The girl looked up and Sam saw her gaze rested on their empty plates.

"Will you eat, Granddaughter?"

Her answer came subdued but instant. "*Ha'ah.*"

Lorraine held out the pot with the fry bread, still puffed and warm, and the stranger took one.

Sam poured coffee, added a sugar cube and milk automatically, set it on the table, then sat and patted the bench next to him. "Rest here, Granddaughter. Eat. Drink. Then we will speak."

Their guest moved forward tentatively, watching, registering every detail. Lorraine handed her a plate of scrambled eggs and sausage. She ignored the invitation to sit and stood, eating quickly, almost in one big swallow. She sipped carefully at the cup first with suspicion, then gulped her coffee with a sigh of pleasure.

"*Łikąą golįh*" (It is sweet), she complimented Lorraine.

Lorraine refilled the cup. The girl took a sip and wrinkled her nose, looked at the table. She gestured with her chin toward the package of sugar cubes, said, "*Eí*" (That).

Lorraine pushed the sugar to the table's edge and the girl selected two cubes, dropped them into her cup. She tasted it, wrinkled her nose again and looked shyly at the father and daughter.

"She likes it sweet, I guess," Sam said and smiled back at her.

The girl raised her chin a second time indicating the milk, said "*Łá*" (There). Father and daughter grinned together, nodded encouragement, and slid the milk across the table.

Sam tipped the sugar box toward her and repeated her words. "*Eí*" (That). "*Łá*" (There). Smiled again.

"You think she's ever had a Starbucks? I'd call that pretty much a latte," Lorraine commented. She watched their visitor pour a large dollop into her cup and offered her more fry bread.

The teenager picked up one more of the puffy fried bread pieces and devoured it. Her eyes continued to sweep the area, her reaction to sounds immediate, intense, even as she chewed and swallowed.

"The sound of our language is good to my ears," the visitor said to them. Looking toward Sam, she saw he wore the necklace of a warrior.

Sam noticed her eyes stopped on his necklace and he grasped it, and said in Apache, "I heard your words in our language. In my dream you said 'come' and we came." He looked around the wooded campground. "Here, our ancestors lived. It is a good place to find you."

"*Ha'ah,*" the girl said, although her face remained blank. She gingerly seated herself on the edge of the bench, both hide-wrapped legs sticking out away from the table. Her eyes continued watching all around; her body poised ready to leap away. She gulped the last mouthful of fry bread and licked her lips, drank the last swallow of coffee.

"I am Juniper Clan, born for Arrow Reed."

Lorraine and Sam looked at one another and blinked, recognizing the formula greeting between Apache who meet for the first time.

Sam cleared his throat. "My child, we are relatives. I, too, am Juniper Clan born for Arrow Reed."

The girl's eyes snapped. "Can it be so, Grandfather?" Her expression showed both relief and doubt.

"I am Red Streak Clan, born for Juniper," Lorraine interjected. "I am born for Juniper because he is Juniper." She raised her chin toward Sam.

Sam nodded. "We are all relatives. How is it we do not know you? Granddaughter. Who are your people?"

"*Nlááyú,*" she answered, lengthening the sound of the double vowels to indicate her people existed far away. She turned south and puckered her lips, pointing them south in the direction of Mexico. "We live in the Blue Mountains high above the broken-voiced people."

Sam shifted his legs so that one foot slid forward. The girl saw the movement and imitated it, ready for flight. "How did you come to be here?" he asked again softly.

"I smelled the cooking meat."

Sam laughed, noting she used their people's way to answer the question truthfully with the least amount of information.

"Yes, Granddaughter, but do you travel alone?"

"*Ha'ah*. Grandmother sent me ahead to find the way to the homeland for all the children."

"Children? There are more of you?"   "*Ha'ah*. The children are with Grandmother." She explained it as if the world might think many groups of Apache children roamed the Blue Mountains. "I am the eldest."

Sam thought, his dream memory still fresh, trying to recall what the people in his dream looked like. Had they all been children, he silently asked himself? He raised his eyes to the newcomer's face, watched as she licked fry bread crumbs from her lips. "Why are there no adults to send for help? How did you come to this place?"

The stranger examined father and daughter, then dropped her gaze to the forest floor. "I walked. I followed my mind map."

Sam and Lorraine stared at her in fascination.

The guest added, "I rode a mule until it ran off."

Sam smiled. "The one with long ears," he said in Apache, "goes its own way."

"I was hurt. The mule ran away, afraid."

"Hurt, Granddaughter?"

The girl, hearing concern in his voice, leaned forward and parted her hair with her fingers. "Here, Grandfather."

Sam and Lorraine saw where blood had dried on top of the girl's scalp and left a long, angry gouge across the top of her head.

Lorraine clucked her tongue in sympathy. "When did this happen?"

"*Adąqdá'*" (Yesterday).

"Well, the mule is no loss if it injured you."

"The mule was good to ride. It was an enemy warrior that hurt me. He took me on his horse. I fought and escaped." The girl hesitated, not sure if more information would be useful. "Another *Indah* warrior with metal legs helped me." Confused with the necessity of explaining how a man with metal legs could help, she tilted her neck to the side, stopped herself. "Not all *Indah* are the same."

Sam nodded sagely. "Of course."

He added in English to Lorraine. "Why would anyone take her on a horse?"

Lorraine asked, "Who would have metal legs?"

Sam saw the girl followed their words without comprehension, registering concern at the tone, and he returned to the Apache language. "You said you are Blue Mountain People. Are you then *Ndee Nnaahi*?" (Nameless Ones?)

The girl's face brightened. "You know our other name?"

"Yes, Granddaughter." He shook his head in amazement. "We feared you were all gone."

"Grandmother tells us now is the time to find our relatives." She studied their faces. "We are the last ones, we children, as Grandmother grows old."

"Only children?" Lorraine repeated. "It doesn't seem possible. Where are your mothers and fathers?"

The girl thought a moment. "Gone. All dead. I hardly remember them at all. Grandmother kept us alive and taught us well. But she grows old and says we must find our relatives. We are the last of the Blue Mountain People."

Lorraine stood up. "You have an injury. We have medicine."

She stepped to the SUV and located the first aid box, red with a white cross, from under the driver's seat. She returned with the kit and heard her father's next question.

"There are no others, then? Your mother and father?"

"*Dah*. I never knew them. All were killed in the Blue Mountains by the *Nakaiyé nowik'edandiihi*, our enemies that walk around."

Lorraine breathed softly in English, turned to her father, stunned. "The Mexican newspaper story is real."

Sam felt his heartbeat increase. "I dreamed it."

The girl's head drooped. Her encounter with Metal Legs and

The Other, the struggle and escape from the enemy on the horse, the long night of walking, caught up with her. She raised her eyes and watched as Lorraine opened the red metal box with the beautiful white design, removed something, and handed it to the old man. As long and thick as a finger, the thing fit in the palm of his hand.

The girl slid off the seat, backed away. "What is it?"

Sam removed the cap on the tube of antibacterial ointment, realized the girl did not understand his intention.

"*Izee*" (medicine), Sam said. He squeezed a tiny bead onto a cotton swab and dabbed it onto the back of his own hand. "It will help your injury heal."

The girl placed one hand over her head, blocking anything from touching her wound.

"I have placed medicine on the wound. Spider web and herbs."

Sam pinched his lip thinking. "Of course, she knows good cures if she comes from the mountains."

"Yes," Lorraine answered, "but best to see a doctor. Looks like a real gash."

Sam nodded. "Not bleeding now, though." He turned back to the girl. "What does your grandmother ask that you do?"

"I am to find our people and ask to bring the others to the homeland."

Sam sat silent, pondering a moment. "It's incredible, truly," he said in English, then remembered to speak in Apache. "You have done as your grandmother asked. We are your people," and he smiled at the girl, "or at least some of them."

The girl flashed a tentative smile and stood up. "Then I will return and bring the others."

Sam and Lorraine said together, shocked, "*Dah!*" (No!). They looked at the girl, and at one another, saw their answer returned her to full alert. "This is a different world," Sam said. "Our people will come to help."

Sam said to Lorraine. "Where's the cell phone? Gotta call Albert."

Lorraine carried the first aid kit to the car, returned with her cell phone, and handed it to her father.

The visitor's eyes locked onto the small black metal thing. Sam held it out on his palm. "We can speak to other people far away with this metal four-sided object."

She said nothing, tipped her head to one side and regarded the item in his hand.

Sam moved into the center of the clearing free of trees and tapped the cell phone on. "No signal," he said in English to Lorraine.

The girl's forehead wrinkled trying to understand.

Lorraine turned slowly and surveyed the area. "Perhaps that higher ground will work."

She pointed with her lips toward the east end of the camp-ground, where a jumble of large rocks matched the height of the canyon wall on the other side of the road.

"It's alright," Sam heard Lorraine reassure their visitor. "He goes to find help from our people."

The Blue Mountain girl kept Sam in sight as he moved higher up a collection of boulders against a rocky cliff, stopped, and raised the black metal four-sided hard thing to the side of his head. She already liked the old man and the woman. She'd never expected to know a grandfather. For the first time since leaving the Blue Mountains and Grandmother, *Her Beads* felt protected.

CHAPTER 51

Night Ride

Raiding Trail. *Chiricahua* Mountains, *Cochise* County, Arizona

TRAPPED. LUCY HAD NOT realized her mistake until too late. In the darkness of the night before, the old raiding trail split. All night long she believed she rode within an hour or two of Loreto's, then within a half hour, then within minutes of reaching the neighbors' ranch. But she and the horse had traveled at an off angle on an old spur of the trail. She had urged her mount forward too rapidly, intent on reaching help and missed the cut-off.

Sometime in the darkest part of the night she understood the path had become far too narrow, too high on the cliffs to be the trail she knew. Impossible, even, to turn the horse. The knowledge of her mistake suddenly made her choke in fear. Every "what if" question invaded her mind. What if they met up with a mountain lion or a bear who wanted passage? What if the horse stumbled? What if the trail ran out blindly into a rock wall? What if she dozed off (she could barely stay awake now) and fell off the horse? How far down to the bottom of the cliff from the winding, slender track?

The soft plop of her horse's shod hooves, an occasional small metallic thud when a hoof hit stone, had been reassuring. But when something swooped above in a rush of wings it kept her nervously alert. No other choice now, but forward. Until she heard a new sound.

The distinctive tones of water trickling over rocks made her lean into the blackness peering ahead. Her horse stopped and jingled its bit, dipping its head. Lucy put an arm out to the west, trying to gauge the space possible for her to dismount. Her fingertips brushed against wet rock, at the same time the horse moved two steps forward, stretching its neck toward the tinkling music of water. The stars shed a hazy light that revealed water dribbling down the cliff face. A split rent in the cliff had a hollow worn into the rock wall by the constant action of water, forming a shallow catchment away from the edge of the path. She let the horse lower its nose and drink. She took a deep breath, swung her right leg over, turning her torso against the saddle, and slid down, directly into the natural pool; cupped a hand of water to her own mouth. Pulling gently on the horse's reins she pulled the animal forward so that he stepped all four hooves into the water. From there it was only a matter of tugging him sideways. She turned the horse and allowed a further long drink before remounting. She didn't trust herself to judge the path but left it to the horse, who moved to retrace its way back to the cutoff.

In the false dawn an hour later, she had a developing view of the downhill slope. Her horse had slowed its pace each time it encountered any bend in the path, where it could not see what lay beyond. Once, it smelled something that made it stop, snort nervously. Lucy held it stationary, softly murmuring, hoping nothing was ahead they didn't want to encounter. But when she saw in the gathering light the slimness of the path, and the dropping slant of the descent, she brought the animal to a halt, filled with the terror of seeing the canyon bottom several hundred rocky feet below.

Dead tired, Lucy felt like giving up, but thoughts of her Uncle Vicente pointing a gun at Nick flared into her exhaustion. She nudged her mount onward, watching for the branch off the trail, keeping the horse's pace slow, trying not to slip her weight forward in the saddle. Each step must be placed just so. Her shoulders were stiff and her neck cracked when she moved it. "Whoa, whoa," she murmured to her mount, whose withers quivered at the snapping sound.

She might have missed the cutoff if the horse didn't stop, as she'd begun to doze in the saddle. When she came to, her chin wobbled on her chest, her torso slumped almost down to the saddle horn. She saw a thin thread of a path climbed up from where the horse halted. She saw it widened as it ascended toward the rim.

She patted the horse's neck, then directed it to move to the side and upward this time with full appreciation of where she found herself. "Hup."

The midmorning sun stood over the Peloncillo Mountains to the east, and cast a promise for the day. Lucy could hardly wait to find her way to the Loreto ranch. She cleared the top of the ridge and dug in her pocket for her cell phone, dropped the reins on the pommel of the saddle and stretched her legs and arms out, groaned in relief. "That feels good." Her horse bent its head and shook it, reached down and cropped at a few strands of grass.

She tapped a finger on the face of the phone, willing it to flash her home screen photo, a picture taken last year with her dad. But no photo came up. Instead, she got a "No Service" message. Disgusted, she turned it off, searched for the opening of her pocket to tuck it away.

Stopped on the rim she caught an unexpected noise. Voices. Her horse shook its head, snuffing the air for danger, alert with both pinnae raised. She curled her body forward, fear charging in her veins, tried to draw her horse's head up. The horse, sensing her alarm, spooked and jerked away, its reins falling forward and out of her reach. The animal burst into a panicked trot, turned completely around as Lucy wildly tried to gather the reins, and brushed her against a Ponderosa pine. She dropped her phone, just before the horse careened a second time against the tree trunk and knocked her out of the saddle.

She hit the earth hard as the horse disappeared into the forest, racing across the top of the mountain. By the time she stood up, checking herself for damage, dust was settling into the pine needles. Relieved to find no broken bones she stepped away from the tree, felt something hard under her boot, and heard the brittle crunch of glass.

"Nooo." Her reaction, unthinking, left the word hanging in the air. She bent to pick up the shattered casing of her phone, then froze. The sound of a drawn-out howl of terror ripped across the canyon. Lucy stopped in her half-risen posture and twisted toward the cutoff trail. Every nerve tingled as she told her feet to move, but something made her stick fast.

There, standing at the top of the path where it led down to the main trail along the mountain, just as the horrible scream bounded back and forth across the canyon, stood Chapo, staring at her. Dumbfounded.

CHAPTER 52

Dress for Success

Chiricahua National Monument Wonderland of Rocks, *Cochise* County, Arizona

SAM DIALED AND HEARD his call begin to ring. He could hardly wait for Albert to answer his phone. From on top of the jumble of rocks he saw Lorraine and their new relative approaching from across the campground, and motioned at them to hurry. When Albert answered, Sam's voice thrilled. "Oh, my friend, I've found a Nameless One!"

"Leatherneck," Albert said, "I think I got one, too! An injured child was found at the border who only speaks Apache!" Their declarations trampled on one another. "Curly says he needs your help."

"Man, I'm calling you and Curly for help, because we got an old-time teenager here on a mission to find her relatives."

"Really!"

"Way old-time clothes, moccasins, everything. She's been walking a while. Wait a minute!" He held the cell phone away and waved at his daughter and the teen to join him on top of the rocks, gestured for them to hurry.

"Is she there? Will she speak?"

Sam pushed the speaker button.

Albert's voice bounced loud against the hard-surfaced boulders. "*Dagot'é!*" (Hello!)

The teen startled, surprised, but held her ground and listened intensely without a muscle moving in her face. Not quite understanding from where the voice sprang, she put her hand out to the cell phone on the rock. She brushed her fingertips across it, breathed out a sigh of relief when nothing happened. "Is the voice a ghost?" the girl asked.

"*Dah*." Sam shook his head. He tried to think how to translate the concept. "There is a wind that carries words long distances straight between one person to another."

The girl kept her eyes on the phone and jumped a second time when Albert's voice, speaking in Apache, asked, "Can you hear me?"

She shook her head in confusion and Sam understood that speaking by cell phone presented a giant leap of faith.

"Devil Dog, ask the questions. She will listen and I will help."

Albert said in Apache, "Where is she from and did she travel with others? The child they found seems to be *Chiricahua*. She's in the hospital in San Enebro."

Sam saw the girl was overwhelmed, but interested. She listened as Albert described the social worker's request for assistance in Apache. "Do you think you might know the child?" Albert asked.

She tipped her head to one side, studied the cell phone before looking at Sam to speak. "*Doo bígonsjh da* (I don't know). Grandmother told the children to wait in the Blue Mountains for my return."

Sam said, "The child who speaks Apache is small. We wish to help her."

The girl thought. "How many days travel to see her?"

Sam smiled, "We will travel swiftly in the *béshnagháí*, and return here tonight." He saw something shift in the girl's expression, recognized the idea of riding in a metal wagon captured her interest.

"*Ha'ah*," she agreed, "I will go with you."

"Okay," Lorraine stepped forward, "but we can't take her to a hospital dressed like this."

Sam looked at the Apache girl. Her worn, ragged-edged leather skirt, her knee-high leg wrappings and moccasins with disks on each toe, her knot of hair folded into a fat dumbbell shape—the *nah-leen* (maiden shape), and her black and white bead necklace. Her entire presentation bore no resemblance to a modern teen's clothing tastes.

"Alright," he addressed his daughter. "What have you got in mind?" and began to explain to their visitor that she needed to wear clothes like themselves, in order to help them. He saw her eyes flash with the novelty of the idea.

"No problem," Lorraine said in English. "We'll have her looking like a regular member of our crew in no time." She motioned the girl to follow and they returned to the camp.

Lorraine rummaged through her own camping clothes and found her spare pair of jeans, a red T-shirt, tennis shoes, socks, panties, a brassiere, and a hooded sweatshirt for their visitor. The teen stared at the clothing as Lorraine presented each item.

"For you," Lorraine said in Apache. "Go ahead and put them on."

The girl just looked at the items neatly placed in her hands, her face blank.

Lorraine, head tilted, tried to figure out the girl's hesitation.

"What is it?" Lorraine asked in Apache, but got no response.

At that moment, the twins returned from their play and burst into the tent. "Grandpa says we need to go," Elsie said.

Susie, right behind, ran into her sister's back and knocked her down, at the same time asking, "Where are we going?" Both little girls tangled on the floor and laughed uproariously at their boisterous entrance.

Their visitor, surprised but composed, stared at the two wordlessly.

"Girls," Lorraine said, "we're going to Douglas to see someone in the hospital."

Two sets of identical warm brown eyes stared up at the older girl, examining her from head to toe. The twins, still giggling, stood, each one stopping to lean, one each, on both sides of their mother.

The teen, arms piled with Lorraine's clothing, regarded the twins silently, then asked, "How is it they are the same?"

Lorraine took a quick gulp of air, realized the teen had probably never seen twins. In the centuries before modern times, twin births often resulted in the death of one child, a survival decision that recognized the harsh reality and difficulty of raising more than one infant at the same time.

Lorraine smiled reassuringly. "You have lived away from here for all your life, but now the real people know how to help a mother keep both babies when there are two or more."

The teen girl drew in her breath in astonishment. "Or more?"

"Yes," Lorraine said, "sometimes even more."

Lorraine placed an arm around each daughter's shoulder and smiled encouragingly, motioned with her lips in a kind of air kiss toward the clothing and said in Apache to the guest, "Those are your clothes now."

The teenager looked at the clothing piled in her arms and Lorraine saw she struggled inwardly; immediately understood the idea of receiving gifts without something to give in return, created an issue.

"*Shidizhe* (younger sister)," Lorraine said, "You have arrived in our camp under the protection of *Ussen*. You have brought us the gift of your presence, and now we need your help. We are relatives. What belongs to one, belongs to the other."

The teen, grateful for Lorraine's understanding, lifted the edges of the pants and shirt. She had seen such clothing before, but only on the bodies of her enemies. Now, she realized, even her own people in this new world wore such things.

"But how, elder sister," she asked, with a wrinkle between her brows, "do you put the leg coverings on? There are no strings to tie them."

Lorraine smiled, saw that dressing her new relative in modern style required some one-on-one assistance. "Okay girls," she said to the twins. "I need you both to step outside and guard the door while our relative changes clothes."

The twins might have complained about their exclusion, but the idea of guarding the door appealed to their sense of helpful participation. "Okay, Mom," they responded together, and left the tent.

Lorraine held the jeans up and displayed the zipper. She worked it up and down several times to show its movement and how it worked as a fastener.

Her audience of one imitated the noise in a hushed and sibilant whisper. "Zzzip. Zzzip," drew out her first word in English.

Lorraine laughed and said, "That's right, zip, zip."

The teen pulled the metal fasteners up and down several times, and rewarded Lorraine's tutoring session with a shy smile.

"Now," Lorraine instructed, "You must take off your moccasins and your skirt."

Without hesitation the teen-ager removed her moccasins and leg wrappings. She slid her knife from her wrappings behind her back under a cord that tied around her waist for carrying pouches.

Lorraine saw the transfer, decided to say nothing. She also noted her new relative wore nothing beneath her skirt, and handed the panties to the girl.

The teen accepted the panties and examined them. She placed her hands through the leg holes and scrutinized the top, bottom, sides, and finally held them up to Lorraine, her eyes puzzled.

Lorraine turned her back to the tent flap and unzipped her own jeans, opened the fly to demonstrate she wore underwear.

The teen watched and immediately understood. She began to

step into the panties, but Lorraine stopped her, explained they fit best when donned with the inside label worn in the back. Panties successfully fitted, Lorraine handed her the jeans, and instructed her to unzip them and place one leg at a time into the garment. The teen did not need further instruction and quickly pulled the jeans up and zipped them closed like a pro. She turned to Lorraine and waited.

"*Enjuh*" (Good), Lorraine said. She sat down on a bedroll and motioned the teen to sit, too. She handed her a pair of socks, and instructed her pupil to put one on each foot.

The teen held them up, looked back and forth between them, turned puzzled eyes to her tutor.

"Either one," Lorraine said and pulled her own jeans' legs up to show the girl how she wore socks.

"*Enjuh*!" (Good!), the girl said, and smiled wide for the first time, pleased with herself as she slipped the socks onto her feet.

Lorraine grinned broadly, repeated, "*Enjuh*!" and set her spare sneakers in front of the girl. Lorraine held her own foot out as a model and the teen stuck her legs and feet out. Then she slipped each shoe on.

The girl lifted the shoestrings, uncertain of her next move, and looked quizzically at Lorraine for instructions. Lorraine untied her own sneaker and demonstrated a slow-motion example of tying a classic bow. It took the girl three times before, on the fourth attempt, her bow held. Delighted, the girl stood and moved her feet back and forth.

"*Enjuh*!" Lorraine celebrated. She poked a finger around the toe area and saw the sneakers were a little big on the teen's feet, but she decided they would have to do, as they were the only shoes available.

The next item of clothing presented the biggest challenge. First Lorraine instructed the teen to remove her no-color shirt. The girl complied without concern about modesty. Bare-chested she waited for Lorraine's next direction.

Lorraine lifted up her own shirt to show how a brassiere fit across her bosom and fastened in the back. The teen looked at the straps, at the hooks in the back, and at the way the lingerie fit across Lorraine's bosom. Her face, mostly still and expressionless, grew a frown. When Lorraine offered her own extra brassiere, the girl refused to take it.

"*Dah*" (No), the teen said. "Women of the *Ndee Nnaahi* do not wear these." Her frown deepened. "*Ąął,*" she said firmly (End of discussion). And she handed it back to Lorraine.

Lorraine bit her lip, considering. She sighed, thinking that at least her mentee was of a slight build. "Well, I guess we'll just have to deal with your free spirit side," she said. She picked up her favorite long-sleeved, blue with white trim, western cowgirl shirt and helped her protégé into it. She showed the girl how to close and open the snaps.

Their click sound provided the teen with a new noise and experience. For a few moments she practiced snapping and unsnapping the fasteners. She smiled with confidence with the sound of the last snap and held her arms out straight to admire the trim.

Other than rejecting the lingerie, the teen accepted the clothing changes without comment. When Lorraine offered to brush out her *nah-leen* (maiden knot), and gathered her hair back into a ponytail, the teen asked to brush it herself. When she finished brushing, the girl carefully removed any loose or stray hair caught in the bristles, placed those leavings in her jeans pocket. Lorraine understood she would burn those hair strands later, in order to remove the risk of someone using something from her body to harm her with witchcraft. She knew from her father that the ancestors had practiced the same kind of care with anything personal. Hair, bits of fingernail, fecal matter, must be destroyed or buried, never left to fall into the hands of an enemy.

The only object the teen refused to take off was her black

and white bead necklace. Otherwise, she had been converted to an (apparently) twenty-first century teenager.

Lorraine took several steps back and looked at her final product. "*Nzhóó*" (Nice), she said, and the girl's eyes brightened.

Outside the tent Lorraine heard her father's voice. "Time to hit the road," he announced.

"We're coming!" Lorraine called back, and then to her daughters, "Open the tent flaps, girls."

She drew the teen outside behind her, announced, "Apache 2.0."

"Oh, you look nice," Susie and Elsie said together.

Sam was slow to chime in as he assessed the girl's transformation. He rubbed his chin and said approvingly, "*Nzhoonigo*" (Very nice). He looked at Lorraine and in English, commented, "I don't know about the shirt. Got a little bit of a Buckle Bunny look going on?" and cocked his head. "Think that's a good idea?"

Lorraine shrugged. "She flat won't put on a brassiere. Says her people do not use them."

Sam nodded. "Can't argue that." He curved his hand and motioned to all. "We need to go."

CHAPTER 53

On a Mission

Chiricahua National Monument Wonderland of Rocks, Cochise County, Arizona

THE TWINS LED THE way to the SUV, where Sam opened the back seat car door and asked them to let their guest enter first. The teen peered inside the open door and surveyed the dimness within. She smelled the interior air, a foreign blend of aromas previously unknown to her; car seat covers, a little metallic zing, a residual scent of canvas left from the folded-up tent that had traveled in the back space. She raised her nose and also breathed in a light tang of fuel and oil, both smells she recognized as belonging to the roads where metal wagons traveled. Her first thought, if I go in, how will I go out? was a natural response to any average entry question in her life. Grandmother taught all of the children to avoid being trapped by ensuring a pathway out remained available under all circumstances. She noted there were four doors into the metal wagon, each with a window, the front window, and the back window which was also part of a door.

Sam, eager to begin their drive, observed her hesitancy and said, "It's just like walking into a house and this is a safe house. It will carry us all."

Sam waited for her to enter but instead she turned, placed a hand on the door, and said, "Must it be closed behind me?"

"It must," said Sam, "or the wind might push you out. But for right now I'll leave the door open until we're ready to go." Then he walked to the other side to settle in the twins.

Susie scooted across the seat and sat in the middle, peering out at her new relative. "Do you like it?" she asked. Elsie climbed in and poked her head around her sister and said, "This is our car, but Grandfather has a pickup truck. I like pickups! What do you like?"

The teen smiled at the girls, without understanding differences or preferences. She had seen many metal wagons on her journey, but without an expectation of what it might be to sit inside one. Her impressions had been formed at distances, and she had thought of them as small bugs running down black trails. Now, she thought to herself, it seems like a big bug.

"C'mon," Susie said.

Gingerly, she picked up one foot and placed it on the floor of the metal wagon.

"Bend down and bring in your other foot," said Elsie, "or you'll bump your head!"

"*Ha'ah*," the teen answered and slowly, carefully, sat.

"*Enjuh!*" the twins approved together.

Lorraine started the vehicle and the teen stiffened at the unfamiliar growl of the engine, the tactile rumble of the seat. She remained sitting on the seat's front edge, ready to leap out if necessary. Outside the car, Grandfather solidly shut all open doors and took his place riding shotgun on the front seat.

The excitement of the information exchanged with Albert left the adults with a buzz combined of equal parts of alarm, exhilaration, and nerves. When Sam turned his head to check on the back seat, he saw a frozen look of uncertainty on their relative's face.

The ponytailed teen stared glassy-eyed out a window at the outside world as it seemed to run the other way past her.

"Granddaughters," Sam said in Apache to all three riders

in the backseat, "Hear what I say. Albert says we're on a tribal mission." Sam's voice carried a tremble. He squinted his eyes, turned to look straight south down the valley toward Mexico. He swept an arm out to encompass the lands that lay directly before them and asked the teen, "Is this the route you traveled?"

The girl craned her neck ahead, then to the side, intimidated at the speed with which things passed by the window in a blur. "*Dah*" (No). "*Nlááyú*" (Over there). She used her mouth to point east, then south, lifting her chin toward the places she had traveled through in past days.

Already the teen's devoted acolytes, Susie and Elsie, watched her closely, repeated to one another the way she elongated words softly, imitated her chin lift.

Sam used English to speak to Lorraine. "We've got to get our plan in place, Daughter. How do we explain our new relative?"

"We can say she's from a conservative family of relatives that only speak Apache. At least we've already got her dressed modern."

Sam turned, again watched their passenger stare out the window.

"Did she tell you her name, Daughter?"

Lorraine concentrated for a moment at reducing speed as the car rounded a curve along the base of the *Chiricahua* Mountains.

"We don't know her well enough, Dad."

Names among the Apache were not shared in the same way that names in other cultures might be. First, names were considered family property and it was the right of families to grant or forbid the use of their property. Next, even when a formal name was chosen, it was generally reserved for use in ceremonies and chants that improved health or prepared someone for coming of age or perhaps for going to war. And then its use was usually made by a medicine man. "Real" names given at birth were to be used only for such moments in sacred ways. Each time the name was spoken out loud it surrendered a piece of its power, and no one wanted to lose the protection of that power through overuse.

"I didn't mean her "real" name," Sam protested. "I mean what does she go by?"

"Ask her," Lorraine urged. "This all happened so fast we never even reached the point of exchanging nicknames."

Sam turned to the girl who couldn't seem to stop peering at the passing countryside. "Is there a nickname we can call you, Granddaughter?"

She pulled her eyes away from the window. "Yes, Grandfather. The children of the Blue Mountain People call me Eldest Sister, but they also call me *Biyoo'*."

Sam and Lorraine both smiled. Sam's eyes flicked at the beads around her neck.

"'Her Beads. Fits her," Lorraine said.

"It's a good nickname." Sam agreed, thought for a moment then asked the girl. "But I will ask you to carry one more nickname, so the *Indah* can say it. Alright?"

"*Ha'ah*." Her Beads saw these *Chiricahua* people understood the rules of names. They knew she could not share her real name. Every use of a real name must be engaged carefully, and only for important things. Nicknames carried no power in her world, and it didn't matter how many a person owned.

"The *Indah* people here will not understand your nickname *Biyoo'*." Sam squinted out the window ahead as he spoke. He turned to Lorraine. "What do you think, Daughter?"

Lorraine scrunched her shoulders together. "A name? I always liked Linda." She looked in the rearview mirror and asked the twins for their opinion.

"Priscilla," Susie said.

"No, Elizabeth," Elsie demanded.

Sam's face curled into exasperation. "Those are too strange

for her. It's got to be something she can remember. Something simple. Something she already knows, more or less."

He thought furiously for several minutes before announcing, "I think I've got a good one. Short and sweet."

He turned around in his seat and looked back at their passenger. "When you came into our camp, you asked for '*Eí*' that and '*Lá*' there." He used his hands to gesture in two different directions, looked at the girl and wrinkled his forehead earnestly. "Say them together."

She hesitantly spoke: "*Eí...Lá,*" performing the same gestures with her hands that Sam made, which sent the twins into giggling fits, hands over their mouths.

"Now put them together, and say them faster, without space between the words."

The girl placed her lips together and compliantly ran the two short words together. "*EíLá,*" her hands moving eloquently through the air.

"*Ha'ah!*" Sam cheered. "That's it."

"What?" Lorraine asked.

"We'll call her Ella," Sam said. "It's simple and she'll remember it because that's what she said to us."

"Ella," Sam pronounced. "Ella. C'mon girls, say it, so she hears it from all of us."

"Hi Ella!" Susie said in English.

"Go ahead," Sam encouraged in Apache. Then in English, "Hi Ella."

The girl immediately said, "Hi Ella," and made the two gestures with her hands.

The twins giggled, and Sam had to quiet them with his sternest eye.

Sam reached back and pushed her hands down. "*Dah*," he smiled, "no hand motions, and no 'Hi'. Just Ella." He nodded his head, "Try it again."

"Ella," she said, but the hands came back up.

"*Dah*, no hands. Here sit on them." He asked the twins to demonstrate, and to say 'Ella' with their passenger.

They practiced saying her name over and over, all three sitting on their hands.

"Now," Sam invited, once he felt sure she knew her new name well. "Ella, tell us about the man with metal legs."

CHAPTER 54

Choices

Abandoned Mining Camp, *Chiricahua* Mountains, *Cochise* County, Arizona

AFTER THE BORDER PATROL ATVs descended the mountain, finding the dispersed men had been a challenge for Chapo. He foraged them out from beneath rocky overhangs and under bushes, wasted a good hour of the new day. He found one slide mark off a rock to the base of a ponderosa pine where a backpack rested against the trunk, with no sign of its carrier. When a few pine needles fell against his cheek he looked up and there sat his quarry, arms wrapped around a branch, eyes wide.

"What are you doing up there, man?"

A face shimmered in the darkness of the tree. *"Tengo meido de osos."*

Chapo choked on a laugh. *"Pendejo* (Fool). C'mon down. No bears around here. Just *La Migra!* (Border guards)."

Chapo collected the men one by one, led them up the slope following deer paths, and eventually reached the clearing where they'd slept the night before. He'd half expected Vicente to be waiting, but the clearing stood empty of all but ATV tracks in the dust and the song of birds. Chapo decided they couldn't wait for Vicente. Too risky and the truck would be waiting. The morning was in full progress and time tight, but Chapo let the porters rest, drink. He dug into his saddlebags and passed out energy bars.

"*Vamos, hombres. Un poco más allá*" (Let's go, men. Not so far now).

The men shouldered their packs, some rubbed bruised arms or legs, some groaned at the prospect of more walking. All shuffled up the ascent toward the path. Chapo threw the reins over his mount's head and picked his way up the steep incline, scrambling just inches ahead of the horse to the ridge. At the top of the ridge the Crest Trail progressed on a north/south passage along the backbone of the *Chiricahua* range. He halted, waited for the porters to assemble. As they fell into line, breathing heavily from a combination of altitude and fatigue, he wished silently he could be anywhere but here. He reminded the men that Vicente would soon be riding drag behind them. One man cursed, spat, and cleared his throat. The men's eyes gauged one another's, exchanged flat looks of regret at where they found themselves.

Chapo saw the disgruntled faces and mounted his horse. The mare sidestepped, a bit wary of the dark mood that hung like a miasma about them. Looking down at the group from the back of Salsa, Chapo directed them to once more check their loads, and ascend the next level of the path.

"*Arriba*" (Onward), Chapo encouraged.

First one, then another checked their packs, shifted the loads on tired shoulders, and moved toward the path. Chapo allowed all to pass by and followed at the end of the line which encouraged their pace to quicken. He counted heads, then asked them to halt while he moved by to the head of the file. His heightened view on horseback gave him an advantage to see the trail ahead and deal with whatever they might encounter.

The path curled across a flat ridge that narrowed, then moved down over the edge, carved into the side of the mountain spine.

Hard to believe that once this slender path, the old Apache raiding trail, provided the main route of passage up and down the range. The porters fell into their walking rhythm, all thoughts focused on reaching the end of their journey and the prospects of what lay after. The trail dipped up and down, occasionally splashed through rivulets of water, constricted in places demanding careful attention for where they placed their feet. A few minutes into trail time Chapo noticed a horse had left shod prints ahead of them. Fresh. He turned in the saddle and looked back. The men's attention was on the increasingly cramped trail. No sign of Vicente yet, a good thing, he thought. And now this. He knew the horse's identity, knew the horseshoe prints of all the Diaz Ranch horses. Vicente's niece Lucy must have ridden this way.

He hoped his horse's tracks and the men coming behind him would cover the prints, destroy them. He didn't know what Vicente might do if he saw the tracks. He couldn't get the picture of Vicente's cousin Nick out of his head. The way Vicente ordered the porters to carry him up to the cliff dwelling, artificial legs thrown aside. He didn't want to think of what Vicente might do to Lucy if he intercepted her riding for help to the nearest ranch. He felt no compunction about the job he worked, but treating kids badly, any kids, felt wrong.

The entire morning he'd been thinking, trying to figure his own way out of the whole mess. All I want, he thought, is to get this load to the truck, collect my pay, and get the hell out of here.

The view of the river below with a backdrop of the Peloncillo Mountains east across the valley that divided Arizona from New Mexico presented a spectacular view. Ponderosa pines created spots of darkest green along the tops of the jagged peaks, darkening the heights of the mountains like waves lapping a shore. Far below, the stream sparkled as it eddied and ran in the clear sunlight. From the tops of ridges to the north, Chapo could see distant formations that paraded into armies of rock columns at the *Chiricahua* National Monument. An uncomfortable tickling slid down his back. The rock towers there always made him feel anxious. Something about their fantastic shapes and thousand variations felt unnatural, ominous. Even the name the early settlers used to describe them, a word he did not like to hear, made his nostrils flare. Hoodoos.

When he reached the trail that diverged upward to the highest ridge, he called a rest. The path diminished to its thinnest eighteen-inch width beyond, and he wanted the men to be as refreshed as possible to tackle it. The packers dropped their loads where they stood, stretched their backs.

Chapo asked the lead porter to hand out the last of the energy bars. "There's water maybe an hour ahead after the trail narrows." Only a couple of hours, he thought to himself, gauged the sun in the sky. This is not the life for me, he reminded himself. Last time, he silently vowed.

He dismounted onto the cutoff trail, left his horse loosely tied to a bush blocking the cutoff's access. He saw that Lucy's horse had taken the trail, and he scuffed away more of the horse prints and ascended, looked back to ensure the men were engaged in resting. He didn't want people wandering about. Good girl, he thought. She's off the raiding path and on her way to Loreto's.

He saw dust hung in the air when his short climb emerged into a lush meadow studded with clumps of white flowers. Scattered ponderosa pines scented a soft breeze. He thought it's like a kind of cowboy paradise up here, then snorted, thinking of the drama that had played out over and over in the *Chiricahua* range.

He knew the Apache used the meadow long ago to graze herds of cattle and horses as they drove them into or out of Mexico. Two paths; one on the west side of the mountains passed above the Loreto ranch, a wide trail, safer. The other path on the east side of the range was thinner, more dangerous, and shorter. Now a truck waited on the east side in an unpopulated canyon. He'd been across the worst part of the raiding trail before, felt the terror of its narrow width, fought the panic of rounding its contours without knowing what lay ahead. He refused to think about the unsightly bones of animals far below at the bottom of the gorge, long dead after just one wrong step.

His eyes automatically scanned the meadow for hoofprints, saw Lucy's horse had headed across the meadow to the other side of the range. He sighed and thought, "at least she's out of the way."

Angry voices, one of them Vicente's, erupted below on the trail and Chapo spun around. As he turned to descend the path, he registered a movement and slammed to a halt.

Then, everything seemed to happen at once.

Lucy hunkered at one side of a ponderosa pine; her expression relieved, even joyful. "Chapo!" she called.

At the same time angry voices below became more strident. Chapo heard the harsh threat of Vicente's shouts lash out. "Get on your feet!" And the sound of scuffling.

Chapo's heart sank and his mind raced in alarm. Where was Lucy's horse? He raised a forefinger to his lips, pointed toward Loreto's and stirred the air frantically, motioning violently that Lucy must go.

Chapo slid across the uneven path to the lower trail toward the excited shouting, watched in horror as Vicente raked his spurs across his blue roan's flanks causing it to plunge and buck against Salsa.

Chapo urged Lucy silently, his neck taut as she scrambled up and ran across the meadow onto the path. Her face, so startled every freckle stood out, burned into his memory. He threw himself down the cutoff to grab at Salsa's reins, at the same moment a wobbling horse scream ricocheted against the far canyon wall.

He registered two things happening at the same time from the top of the trail. Looking north he saw Lucy pause at the edge of the forest, her face terrified. At the same time to the east he saw Vicente on his mount teeter off the trail and fall into the chasm of the canyon. Lucy turned and ran down the trail away from the tumult while Vicente and his horse seemed to hesitate on the edge, drop in slow motion, then plummet to the bottom.

Birds stopped singing. The low undercurrent of sound from the river disappeared. The trail, captured in an envelope of shocking disquiet, waited for someone, anyone, to break into the unnatural silence.

The slowed world regained speed as Chapo saw Vicente and horse smash together onto the rocks. Blood gushed from the horse, the man's body flapping like a rag doll, twirled away and out of sight, leaving one torn-off sleeve fluttering on the ground. The babble of frightened voices beside him blended with a glissade of rocks gathering momentum, ended in the tumultuous crashing of stones that roiled the water in the rocky river below. Next came long, ragged screams of the injured horse.

The men clustered along the edge of the trail, craned their necks over the empty space to examine the bottom of the canyon and the river that ran below.

"What . . .?" Chapo demanded. He couldn't form the words.

A jumble of voices responded, mixed with the grating and anguished suffering of the horse, and created a tortuous blend of horror. Chapo stepped too close to the edge and crumbled earth fell away. Several arms reached out and pulled him from the edge. He shuffled backward until he could feel the wall behind him, solid. What he'd seen below turned his mouth to dry sand. He squared his shoulders, focused on slowing his breath, still seeing a replay of the entire fall. He could still see the horse as it hit the ground, the blood spatter and pieces of the saddle; and something else flying off high toward the edge of the forest.

"Pray for his soul," a porter said and made the sign of the cross on his chest. Down the line of men, a cascade of head and shoulder touches followed.

Chapo grimaced, asked, "Is everyone else okay?"

"*Si, bueno*" (good), said the lead packer in a tight voice. "Can you see if he's moving down there?"

A jumble of boulders blocked the view of where Vicente's body must be. His hat lay in sight and a blue denim sleeve jutted out from the reef of stones. But no movement. The horse kept trying to rise unsuccessfully, one leg dangling, blood splattered all around.

"Only thing moving is the horse, jefe."

Intermittent horse squeals, discordant, painful to hear, continued from below. The men flinched as they watched it try to right itself, legs flailing, and slip farther down.

"Got to do something." Chapo saw his own horse had pulled his reins from the bush and trotted farther along the thinning trail during the commotion. He watched as the horse rounded a curve almost out of sight. "Someone get Salsa back. We'll use the horse to hold a line and lower a man down."

A thick chested porter immediately jogged away after the horse. Meanwhile the sounds of the injured animal at the canyon bottom continued, making Chapo grit his teeth each time it squealed. "Anybody see anything of El Patron?"

The men scanned the canyon side where the shirt sleeve continued to flap lightly in a breeze, but no part of the boss's body protruded from behind the boulder. The pack from the horse had split and spilled against the rocks of the escarpment; the contents strewn across the area.

"What took you so long?" Chapo demanded when the man returned leading Salsa.

"No place to turn around, jefe." The thick chested man stroked the horse's nose, seemed troubled. "Someone turned around at the same place before me. Maybe . . .," and his eyes moved to the cutoff trail.

Chapo hissed, wanting no attention brought to sighting Lucy, grabbed the reins, caught the bridle, and jerked Salsa into position.

"*Calmaté*" (be calm), he crooned, patting his mount's neck.

The horse rolled its eyes back, shifted weight onto its back hooves, huffed nervously but stood solid. Chapo grabbed a looped rope from his saddle, rejoined the porters who gingerly leaned and peered from the trail edge, examining the canyon below.

The horse sounds formed a rhythm of disharmony out of synch with the purling river below and the rustle of pines above in the meadow. Each time the horse screeched Chapo grimaced. His stomach flipped again as the blue sleeve waved against the boulder. He raised one hand to his lips and rubbed his mouth. He knew the saddle rope was too short to reach Vicente.

He contemplated his choices, calculated the time it would take: an hour back down the trail for anyone to reach the bottom; at least a half-hour along the river to where they could access the man and horse; then Vicente might already be dead. Meanwhile, what could they do to help him? And the horse's shrieking continued, interspersed with shudders and moans of pain. Some of the packers held hands over their ears.

The thick-chested man said, "I'll go down, jefe."

"We only got one rope, and it's too short."

"A man should not have to die alone, jefe. Drop me to the ledge," the thick-chested man offered, "I will climb down from there."

Chapo unlooped the coiled lariat. He let it fall to its full length over the cliff. He leaned out to see how far it reached. He saw it was short of the canyon floor by at least fifty feet. The men around him groaned.

No, Chapo decided. He knew whose job it was to clean up any messes. Knew who'd get blamed for whatever went wrong, no matter what. "No, I will go." He instructed the thick-chested man: "Send two down the trail to come back along the river. They can help me carry him out." Or bury him, he thought, grinding his teeth.

Through it all, the injured horse continued to struggle and squeal.

"Can't you put him out of his misery?" one of the vaqueros asked.

Chapo shook his head miserably from side to side. "We can't see where Vicente is. No, don't shoot from here. If a bullet hits a stone, it could ricochet and hurt Vicente."

Looking down, Chapo thought of being in Vicente's place below. It could have been him, or any one of them. Chapo knew if Vicente survived and found out he'd hesitated to help him, he was as good as dead. The queasy roll in his belly twisted.

Two men left in a trot and Chapo covered his ears. After a quarter of an hour, he could not wait longer. "I got to do something now," he thought. "Somebody else will hear that horse and there'll be a lot more problems."

He turned to Salsa, gingerly reached into the saddlebag for the packet containing the first aid kit, and stuffed it inside his shirt. He checked that his sidearm was firmly belted at his waist and secured in its holster. He held up his arms for a loop in the rope to let him down the cliff face, secured the other end to Salsa's saddle horn.

The thick-chested porter held the horse's head tightly, humming softly, reassuringly. "*A sus órdenes, hombre*" (At your service, man). "*Lento*" (Slow).

Chapo tested the hold of the rope against his weight and Salsa braced and held strong. Chapo placed one foot carefully, then the other, and began to descend, cursing. And praying.

CHAPTER 55

Wisdom Sits in Places

On the Road to San Enebro, Hidalgo County, New Mexico

SAM POINTED WITH A thumb, indicating smoke curling far down the valley to the southwest in Mexico from the Cananea smokestacks. "The Land of Those Who Walk Around," he said in Apache.

"Look at that border wall." Lorraine's voice carried awe. "Looks like they're trying to keep out King Kong."

The twins craned their necks.

"What do you see, Granddaughters, beyond the wall?"

Susie stared south into the seared plains of the open Sonoran Desert.

"A mountain all alone." She leaned back in her seat.

Elsie placed her chin on the rim of the front seat, added, "With rocks on top."

"*Enjuh*" (Good). "My Blue Mountain granddaughter, how do you call the name of that mountain?" Sam pointed with his lips to the south again.

Ella, *Biyoo'*, dipped her head to get a better view through the front window. Without hesitation she answered, "Rocks All Around is the name the ancestors used." She thought a moment. "No good water there."

"Over there," he continued, using his chin to point east and inside the United States
border, "See that other mountain?"

"It looks rocky, too," Elsie said. "What's that one?"

Ella answered. "Grandmother told us it was a good place to know because it is seen well from all directions. See the notch? There is always water there. The ancestors called it *Dzil Nii'leezhé Bigowa*."

The girls' heads tilted as they scrutinized it intently.

"Prairie Dogs' Home Mountain," Elsie translated.

"It is where the ancestors fooled the Buffalo Soldiers," Ella explained further.

"I remember that story," Susie said, her face filled with the light of discovery. "I didn't know it was real."

Grandfather laughed. "Of course, it's real! We use names to help us remember places. What do we call the naming of places?"

The girls looked at one another. "Naming?" ventured Susie.

Ella spoke. "In the Blue Mountains, Grandmother taught us to call it, 'Wisdom Sits in Places.'"

Sam turned and smiled at Ella. "*Ha'ah*. That is the way of the ancestors."

She leaned toward the twins. "Tell me the story of the mountain. I was there two days ago," she said, remembering the spring. "That is where I saw the warrior with metal legs the first time." The girls began to ask more questions about the warrior but she stopped them. "I will give you an idea. Grandmother said it's not a good place to ride horses fast."

"Oh!" Susie said, and showed delight. "The Buffalo Soldiers' horses broke their legs in the prairie dog holes. The soldiers were chasing the ancestors." The little girl's face showed delight at recalling the story after Ella's hint.

Sam started to hum one of the old Apache traveling songs the girls knew, and grinned with delight when Ella joined into the song, same words and melody. His deep voice offset the high-pitched piping of the girls, while Lorraine patted a soft beat on her knee and Ella's soprano connected it all.

When the song ended, they traveled quietly. Driving south, they surveyed the long-distance views, the immensity of space within the horizons.

"That music sounds right for a journey." Lorraine spoke matter-of-factly, her tone glum. "All of this land used to be Apache territory, but not anymore."

"That is the way it has always been for the Blue Mountain People," Ella said.

"Wrong, my daughters," Sam said and smiled. "It's all still ours, just not exclusively."

"Humph," Lorraine disagreed, but softly.

Ella considered the wide expanses into Mexico. "It is hard to find water that way. Better to travel the other trail anyway," and she pointed to the notched mountain again.

"How well do you know the way, Granddaughter? How many times have you traveled in those places?"

Ella studied the territory east, then south. "Just once. Only from the Blue Mountains to the Land of Standing Up Rocks."

"And yet, you seem to know what is there." Sam indicated the uneven plain sloping toward the mountains and valleys of Mexico.

"It is as Grandmother said. 'Wisdom Sits in Places.' We learn the stories and know what is there. All of the Blue Mountain children know the lands of our people, whether they have stood at those exact places or not."

CHAPTER 56

Death Drop

Raiding Trail Cut-Off, *Chiricahua* Mountains, *Cochise* County, Arizona

TIME SLOWED AS CHAPO faced the cliffside, held tight to the rope, and stiff-legged his boots down the mountain wall. More minutes ticked by when the rope caught in some manzanita bushes. Chapo dangled too far down to unravel himself from entanglement, and had to wait uncomfortably for the crew above to free the rope. When they accomplished that, they swung him twenty feet to the south to avoid the manzanita, resulting in his hanging over a lip of the canyon. Chapo hung quietly, lips pressed together, as the crew slowly lowered him. It seemed forever before the rope slacked and he reached solid footing.

Once his feet stood on solid rock, Chapo leaned out over the precipice. He looked up and saw heads at the top. "I am on an island of rock," he shouted to those above him, "too high to jump." He shook his head. "Too straight up and down to climb."

The lead packer cupped his hands around his mouth. "Is there rope on the injured horse?"

Chapo leaned out to see, but the angle of his sight provided no information. He heaved a heavy sigh to himself, shook his head, and raised his arms in consternation.

A breeze continued to ruffle the blue sleeve that lay next to the rocks. Chapo saw a flash of something colored at the edge of the forest beyond the thrashing horse and thought, "There he is! He's still alive!" He worked his way again around the edge of the precipice, searching for a way down; but without more rope it seemed impossible and he sat on the ledge to think. He could not get down alone and he must wait for the two others to arrive from below. So close, he thought and gritted his teeth; but not close enough.

The men on top cheered almost an hour later when the packers appeared far below, scrambling clumsily along the river. They immediately veered toward Chapo, shoes sliding on the loose shale, cursing when the glissade of rocks carried them like surfers back into the shallow stream below. Their shouts bounced against the canyon walls. At the sound of more voices the injured horse's panicked complaint of pain renewed, loud and distressing.

Chapo called to the men, *"Oye! Puerlo verlo?"* (Hey! Can you see him?) Chapo pointed to the rocks.

The two packers, wet up to their thighs from walking in the stream, adjusted their path and made their way to where the flapping sleeve snapped in the wind against the rocks. In seconds they returned into view, their faces frightened. They both shook their heads in a negative back and forth, peered up and down the slope, shrugged.

Chapo called, "Is he alive?"

At the same time the packers above shouted *"Cuerdo! Cuerdo!"* (Rope!)

The men scrambled across the scree working their way past the tortured horse, staying clear of the thrashing, called up to the packers on the trail *"No cuerdo."* (No rope.)

When they reached the rock face below Chapo, they reported: "Horse's got two broken legs."

Chapo gritted his teeth. "Vicente. Is Vicente dead?"

"Don't see him, jefe."

Chapo felt as if he might go crazy. "HOW IS IT POSSIBLE NOT TO SEE HIM?"

"Nobody under the boulder, jefe. Just a piece of his shirt."

At the same time the horse reacted by screaming louder.

"CHECK THE FOREST AND BUSHES!" Chapo yelled at the men, motioning them toward the forest edge where he thought he'd seen some movement.

The two peeled off, skirting the woods, peering around and into the darkness of the massed trees.

Chapo watched from his rock as he waited in agony as the horse seemingly endlessly screamed. In a frenzy, goaded by the horse's shrill squeals, Chapo slipped out of the rope holding him in place. He took off his boots, removed his belt, pulled his weapon from the holster, and stripped off his shirt and pants. He tied one leg of his jeans to the rope end and the other leg to the belt; next, the belt to the shirt; and let the length of rope, pants, belt, and shirt fall. He saw his rescue line still lacked thirty feet to reach the men.

"WHAT DO YOU SEE?" Chapo roared.

Both men reappeared at the forest line. *"Nada y nadie"* (Nothing and no one), one of them called back.

Through the continuing torment of the shrieking horse, Chapo raised his head and yelled through gritted teeth, "COME HERE NOW."

The men made their way back across the scree, halted at the bottom below the rock. They threw their heads back and looked up the sides of the sheer cliff face at Chapo's wild movements, alarmed.

He'd quickly begun to untie the jeans from the rope, with a new plan in mind. He laid flat on his bare chest and stomach and dangled his shirt-wrapped gun from his rigged cord of jeans and belt over the edge. He'd gained only a few more feet.

"Get ready!" he warned. "I've got to drop it and I don't want my gun hitting the rocks."

They caught it. Within minutes they left him standing almost naked on the rock and made their way back to the struggling animal. At the sound of one gunshot, the horse screams ended mid-shriek.

"*Gracias a Dios!*" Chapo said. He turned away in a meltdown of emotion and fear. Red-faced and breathing hard, he held onto his hat's brim as he leaned over the cliff, suddenly too tired to stay on his feet. Cold, too.

"Get me out of here," he yelled up in a raw voice. "*Nadie está alla*" (No one's there).

At that moment, someone above, feeling the slack in the rope, hauled it up about ten feet. Someone else grabbed it and as they unwittingly tugged against one another, both lost hold of the rope. It slithered down, caught on the manzanita, and pulled away from Chapo's ledge, dropping all the way to the canyon floor. It left Chapo marooned, bare in his underwear, socks, and

hat, pulling on his cowboy boots, and no idea of how to solve his predicament.

CHAPTER 57

Reunion

Medicine House (Mercy Regional Hospital, San Enebro, New Mexico) *Chiricahua* Apache Homeland

CAT HAD BEEN WATCHING and waiting for a moment to somehow creep off the high shelf where she lay and disappear when Brown Woman brought the kitten. Cat knew her mission must be to escape, but quickly decided she wanted to take the kitten with her. As she dangled a thread in front of it, a small paw batted frustratingly on empty space. When the kitten mewed, Cat giggled and held it to her nose, rubbing its softness against her cheek. Her leg rolled a bit as the tiny animal twisted in her lap and mewed. *"Gidi, gidi, gidi,"* Cat teased the bit of fluff. "You are such a nice *gidi*."

Busy with the kitten, it took Cat a moment to realize people stood in the doorway, silently watching her play. She closed the smile from her face. Cat tucked the kitten under the blanket, drew the pillow over her head— motions that caused her leg to slip farther off the pillows. Brown Woman stepped forward, tucked and lifted so that her patient's neck was supported and made sure her leg was propped up.

Cat did not like to be touched by enemy ghosts, but tolerated Brown Woman because she knew who had brought the kitten. Cat saw Brown Woman would not let her hide. Neither would

316

the kitten that already had one paw out from under the sheet and complained loudly. Cat looked at the people through eyes almost squeezed shut. That made the old man who stood beside the bed smile. He covered his mouth with one hand, but his grin escaped the edges of his palm. She thought to herself she did not know that men could live to be so old. An enemy woman with metal circles in her ears stood next to the old man.

The kitten mewed and suddenly escaped from beneath the linens, its little claws scrambling against the smoothness of the sheets. Cat expelled a breath of exasperation which made the hair around her face wisp upward. The man swallowed hard, as if something was stuck in his throat. At home in the Blue Mountains, Cat knew she made Grandmother laugh sometimes. But she didn't know this man. She saw movement of other people in the entry, and had a flash of anger that they stared at her so rudely.

"You are enemy strangers." She bit each word off in Apache like a wolf at its meat, "And when you laugh you sound like coyotes." It was one of the worst things she could think to say. The man's hand failed to cover a snort. Cat bristled with indignation.

"Sąh!" (Listen!), a voice commanded. "Ncho'go natsíńkees da!" (Don't think
unpleasant thoughts!)

Cat's eyes widened. She must be mistaken. No one here spoke her language. The enemy with metal circles in her ears stared disapprovingly. Her bright pink cheeks and lips made Cat wonder if she'd eaten berries. Cat would like to eat some berries, but she had seen none. Even if there were berries, she decided, they'd probably be poisoned. The woman spoke in a waterfall of incomprehensible words that washed around Cat, and the child drew the pillow over her head again. She despised and feared the meaningless sounds of those enemy words.

She felt a tug on the pillow and a voice asked softly: "Shidizhé" (Little sister), "is it you?"

Hearing the language of her own people by a familiar voice felt like a clear stream of water had suddenly rushed through a dry arroyo to quench her thirst. Cat wanted to drink more of her people's words.

She knew it could not be *Biyoo'*, Her Beads. Cat had watched her older sister descend the Zig Zag Trail a long time ago, on her journey to find the path to the homeland. She'd watched her walk down the trail and disappear going north.

Cat thought desperately of Grandmother and her teachings. She decided to become the desert tortoise and went still. Perhaps these strange people in this white and metal place would think her a rock or something dead. Maybe she could crawl away when no one watched. If she kept herself without motion, they might forget her. If she could hold her breath long enough, they might give her time to become invisible. She took a slow deep breath and held it.

A hand crept under the blanket and ran tickling fingers along her jaw up to her ear lobe. Surprised, Cat expelled her breath in a noisy splutter.

"*Gidi*," Cat, the voice said in her own tongue. "Do you not know your elder sister?"

Could it be? Slowly *Cat* allowed the tickling hand to pull away the blanket. Wide-eyed, she watched as the smiling face of *Her Beads* appeared.

"*Ashch'ishégo*, Small One, Where are our people?" The old man asked.

Her Beads quickly clasped *Cat* in her arms and held her in a strong embrace. She had only a moment to say, "He is our grandfather, here from the *Chokonen*, Rising Sun People, to help us."

Cat turned a smile toward Sam that nearly blinded him with its brilliance.

"She knows you!" Metal Circles Woman's voice cried out. Sam smiled agreeably.

Cat hugged *Her Beads* tightly, buried her face in her neck.

"Answer our relative, *Shidizhé* (Little Sister)."

Cat clung to Her Beads, her arms tight around her older sister's neck.

"*Doo bígonsih da*" (I don't know), she said in a small voice. "*Shich'á' ch'a'okíí*" (I lost them).

"Says she got lost," Sam translated to Lydia Castillo.

The social worker's face registered empathy. "Oh, the poor little thing."

"We are *Chokonen* together," the old man said in Apache. "We will find the others." He nodded reassuringly, and moved sideways to allow a woman and two girls behind him through the door. "Here are more *Chokonen* relatives."

Cat stretched her neck in search of relatives. She wasn't sure she'd ever known any relatives before.

Elsie and Susie squeezed into the room ahead of their mother, went directly to the hospital bed. They bent around Her Beads and greeted Cat. The little girl's eyes swept over Lorraine and her two daughters with the same faces.

Sam turned to the social worker. "We are grateful for your call to the tribal president. I'll be talking with him soon to report we've found the child and she is ours."

The social worker placed a hand over her heart, tears building in her eyes. "I'm so glad to have been of help; so relieved she belongs to you."

She stepped closer to the bed, reached and stroked the little girl's hair, moved her hand down her cheek. "It's wonderful, sweetie, to know we found your people."

Cat shrank from the woman's outstretched hand, staring at the red painted nails, thought of monsters dipping their fingertips in blood from the winter stories in the Blue Mountains. She rolled her body away from the woman's hands, tried to roll her leg back on top of the pillow.

Her Beads placed a hand on the stranger's shoulder and pushed lightly, but firmly, away.

"She didn't mean to scare you, Cat," Sam said in Apache to the child, as Lydia Castillo bit her lip.

Lydia, embarrassed at the discomfort her touch engendered, wrinkled her brow, turned to walk away, stopped, called back to Sam. "What is the child's name?"

Sam looked up with guarded eyes and quickly translated into English. "Cat."

"Ohhhh," Lydia said, in a tone of discovery. "Is that short for Catherine, such a beautiful name."

Sam nodded easily. "Yes."

Lydia Castillo stepped down the corridor. "Oh, and the child's last name?"

The loudspeaker chimed, followed by an overhead voice calling Lydia Castillo's name.

"I must check on that," she said, waving upward at the unseen loudspeaker. "Stop in to see me in my office so we can finish paperwork for Catherine's release." She turned and hurried off.

Meanwhile, the three little girls had engaged in a communal appreciation of the kitten's antics.

Cat addressed the twins. "You are not Blue Mountain People," she stated factually. "How do you look so much like one another?"

"*Naki gozlįį' néé*" (We are twins), Elsie replied. The two sisters smiled identically at Cat.

"Both of the same birth?" Cat drew back a little. "How did it happen you both live?" Cat thought everyone knew that only one of two born together could live.

The twins shrugged. Susie used one finger to trace the kitten lightly over its head, down its back, and to the tip of its tail. "*Dédí'iléí*" (Soft).

Sam joined the others next to the hospital bed. "Little One, that was the old way. Our people no longer believe it."

Cat knew what Grandmother had taught them. She kept

her face blank, looked at *Her Beads* who tilted her head to one side, nodded slightly.

"Does your leg hurt?" the old man asked.

Cat turned her bottom lip out. "Not now."

"How did you get to this place?" *Her Beads* asked.

"Enemy people brought me in a metal wagon."

Her Beads's face did not betray emotion when she asked, "Why did the Blue Mountain People leave before my return?"

"Grandmother told us to go."

The adults exchanged a look of alarm.

"Ah, and where is your grandmother?" Sam asked.

Cat struggled to remember. She tilted her head. "It was a long time ago. Eldest Brother said Grandmother would follow, but she never came." Her voice faded.

Lorraine raised her eyebrows at her father. "We must find the others."

Sam patted Cat's hand. "Do you know where they might be? We'll find them so we can know our relatives."

"I am not your relative. I am one of the Blue Mountain People." Cat spoke before she knew her words had left her mind and entered her mouth. "We have no old men in the Blue Mountain People."

"I am your *Chokonen* grandfather," Sam straightened his shoulders. "You just did not know me before now. My grandfather was one of the *Ndee Nnaahi,* the Nameless Ones." He looked steadily at Cat until she lowered her eyes. "I am your grandfather, and I am grandfather to all of the children of my people. Did your grandmother not teach you our ways?"

Even under reproach *Cat* drank the sound of his words, music to hear her own language.

"Do you know where they travel?"

"Of course, Grandfather," *Cat* replied using the relative term carefully, "I know the map in my head."

"But have they followed the trail the way we learned?" *Her Beads* asked the question thinking of her own path, its changes in direction to avoid discovery.

Cat snuggled against the older girl. "That is how I fell off the horse," she confessed, "when the journey moved to a different path." She examined *Her Beads's* familiar face. "*Édįhi Lashí*" (Maybe they're dead). Her lower lip trembled.

"*Dah*, no, little sister," *Her Beads* said. "We'll find our people. They're looking for us."

Cat thought: *Ussen* has chosen. He has brought me *Her Beads* and Grandfather.

She watched Grandfather solemnly bring a small leather pouch hanging on a cord from inside his shirt. He reached inside the pouch. Four times he pinched *hoddentin* from the little suede bag and tossed it to one of the four directions. Cat watched his hands and the floating bits of sacred cattail pollen as each sprinkling puffed into the air and gently wafted down around them. A collective sigh of release dissipated with the dust and a feeling of rightness settled around Cat.

"Now," Sam said. "*Ussen* has brought us together. *Ussen* will find the others. *Ussen* is all powerful. *Ussen* will protect us."

Together Cat and *Her Beads* murmured softly. "May it soon be usefully so."

CHAPTER 58

If It Isn't One Thing It's Another

Dry Gully, *Chiricahua* Mountains, *Cochise* County, Arizona

NICK AND TOMÁS STOOD, heads swiveling, trying to determine where the girl went. She'd disappeared in an instant. They'd been shocked when they turned and found her gone. Like watching a magic trick.

"Now what?" Tomás asked, throwing his hands up in question.

"Wish I had time to check her wound." Nick worried. "She was bleeding." Vicente on the loose, he thought, and up to major no good, but the girl had managed to get away on her own. He chewed the inside of his cheek. Where, he wondered, could she be going?

Tomás dug into a pocket and tried his cell phone. Nothing. "Of course," he protested in a disgusted tone, "why would I expect it to work here?"

"You could climb a mountain and try a call, but it'll probably be the same." Nick surveyed their surroundings. He moved to find better footing near the bank, but a tangled mess of mesquite made it impossible to keep pace and he returned to the soft sand of the empty river bed.

"Loreto Ranch is still closest on the old Apache trail cut-off. They got a landline."

Tomás agreed and both returned to trudging through the sand. Nick could not stop thinking about the girl. Not much I can do right now for her, he thought. No way to tell how long my leg charge will last either; walking on borrowed time. Once I lose the charge, I'll be the one needing assistance. Stay focused, he chided himself. Find the nearest help and report to the authorities. He knew the girl to be capable, yet he thought earnestly, still so feminine, even elegant in her strange garb and black and white beads, so . . . lovely.

"Walking will take forever," Tomás complained, interrupting Nick's musings.

"The lament of the cowboy on foot." Nick's tone registered no sympathy at all. "What can I say except I'll keep moving as long as I can."

"I don't mean you, Nick. I mean it's just too slow. And I keep thinking Vicente may circle back. I think he'd like us to be . . ." and he searched for a word.

"Gone?" Nick tried. "Yeah, no question there."

They soldiered on for another half mile along the river bed, when the crackling sound of a large animal moving through brush on the bank ahead brought them to a dead halt. Tomás tapped his own chest and motioned he'd climb the bank. Nick nodded, shuffled to the inside of the wash, still moving slowly forward.

Nick watched as Tomás reached the edge of the bank, crouched and ran bent over into the brush. A few minutes passed with no sounds beyond some bird calls and the susurration of Nick's footsteps through the loose arroyo sand. A sudden explosion of noise on the bank above ripped through the quiet. Brush snapped, thuds vibrated the earth, and Tomás whooped.

Nick plowed through the sand, following the commotion, seeking a way up. His left leg faltered, then stopped. He snapped the knee into lock position, and stiff-legged on, eyes searching the rim of the bank, listening to what sounded like a punching fight in the brush above. Silence settled suddenly above him.

"Hey," Tomás called down, leaning out from an overhang of the wash. He wiggled his eyebrows comically at Nick.

Nick looked up and snorted. Tomás, mounted on Larry, grinned triumphantly down at him.

"I can't believe how that mule keeps turning up," Nick said. Tomás slid off Larry as Nick struggled to climb onto the edge of the arroyo. Nick planned each step up the bank, clumsily dragging the locked leg. Tomás reached to hoist him up the last few feet.

Beads of sweat rolled down Nick's face as he caught his breath. "Thanks, primo. Now I know what it feels like to be peg-legged."

"Your transportation has arrived," Tomás said, bowed and held out one arm as if inviting Nick to enter a limousine.

He folded his fingers into a cup and formed a step to vault Nick up onto the mule's back, then held Larry's reins while Nick settled on the broad flanks. Tomás jumped and swung one leg up behind Nick on the mule, dragged himself forward to hold Nick's waist.

Nick gathered the reins in his hands and pointed the mule north toward Loreto Ranch. He clucked to quicken Larry's pace and the mule went into a trot. Nick kept scanning, watching for Vicente, but hoping he might see the girl. He wanted to find her. To help her. To protect her. Or, he criticized himself, maybe she could help him. Eh, he thought, she probably had no interest. They couldn't even understand one another's languages. Although, he mused, all things considered, they'd communicated pretty well. He thought about the way she formed her lips around the words she tried to teach him. Her mouth had puckered almost into a kiss when she was teaching him her word for water. It occurred to him he'd like to know what it was like to kiss her. *"Twoh,"* Nick said aloud to himself, thinking of how soft her mouth looked, how kissable her lips would be, how....

"What?" Tomás asked.

Larry knocked a hoof against a stone, spooked himself, shied sideways. Nick wrestled the reins and redirected the mule forward, but didn't answer his cousin.

"Why do you think she took off like that?" Nick asked instead, his words jigging with the mule's pace. "You'd think she'd feel safer to stay with us."

"I'd feel safer if she'd stuck around." Tomás rotated his neck and looked behind them, saw no one. "She knows stuff."

"Yeah." Nick searched the landscape ahead. He wrenched his mind away

from the girl. Focus on the problem, he told himself, then out loud said, "You think Vicente is hanging around?"

"Dunno. Whatever he's doing it's probably not good. That's the way it's been since Roberto disappeared." Tomás stomach growled.

Larry plodded past a forest sign: "Loreto Ranch: 3 miles," with an arrow pointing to a path leading northwest; "Old Fort Bowie: 12 miles," the arrow pointing north toward a cut into a fold of the hills; "Diaz Ranch," the name slashed by an X, with a poor attempt to carve the word "Dog" and an amateurly drawn three-peaked mountain after it; then: "6.5 miles," an arrow indicating due east. The last sign listed "Rucker's Canyon: 2.1 miles," followed by a warning: "Steep trail: no upkeep."

Nick tried to figure how long it would take to reach Loreto's as they turned onto the path. "What do you think, Tomás? Two hours to get to Loreto's?"

Larry's hooves plopped softly on the sand of the path.

"At least," Tomás answered. "Mostly uphill, so probably closer to three hours. Plus, Larry's carrying both of us."

They rode on in the sunlight. Nick rolled his lips together, patted a pocket seeking lip balm, found none. Probably fell out, he thought when they manhandled him up the hill.

Tomás sighed. "If only Roberto had stayed," he said sadly. "None of this stuff would be happening."

Nick heard the suffering in Tomás's voice, felt the weight of his longing for better times. "We all miss him," he began, when Larry stopped and jerked up his head, jingling the metal of his bridle. He snorted and backed up, eyes rolling, showing the whites.

"Whoa, whoa there." Nick's automatic reaction was to scan the area quickly all around and behind them, searching for the threat.

Tomás facing forward looked straight over Nick's shoulder. His voice incredulous, he said, "Look! Look ahead! See that?" He tuned his words into a whisper, "People, kids, running across the trail."

Nick turned, eyes darting. "People? Vicente with them?"

Tomás swallowed hard before replying in a thin voice, "No. It was," and he held his words for a few seconds in his throat, stared ahead. "It was . . . Indians."

"What do you mean, Indians?" Nick kept sweeping his eyes across the hills, the path, the arroyo behind them.

"Man, they had bows and arrows." Tomás wiped his nose with the back of a hand.

"Maybe it was hunters."

"Bow season's over. Rifle season doesn't start for another week." Tomás shook his head as if to rattle his brain into place. "Besides, they were kids, dressed really funny, like that girl. Nick, it was kids!" He pushed on Nick's back, urging him forward. "Quick, maybe we can get up closer."

Nick pressed his heels into Larry's side, pulled the reins to the right, and angled the mule off the Loreto trail. Thought eagerly, "Maybe she's with them."

"Hurry," Tomás urged. "C'mon, c'mon." He pressed his heels against the mule's barrel.

As the mule strode across the curve of the hill, they saw the trail winding along the bottom through the trees.

"Here it is, Nick. This is where they crossed." Tomás slid

off Larry's rump. "Look!" Tomás pointed at soft squiggles in the loose dust of the trail.

"Or . . .," Nick said, studying the marks, "maybe just wind blowing."

Nick dismounted slowly, raising his frozen leg over the horn and slipping down, gently settling both feet on the ground and continuing to scan the area around them. Larry's reins in one hand, he leaned over to examine the dust carefully. "No tracks." He shifted his view between where the marks began and ended. "Per se," he added.

"That's unreal." Tomás, a little pale, looked confused. "I saw them, Nick! Kids! Really, I did! Who ARE they?"

Nick passed the reins to Tomás. He lurched to the edge of the trail, stuck his stiff leg out to one side, and squatted on the other leg. Where the hill lapped along the dirt of the trail, several places showed flattened grass. "I don't know, but it's a mystery I want to solve." He examined the flat places carefully, then found he couldn't raise himself to stand with his one leg locked. "Help me up, Tomás."

Tomás caught Nick's hand and pulled him up. Both grunted with the effort.

"Look right there." Nick pointed past the bent grass, to a small patch of earth surrounded by leaves. "You see what almost looks like half of the upside of a circle?"

Tomás leaned over, then squatted for a closer look. "Yeah. What is it?"

"That is the toe print of a very soft shoe."

Tomás' eyes flicked up at Nick. "Like a moccasin?"

Nick's gaze climbed up the hillside. "Exactly like a moccasin," he confirmed, eyes searching. He saw trees and grass and leaves, but nothing more. "Almost like they're invisible."

CHAPTER 59

Moccasin Travel

Raiding Trail, *Chiricahua* Mountains, *Chiricahua* Apache Homeland

THE HORSES HAD BECOME a problem. The children crossed the valley in the night, slipping into and out of gullies that concealed their movements, right up to the edge of the canyon leading into the *Chiricahua* Mountains. When the group encountered a hard, black river, the horses spooked at the sound of their own hooves striking the black path. The noise of occasional passing metal wagons intimidated humans and beasts. Twice, children scattered from their mounts and landed hard on the ground, due to the terrifying whoosh of rushing metal wagons passing by and creating gusts of wind.

An hour before dawn the group neared a cluster of ranch buildings tucked into a fold of the mountains. The ranch house, lit front and back by yard lights, sat illuminated in the darkness. The scouts rejoined them and reported the small width of the old raiding trails ahead.

Naadiktaz, It Wiggles, called the *dikohe* together to consider their situation. The children clustered within a grove of mature manzanita bushes and It Wiggles quietly stated the problem. "We move now into the mountains. We must leave the horses behind."

The smaller children lifted questioning faces to the older ones. All of the children liked to pet the velvet of the horses' noses, to trade warm breaths with the large animals, to inhale the rich equine aroma. Each had gathered handfuls of grasses as they walked, scooped withered crabapples from stunted trees, brought branches with mesquite beans to the horses to add to their grazing.

It Wiggles looked around and saw that *Dahsts'aa'*, Strawberry, lead handler, sat staring forlornly at the ground. He knew she loved the horses. The little ones, who often sat comfortably on the warm bare back of a horse while Strawberry checked hooves or brushed away trail dirt from dusty coats, now looked to her for answers. It Wiggles placed a consoling hand on Strawberry's shoulder and she looked up. "I will tell them," she said.

It Wiggles looked on as Strawberry explained to the younger children the necessity of leaving the animals behind. "The horses helped us move quickly," Strawberry said. Her long hair woven into a braid at the beginning of the evening had loosened in the wind. She pulled an errant strand, tucked it behind one ear, and addressed her words to It Wiggles. "They are useful to carry food and small children."

It Wiggles nodded. "And now on these narrow trails they are too big. It will be harder to feed them. Here they can rest after serving us well. We can leave them by the enemy place."

The other *dikohe* nodded in soft agreement. Even Pretty One joined in with a soft "*Ha'ah.*"

Strawberry hung her head. "If they must be left behind, may it be usefully so."

It Wiggles swept one hand toward the packs that had been removed from the horses' backs. "Ready them for carrying on our own backs." He saw Strawberry's shoulders straighten and watched her move off, the smallest children following to where the tired horses waited.

Strawberry rubbed noses, patted flanks, spoke gently to each horse. With the help of the children, she set about repacking bundles for humans to carry. Red One, pulling the last pack from her favorite, a bay, threw her arms around its neck and wept.

Strawberry leaned over the girl and said, "That is not allowed. What will the small ones learn?"

Red One recovered herself, patted the long neck of the bay, and stepped back.

It Wiggles stood nearby, hoping his presence reassured. He held two of the smaller children up to pet the manes of the horses, and to softly lisp their goodbyes to the animals. The horses, spoken to one by one, held their pinnae erect, alert to the children's messages.

The older children shrugged into their packs as the group gathered itself in the dark before the first hint of light in the sky. Little food remained to be carried, by now mostly consumed. His Big Toe led the Blue Mountain People forward on foot as they resumed their journey out of the valley and into the canyons.

It Wiggles and Strawberry held the horses as the line of children passed and waited until certain the children had topped a rise and disappeared from sight. They each jumped to the back of a horse, gathered the reins of the other animals, and led them downhill.

The sun's rim had reached the horizon when they arrived at the fence line of the ranch. A water tank, full to the brim underneath the structure of a windmill and inside a barbed wire fence, attracted the small herd. It Wiggles removed halters as the horses dipped their muzzles into the tank, while Strawberry kept watch all around. A quarter of a mile away the ranch house still appeared to sleep. It Wiggles and Strawberry froze when they heard a dog bark.

They fell to the ground and moved low to a near ditch, taking the halters with them. It Wiggles pulled out a large rock, laid the halters into the earth in case there might be a need to recover them, and placed the rock back. They moved outside the fenced water tank pasture as quickly as they could to put space between themselves and the ranch house.

One of the horses whickered a query after them, but neither child looked back.

The travelers found the trail as mist left the mountains in the full light of early morning.

Two scouts, nine-year-old *Baishan,* Knife, and seven-year-old *Na'iłł'oolé,* Spider, had explored ahead the night before on the path before them, discovered the trail curled along the underside of a cliff, a stream frothing below. Thick brush offered an area of concealment as they'd also discovered enemy houses, one of them close to the trail. When It Wiggles and Strawberry rejoined the group they moved among the children, making the follow sign. One by one, they moved into the brambles and made their way to a grove of stunted oak where they could rest. The children clumped together in silence, staying close to the ground. They waited there as It Wiggles explored the threat of the houses.

He had quietly looped around the closest structure, found no enemy present. He checked the bunched leaves at the base of the doors, within seconds quite certain it held no present occupants. On his return to the children, It Wiggles scanned where they'd rested, found only a few bent grass blades to show anyone had passed. He smiled, pleased with the way the Blue Mountain People left no mark on the earth.

It Wiggles waited as the group gathered silently about him, his heart filled with tenderness for their patience. "Our scouts have seen the path ahead. Watch for the Two Tails!"

The children turned and looked north, but they were still in the lower canyons, with no view of the mountains ahead. An early morning breeze wafted through the leaves of the forest, shaking the earth gently awake. Far off, the children heard human voices.

It Wiggles's head came up listening. "Far off," he noted quietly. "Today we use only warning calls. We will not speak when we leave here." He looked about him and selected eight-year-old *Izee*, Medicine. "We are close to the enemy. What is your warning call?"

The girl answered promptly with a sharp "peep," the sound of a female Arizona woodpecker tending her young.

It Wiggles gave her an approving glance, and turned to the children. "Softly now, each one make your warning sound to another." The manzanita thicket shimmered softly for a moment with the muted sounds of birds, chirping, warbling, tweeting, chocking. All eyes were on It Wiggles as he moved to the front of the group. "*Enjuh*" (It is good). The music stopped.

"We lost a small sister. If you are lost, what will you do, *In'lt'áni?*"

Cricket's husky voice rasped shyly. "I'll find the way to the Land of Standing Up Rocks and look for Blue Mountain People trail sign. If I do not find it, I'll go to the spring called Standing Water. Someone will leave sign there." She looked up from her recitation at It Wiggles's face, trusting she'd given the correct response.

"*Enjuh*. May it be usefully so," It Wiggles confirmed. The group gathered around him replied in a murmur, "*Enjuh*."

He led them carefully to the edge of a stream and they all drank, then filled their gourds. No one splashed another. No one spoke. It Wiggles waited until all had secured their gourds to their belts. He made the follow sign and led them uphill, away from the stream, sending Knife a solid quarter mile forward, watching, listening, moving north; assigning His Big Toe and Left Hand to the rear, brushing footprints from the sand, putting any overturned rocks back in place, ensuring no tracks revealed the group's passage.

The Blue Mountain children walked noiselessly along the trail, their line rippling like a caterpillar between the canyon walls. It Wiggles knew they needed to cover as much territory as they could before the sun rose high. He saw sign from the day before that people had passed. Enemy shoe prints, overlapped by the tracks of dogs, horses, javelina, deer, even coatimundi, marked the path. One print he did not know. A fresh print, a straight line with tracks superimposed over the others, something like a quail, but not a quail, unless it had a very long tail. Puzzled to see so many animal tracks interspersed with human, he pondered the reasons. It seemed like a rich hunting ground. Too rich, he thought. Perhaps hunters walked here. They'd been moving on the trail for only the time it took the morning sun to lighten the canyon tops when Knife, the lead scout, called out a warning in bird song, and the whole group scattered noiselessly behind boulders that balanced along the creek.

Within seconds voices laughed nearby, and the children saw two enemies bumping down the trail, legs churning; boys, not men; unarmed. They sat on metal things that had no head or tail, with two of the round legs that metal wagons had. The enemies, oblivious to the tracks on the path, unaware of the trees, of bushes, of all about them, passed without seeing anything beyond the next few feet before them. Their voices floated back, diminishing even when they yelled in excitement at a rapid downgrade. It Wiggles gave a songbird warble and the group rose from the shadows and returned to the trail. It Wiggles observed the straight line with quail tracks was left by the enemies circling legs. He stared hard, memorizing everything about the marks, and motioned the children forward.

CHAPTER 60

Border Passage

United States/Mexico International Border, Near Hog Crossing Border Patrol Checkpoint, Hidalgo County, New Mexico

IGNACIO REBELLED FROM THE first moment they discussed the topic.

"Very well," Esteban replied. "Every man must decide for himself. For me, I must go."

"I cannot stand the idea of being close to it." Ignacio's voice curled with loathing.

"You suffered as a boy, I understand. But they are my horses and I will have them back." Esteban looked at his son with empathy. "They will not expect anyone so crazy as to cross through cholla." He drove in the nail he'd held back. "And you are not on horseback now."

He watched as Ignacio turned away, seething with anger, stuck in the bad dream of pulling trillions of cholla stickers for months from his legs and arms. Esteban remembered the day well when the boy's horse bumped against a cholla cactus and went mad with pain, throwing his rider into more cholla.

Ellsworth held out two packets. "Perhaps these will help," he said.

Each Garcia took one. Esteban opened his and found a thin poncho made of military desert camo material, tightly woven, light in weight. He ran a hand across it, did not hear even a whisper of sound. He looked at Ellsworth and smiled.

"Bury it under a rock on the other side," Ellsworth rumbled. "You can't reuse it because it may have stickers. But we don't want *La Migra* to know you went through."

"So, these ponchos have worked before?" Ignacio's face lightened.

"You see, things can work out," Ellsworth said, not answering the question. "Now we just wait for dark. We'll pick you up at Ojo de Diablo."

Esteban knew the *tinaja* (The Devil's Eye), a muddy tank in rocks at the base of the Peloncillo Mountains. "*D'accuerdo*" (Agreed), he affirmed.

As dusk descended the four men ate the last burritos from the *colonia* and drank water. Ignacio made no more protests and Garcia father and son slipped the ponchos over their heads. Esteban held his hand out to Ellsworth and Lucero. "See you at the *tinaja, si Dios aprueba*" (if God approves).

"HE will approve, because it is time for justice. And we will get your horses."

"*Si*, Don Rafael." Esteban reached out a hand and shook both Don Rafael's and Lucero's. "At long last the Broncos will be stopped, their raiding and killing ended. The wild ones must be finished. We will do it."

The men's individual features faded in the gathering darkness, and the two walkers, shapeless in their ponchos, walked away toward the border. The SUV slowly moved back to the highway, no lights, its motor a low mechanical murmur broken by the hills.

The high desert returned to silence.

CHAPTER 61

Almost Home

The Raiding Path, *Chiricahua* Mountains, *Chiricahua* Apache Homeland

NAADIKTAZ, IT WIGGLES, KNEW it had to happen sometime. The Blue Mountain People had crossed the path safely, but they'd been seen. *Dahsts'aa'*, Strawberry, changing off with Knife and others to lead the line of children, could not be faulted. He'd watched her check the trail for threats. She'd sent scouts in the four directions. All returned with no warnings of danger. Sometimes, It Wiggles knew, things could not be predicted.

Now, as he brought up the tail of the group, helping *Bikécho*, His Big Toe sweep for sign, It Wiggles found himself caught in the unexpected arrival of strangers. He quickly dropped and draped himself on his stomach along the uneven and shadowed points where boulders tangled with trees high up on the side of a hill. He knew his body line lay concealed in shadows so long as he kept still, and he watched the two men below examine the path.

It Wiggles saw the tallest one had a stiff leg. Vulnerable. Slow. *Enjuh* (Good), he thought. Above him from the top of the hill, hidden in the timber, he heard a query in the voice of a redstart. His Big Toe evidently could not see him and wanted reassurance. Any noise at all would bring attention to It Wiggles's hiding place, and he did not respond.

The stiff-legged enemy below heard the redstart, too. It Wiggles watched him scan the mountain side. He thought of the way a jaguar in the Blue Mountains blends into shadow and light, unseen until it moves. He tried to lay without even breathing, just a shadow of stillness against stones and leaves, trees and brush. He watched the enemy's dark eyes sweep across him.

The redstart called again, insistent. Down below, the men both sought the bird's location, apparently saw nothing. It Wiggles remained frozen so that his left foot, hooked into a dead tree notch, grew numb. He wondered if he could run away, if necessary; he tried bending his toes, but only when the men below looked elsewhere.

Finally, the two men mounted their mule and moved along the path. It Wiggles waited until certain they'd traveled away. When he unclamped his foot from the tree fork, he dragged the branch a bit downhill, starting a roll of pebbles and leaves that rattled into the silence. A light puff of dust rose in the air. Startling himself, he jumped to his feet, found purchase on the slant of the hill, all the time looking north along the path after the men.

The redstart warbled once more, and this time It Wiggles warbled back. He moved away from his hiding place, stepped carefully uphill, brushing his tracks with a leafy branch, leaving no indication of his passing. His foot stung as it came awake from its sleep. It felt as if he'd stepped into a red ant hill before he reached the top. There His Big Toe materialized and slid in behind him. They exchanged no words. They both knew the way now. On top of the hill the view of the mountain range opened up.

Far in the distance ahead, along the extended line of a purple ridged mountain, It Wiggles recognized a geographic marker: Two Tails. Excitement pulsed through his body, and he reached out to include His Big Toe in the moment. But His Big Toe had moved soundlessly away from him, exploring the forest floor for any sign left by the Blue Mountain People. It Wiggles waited until His Big Toe looked up, and motioned at the mountain. The expression on the face of his lieutenant brightened, and the two boys exchanged a triumphant moment of silent glee.

It Wiggles felt relief he'd not been discovered by the stiff-legged man. Since leaving the Blue Mountains his days had become heavy with the burden of guiding the children safely to the homeland. The increased pressure of travel in enemy places had convinced him it might become impossible to remain invisible. Yet, he thought, he'd watched the stiff-legged man examine the hillside without seeing him, hidden in plain sight.

Pleased and reassured, he examined the trail markings the *dikohe* Knife had used. He understood now the children could succeed in reaching their destination, with or without him. They knew their skills. Now, he thought, if we can find *Biyoo'*, Her Beads, all will be well. And *Gidi*, Cat. He could not stop worrying about Cat.

When the children found their way blocked from following the ancient trail, they'd been forced away from the mountain spring on the slopes of Prairie Dogs' Home Mountain. The alternate route, the one called They Go Raiding Quickly, would get them to the same place at the end of the mountain range where Two Tails rose.

It Wiggles and His Big Toe found the children resting among the rocks, mostly asleep, as they waited out the afternoon for the cover of night. One expelled a slumbering mew, and It Wiggles curled his own body protectively around him. Sleep came quickly, although the sting of a pebble a half hour later against It Wiggles's back brought him instantly onto his feet in a crouch. Behind him Knife and His Big Toe pointed with their lips up the hillside.

It Wiggles felt it before he heard it, a slight tremble in the earth, recognized the feel and sound of human movement on the land. Birds called, passed their message from one throat to the next, warned the forest that intruders approached. It Wiggles signaled to the boys behind him to take shelter.

Just under the ridge line above, two men picked their way along a deer trail slanting down the hill side. *Nakaiyé*, Those Who Walk. The men hurried, made too much noise in the broken-voice language of the enemy. It Wiggles saw the men, both unaware of their own noise and surroundings, kick small stones and dirt that rolled down as they passed. He wondered at their ignorance in making noise in the quiet of the forested hills.

Once the *Nakaiyé* continued out of sight, It Wiggles signaled His Big Toe to check where the walkers came from, and Knife to see where they headed. He sat on his haunches and patiently watched the light fade as the sun began its afternoon descent behind the ridgeline. The boys returned from their scout as shadows in the dull late afternoon light.

Knife reported, "It is not far to the bottom of a canyon in the next valley. It has a small river. They walked north on the west side of the river."

His Big Toe nodded at Knife in agreement. "Two ridges above, there is a well-used path, the same way we are traveling, I think the ancestors' raiding path. It climbs up above the canyons and I could see that small river below."

The three considered their combined information.

A slow smile spread across It Wiggles's face. "We've found the trail called They Go Raiding Quickly."

The boys' faces, drawn with weariness, relaxed for a moment. Their eyes brightened as they realized they now traveled in the home territory of the ancestors.

CHAPTER 62

Chuck You Farley

Loreto Ranch, West Side *Chiricahua* Mountains, *Cochise* County, Arizona

LUCY COULD HEAR BIRDS overhead as the Loreto Ranch came into view in the canyon below.

She looked up, impressed with the circling flocks. She'd walked several hours, gulped hard at the dry air, and thought of her canteen dangling from her horse's pommel as it thundered away.

Far below she saw a man exit the barn and stride across the ranch yard toward the house. The figure, tiny in the distance, paused and looked at the cloud of shrieking birds, then up the trail. Lucy jumped up and down, waving, sure it must be Mr. Loreto. She knew he'd help her.

But he didn't see her. Too late she understood her figure went unseen in deep shade, too far away. He tipped his cowboy hat up looking to the top of the ridge and the noisy birds. She raised her hand to her mouth, placed two fingers between her lips, just like Tomás had taught her, and whistled. But it fizzled. She held her mouth open, her tongue so dry it felt like an emery board. Meanwhile Mr. Loreto turned and continued across the yard. "Fzzzt," she tried again.

Exasperated, she moved into a stumbling trot, mumbling under her breath. She knew all the cowboy cuss words, but never dreamed of using one. Instead, she reverted to an expression currently in vogue in her middle school. She opened her mouth and yelled with all her might.

"Chuck You Farley!"

For a moment she was shocked she'd said it, and clamped her hand over her mouth, exactly what Tia Elena would do if she said such a thing in her presence. Desperate to contact the man below, Lucy screeched it a second time and tripped because she'd begun to run. She managed to point herself toward the inside of the canyon wall, but scraped an arm against the rocky wall as she hurried, raising blood. By the time the path lost its altitude and flattened, she had run out of breath and slowed, covered in dust and blood transferred unknowingly from her arm to her face.

She heard an engine start up. Lucy's voice swelled into a cry both loud and alarmed as she ran around a corner of the ranch house in time to see a pickup truck disappear down the road. She whooped but the truck kept going. Chest heaving, she stopped forlornly, hands clenched, as she watched the truck weave around the side of a hill and fade into the trees.

"Now what am I supposed to do?" she demanded of the barn and surroundings. Done with middle school curses, she slumped to the ground next to the corral, sobbing.

The silence spread out around her. Even the cloud of birds dissipated.

She heard the clump of plodding hooves and looked up to see her horse, unsaddled and already curried, exit the open barn into the corral. Tears coursed down her cheeks as she extended a hand toward her horse. It placed its muzzle into her hand through the corral poles and whickered in greeting.

Behind her a door slammed and she turned to see a familiar form on the kitchen steps.

"What's going on out here?" a voice called.

Lucy's breath caught in a hiccup of emotion. Looking like a whirlwind of dust, Lucy ran for Belen and threw herself into the safety of her neighbor's arms.

CHAPTER 63

The Trouble with Cholla

United States/Mexico International Border, at Hog Crossing Border Station, Hidalgo County, New Mexico

ALL WENT SMOOTHLY UNTIL father and son reached the last few steps at the border fence. Ignacio's right foot landed on an uneven rock throwing him off balance. His body automatically corrected by moving just one step left, brushing him against a cluster of cholla buds with one poncho covered shoulder. The bud flipped off the cactus against the poncho but bounced across to his nose, where it hung. The tiny cactus needle barbs dug in.

Ignacio swiped the bud from his face which then stuck to his hand. He yelped in real pain, waving the impaled hand and flicking it about, but the bud did not shake away. Esteban hissed for silence. Reacting blindly, Ignacio searched for anywhere to wipe his hand and free it of the cholla bud. He ended by swiping it against his father's poncho which hurt his hand so much he no longer knew or cared about noise. Esteban, surprised at the rapid deterioration of their situation, attempted to flick the bud from his own poncho but instead managed only to dust the back of his neck with tines that somehow also settled on his face. The two men bristled with stickers, the initial whole bud returning in the chaos to Ignacio's hand.

Ignacio cursed, breathing hard. "I told you," he seethed, teeth clenched, "I told you!"

Esteban said nothing, went back to finding his way to the fence, and used one foot to hold down the lower of the wire strands so his son could climb through to the U.S. side.

Ignacio, feeling each sticker as if it were a knife point, panted in pain when he crawled between the fence strands held open by Esteban.

Entry onto the U.S. side proved to be a hollow victory. They blundered a short way to the dirt road, where the condition of Ignacio's hand, face, and legs ("How did they get on my legs?" he said pitifully) overcame him. His curses increased in intensity and volume.

Esteban said nothing. A lifetime of ranching in the Sierra Madres had taught him silent suffering. He ignored the pain, focused on his purpose. He wanted his horses.

Esteban instructed Ignacio to take off his poncho, an excruciating but necessary maneuver. The two moved toward a jumble of rocks where they ditched the ponchos together under several small boulders. The bending and moving managed to transfer tines into their clothing, and soon both found themselves limping along the dirt border track, keeping a look out for *La Migra* (Border Patrol). Every movement, every step caused the scattering of cholla needles to dig into their flesh, an infinite torture.

A short hike along the border dirt road of less than a mile felt like a hundred before they reached a deserted two-way road, empty in the night. Even in the dark, Esteban could feel himself under the bulk of hills leading into mountains he knew were there: the Peloncillos. But they didn't make it to the meet-up place with Ellsworth and Lucero at Devil's Eye Spring. Each focused on his own pain so entirely that neither heard the approaching crunch of wheels behind them. When the vehicle flicked its lights on, both father and son stiffly turned like old men, blinded by the headlights of the Border Patrol.

CHAPTER 64

San Enebro Emergency

United States/Mexico International Border, Hidalgo County, New Mexico

BENNY CORTEZ, BEHIND THE wheel of the Border Patrol van, pulled over to the side of the road, flipped on bright lights that lit up two men. He played the spotlights at and around them, puzzled at the way the men kept moving.

His partner saw it too. "What's wrong with them? Why they moving like that?" Fuentes grabbed the van's mic and his voice reverberated against the rocky terrain, making his words rattle together. "BORDER PATROL." Benny stopped, pushed the button to lower his window and yelled out, "*¡Patrulla Fronteriza. Las manos por encima de la cabeza!*" (Hands above your heads!)

The men seemed to try to follow instructions, but neither could hold their arms up long, and they wouldn't keep still.

Fuentes left the van's cab ready to draw his weapon. He ordered them to separate farther apart and face away as he neared. He reached behind for handcuffs as he approached them, suddenly stopped and backed up. "Shit." He returned to the driver's side of the vehicle where Cortez waited. "No way I'm getting close enough to cuff those guys."

Cortez's spotlight beamed on the men in a way that parodied a stage performance. Their raised arms quivered, their faces glistened. They kept moving. Virtually dusted in cholla needles

345

and spines, they looked as if painted with glimmering highlights.

Cortez exited the truck. *"Entonces, ¿qué pasó con ustedes?"* (So, what happened to you?)

Ignacio ground his teeth. Managed to say, "Cholla."

Esteban complained, *"'Stamos buscando nuestros caballos que fueron robados dos noches atrás"* (We're looking for our horses that were stolen two nights ago).

Cortez and Fuentes exchanged a look.

"¿Cuántos caballos, hombre?" (How many horses, man?)

Benny moved to the back of the van and opened the double doors.

"Seis" (Six). Esteban was ready to describe each one.

The faces of the two Border Patrol officers tightened.

Benny spoke to the older man, the calm one. *"Los caballos entraron en la cholla?"* (The horses went into the cholla?)

"Pues, no sé" (I don't know). The older man shrugged, his words muffled through clenched teeth. *"Los seguimos hasta aquí"* (We followed them to here).

The Garcias kept moving in place, their bodies quivering with the pain of thousands of cholla barbs.

"¿Quién los robó?" (Who stole them?)

"No sé, pero creo que ... los Indios" (I don't know, but I think . . . Indians). Esteban's statement was delivered in a straightforward way. He clenched his teeth and clamped his jaws together in determination. He held his hands out from his body, tried not to let them shake.

Cortez and Fuentes stared at him. *"¿Indios?"*

"Si, los Broncos del Sierra Madre."

"What's he talking about?" Juan asked his partner. "The wild ones from the Sierra Madre. Who's that?"

Cortez circled them, using his flashlight. "Not sure, but I think we saw their horses the other night."

"The horses that ran through the checkpoint?"

Cortez nodded. "Let's get these guys into San Enebro

Emergency. You ever get cholla stuck on you?" Benny noticed the young guy with sticker-covered cheeks glared in fury at him when he named the cactus.

Juan hunched his neck. "Thank God, no." He stood alert, watched the men, shook his head. He motioned them toward the back of the open van. "*Caballeros*, move very carefully to the back of the van. Nice and slow."

The injured men hobbled to the rear, gingerly pulled themselves inside.

Cortez drove the van as gently as possible into San Enebro. Moans and protests from the back of the van punctuated the drive. When the van hit a bump in the road or turned a curve too sharply, the volume increased and Cortez slowed to accommodate his human cargo. Light edged the horizon when the van finally pulled into the hospital entrance and rolled to a stop in front of the emergency entrance.

After the patrol van stopped Fuentes flung the rear doors wide open and backed away.

Esteban wavered for a moment before scooting himself out. The spines in his clothing found new places to latch into skin at his every motion. Barbs already piercing the skin broke off and dug in deeper. Ignacio crept out sucking air through his teeth, tears running from his eyes.

Cortez and Fuentes kept their distance, shooed the men forward through the automatic emergency doors. The detainees hovered inside the door, arms raised stiffly forward, as staff mobilized without getting too close. An orderly pushing a wheelchair forward called to Cortez, "Where'd you find the zombies?" He stopped and backed away when the shambling men got close.

A triage doctor arrived almost immediately. "What on earth have you brought in?" he asked.

"An example," Cortez said, "of who wins in a fight with cholla."

Within a few minutes Benny watched the doctor begin to remove cholla spines. The doctor hovered intently above a microscope, selecting an inch of skin on the back of Esteban's hand to clear the barbs. Esteban sucked in his cheeks and blew out air as the doctor plunged his tweezers down, gripped and tore out a single, shiny spine. Tough old guy, Benny thought.

"How do you get all those stickers out?" Cortez asked.

"Never really do," the doctor said, "These spiny little hairs? We call 'em glochids. Eventually they'll dissolve into the body." He sat up straight for a moment to rest his back. "Usually within six weeks."

Esteban, face taut with strain, flinched. He understood enough English to follow the doctor's words. Beads of sweat ran down from his hairline.

The doctor pushed his stool back, bent his neck with a pop each way and looked at Cortez. "What happened? How did these guys walk into cholla?"

Cortez shifted his standing posture, setting every piece of equipment on his uniform to jingling. "'Course it was night and dark. He said somebody stole his horses and they were trying to get them back."

The doctor nodded. "Hog Crossing's been busy this week. Didn't you bring in that kid with a broken leg?"

"Yeah, my partner and I found her. How's she doing?" Benny remembered how solemn the child had been on the ambulance ride to the hospital.

"Leg's set. Clean break."

Cortez saw Esteban show interest at the mention of horses, wondered how much English he knew, raised his eyebrows. *"Pregunta?"* (Question?), he asked.

"Sí," he responded in Spanish, "has anyone found our horses? We lost six. One buckskin, one black, four bays."

Cortez shook his head no.

Esteban nodded philosophically. *"Tengo sed."*

Cortez turned, reached for a cup and straw, only to be elbowed away by the doctor.

"Not yet. First, we examine and clear hands, eyes, lips, mouths, noses, and clear away every single glochid we can." He frowned as he returned to his careful tweezing. "Seriously. Life threatening. Best scene scenario is a bad case of dermatitis. Worst scene, no kidding, blindness if it's in the eyes; even death, if barbs lodge in the throat."

Cortez's eyebrows looped over his eyes. He brought up both hands in front of his chest, explained to Esteban why he must wait.

"We'll be tweezing for another hour or two at least, then we'll wrap all punctured skin in gauze, soak it in white glue, and let it dry and..." The doctor looked at his patient. "...rip it off." The doctor tried to gauge his patient's pain tolerance, amazed at the man's stoic endurance.

Benny watched from six feet away, a little nauseated. "Maybe you should check me out."

The doctor paused, ran his eyes over Benny's face and arms, saw no glochids and raised his eyebrows in question.

"Oh no, I don't have any of the cholla on me," Benny said, "but this is all starting to make me feel sick."

By noon, Esteban and Ignacio had been tweezed, glued, the remaining glochids ripped from their skin. Spine-filled clothing, even boots (much lamented by Ignacio who'd worn his favorite hand-tooled pair) disappeared into ashes in the hospital incinerator. The men waited in their backless hospital gowns, their suffering tamped down by intravenously administered drugs. Finally, the doctor approved food and drink, assigned them to a one-night stay for observation.

Glumly, Cortez informed Fuentes they were stuck on duty until their supervisor could find someone to take their place. "He mentioned they've got a big operation going down. Oh well, it'll be overtime."

In the secure hall of the hospital, Ignacio slept, exhausted.

Esteban stared off into space, gnawed at the inside of his cheek.

Cortez glanced at Esteban, thought of the sound when the glued gauze ripped the glochids from the man's face, and winced in empathy. Cortez wondered what ran through Esteban's mind during the procedure, as his manner continued calm and uncomplaining. Cortez doubted he himself could have remained silent.

Cortez would have been surprised to learn Esteban had ignored everything between himself and the world as he and his son endured their cholla encounter. In fact, Esteban's entire conscious being consisted of but one thought running constantly across his brain like a movie house neon ribbon sign that repeated over and over: "I want my horses. I want my horses."

HOME IS IN THE HEART

CHAPTER 65

Off the Raiding Path

Land of Standing Up Rocks, *Chiricahua* Mountains, *Chiricahua* Apache Homeland

WHEN THE SCOUTS REPORTED the path They Go Raiding Quickly had been recently traveled by heavily laden people on foot, *Naadiktaz,* It Wiggles, ordered the children off the trail. *Bikécho,* His Big Toe, moved into advance position, swung the group to the west wall of the canyon. He located a game trail, signaled the others to wait, while he scrambled up the cleft created by a fissure in the cliff side. On top of the ridge he surveyed the surroundings, recognized the height placed him well above sight from the trail. Again, seeing the Two Tails in the distance heartened him.

He returned to the edge of the crack and tossed a pebble down. Soon the children, each small one helped by an older one, crawled up and onto the higher ground. The children moved directly outward to watch for trouble as the rest of the group followed. Each team of children discovered the Two Tails and silent smiles bloomed throughout the maneuver.

It Wiggles counted heads, feeling sad his Blue Mountain People amounted to so few. He felt sure they would find *Biyoo',* Her Beads, but wondered once again if *Gidi,* Cat, was forever lost. He must trust in their abilities. He must trust *Ussen* to protect them.

It Wiggles nodded to His Big Toe to send the scouts forward. The group moved ahead silently.

A solid afternoon of walking, snaking through narrow jumbles of rocks just under the edge of ridges, sometimes reverting to carrying smaller children through difficult terrain, until the scouts reported voices ahead. It Wiggles made the stay sign, flat palm pushed down, and crept forward carefully to a ridge that opened into a narrow park. Trees, surrounded by scattered pine cones framed a small meadow. It Wiggles heard voices bouncing against the rock walls of the canyon and saw a cut-off path emerge from the lower old raiding trail. He lay behind cover while surveying the area and watched as an enemy appeared and ascended a path that stretched across the meadow.

The man, who peered ahead at the trunk of a tree, suddenly stopped, gestured emphatically with one hand, staring at something It Wiggles could not see. As the man pushed his arm in a "go away" gesture, a girl emerged from the shade.

It Wiggles heart pumped hard. The dark-haired girl stood about the size of *Her Beads*. It took only a moment more to discern her as an enemy stranger, and he heard her call out one word.

It Wiggles saw the enemy man place one hand over his mouth, a gesture warning silence, and signaled to the girl to quickly leave the meadow. Then from the canyon an angry voice erupted and a horse squealed in terror.

It Wiggles had frozen at the animal's scream, could still hear voices below, and did not move. The enemy man and girl shared a wide-eyed glance. Suddenly the girl burst into full speed and ran from the clearing as if chased by spirits, while the man turned away and hurried down the path to the trail below.

It Wiggles lay and listened to the sounds over the edge of the cliff. Enemy voices, loud and angry; words he could not understand. The sound of a horse snorting, neighing, and men yelling, alerted him to trouble. The babble increased and he knew he must keep the children away from an encounter with these people. In his head he traced his mind map toward the Land of Standing Up Rocks. If they could stay on the mountains' backbone, perhaps they could avoid trouble on the trail.

It Wiggles approached the canyon rim and peered over the cliff edge into the canyon where the trail They Go Raiding Quickly wound along the canyon wall. He saw only one nervous horse stamping and blowing through wide nostrils. An enemy man was trying to calm the horse. Other enemies stood along the trail's edge, peering down, talking in excited words. It Wiggles recognized the language of the broken-voiced people. He noted the backpacks left along the cliff wall and knew they carried packs of bad medicine. Dismayed at the enemies' activity, he withdrew to the meadow and followed the girl's footprints to the edge of the forest. He studied the ground and area intently, returned along the meadow opposite the canyon, and crept back to where the Blue Mountain People waited.

"There is a path that leads north to Water Standing. It will take us on the ridge above the enemy who occupy the raiding path. Enemies are near, stay invisible," he told them.

It Wiggles saw the eyes of the children brighten. He took the lead, kept the Blue Mountain People to the west edge of the meadow in the shadows of dark trees. Noises from the east side of the meadow wafted their way, but the bedlam had ended and what they heard were single voices calling back and forth. When the dozen children reached the alternate trail, he pointed them forward, sending his apprentices hurrying ahead, intent on finding water before dusk. Their supplies used up, they all watched for trail food that might be gathered along the way; nuts, roots, berries, small animals. He lagged behind, watching the tail of their group, guarding against discovery by the enemy. His stomach rumbled as the afternoon waned. They must find their relatives soon. But before that, they must find food enough to keep them strong.

As they followed the ridge path, he noted the fresh tracks of another walker with hard-edged shoes. Enemy tracks. It must be the girl he'd seen rush away from the man above the raiding trail. He knew His Big Toe must see the tracks as well, and would not be tricked. The sun had passed overhead when he saw the single set of tracks diverge to descend into a valley on the west side of the mountains. Far below he made out a solitary figure rounding a curve, and thought, one more enemy avoided.

It made their discovery all the more a surprise when they found themselves, sometimes on game trails above the raiding path, sometimes walking with no path through brush, finally approaching an area even the youngest could recognize. Identifying the Land of Standing Up Rocks came naturally. So taken with the scenery of their ancestors' unmistakable homeland, the group gazed onto a lower plateau, saw the glint of stopped metal wagons, and people the size of ants in the distance, missed seeing an approaching figure on the path ahead.

It Wiggles made the call of a roadrunner, their group danger alert. The Blue Mountain People understood they must disappear immediately. Put to flight, the children flung themselves into cover and disappeared.

At that moment a voice rang out. An *Indah,* a Pale Eye, a man with a small, square, black four-sided stone in his hand, stood down the slope where canyons, covered with scattered standing stones, reached tall into the sky. The man's voice called out a second time, and he held the black four-sided stone before his eyes. The Blue Mountain People waited.

It Wiggles could not believe they'd been discovered. Last in line, he looked back to see the *Indah* puffing as he sprinted uphill to reach them. His mind automatically registered the man had no obvious weapon except for the black stone. *Enjuh* (Good), he thought. Easier to kill if I must. He'd reached a point where he could easily disappear into the rocks, looked back, saw the man leaning with hands on knees, winded. It Wiggles slipped away before the man raised his head again.

As he continued forward It Wiggles assembled the children one by one. They put space between themselves and the Land of Standing Up Rocks, not stopping to rest until they located a shaded dell where a lookout could be kept all around. Examining the children slumped against and behind rocks he thought of what he could say. Fatigue and hunger showed clearly on their faces.

"*Ussen* protects us. You have come a long way and you have done well. Soon we will rest." He looked at Pretty One who understood his silent inquiry for remaining food. She formed the word *"Dah"* (No), on her lips without speaking aloud. It Wiggles looked at the group of children. "Let us share what we have found this day. The nuts will be our meat. Sweet berries will color our tongues. We are in our people's mountains. Who can tell me where to find water?"

Seven-year-old *Na'iłtł'oolé*, Spider, raised his chin. "Younger brother, speak," It Wiggles said.

Spider kept his voice low, said softly, "At Water Standing."

"And so it is," It Wiggles said. "How far until we drink our fill?"

Spider thought, then said, "If we walk fast, we can drink before darkness comes." He cast his eyes on the ground, hoping his mind map was correct.

"It is as if you have always been here in our people's homeland," It Wiggles said and Spider glowed with pleasure.

CHAPTER 66

Shortcut to Help

Rucker Canyon, *Chiricahua* Mountains, *Cochise* County, Arizona

NICK SAW THE TWO men moving across the mountain and thought they might have been the same ones who carried him on Vicente's orders into the cliff dwelling. Rough looking men in a hurry to get somewhere, but where, he wondered, and why? Dealing with Vicente, the kidnapping of the girl, the strange group of kids that crossed their path, had all rolled into one threat too many, and now these guys.

"It's getting crowded around here," he said softly to his cousin.

Tomás agreed.

"We gotta find help fast. Everybody seems to be moving toward Loreto's. Maybe we should try the opposite. It's kind of straight down the mountain to Rucker Canyon Road, but I'm up for it if you are."

Tomás nodded. "Let's do it."

For the second time since losing the girl, Nick needed help to mount Larry. Larry's height stopped him from using just his forearms to spring on to the mule's back. He couldn't get his frozen leg far enough out to use a pendulum motion upward. Tomás again joined his hands into a step and lifted Nick onto the mule's back. Nick's unbendable leg stuck out at an odd angle off the left side of the mule.

Nick looked down at the ground. "Long way down. I don't think the leg engineer ever thought about riding a mule. I can see it's just one bump away from hitting against a tree trunk and I'll end up taking a nose dive five feet off Larry."

Tomás looked around. "Hate to mention it, Nick, but we're surrounded by trees. Hang on."

Nick kept Larry still as Tomás swung up and looped his arms around his cousin's middle.

Nick pressed himself forward to give Tomás as much room as possible, allowed Tomás a moment to settle, then clicked his tongue. The mule responded with a slow start up and plodded forward.

"At this rate we'll hit Rucker Canyon Road by midnight. I'm gonna ask Larry for a little speed." Nick gathered the reins tighter. "Ready?"

Tomás kept one hand around Nick's waist, and his other hand flat against the mule's back, ready to grab at anything for balance. "Do it."

Nick urged Larry into a trot. Tomás slid to one side, hung midair for a breathless moment off the mule's croup, balanced himself quickly by shifting his weight, and re-clamped his thighs around Larry's barrel. Larry eased into a smooth lope, and they moved swiftly forward.

CHAPTER 67

Hot Tips

Border Patrol Regional Headquarters, Douglas, *Cochise* County, Arizona

THE DOUGLAS OFFICE OF the Border Patrol received two messages within minutes of one another, one by landline telephone, the other by radio. The first, via the *Cochise* County Sheriff's Station, came from a rancher at the base of the *Chiricahuas.*

"Just found a half dozen horses in my west fenced pasture. You have any complaints somebody lost some horses? They weren't there last night, but they sure helped themselves to my best meadow grass. Like to find the S.O.B. left 'em without letting me know. No brand. Two v-cuts on top of each left ear." The rancher's voice fumed with the anger of one who'd suffered the indignities of his unthinking fellow man. "It's not like you can't see the ranch house from the field. If they wanted help, they should've asked."

Dispatch responded, "No reports. I'll let the county vet know. May take a few days to run down the owners. Stop and file a complaint so we can make it official."

The second message arrived by radio from a ranger at the *Chiricahua* National Monument. The ranger described a tourist's report about sighting a group of wild Indians.

Dispatch managed to contain herself and not laugh aloud.

"What made your tourist think they were seeing wild Indians? Over."

Long pause. "Tourist said they wore moccasins and looked like an episode from that old serial *Gunsmoke*. At least ten of 'em. He swears he took a photo but it didn't turn out. Over."

Dispatch swallowed a guffaw. "Ten Little Indians, huh? Anything else? Over."

"He says the Indians ran like crazy when they saw him. He was taking photos of the hoodoos at the highest point in the park, and they hid in the rocks. Said they took off fast and he couldn't keep up. Says they had gear strapped on 'em. Over."

Dispatch thought of the steep paths at the top of the monument, the rocky pathways that slipped under the foot, skidding hikers into sometimes perilous situations, the scattered boulders that made it difficult to see directions, deep canyons with sheer drop-offs, rough surroundings. "He tried to follow them? Why? That's awful rugged backcountry. Over."

"He said he thought they might be lost and he's worried. Over."

Dispatch snorted. "I'll bite. Why does he think they're lost? Over."

"They were kids, he says; some of 'em little. Over."

Second long pause. "Any school groups in the monument? Over."

The radio crackled. "Negative." More crackling. "Far as we know, but they don't always check in here first. Over."

Dispatch took a swig of coffee, found it cold, grimaced. The report went into the basket, the information ready for distribution at afternoon roll call.

CHAPTER 68

Taking Care of Business

Mercy Regional Hospital, San Enebro, Hidalgo County, New Mexico

MID-AFTERNOON AND CORTEZ STILL sat in the hospital's security corridor, waiting for Fuentes to relieve him. Juan had probably found a cot somewhere to sleep, he thought, feeling his own gathering fatigue of what had become a twenty-four-hour day. He began to dream of something hot to eat, something cold to drink, a soft pillow to rest. The elevator opened and a familiar voice addressed him.

"Benny!" the voice called out.

Cortez looked up to see Rafael Ellsworth and a man dressed like a vaquero he knew as Rafael's foreman. He stood up, put out his hand. "Well, where'd you come from?"

Cortez had known Ellsworth for a decade as a *Chihuahua* rancher of fundamentalist heritage from a big spread on the east side of the Sierra Madre. The rancher had worked closely with Border Patrol on numerous occasions. He traveled frequently between the two countries, usually trips associated with cattle and horse sales. He was rumored to have eight or nine wives, a topic discussed often on long duty nights among the border officers.

Ellsworth grinned broadly, shook the extended hand. "You know Lucero, right? Missed you last night when we came through

Hogs' Crossing." He ran a hand from his forehead over the crown of his head, leaving a chunk of red hair standing straight up.

"I was on fence duty last night," Cortez said, smiling.

"What're you doing here?"

Cortez stretched his back. "Mostly waiting for somebody to relieve me." He jerked a thumb behind him. "Picked up two guys from a cholla patch before light this morning. They're under detention 'til we figure out their situation."

Ellsworth and Lucero exchanged a guarded look that Cortez could not decipher.

"Wait!" Ellsworth said, "Is that the Garcias? Esteban and Ignacio?"

"Yeah?" Cortez looked quizzically at Ellsworth.

"They okay?"

Cortez laughed. "They'll live alright, but they got a hell of a story explaining themselves." Cortez slapped a friendly arm around Ellsworth's shoulders. "The human pincushions are your people?"

Ellsworth's eyebrows went up. He had not risen to leadership of his *colonia* without being fast on his feet. "Yeah. We all started out together."

"They say they were chasing stolen horses." Cortez watched Ellsworth's face.

"True enough."

"And...?"

Ellsworth cleared his throat. "Didn't find them. Yet. Yeah, we're all together. They turned up two days ago asking for help to track some stolen horses. Thieves raided their place, took all six horses, stole some supplies. The four of us followed the trail from the Sierra Madres to Enmedios yesterday. The thieves are good. Really moved the horses right along; running them 'cross country, no less. No vehicles. Last night we put the Garcias on foot to try and figure where the horses went across the border.

They didn't have papers anyway. But Lucero and I did and we came onto the U.S. side, trying to find horse tracks. We thought we'd be able to talk over the fence, but they weren't there. So, we came into town, stopped at the Border Patrol office and heard a couple of illegals were picked up and taken to the hospital. We're here, seeing if it's our guys." He stood shaking his head. "And I guess they are."

Cortez would not have believed the story from anyone else, but from Rafael Ellsworth it made sense. Still, it didn't explain how the guys ended up on the wrong side of the fence.

"C'mon, Rafael. What got 'em to our side of the fence?"

"Maybe pain, Benny." Ellsworth's tone went sarcastic. "Maybe they were looking for help. What'd they say?"

"They said Indians stole their horses." Cortez laughed. "Tell me that's true!"

"That," Ellsworth replied, looking up and beyond Cortez's shoulder, "I do not know. What I do know is we've tracked a half dozen stolen horses for the last two days that belong to my good neighbors, the Garcias, from near Nacori Chico in Sonora."

"And . . . what's with the Indians?"

"Oh, you know the old stories," Ellsworth said. "You seen any Indians lately?"

Cortez laughed. "The only border crossers I've seen in the last week are your two pincushions," and he raised his eyebrows. "'Course if they were really chasing horses, that shouldn't be hard to settle. Oh, and that little kid," and his voice slowed down while he thought. "Nah, she's just a little thing. Little odd, but she couldn't be anybody you tracked."

"What about a kid? How little is she? What do you mean, odd?" Ellsworth asked.

Cortez looked at him curiously. "Odd that she didn't like Popsicles and we had to bring her in with a broken leg. Me and Fuentes picked her up at the border." He paused, remembering the sequence of events when they found the little girl. "I guess it's possible she could have got there on a horse, because we had a few spooked ones, a good half dozen, raced across."

"Half dozen, huh? 'Cause that's what we're looking for." Rafael Ellsworth sighed. "But I don't know what a kid might have to do with it all. Probably unconnected."

Cortez shrugged. "We have occasional coyotes or javelinas cross, once in a while some livestock; but this was a first for horses. And definitely a first for a little kid all on her own." His voice trickled out to silence as he thought. "She did have some funny shoes." He thought some more. "She never said a word to anyone. No English. No Spanish. You think she might be connected?" Cortez noted Ellsworth flinched.

Ellsworth moved his cowboy hat from one hand to the other. "Don't see how," and he sighed. "So where does that leave the Garcias? I'll vouch for them. They're good mountain ranchers from the Sonora side, just trying to get back their horses."

"Rafael, they're already in the chute. But it shouldn't be too hard to straighten it out once the doctor releases them. You'll vouch for them?"

Ellsworth nodded yes, hands on his hips.

"Okay, let me see what we can work out," Benny said.

"Good. That's a relief," Ellsworth said in a conversational tone. He added, "We were afraid they'd gotten lost in the desert." Ellsworth changed his stance and stretched his shoulders, asked casually, "What happened to the kid? Where'd she end up?"

Cortez noted his acquaintance might be trying a little too hard not to seem interested. But this was Rafael Ellsworth, respectable rancher. What could he possibly want with a little kid who didn't seem to speak English or Spanish? No harm at all, he thought to himself, then replied, "Last time I knew, upstairs in the children's ward."

CHAPTER 69

Keeping the Family Together

Mercy Regional Hospital, San Enebro,
Hidalgo County, New Mexico

SAM CHARLEY WAS ABOUT to leave Lydia Castillo's third floor office. They'd called Albert who officially confirmed Sam's authority. They had just spent a half hour with Sam's signing his name as a member of the Mescalero Tribal Council on behalf of the hospitalized child, verifying her as a Mescalero, and releasing her to his custody.

"Ignorant as all get out about the history of right where she sat," Sam thought, "or of anything to do about Apache. Just like the rest of the world."

The social worker had required his signature on approximately every page of what must have amounted to a full ream of paper. Sheaf of papers in hand, he muttered profanities under his breath he'd not thought of in years. Now all he had to do was get the doctor's signature on the medical release.

Sam thanked her and turned to leave at the same moment the phone rang. "Thanks again!" he said as he stepped into the hall.

Hands full, Lydia clumsily punched the speaker button, and Sam heard her say, "Lydia Castillo."

A voice identified itself. "Front Desk. A gentleman is here requesting access to a hospital patient." Sam held the door from closing, and listened as Lydia asked, "Why is the visitor asking for access?"

"He says he's looking for a lost child with a broken leg, an Indian, he thinks, who was brought in by Border Patrol. I asked if the child is a relative and he said no. He says he's a neighbor." The voice paused. "He's rather insistent."

"Oh! Send him up to me, please, and I'll speak with him," Lydia said. "I don't know why your tribal member is so popular," and she looked up to find Sam had left. "Well!" she said out-loud, "Everybody's always in a hurry." She sighed. No problem, she reasoned. I'll let this neighbor know the child is in safe care, and that should wrap it up.

Meanwhile Sam Charley was moving swiftly down the hall toward the elevator. Twenty feet away the elevator chimed and a light above the door blinked brightly on the number 3. As Sam neared it the door opened silently and a large man stepped out, taking up all the space in the hall. Tall and red-haired, the man carried a cowboy hat in one hand against his chest. He met Sam's gaze and held it, moved to stand against the wall in the narrow corridor.

Sam brushed by. "'Scuse me." Sam could feel eyes on his back as he moved away.

"You happen to know if this is the right direction for the Social Services Office?" the red-haired man asked.

Sam's dream suddenly pushed into his consciousness and he heard the dream woman say again, "Come," her dream voice distinct, urgent.

Sam turned. "What?" he asked.

"Social Services?"

He tipped his head to the right, looked at the man. The dream woman resurfaced insistently. "Come," she repeated, "*Kad'i*" (Right now).

"Oh." Sam looked both ways, swallowed hard, pointed with

his chin at a sign on the wall in front of the elevator. "I believe it is to the left."

The red-haired man read the sign and nodded, "Appreciate it. It's like pulling teeth around here to get information." He turned and resumed his way.

Sam placed one hand over the warrior's necklace which lay under his shirt against his chest. A thick pressure gathered in his belly, a feeling of impending peril. "Protect us all," he prayed silently as he threw open the stairwell door and raced up toward the fifth-floor children's wing, his bundle of papers held tight to his chest.

As he burst into the hospital room where his family waited with *Biyoo'*, Her Beads, and *Gidi*, Cat, he decided to blow off the official medical dismissal. A circle of faces lifted toward him in surprise.

"Gotta go!"

"Now?" Lorraine hushed the twins as they began to protest. "*Dagoshch'i'*" (Quickly).

Cat's lower lip extended.

Sam said, "*Dakówa*" *(*Everyone). "*Doo dahiłts' da*" (Absolute silence).

Cat's lip folded into an eager smile and she sat up from her pillows.

Sam pointed with his lips at Ella, indicating the pillows. "Take them," he said. Ella quickly grabbed the pillows. Sam handed off the papers he carried to Lorraine, gathered the little girl gently into his arms, who at the same time grabbed at the kitten. The ball of fluff jumped through her hands and the twins scrambled to catch it, scooped it inside Susie's zipped up hoodie.

Sam's harsh "Sssssssst!" kept everyone silent.

Sam peered into the hallway noting one nurse far down the wing walking away with her back to them; indicated with a toss of his head that all should follow. The group snaked out in a single line. Noiselessly the family padded down the corridor to an EXIT sign. Sam heard the elevator chime farther along the hall. The group rippled through the door, down the stairwell, the door closing automatically behind them with a swoosh.

Cat squirmed in Sam's arms looking about when they entered the parking lot, surprised at the alien terrain of rows of parked cars. He felt her body stiffen and reassured her softly. When they reached the SUV Sam motioned with his head at the twins. The girls tumbled in, followed by Ella, while Lorraine climbed into the driver's seat.

Sam placed the child carefully next to Ella, her cast leg comfortably extended across the pillows on her big sister's knees. Cat looked around the interior, ducked her head, eyes flashing between elation and fear.

Lorraine backed out of the parking place, moved the vehicle sedately to the road. Sam watched the exit door they'd just used until they turned out of the lot. No one broke the silence until Sam turned around.

"No one follows, Daughter," and he patted her shoulder. Get us onto Highway 80," he said in English. "Albert's coming." Sam lay his head against the seat back and took a deep breath. "Whew."

"Okay," Lorraine answered in English, expelling a breath as well. "Explain what just happened there, please. I thought Albert was in Albuquerque for the weekend." She guided the car to a stop sign, veered north at a signal.

"He's on his way to Where They Cut the Tent, to meet up. Some interesting things are going on around us. Including that hospital. People are asking about illegals crossing the border, in particular about a child with a broken leg." Sam paused. "I just hope the van Albert brings is big enough."

Sam twisted his head so he could see Ella and Cat together. He smiled broadly and spoke in Apache. "You did well."

Ella held Cat's leg steady, hugged her. "Ella, how many Blue Mountain People came with *Gidi*?" Sam's question hung in the air.

Ella squeezed Cat's small hand and asked, but *Cat* didn't know. "Let us name them," Ella said, and the two girls ticked off the names of each Blue Mountain person on their fingers. Sam and Lorraine attempted to follow the names but lost track. Sam asked them to start over and wrote the names on a list. When finished, he read the list back to the girls.

"And Grandmother," Ella added.

"*Dah*," Cat said, her expression bleak. "She did not come."

Ella's eyes flashed, then welled. Sam looked back with empathy and saw she sat stiffly. She swallowed hard and hugged *Cat*.

"And *Jeeh*, Piñon Pitch, is teaching *Ch'a banné*, Big Ears, to make a living," *Cat* informed everyone. "They went raiding before we left." The little girl looked earnestly at the older girl. "The *dikohe* left signs for them to follow." She peeped shyly at her older sister. "I am to go with them next time."

Still digesting the information that Grandmother had not traveled, Ella said quietly, "Yes, it's time for you to learn your warrior skills."

Sam watched the yellow grasses of the San Bernadino Valley fly past. "So, two of the Blue Mountain People are making a living." The old phrase describing raiding felt full on his tongue.

Sam began to compute out loud in Apache, adding up the names. "I count eighteen, but not Grandmother, equals seventeen; minus two girls on a raid, leaves fifteen. *Her Beads* and *Cat* are here. I'm coming up with a total of . . . thirteen other Blue Mountain children traveling north." Sam nodded his head up and down as if arguing with himself. "Yes?"

"*Ha'ah*." Ella agreed.

"So now the big question." Lorraine's hands on the wheel moved left as she followed the curve of the highway. "WHERE are those thirteen Blue Mountain People?"

Cat's voice piped. "I know. They will look for a message at the spring called Water Standing."

"That's at old Ft. Bowie. They call it Apache Spring in

English," Sam said, shook his head. "It's almost too good. Water Standing is just a short walk from Where They Cut the Tent."

"It's history, Dad. It's where the rubber met the road between our ancestors and the *Indah*."

Lorraine had steered them past Douglas and cut onto the northern highway. A Border Patrol car, lights flashing, came up fast behind them, and the whole vehicle went silent. *Cat* buried her face in *Her Beads's* shoulder. The Border Patrol car blinked its passing signal, pulled out and went around, speeded ahead.

Sam and Lorraine both let out their breaths.

"Had me for a second there," Sam said. "At the social worker's office, we called Albert to get clearance to release *Cat* to me."

"And?" Lorraine's voice sounded thin.

Sam sighed. "I got permission to take *Cat*, but Albert told me the tribal president got a message from Border Patrol. A tourist saw some Indian kids in the *Chiricahua* Monument, and Border Patrol already knew about *Cat* and how she was found with a broken leg. They thought there might be a connection."

"Who knew they could actually use some logic?" Lorraine's words dripped scorn.

Sam continued in Apache. "Some *Nakaiyé* men caught in cholla on the border were brought to the hospital. They said Indians stole their horses." He rubbed one side of his face, feeling numb with so many things happening. "They were looking for the little girl who broke her leg."

Lorraine broke into explosive Apache. "What men are they?"

Ella/*Biyoo'* looked squarely into Cat's face. "Did you raid horses?"

Cat's face reflected competence. "We had six horses when we ran through the fence." Her expression went flat. "I fell off, but we rode very fast."

"It is as I thought," Sam said. "And just now a red-haired man was at the hospital looking for *Cat*." He looked over his shoulder at Ella/Biyoo'. "Do you know a red-haired man?"

"*Dah*, although there are red-haired enemy people in the Blue Mountains."

"Will he come after us?" Lorraine's foot went down on the pedal and the SUV surged forward.

"Maybe. He might learn where we're from." Sam relaxed a little, turned, and spoke in Apache. "Albert says he's on his way and bringing a big van. If we can get everybody to *Mescalero*, I think we may be able to make this all go away."

Sam changed to English. "Albert reminded me of how long *Cochise* County has held a grudge against the Apache. You know, our *Ndee* people fought a long time for their lands. The *Ndee* really are the Dead in *Cochise* County. And the *Indah* fought back so hard to become The Living. Even when Albert and I came for the centennial of Geronimo's final surrender, there was a nervous feeling. We're not sure how they might feel about a group of Bronco Apaches back in the homeland."

Lorraine's answer took a moment. "Point taken. But they're KIDS."

"Nobody'd hurt a kid, would they Mom?" Susie's plaintive question reminded Sam again that two others in the vehicle understood English.

Lorraine used honesty tinged with caution. "People love children of every kind. Grandfather and I will always protect you."

Sam's shoulders moved up, as if he had an itch. "We need to find the rest of the Blue Mountain People. We'll get them to *Mescalero* and everyone there will protect them."

"How can you protect them?" Lorraine insisted in English. "They don't speak English or Spanish. They come from the mountain peaks in another country! They've been living the old way, raiding, rustling, fighting. Somebody's going to come looking for them." Lorraine's fear made her voice rise higher.

"They can't go back. There's nobody left." Sam shook his head. "We're all they've got now. They're kids. They need us, and we're their relatives."

"Why can't they just BE us? Cat looks like us." Elsie said.

Sam rubbed one ear against a shoulder. "Yes, they are my grandchildren just like you. And they are your cousins. They are us!" Sam sighed, thinking his way through complications. "They are the last of the old ways, and their people's country is our people's country. Of course, they belong with us." Sam pulled at his upper lip.

Lorraine smiled as she drove. "Yes, Dad, they are us. I just can't see how we can get so many past the authorities."

"Yes, Daughter, but I am thinking there may be a way. They are us. The way I figure it, we hide our relatives . . . in full view."

"Ahhh," Lorraine said, "a redstart among the redstarts." She looked in her rearview mirror at Ella/Biyoo' dressed in modern clothing. "And Ella is the first redstart."

Sam nodded. "As long as she doesn't speak. The sound of Apache around here is not a good strategy."

Lorraine drummed her fingers on the wheel. "Where do we get more disguises to hide them in plain sight?"

"That's already covered. Albert was to stop at Tribal Services and bring clothes. We'll see what he's got when he gets here." He rubbed his nose. "I hope he remembers hats. They've probably all got long hair. Bunch of baseball hats would be a nice touch."

Lorraine sputtered. "I can see it now. Blue baseball caps with a mountain design, and a name: The Blue Mountain Scouts. Love it, Dad."

"Not bad, Daughter," he said. "But here's the way it is: Our people have been flat told we must never come back here. Never. And the enemy didn't care about any difference between adults and kids." Sam chewed on his lip. "It's not going to be an easy thing if outsiders learn about it. It doesn't take much for nervous minds to do nervous things." He wrinkled his forehead. "We've got to find them and get them home to *Mescalero*. Safely. Quietly. Lookin' like they belong."

He lowered his voice. "And that red-haired guy at the

hospital. He was all business and I don't want to learn what kind of business."

"Over my dead body," Lorraine said biting off the words.

"Over NO dead bodies, my daughter." And he switched to Apache. "We want the Dead to be alive and well."

．●●

A quarter hour passed before Ellsworth made it back to the hospital's security floor. Red-faced with frustration, Ellsworth found Esteban and Ignacio Garcia had been released from the hospital to the custody of a Border Patrol officer. Lucero waited with them, drumming his fingers.

"Which way?" Esteban asked, when Ellsworth appeared.

Ellsworth planted one cowboy boot in front of the other, head shaking in dismay. "Turns out the patient brought in from Hog Crossing the night horses ran across the border was treated for a broken leg, and released. Gone. Never even got to see the kid or ask a question."

Esteban, his skin inflamed and painful from his cholla encounters, anxious to return to the chase said, "The horses. What about the horses?" He felt as if his skin might burst from the left-over pain, sought relief with movement. "I want my horses."

Ellsworth raised a hand to offer a calming pat on Esteban's shoulder, withdrew it unsure of where pain lay.

Esteban said, "I'm not going back without my horses," and his son Ignacio nodded.

"Guess we'll see when we get to Douglas," Ellsworth said. "The officer here just informed me we're expected to go to the Border Patrol offices in Douglas, fill out some claims paperwork, answer any questions they have, and then return to Mexico."

Esteban felt driven to turn and walk around the small room. In a determined voice he said, "What about the problem? I want to settle the problem." He stopped and spoke directly to Ellsworth. "You said, Don Rafael, once and for all."

Lucero looked up, shook his head yes, but Ellsworth studied the wall.

"Yep." Ellsworth turned to look out the window down at a large parking lot. "And that's how everyone feels in the Sierra Madre. Too much of a problem for way too long." He took a deep breath. "But there's something else."

The Garcias' eyes locked on Ellsworth's face.

"It's crazy, but the patient they brought in from the border was a child. Nurse thought maybe four or five years old." He contorted his mouth in frustration. "A little girl," and his eyes bulged in frustration.

The other three stared at him in disbelief.

"The thieves are children?" Esteban's mind reeled. "They dropped their devil necklace in my corral while they stole my horses. They slit my dogs' throats. Children?" He shook his head. "No, it could not be the thieves are children. How could children make such a journey?" He looked at Ellsworth. "How far would they have come? That would have been down the spine of the Sierra Madre and across the desert." He shook his head again, asked, "How far would that be?"

Ellsworth thought. "Something over 350 kilometers, I'd think. More than 200 miles at the least." His forehead wrinkled. "No wonder they stole horses. That's a long way to walk." It was Ellsworth's turn to shake his head. "Well, it gets even better."

Esteban stubbornly repeated, "I know we are supposed to leave, but I want my horses."

"That's why we're going to Douglas. Horses that sound like yours turned up in a rancher's paddock last night and we have to identify and claim them."

"I don't understand," Esteban said.

"Neither do I, Don Esteban. After I talked with Benny Cortez,

I went to find the child. But she's already gone, picked up by her family.

Esteban's heart pounded with anger. "Where is this family?" he demanded.

"Somewhere in New Mexico," Ellsworth said, "according to the social worker." He looked at the other three. "I can't believe that we may have been dealing with kids. How can that be?" He stared out a window with hard eyes. "Why would that be?" He rubbed his eyes, fatigued with loss of sleep and frustration. "What can we do with kids?" He shook his head, puzzled, looked at father and son Garcia, ground his teeth. "For now, hombres, let's see if we can recover the horses. After that, there may be other decisions to make."

He looked around the room, saw they agreed; at least for the moment.

CHAPTER 70

Water Standing

Water Standing, *Chiricahua* Mountains, *Chiricahua* Apache Homeland

NAADIKTAZ, IT WIGGLES, URGED the children forward along the mountain crest. *Dikohe* traveling ahead had already reported their destination lay close. As they neared the never-failing spring called Water Standing, It Wiggles watched for the water source, so copious it formed a small pool before spilling out to create a flowing stream.

Grandmother had warned them the *Indah* enemies had made a permanent soldier camp nearby and the water must be approached with caution. He could see her in his mind, smoothing the sand with her hands, using a stick to draw the spring and creek in a basin surrounded by tall hills.

"Here," she told the children as she drew in the earth, "is where you will find a message; where you may leave a message."

Leaving the children to rest in cover, It Wiggles bade *Bee eshgané*, Left Hand, and *Baishan*, Knife, follow him. Carefully they approached the running spring they knew must be Water Standing. Pleased with its abundance, they searched the immediate area for messages.

The three scattered, eyes searching the rocks, the mosses, the very ground that surrounded the mountain glen. Water gushed over rocks above and tumbled in a waterfall down into a sylvan pool that invited thirsty travelers to refresh themselves. After a few fruitless moments of searching, It Wiggles motioned the boys toward the pool while he stood guard. The boys lay down flat on the pool rim and drank the cold water in long, thirsty gulps. As they drank, It Wiggles cast his gaze in and around the spring, admired the trees that cast their shade across the water, thought of all the ancestors who must have gulped just like the boys in deep, satisfying swallows.

The boys rose up satiated and immediately filled the water gourds they carried, an old rule that all of the Blue Mountain People followed at every spring or tank or stream. They knew that water was *Ussen's* greatest gift to the real people. They also knew that places where water existed were the most dangerous places of all. It Wiggles kept his eyes searching and his head turning, protecting the boys as they drank from the spring of their ancestors.

It Wiggles thought of all the stories he'd heard about this special place in his people's history. Here, Chiricahua had found a never-ending water source in a dry land. It was *Ussen's* gift to His people, the source of all life. Because of the reliability of its never-ending water the ancestors had used it as a place of communication, knowing that other Chiricahua would visit.

It Wiggles looked at the boys, faces wet and bellies filled with *Ussen's* gift. "Let us find Biyoo's, Her Beads's, message," he said.

They found nothing in their first circling, except the hard prints of *Indah* shoes that passed by on a path under trees that shaded the mountain dell. The tracks moved both ways and showed heavy use. It Wiggles silently indicated with a hand gesture that the boys fan out farther. The *Indah* tracks made him leery of using his voice. He sent one boy along the stream's edge, and the other up the small waterfall. Left Hand returned triumphantly in minutes. He leaned over the waterfall edge and signaled Knife and It Wiggles to follow.

A slender tree sat a stone's throw from the pool, and above

the waterfall, at the very point where a hill stretched suddenly upward. Left Hand parted the branches of the tree's lower limbs and displayed a circle of clover-shaped links of woven grasses resting there, still green and fresh. The three grinned at one another in discovery.

How many times, It Wiggles thought, have ancestors used this same method of communication in the past? And how well Grandmother had prepared them to find their own way.

The boys silently split their search three ways, examined the ground beneath and away from the tree. Within minutes Knife's call, the low warble of a songbird, brought the boys back together. Knife stood on the northeastern hillside that ascended above the pool and across from the trail that looped away from the spring.

All three read the message clearly. Four sticks lay slightly out of line, the first pointed north up the valley. A large pebble and a small pebble lay inches ahead of the sticks. A handful of pebbles lay scattered behind.

They looked at one another in silent agreement. It Wiggles nodded to the north and sent Knife forward. It Wiggles bent down, picked up the scattered pebbles, replaced them several steps away. If the messenger who'd left the sticks and pebbles returned, the movement of the pebbles would confirm the communication had been read. It Wiggles signaled Left Hand to follow Knife at a distance, waited, then crossed to the opposite side of the stream bed and followed behind the boys' route north, as the message had instructed.

As It Wiggles moved into the trees that followed the mostly dry streambed descending from Water Standing, he became a shadow among the tree trunks. He picked his way silently through scattered leaves along the waterway's curves, and watched for sign leading the way. After a half mile he came to a sudden halt. Stopped, slid into the underbrush, readied his weapon.

Ahead, Knife crouched, attention riveted on a small valley

snaking between hills. A stick, jammed in the earth next to a tree where the valley opened, stood with a white fluttering cloth tied to it.

It Wiggles felt a surge of hope. Her Beads had carried a white cloth to use as a message when she left the Blue Mountains.

"*Ussen*," he prayed unspoken, "protect the Blue Mountain People, shield us from harm, preserve our well-being, and give us power to find our way."

Even as he prayed his eyes watched Knife change his position. The young *dikohe* moved on his stomach through the valley grasses toward a cluster of stunted oak trees along the bottom of the larger hill. In the distance beyond something moved. Knife halted, laid still. It Wiggles' eyes fastened onto the movement in the quiet land.

Her Beads picked her way along the valley bottom and came to a halt where the white cloth rippled. It Wiggles thought she must have lost her own clothes, although he saw her black and white beads still circled her neck. He watched her touch the white cloth. She bent her head and examined the earth around the stake. She looked up and moved her eyes over the valley and surrounding hills. It Wiggles did not move, and her eyes did not stop at his concealed place. But her examination returned to the closer space around her and stopped at the clump of low oak where Knife waited.

The distinctive chirrup of a quail sounded and It Wiggles watched Her Beads as she concentrated on the sound's origin, then cheeped back. Waited.

It Wiggles watched as Knife slowly rose; approved Knife's decision to reveal himself. Finally, It Wiggles thought, the Blue Mountain People come together. His heart pounded in relief and joy. He quietly maintained his position, wary of the unknown, prudent until the all-clear signal. He watched as Left Hand used his quail signal before rising to move toward joining the others.

Her Beads raised her arm, clench-fisted, but It Wiggles stayed unmoving. At the same moment Knife and Left Hand stood next to Her Beads, It Wiggles glimpsed a movement behind the girl.

There again, another movement that parted the grasses. He almost jumped, as he recognized a human form approach. A white-haired man emerged from the valley's distance. The figure wore the pants and clothing of the *Indah,* the Pale Eyes. It Wiggles searched all around and behind the man, looking for other enemies. His mind raced as he considered that Her Beads might be a prisoner, forced to entrap them. But he saw nothing to confirm his suspicion.

Instead, the stranger moved forward, showing his hands open. No weapon. Behind him Her Beads head turned, continued to scan the valley area. "Here is our grandfather," she called out. "Our relative."

The man joined Her Beads at the white cloth signal. Birds called. Wind sighed through the trees. Fallen leaves skittered along the gravel streambed blending into a background of sylvan quiet. The world waited.

It Wiggles raised himself and stepped into the sunlight.

CHAPTER 71

Vicente's Trail

Rucker Canyon, *Chiricahua* Mountains, *Cochise* County, Arizona

NICK RECOGNIZED THE SOUND of Border Patrol ATVs at Rucker Canyon a quarter mile away beyond the hill above the valley.

So did Larry, who connected the sound with salt and fodder cake deliveries to the field. The mule quickened its pace, cutting sideways across the steep hill that turned into a slow and irreversible slide.

Tomás grabbed Nick tighter around the waist, feeling himself slipping. Mule and riders leaned into the hillside to keep from falling and slid to the bottom in a billowing cloud of dust. Larry found his hooves on a flat surface, flexed his heels, and stopped abruptly in front of the ATVs, refusing to move even when Nick and Tomás both gouged him in the side with their heels.

"Damn mule!" Tomás choked. He bounced down from Larry's rump.

Larry sidestepped toward where the boiling dust parted. Tomás stumbled out of the cloud behind the mule, removed his hat, and slapped at his clothing. Dust everywhere. Nick and Tomás choking. Mule braying. Horns honking.

Horns honking? Nick realized they'd landed more or less in the middle of a road and created a traffic jam. A half dozen vehicles waited as the air cleared, stopped by the dust cloud in the road. Several drivers peered from behind closed windows, regarded the emergence of the mule and two men from the billowing dust with astonishment.

Tears from the dust streaming down his face Tomás said, "Can't see. Where are you, Nick?" Tomás bumped blindly into one of the stopped vehicles. He swiped at his eyes with the sleeve of his shirt, hands moving along a car door.

Nick kept his seat for the moment, his left leg awkward in its frozen position. He clicked his tongue, moved Larry away from the cars.

"I've got some water," a voice said. "Stand still, lean your head forward. Let me pour some on your face." Nick peered from the edge of the cloud as the dust parted and Benny Cortez emerged, water bottle in hand to pour across Tomás's eyes.

"Hey!" Tomás yelled, as he blinked and sputtered. "Are we glad to see you, or what!" The dust ran down his face in muddy streaks.

Benny laughed good naturedly. "Usually people are running away when they see me," He held the remaining half bottle up to Nick, on the mule. "What the heck were you guys thinking coming off the mountain like that?"

Nick took the water, splashed his face, dabbed at it with the tail of his shirt and grinned sheepishly. His unwieldy left leg stuck straight out, making him feel especially vulnerable. "Coming down," he announced, and heaved his other leg over the saddle so he could slide off. He landed, brought the reins over Larry's head, and led the mule to the roadside. His gait, peg-legged because of the frozen leg, rocked his entire body side to side.

Watching Nick's painful-appearing gait, Benny asked, "You injured, Nick?"

"Nah," Nick said, "Unless you count my sanity. Need a charge for my leg. That's all."

"Sure looks like something hurts," Benny said, but his tone was relieved.

Tomás shaded his eyes from the sun and peered up the steep mountain side. "That was some shortcut."

Nick followed his gaze and nodded. "Let's not EVER do that again." He looked at Cortez. "You got a radio?"

Cortez waved through the thinning dust at the vehicles to move on. "Let's report you as found. Gotta APB out looking for you."

"What about my niece, Lucy?" Nick asked.

Benny stopped in mid-stride. Smiled. "Safe at Loreto's. That came in a couple of hours ago. What's going on? I can't keep up with everything."

Nick and Tomás heaved out a long sigh of relief together. Nick said, "That's a huge relief."

Tomás's voice quavered. "Did you find Vicente, my brother?"

Benny put a hand up in a stop gesture. "Wait. First things first." He grabbed the mic, pulled it out on the cord and spoke, handing the Diaz cousins granola bars as he talked.

Nick heard dispatch ask if they'd seen any smugglers in the last two days. Benny looked at the two young men, asked, "See any?"

"Yep, we saw some."

"Think you can recognize 'em?"

"Oh yeah."

Tomás nodded, added, "And Vicente tried to kill us. And he tried to kidnap us!"

Benny's face registered surprise. He cut Tomás off. "Kill? Kidnap? Wait a minute." He reported both Nick and Tomás could identify the smugglers and the radio crackled with instructions before he signed off.

Tomás continued, "Vicente wanted to take this really hot girl who helped us."

Nick interrupted Tomás with an elbow jab. "But mostly BIG trouble with Vicente. How about you guys. Seen him?"

"Haven't heard. Been at the hospital all night with some

guys that got stuck in cholla at the border. Been out of the loop, except I did hear the word on Lucy earlier. How many smugglers did you see before you rolled down the mountain on a mule?"

Nick's face twitched. "Probably fifteen. They carried something in backpacks. I never saw what, but it was wrapped in plastic. I think Vicente brought them in night before last and they stayed at the ranch." He breathed deep. "Since then, we've been kidnapped, tied up, shot at, my leg's out of juice, worried as hell for Lucy. It's been a long couple of days."

"What about the hot girl," Tomás asked. "Anybody seen her because she just disa...."

Nick stopped him with a glowering frown, turned to Benny. "She went her way after we had a run-in with Vicente. Watch out for him. Something major's wrong there."

Cortez nodded. "Okay. I keep hearing his name. Let me ask the station." He spoke to headquarters requesting location and status of Vicente Diaz. The answer came back swiftly. "Missing. Last seen on a horse going over a cliff on the old Apache raiding trail. Horse dead and no body found.

Nick and Tomás exchanged puzzled looks.

"This has got to be one of the craziest things ever," Tomás said. He looked at Nick. "And what about a group of kids we saw today who ran across the path."

"Kid smugglers?" Cortez asked, mystified.

Nick grinned. "Not smugglers, just kids. About a dozen of 'em, headed straight up hill."

"Yeah, a dozen," Tomás agreed. "They disa...."

Nick frowned again. "They were ahead of us crossing the trail, and we just saw them, that's all."

Nick gauged Benny's expression, but he didn't mention the girl or the children's appearance. A question formed in his mind: Who am I protecting? And why? He thought of the girl, wondered if he'd ever see her again. Shook his head. Thought, guess I'm just hopeful.

"Didn't resemble wild Indians, did they?" Benny's mouth curled at the corners. "Had a report from a tourist around noon of seeing wild Indians at the *Chiricahua* National Monument."

Nick's brow furrowed, thought of the girl's odd clothing, the children disappearing after crossing the trail, but said, "Really? Vicente's been our main problem."

"Well, if you see the girl or the kids again, let us know." Benny looked up the side of the mountain, ticked off the week's events. "Some week. Between finding a little kid with a broken leg and those cholla guys, we just picked up a couple of *pollos,* said they tried to help a man who went over a cliff on a bucking horse. Found the horse but no man. Reports of wild Indians, etcetera. We've got ATVs up on the ridge trail after the smugglers." He paused, rubbed an eye, laughed quietly. "Will you help us identify the smugglers? They're bringing them in near Old Ft. Bowie at Apache Pass. I'll take you and bring you back." He looked at his watch.

Nick reached to rub his left thigh, muscles sore from supporting the weight of the locked artificial leg. He hesitated. "We can go, but can we stop at the ranch, pick up my portable recharger? Be nice to have my leg usable. And, what do we do with the mule?" He turned to pat Larry on the neck. Each pat raised a small dust cloud into the air. "He's the kind of friend you don't desert, not after all he did for us."

"We can stop at the ranch," Cortez said, "and you can recharge as we go." Benny opened the door of his SUV. "Climb aboard." He motioned two ATVs forward and handed off the mule. "They'll get a horse trailer brought in, get the mule back to the ranch." One of the ATV officers pulled an apple from a pocket.

"Now you've made a friend for life," Nick told him.

Nick and Tomás sat in the back seat as Benny pulled his vehicle out. "When did you last see Vicente?"

"Believe it or not yesterday in Hackberry Canyon he clubbed

me, knocked me out. Had me hog-tied and carried into that old cliff dwelling and threw away my legs. But the last time we saw him was early this morning, after Tomás got there. Tomás was looking for Lucy, but he found me instead. Then Vicente came back and went after us with a rifle."

Tomás listened, nodded his head. "And the girl," he said. "Vicente tried to take the girl."

"Why? Who's the girl?" Benny's eyes flipped to look back at them in the rearview mirror.

Tomás shifted on the hard seat and echoed the Border Officer. "Why? Why did Vicente do all this to her and to us, Nick?"

Nick put an arm around his cousin's shoulders. "I think it's because of Roberto."

Tomás' face went blank.

Nick paused, thought: There'll never be a better time. Wished fervently he didn't have to tell Tomás what he'd seen in the back of the cliff dwelling behind the ledge.

"Tomás, I gotta tell you something hard. You listen, too, Benny."

Tomás straightened his back, turned a worried face toward his cousin. "O.K."

"You know, in the cliff dwelling?" Nick couldn't keep the sorrow from his voice. "I think I found where Roberto is."

A long moment of silence followed. Tomás's back changed from straight to rigid.

"When you rode up this morning, I thought you were Vicente, come back to kill me without witnesses. By then the girl was there, too. I tried to hide her behind the big rock at the back of the cliff dwelling. Couldn't do it because there was a body there. Pretty sure it's Roberto." Nick looked ahead at the trail, swallowed. "And I think probably Vicente put him there."

Tomás closed his eyes, leaned his head back on the hard-surfaced seat. "How could Vicente do that? To his own brother?"

"I could be wrong, primo. Jeez, I want to be wrong." Nick

looked out the window as the Border Patrol vehicle hit pavement. "Really dark in there. Couldn't see well. Maybe . . ." and his voice trailed away.

Tomás fought tears back, but lost; within a few moments rasping, choking sobs poured from his throat. "Vicente never got along with Roberto. Never. He always said Roberto cheated when he was born first. Vicente wanted to be the eldest." Tomás tried to regain his composure, raised a hand to swipe at his face. "Sorry, Nick. Can't help it. Guess I knew it somehow."

"Aw, you've got a right to do whatever you want to do." Nick said. "Don't forget he was coming back to kill me. S'pose he would have killed you, too." Nick gripped Tomás's shoulder hard. "We were all in Vicente's way."

Tomás bit his lip to stay tearless.

Benny asked, "What was Vicente's way?"

"Who knows, Benny? When I first talked to him, he thought he'd created his own country. Named the ranch Republic of Dog Mountain. He had a manifesto, declared he'd seceded from Arizona, and it was his kingdom."

"I knew he could be a little off the wall, but I never heard about that." Cortez pulled up to the ranch gate that proclaimed Republic of Dog Mountain with its trespassing signs and warnings. He shook his head in consternation. "So that's what this is?"

"We've been trying to figure it out, too. Part of Vicente's master plan, I guess." Nick looked at Tomás. "Want to get the gate, primo?"

Tomás, face forlorn, waited for Benny to release the vehicle's rear locked door, stepped out. He dug his key from a front pocket and approached the gate.

"Sorry to ask upsetting questions, Nick. He's a nice kid."

"He's good, Benny. Been through a lot." Nick took a deep breath, watching as Tomás swung the gate open and Benny drove through. "Some awful stuff. Who else could it be in the back of the cliff dwelling but Roberto? When Vicente came back, I think he was surprised to see me with Tomás and the girl. I don't know why he went after the girl. He's crazy. Then he came after us. He shot at us, creased the girl's head, grabbed her, but she got away."

Nick stopped as Tomás re-entered the patrol vehicle. They drove and came to the curve that overlooked the box canyon and the ranch house.

"I'd like to know more about the girl and how she fits in," Benny said.

So would I, Nick thought to himself. "She helped us when we needed help." He thought of her face, so alert, so calm, so lovely. "Didn't get her name."

"You should have seen her handle Vicente!" Tomás said, admiration in his voice.

Yep, Nick thought. Beautiful. Strong. Where the heck did she go?

Back on the road within minutes, recharger plugged into the dashboard, Nick looked across the San Bernadino Valley, stretched golden in the afternoon light. "So how does Apache Pass get involved in all this?" he asked.

"That's where it all started this morning. Park ranger at Old Ft. Bowie found an empty semitruck trailer in the canyon bottom, off the road by Siphon Canyon. You know the area where the Bascom Affair happened. And that put us ahead of the curve." Benny turned west onto a dirt road, reduced his speed to match road conditions. "The truck driver took a plea deal and went witness. Says he's waiting for a drop today. We've had reports of men with packs near old Ft. Bowie over the past month, been watching. And today a tourist over in the Wonderland of Rocks says he saw a group of kids, dressed funny, like they were playing at being Indians or something. He thought they must be some kind of a school club. Don't know how it comes together, or even if it does. When those two smugglers walked out of the mountains, said they didn't want to be *pollos* anymore, the captain kicked the whole shebang into high gear. This is the first time we've got a whack at actually figuring it out, stopping it."

The road reached an unmarked turnoff, went south into a shaded coulee, the entrance to Siphon Canyon. A semitruck trailer waited, backed in with nose to the road, posed for an easy exit. Next to it two Border Patrol vehicles sat in the shade under scrub oaks. On the far side of the truck a private SUV sheltered under a separate tree, where its passengers craned their necks to see who joined them.

Nick and Tomás stared, electrified.

The passengers, a collection of adults and children, observed the newcomers' arrival. In their middle, a slender young woman in jeans and sweatshirt studied their faces as they exited the back seat. She stared, slowly placed a hand at her throat, adjusted a string of black and white beads that circled her neck. As she recognized the two young men, her face opened in welcome.

CHAPTER 72

Apache Pass

Where They Cut the Tent, Water Standing, *Chiricahua* Apache Homeland

BIYOO', HER BEADS, AND Nick locked eyes at the same moment. She turned away and spoke to a tall, white-haired man beside her. They stepped forward as Nick approached, trailed by Tomás a foot behind, and by Benny Cortez who held back even farther. Tomás quickened his pace just before reaching the girl, coming up even with his cousin. Both young men grinned broadly, halted, suddenly shy. Cortez waited in the background, but turned away as other Border Patrol vehicles arrived.

Her Beads looked down at the warrior's legs, then back up to his face. She wrinkled her brow. "O-kay," she enunciated carefully, flat-toned.

"*Ha'ah*," he said and tipped his head.

She observed Grandfather thrust an arm out. Palm met palm as the three men clasped one
another's hands. *Her Beads* heard words, without understanding; but the warrior's voice trembled ever so slightly and his tone warmed her heart. His voice, she thought, I want to hear more of it.

Beside *Her Beads*, Grandfather translated the warrior's words. "I'm glad to see you again, and Nick reached out to grasp *Her Beads*'s hand, then didn't let go.

Ła'ihíí, The Other, extended his hand to the girl at the same time, jumped when the old man took it instead.

Grandfather smiled. "We know you two." He looked past the cousins to Cortez, who had turned away to the other arriving metal wagons.

Her Beads saw the warrior, *Béshbijád*, Metal Legs, look at Grandfather, eyebrows raised. Grandfather extended a hand indicating the others by the SUV. "My family. We are very grateful for the help you gave my granddaughter. She has told us about you."

"Ah." The warrior released the girl's hand after Grandfather's first two words, stepped back a little. For several moments, *Her Beads's* palm remained warm from the touch of the warrior's strong hand. She had to fight herself.

Her Beads followed Grandfather's actions, understood he introduced the others. "I'm Sam Charley, grandfather to the children," he said.

Her Beads saw the warrior examine the surroundings as he listened. His glance encompassed Lorraine and the girls, as well as two young boys who sat on their heels, dressed in old style clothing. *Her Beads* watched as Metal Legs nodded at them. The boys sat still as rabbits frozen under the eye of a coyote, but they watched back, faces without expression. *Her Beads* saw the warrior studied their clothing and footgear. His eyes came back to her and she said something to the old man.

In Apache, the old man answered her. "He is a man who notices things. Your clothing is easy to explain."

He changed to English and *Biyoo'*/Ella, listened without understanding.

"Ella says you had a dangerous time with some bad people." Ella heard Grandfather's use of her new name, and then the warrior repeated it.

"Ella, is it?" The warrior turned and looked intently at her. "I didn't know her name."

Ła'ihíí, The Other, waved one hand in front of his chest. "Hey Ella," he said, which earned a frown from the warrior.

Grandfather seemed amused. "She's usually shy," he translated his words to *Her Beads,* his mouth curved into a smile. "I hear you've been through a few things together," he said to the warrior.

Ella saw the warrior's eyes soften. "Yeah, a few things," he said. "Tell us more about Ella. Who is she? What was she doing in the mountains?"

Grandfather answered, "One question at a time. She's Apache."

The Other widened his eyes in surprise, exclaimed, "No way."

Grandfather answered, "Yes way."

The warrior mouthed an almost whispered, "Wow!" his eyes on Ella's.

Ella saw the words elicited excitement from the warrior, Metal Legs. She remembered Grandmother's stories about the Blue Mountain People and their ancestors, known and feared for their bravery and survival skills. The words faded from her hearing as she examined his dark hair and eyes, thought he could easily be one of her own people. And the way he stood tall. Ready. She had a distant memory of other men, standing just so. His presence made her feel glad, safe. She felt her face grow warm.

Grandfather continued his translation to Ella. "He asks from where you came. I have told him *Mescalero,* because I can answer anything about it."

"Ah," the warrior puzzled. "And what brought her here?"

An exchange of words followed before Grandfather spoke. "She says she is returning to the land of the ancestors."

The warrior leaned forward, asked, "Where IS that?"

Grandfather answered, "*Nahétaqhi, kúde*" (Where we are, right here). And he made a sweeping gesture that embraced the entire area. "We brought our young people to see where the ancestors lived, to help them understand the old ways." Grandfather grinned. "Everybody loves a road trip, especially to the ancestors' homeland." His eyes flicked to Ella. "She's the oldest one

of the group. It was her job to set up a trail for the rest to follow when she found you instead."

The warrior nodded, regarded Ella thoughtfully. "Can you tell her I appreciated her help? Especially since she didn't know me." And he placed a hand over his heart.

As Grandfather relayed the message, *Her Beads* rested her eyes peacefully on the warrior, her face composed. She thought, "My heart is glad to see him," and raised her own hand to her heart.

· · ·

Sam began to feel like a third wheel, but interpreted Ella's next question. "She wants to know how your legs work." He fixed an inquisitive eye on Nick. "How'd you lose them, son?"

Nick looked down at his jeans covered legs, shifted his weight. "The legs work fine when they're charged. Lucky to get out of Afghanistan alive is what I figure."

Sam's eyes widened as he heard the word Afghanistan. "Could've been your grape!" and he tapped his own head. Ella asked what he said.

"Granddaughter," he replied, "this man and I have fought as warriors in the same way. Not together, but in the same way. We know one another's ancestors."

When Nick heard Sam use the word "grape" for a head, he recognized a fellow Marine, and laughed. "I thought the worst was trying to digest MREs, but I went on a Marine Proof Mission, that went FUBAR."

"Congratulations! You survived 'the Four Fingers of Death!'" It was Sam Charley's turn to laugh. "I like your style, Gyrene!" Sam thumped him hard on the back. Dust floated up.

Nick broke away from the back pounding. "Where did you serve, Devil Dog?"

"'Nam! Talk about FUBAR!"

Tomás's head moved back and forth between the two, his eyes and expression confounded. "What are you guys talking about?"

Sam and Nick linked arms across one another's shoulders, chorused, "Semper Fi!"

"Ohhhh," Tomás breathed out. "Oh man."

Nick aimed his thumb at his cousin. "Wannabee future trigger puller." He smiled and looked over at the woman and children waiting by the civilian SUV. "Your family," Nick said, "Ella's in your family?"

Sam grinned. "We came to camp out where our people once lived and to support the youth group. Wanted to give everybody an idea of the old homeland."

Nick nodded pleasantly. "The boys," and he bent his head toward the two with disk-toed moccasins like Ella's, "Are they your family, too?" He noticed both kept intense attention on him as he spoke.

Sam looked around in a long gaze that included the whole of Siphon Canyon at Apache Pass and beyond to Apache Springs, the hills, the rocks, and the sky. "We're all related, more or less. This is where we're supposed to pick up the rest of the kids. They've been practicing their trail skills. Just sent one back to tell them it's time to come in, load up, go home. Border Patrol's got us sitting here because they got a situation. We're waiting for the all clear." He waited a beat. "You?"

Nick eyed the semitruck. "Long story. Just got home after a couple of years at Walter Reed."

Sam cocked his head and nodded in empathy.

"Found my cousin Tomás here," and Nick indicated Tomás beside him, "has been living with a lot of changes and lots of trouble."

Tomás bent his head, hooked his thumbs in his Levi pockets. Nick looked past Sam's shoulder and down the canyon. "I ran into Ella on my favorite mountain." He looked at her, started to say more, stopped. Started again, "Happened into some smugglers the next day. They took my horse and my legs, left me hog-tied in a cliff dwelling." His eyes flashed to the girl. "And Ella found me." His eyes stopped on her face, and he repeated. "Ella," enjoyed the roll of it across his tongue. "If it weren't for her, I'm not sure what might have happened."

Hearing her new name linger on Nick's tongue, *Biyoo'*/Ella's eyes lit with a spark of pleasure.

"Can you explain what . . ." and Nick smoothed his tongue across the girl's name again, "Ella was doing? I kept running into her, which turned out to be damn lucky for me."

"She was laying trail," Sam said, "helping the others practice the old skills."

They heard the crunch of tires on leaves and rocks and saw two more Border Patrol vehicles arrive. They watched as uniformed men exited the vehicles.

Sam lowered his voice. "I think we've turned out to be in the right place at the wrong time. Our tribal van's due any minute. We want to get our kids loaded and safely on their way home to the Rez. Don't need any complications."

Nick heard an unspoken request from his fellow Marine, looked directly into Sam's eyes. "Whatever we can do to help, let us know. We're here until somebody drives us home, too."

Sam translated Nick's words to Ella as the young Marine's eyes roamed Ella's face.

The three watched as Benny Cortez moved to meet the men from the Border Patrol vehicles. Cortez spoke with them, helped them shoulder small packs before they left the canyon bottom, walking up a trail on the steep hillside. All were armed.

As the officers exited the area, Cortez returned to where he'd left Nick and Tomás. Sam murmured something in Apache to

Ella before he took a step forward and extended a hand and the border agent finally introduced himself.

Ella paid attention to Grandfather's warning in Apache and returned to where the children waited.

"Don't worry, Leatherneck," Sam told Nick. "She'll be back."

"Benny Cortez. Appreciate you waiting this out. Hopefully won't be too long."

Sam's smile flickered. "Sam Charley, *Mescalero* Apache Council. I told the patrol guys we got a group of kids coming in from a day hike past Apache Spring. They told us we had to stay in place for safety. Plus, our van is due now. The kids should be walking up this creek bed any minute."

"Yeah, I got the info, but why didn't you register your visit at the Rangers' Station? We had no idea there was a group of kids on the trails."

"Register for a day hike?" Sam said, looking surprised.

Cortez shook his head. "Oh, didn't you stay in the campground?"

"Just my family. The kids stopped somewhere else. They came just for today."

"Okay, now I get it. I got the wrong message. Couldn't figure out why a group of kids weren't registered." He looked around, checked his watch. "Got the message from the *Chiricahua* Monument rangers about the kids. Kind of funny some of the park visitors reported them as 'wild Indians'!"

Sam blinked his eyes slowly, smiled. "Well, they dressed 'old-style' to give them a real experience. But I'll bet the kids will get a kick out of that!" He motioned with his chin toward Nick. "Just explaining to Nick here how we do this for our tribal youth, get them into the Land of the Ancestors. Looks like we picked a busy day! Be happy to get out of the way as soon as the kids arrive and it's okay with you guys for us to leave."

Hands resting on either side of his waist, Cortez turned toward a faint call from the hilltop, and regarded the eastern slope of Siphon Canyon. Against the curve of the skyline, a queue of men crested the hill, a horse trailing at the end. Dust followed the file like a low fog.

"Appreciate your understanding. For safety, everybody stay this side of the truck, please. We'll get through it as fast as we can." Raising his eyes at Nick and Tomás and tilting his head toward the descending file of men, he moved toward the base of the path. "Let's see if you recognize anybody."

Nick looked back at Ella standing beside the Suburban, asked Sam. "You're not going anywhere yet, right?"

Sam shook his head. "We'll be here, Jarhead. Waiting for the kids and van."

Nick put his palm out flat toward Ella. She responded with a dip of her chin.

"Know a little sign talk, do you?" Sam grinned, and called words in Apache to the girl, telling her Nick would be back.

Ella nodded, placed a hand on her chest and answered, "*Ha'ah.*"

Nick and Tomás followed Cortez to where the line of men had begun to reach the canyon floor.

"Look." Tomás said, watching as Chapo hobbled naked except for cowboy boots and jockey shorts at the head of the line. "We know him. Chapo works for my brother, Vicente."

"What happened to his clothes?" Nick asked.

Benny shook his head, stopped the first agent leading the file of men. The agent described Chapo's unclothed condition. "Says he cut his clothes apart to make a rope, trying to help a guy who rode off the cliff." He snorted. "Who should have been splattered and broken near the horse that had to be put down. But the guy wasn't there. Just poof! Gone."

Nick and Tomás exchanged a long look from puzzled faces. "Who was the guy?" Nick asked the agent.

The agent shrugged, "Vicente somebody?"

"Vicente disappeared?" Tomás and Nick said together.

"Try to do a good deed and look where it gets you." The agent led the line of dejected men away to a patch of shade on the close side of the semi. The trailing horse, loaded with packs, nuzzled the leaves under the trees, as men slumped to the ground. Within minutes a few were rousted by the guards to unload the plastic-wrapped packs from the horse, and heave them into the semi.

"There's more of this coming," a guard called. "They had an underground stash the other side of the old fort. Tarps made it look like the side of a hill. Too much stash, though, for one carry."

Nick and Tomás watched as the men worked.

"That's the guys I saw with my brother Vicente early yesterday on their way north" said Tomás. "The horse is from our remuda; he's named Salsa."

"Yeah. Chapo was riding him yesterday," Nick said, "and for the record, we saw the same camouflage trick up in Hackberry Canyon." He scanned the dismal looking faces, saw Chapo catch his eye and look down. He noticed other faces he'd seen, including the men who'd carried him into the cliff dwelling. They turned their faces away from him. "Yeah," Nick confirmed, "these are the men. Seems a couple short in number?"

"Right," Benny agreed. "Border Patrol found two guys hitchhiking north on the San Bernadino Valley highway, took them into custody and delivered them to the county jail in Douglas. They were the ones who tried to help the guy, I guess it was Vicente, who went over the cliff, but he wasn't there when they got down to the bottom." He stopped. Benny raised his eyebrows and tweaked his lips into an expression of doubt. "So they took off, but didn't get too far."

"Except that still doesn't help us with finding Vicente," Nick said. "How could he just disappear?"

Cortez frowned. "That's the big question, buddy. For now, he's reported missing. We're labeling him armed and dangerous." He resettled the brim of his hat lower over his eyes.

Tomás startled. "I don't get it." He leaned forward. "Where could he be? How could he live through a fall like that?"

Cortez shrugged. "We won't know until we find him, if and when. So far, no tracks, no indicators. Know where he might look for refuge?"

Nick and Tomás shook their heads. "Well, he might go home."

"If he shows up, let us know immediately," Benny said.

"If we see him, believe it, we'll be calling you." Nick ran a hand across the back of his neck. He reached an arm around his cousin's shoulders. "Vicente's part of our family, but he's put us through some rough stuff. I know he intended to kill me," He looked at Tomás and thought of Roberto's body in the cave dwelling. "And probably Tomás. We'll do what we can to help bring him in."

They watched as the loaded vehicles pulled out of the canyon bottom toward Apache Pass Road, glum faces peering from windows. The wind stirred the trees, and the engine sounds diminished.

Cortez's voice broke the silence. "Should be a horse trailer soon; then we'll be on our way."

CHAPTER 73

Meet the WHOLE Family

Siphon Canyon, Apache Pass, Ft. Bowie National Historic Site, *Cochise* County, Arizona

THE SHARP WHISTLE OF a hawk sounded. Nick looked up expecting to see a bird of prey in pursuit of a song bird. A clear blue sky hung above. He wrinkled his brow, swung his gaze back to the trees, then dropped his eyes to Ella's face. As the whistle faded, she brought her hand to her mouth and produced a similar sound. Nick realized she answered the hawk's cry. He saw she gazed directly at him. Neither flinched.

Sam, looking back and forth between them, flashed a bright grin, which he concealed by lowering his head and rubbing his upper lip. Nick's voice brought him back to himself.

"Devil Dog," Nick addressed Sam Charley, "Translate for me?"

"Sure, but hold off a second." Sam raised his head, his face straight.

"Father!" Lorraine exclaimed in warning.

Everyone's heads turned south.

A single-file line of walkers approached the edge of the canyon bottom. The last afternoon light flickered through tree shadows creating the effect of an old-time, stop-action movie film.

A slight girl confidently led a line of children, her leather skirt swaying against her legs; smaller girls in similar clothing kept a few paces behind. Boys followed in stained and ragged cloth breeches and waist flaps, their hair held back by headbands made of torn strips of cloth. All wore faded cotton shirts of different colors and carried small leather bags at the waist and on their backs, each with a blanket wound diagonally across their bodies, tied with a cord. Most had a carved horn or dried half gourd dangling from waist or neck for use as a bowl or spoon; all carried water gourds. The older children carried bows and arrow containers.

"Grandfather," *Biyoo', Her Beads,* said in a low voice, "let me greet them first."

Sam stepped back, placed a hand on Nick's arm to move behind the girl.

Her Beads saw *Zhonne,* Pretty One, in the lead. The girl looked ahead of the line, her face flashing alarm which brought her to a halt; next she looked confused, as she saw *Her Beads* standing among strangers; finally, relief as *Her Beads* called out.

"It is well," *Her Beads* reassured them. "Here stand our relatives. Come. Come."

A child's voice floated out from where the Suburban was parked in the trees in a reedy salute to the file of children. "Finally, you have found us!"

The silent line burst into a surprised murmur. Voices in Apache called, "*Gidi?* Cat? Where have you been? What happened to you?"

The children broke into an eager rush toward Lorraine's SUV, clustering around their recovered member. "We thought you might be gone," someone said. Another child seeing *Cat's* white leg cast asked "Why do you have a stone on your leg?"

Naadiktaz, It Wiggles, beamed. He'd returned to the rocks to lead the children after speaking with *Her Beads* and Grandfather. He'd sent Pretty One forward to lead the group in. Now he swept his arms outward releasing the last two Blue Mountain children who swept away the tracks of their group's passage, and took on the job himself. He placed a hand on each child's shoulder. "*Enjuh*" (Good).

Her Beads embraced each one as they arrived. She moved through the children, a pat here, a word there, and *Cat* settled into directing the children forward to gather by the vehicle. *Her Beads* beckoned to Sam, Nick, and Tomás, and brought them to the assembling children.

Sam translated as *Her Beads* spoke. "Here are our relatives," she told the children, standing next to Sam and his family near the vehicle. She moved and stopped between Nick and Tomás, "and our friends."

"Pretty cool," Tomás, grinning ear to ear, said to Nick.

The children regarded the adults, then examined Lorraine and the twins. Several of the children's breath caught when they saw Elsie and Susie shared the same face. They looked at one another and then *Her Beads,* with unspoken questions.

"Can you explain, Grandfather?"

"Soon there will be a place to rest and talk," Sam told them, "but first something to eat and drink."

The children's attention immediately refocused, all eyes riveted on *Her Beads.*

"Eldest sister, is there meat?" squeaked *Na'iłt'oolé,* Spider.

Her Beads turned to Lorraine, who held up handfuls of packaged jerky.

"Yes, there is meat. It will be shared."

Lorraine helped *Her Beads* pass a package to each child, showing how to unwrap the cellophane bags. The men handed out water bottles.

One girl with long, braided hair accepted her jerky and broke away to examine the horse tied to a tree.

"Strawberry," *Her Beads* called. "Come, drink and eat."

The girl switched her braid with a flick of her head, tucked it into the front of her belt. She seemed to swallow her jerky whole. "This horse needs water."

"What's going on?" Nick asked Sam.

"Ella says, horses are that girl's heart," Sam said, pointing his lips toward Strawberry.

Her Beads consulted Sam, turned back to Strawberry. "Go quickly to water the horse and return the horse to the tree. The horse belongs to these friends," and she looked at Nick and Tomás. "The Water Standing is . . ."

Strawberry frowned. "Sister, I know where Water Standing is." She grumbled a bit to the horse as she removed its saddle, used its saddle blanket to rub it quickly down, replaced the blanket, then swung up on its back.

Sam spoke softly to *Her Beads*, and she motioned to *Bikécho*, His Big Toe, to follow the horse and girl. "Go to Water Standing with Strawberry," she instructed. "It is just there . . ."

"I know where Water Standing is, Sister," he interrupted her. He looked to see if there might be more jerky, saw nothing, swung up behind Strawberry.

Sam listened, aware that the children knew where they were, just as he had always imagined they would.

Nick watched, impressed that two children could mount an unsaddled horse so easily.

Sam noted the jerky had been totally consumed. "Jarhead, see if the Border Patrol has anything more the kids might eat."

Cortez had stood back at the arrival of the children but smiled pleasantly as Nick and Sam approached. He wasted no time in offering his supply of granola bars and water, helped pass it out. "Hungry group!" he said.

"Hiking whets the appetite alright," Sam responded.

"Who are they, anyway?" Benny asked, watching the granola bars and water bottles disappear. "Why are they dressed like that?"

Sam and Nick responded at the same time, their explanation and words on top of one another.

"Kind of a hiking group. They've hiked the whole area all

day," Sam said, and thought to himself, and for at least four or five weeks before now.

"Visiting the land of their people, you said?" Nick confirmed with Sam, who nodded agreeably.

"Oh," Benny said. "I get it. So, these are the "wild Indians" the tourist reported." He watched the kids eat and drink. "Why are they dressed like that?"

"Not all of 'em," Sam pointed out, indicating Ella and Cat. "There's a couple there wearing regular clothes." He looked sideways at Nick.

"They look good either way," Nick said, trying to help, not knowing what or how much to say.

"Yeah," Sam added. "They want to know how their ancestors lived."

Cortez nodded. "I got kids. I get it. Stylin'." He listened to the group talking and noticed they did not speak in English. "What language is that?"

"Apache. We try to get them to use it or lose it," Sam said. "This," and he swung one arm out embracing the landscape around them, "is the perfect place to use it."

Benny answered a call on his radio, then reported to Nick, "Horse trailer left the I-10 at Bowie. About fifteen minutes out."

"Great," Nick felt daunted by the minutes now ticking away, about to take him far from Ella. She'd remained across the clearing to help distribute food. "Gyrene!" and he raised his eyebrows at the older man.

"Oh, right!" Sam lifted one arm toward *Her Beads,* caught her eye, and she separated from the children.

The two men moved together in the same kind of long-legged stride across the clearing.

Nick stopped a few paces from her, cleared his throat, and squared his shoulders. He addressed Ella in English while Sam translated.

"I'd like to visit you at *Mescalero,* if that's alright."

Sam's chin pulled in. "Son," Sam said, without translating, "I don't need to translate that. You're welcome to visit."

"No. Translate to HER."

Sam grinned, spoke in Apache, with Nick listening to the unfamiliar clicks pop and tones surge.

Ella focused on Nick's face as Sam spoke, her lips straight, unsmiling. She began to speak, her answer fluid in a return stream of clicks and tone curls.

It seemed to Nick she must be telling Sam an awful lot of things to say, and because her face remained without expression, the answer must be no. Still, he loved the sound of her voice, a bit husky, a river of lush and exotic changing sound. He watched her mouth form the music of her language and he thought it the most beautiful mouth he'd ever seen. He willed her to speak on, wanting to gather into his memory as much of the sound of her as he could.

As Ella's words flowed, Nick's heart sank. Obviously, he thought, he'd misunderstood their shared survival experience. Maybe their entire meeting meant nothing to her.

Ella stopped speaking. "Áqł" (I am finished).

Sam turned slowly to Nick. "Well," he drawled, with a look of concern, "She's pretty sure of her answer."

Nick tried to keep his posture straight, but felt as if an iron bar lay across his shoulders. Maybe he should have just let her carve out his heart with her knife the first time he saw her. He looked at Sam, then again at Ella.

Ella stepped forward, extending a hand to Nick. "*Ha-ah*," she said.

CHAPTER 74

Never Give Up Your Knife

Siphon Canyon, Apache Pass, Ft. Bowie National Historic Site, *Cochise* County, Arizona

NICK'S SMILE STRETCHED WIDE as he reached a hand to Ella. She placed her own hand palm to palm with his. Nick sounded out her name in two syllables. "EL-LA. *Ha'ah.*" Then he placed his hand on his own chest, said "Nick."

"*Béshbijád,*" Metal Legs, she replied, "*Ha'ah.*"

Nick repeated his name.

Sam helped. "Son, she thinks your name is like our personal names and not to be used all the time. I'd say go with the flow for now."

Nick shrugged. "She can call me whatever she likes."

The arrival of the Border Patrol pickup truck and horse trailer ended further conversation. At the same time, Strawberry and His Big Toe returned the watered horse to the head of the draw. The children gathered to watch the loading of the horse into the trailer, observing and commenting quietly in their own language to one another on each aspect of the strange metal wagon.

"It is well," Strawberry approved of men tying a food bag on the horse's nose, "Those men understand horses."

Satisfied with the welfare of the animal, Strawberry and His Big Toe accepted granola bars and bottles of water, examined the paper wrappers of the bars in minute detail, unsure of how to access the food within.

"Like this," five-year-old *Binat'izh*, Eyebrows, said, "Pull hard!" and she drew the bar from its red and blue paper jacket in one motion. She looked proudly at the two. "I am saving these flat skins," and she reached into her skirt band and pulled out several wrinkled wrappers.

"They have a nice color," His Big Toe said. "I will save mine, too."

On the other side of the clearing the Border Patrol agents readied their vehicles to leave.

"I don't really want to go now," Tomás said to Nick. "We're just beginning to know these people." His eyes roamed past Nick, paused on *Zhonne*, Pretty One, and *Naadiktaz*, It Wiggles, as they sat talking to Lorraine.

"I hear you," Nick responded, his own eyes on Ella. He sighed deeply. "For right now we're going to help clean up whatever part of this mess we can and see the captain tomorrow in San Enebro. Tia Elena and Lucy are waiting for us, too."

Tomás thought. "Maybe we could stay here for a while, you know, help out."

Nick looked at Sam, who barely shook his head no, but said nothing.

"They know we'll help, but they have to get the kids home. At this point we'd just be in the way."

Cortez waved at Nick and Tomás, signaling it was time to go.

Nick offered his hand to Sam, and they each raised opposite arms to embrace the shoulder of the other. Sam stepped back.

"Thank you, Gyrene," Sam said. "For everything."

Nick smiled, "I'll be seeing you soon, Jarhead."

Nick took Ella's hand once more, pressed it warmly, received an equal pressure back. He turned and Tomás followed, looking back, and stumbling. They entered the back seat of the Border Patrol vehicle. Nick turned his neck, watched the figures of Ella and Sam recede as the Border Patrol car followed the horse trailer slowly over the dirt road.

Both Ella and Sam watched until the vehicle disappeared into the canyon. The two stood together without touching. "He's a warrior." Sam said. "Strong." He cleared his throat. "Even if he isn't Apache."

"Yes. That is true," Ella confirmed.

"He says he'll visit soon at *Mescalero*."

Ella turned and looked earnestly at Sam. "Does he have one of those small black four-sided boxes?"

"I do not know, but most people do."

"Do you think he knows how to use one so the wind will carry a message?"

"Yes, he knows."

* * *

Albert turned off the dirt road into Siphon Canyon, returned the friendly wave of the Border Patrol driver. Albert saw two men in the back seat and wondered if they were prisoners. He stopped, spoke through his open window. "Looking for a group of hikers. Have you seen 'em?"

The Border Patrol driver, nodded, waved one hand indicating behind him. "Just follow the valley here to the clearing." He checked out the emblem and words inscribed on the side of the van. It read: *Mescalero* Apache Tribe, with a round, spiked seal. "*Mescalero*, huh? You're a long way from home."

Albert could tell the man meant no criticism. "Actually, right here used to be our peoples' home," and he smiled broadly.

The Border Patrol agent tipped his head to the side. "They're waiting for you." He continued past Albert's vehicle and swung onto the main dirt road.

Albert pulled forward, thinking of all those who'd come before him. He said a silent prayer in gratitude, felt honored to be entering the canyon Where He Cut the Tent. It was here the last Apache Wars began when *Cochise,* wrongfully accused of kidnapping, sliced his way from a prison tent. The entire canyon represented sacred space to Albert.

As he climbed out of the *Mescalero* tribal van, he turned to the canyon side he knew to be the site of the tent cutting. He placed his hand around his medicine bag that hung under his shirt and repeated a prayer four times. Only then did he turn and face the people gathered in the valley.

Although he'd arrived with the intention of picking up passengers, he felt unprepared for the scene before him. Lorraine and her girls stood surrounded by a group of children near the family SUV. A small girl with one leg in a cast sat in the vehicle.

"*Dagot'é, shiłt'ii*" (Hello, my friend), Albert said to Sam, shaking hands. He raised his eyes toward the children who examined Albert's person minutely. "*Dagot'é* to you also," he greeted them.

The twins popped up and ran toward him. One grabbed each hand and pulled him toward the children.

"C'mon and meet them!" Elsie urged.

The children seated around Lorraine formed a picture out of history, almost a photograph in their stillness and silence. The children wore buckskin moccasins with the distinctive toe disks of the *Chiricahua* band.

Albert punched Sam in the arm. "Bet you haven't seen those except in museums!"

"No kidding!"

"Dressed the old way! It's real!" Albert could barely contain himself. "I hoped it was so," he told the group. "I wanted to know you."

Her Beads moved gracefully toward Albert. She returned his traditional greeting, then added in English "Hi," and switched into Apache to say, "*Shichóyé,*" my grandfather. "We have come a long way to find you."

He heard the quaintness of her accent and listened; his face delighted. Albert twisted his head back to Sam, stuck out one arm and grasped Sam's wrist, the greeting returned in kind. The two grabbed one another's opposite shoulder with a free hand.

"I dreamed it," Sam said.

He released Albert's wrist to turn around. "These are the Blue Mountain People, the *Ndee Nnaahi*, Nameless no longer."

"I never thought we'd ever find them. Not really." Albert shook his head in amazement.

"You go ahead and admire them, because we need to get them changed into some other clothes. What'd you bring?"

"Social Services piled stuff in the van. T-shirts, jeans, jackets, tennis shoes. All kinds of sizes."

Sam asked *Her Beads* to organize the children to change into new clothing. "Tell them they can keep their old things. Put them in the bags and we'll take them along. And while you're at it, tell them we're going for a ride in a metal wagon. There's a whole bunch of new relatives waiting to meet them." Sam smiled broadly.

Even as he spoke, *Her Beads* had already enlisted Pretty One, in gathering the girls and It Wiggles called the boys.

"Hard to believe how quiet they are," Albert said.

Within a few minutes all of the children had changed their form of dress. Lorraine stood by with a brush to untangle hair snarls, provided hair bands to tie hair back from faces. Susie and Elsie wandered, ensuring T-shirt designs correctly displayed on the front or back, giggling as they tied tennis shoes for the newcomers. Sam and Albert viewed the children one by one as each came forward, now garbed in jeans. The smaller boys especially registered unhappiness when told they must place their bows with their mountain clothes. The children en masse refused to turn over the knives each carried concealed in their moccasin wrappings, instead placing them inside their jeans' legs, knife-tip into their tennis shoes. Even *Her Beads* could not convince them of the necessity of turning over their knives, and looked to *It Wiggles* for support.

"How else, sister, will they protect themselves?" It Wiggles pointed out.

Hearing the conversation, Sam, Albert, and Lorraine regarded one another and came to silent agreement.

"It is as you say," Sam addressed It Wiggles, and a quiet satisfaction fell over the group. "But no one must show a knife without true reason." He looked at each child's face and saw agreement. He looked at Albert. "We grandfathers protect the group. No one will harm you. If we are attacked, you may only show your knives AFTER we two die."

Albert nudged Sam and together the two chorused: "Semper Fi."

The children watched with interest. "That is our sacred oath," Albert affirmed.

Sam looked around the group. "Now, finish eating and drinking. It is the end of the day and perhaps you will be able to sleep in the metal wagon as we travel to *Mescalero*."

A scan of the children's expressions, bright with interest, made Sam turn to Albert. "But maybe not."

"Lima Charlie," Albert muttered. "Loud and Clear."

• • •

As Nick rode in the back seat to the home ranch, already restored in his own mind to its original name as the Diaz Ranch, he dreamed of Ella, and of the sights and scenes of the past few days. He did not believe that Sam and his family had come to *Cochise* County to train their youth in ancient ways. He felt certain the children somehow came *from* ancient ways. He recognized the same look of authentic characteristics that rural Afghans displayed: eyes always watching; bodies ready to react instantly; clothing used as part of their survival, existence, and identity. When the Border Patrol car reached pavement, Nick watched the mountain and valley scenes slide smoothly away under a blue sky tinting toward lavender. He closed his eyes and nodded off.

Nick dreamed himself traveling to visit Ella and the others. His dream followed his hopes, a remote stirring of thoughts and images that flickered past his family's ranch to the high country of New Mexico, where he searched through the wide distances of plains and mountains. He laid his head back and drowsed, dreaming of a horse. It galloped toward him, mane and tail streaming, scattering sprays of sand as hooves cut into earth. A slender female figure entered his dream, head pressed against the horse's neck, legs wrapped tightly about the horse's barrel, leaving an impression almost of flying. The rider, neck wreathed by a necklace of black and white beads, skimmed over a river, and mountains, and cliffs, and mesas, gliding toward Nick from the past, moving in clear sunlight into the future.

Shigo shk'anni sidja.

Here lies my yucca fruit—the Apache phrase that ends a story.

- FINIS -

ACKNOWLEDGMENTS

I AM GRATEFUL FOR the help and support of so many people in writing this book. The seeds were first planted by my parents, Ruth and Ralph Jenkins. They introduced me to Apache culture and history by camping in Cochise Stronghold in the Dragoon Mountains of southern Arizona under the same oak trees that once sheltered Cochise and his people. Thanks, Mom and Dad! Look where it took us! Husband, Ray Galvin, and our daughter, Alexandra Rachell, lived with the writing of this novel through various forms and drafts and led the parade of first readers who also include sister Vicki MacPhee, cousin Judy Kahl, friend Lian Morris, and writers Martha Blue, Kate Cross, and Amy McLane. Kris Horn was invaluable with advice and expertise in creating maps and a website (lynngalvin.com). Thanks to Nick Rachell, esteemed son-in-law, for digital resources and beyond.

I am also grateful to authors/writing teachers James Sallis, Ted Schwarz, Beth Kendrick, and Jeanne Williams for classes, critiques, kind evaluations, and counsel. I appreciated analysis and critiques by members of my writing group: Ruth Chavez, Patricia Cox, Roxanne Doty, Donna Ockinga, and Karen Reed.

Kudos to the originating park ranger extraordinaire Bill Hoy at Old Ft. Bowie, Cochise County, Arizona, for sharing knowledge and historic viewpoints of contact between the Apache and the rest of the world. He is missed.

And finally, thanks to Edgar Perry, R.I.P., tribal historian and cultural preservationist of the White Mountain Apache. I am privileged to have known him.

CHARACTERS

Characters in the United States

Nick Diaz, aka *Béshbijád*, Metal Legs, and Marine veteran
Roberto Diaz, missing eldest cousin of Nick
Tomás Diaz, youngest cousin, age 16, aka *Ła'ihíí*, The Other
Vicente Diaz, middle cousin who controls ranch, aka *Bidáá' łichii'*,
    Bloodshot Eyes
Tia Elena, aunt to the four Diaz cousins
Loreto family members, neighboring ranch family
Chapo Morales, Vicente's right-hand man

U.S. Border Guards
Beneficio (Benny) Cortez and Juan Fuentes

Hospital Personnel
Brown Woman (as called by Cat), nurse
Lydia Castillo, social worker

Mescalero Apache Reservation
Lorraine Albertson, granddaughter of Sam Charley
Susie and Elsie, identical twins, age 6, of Lorraine Albertson
Sam Charley, aka *Doo yidah da*, He Does Not Forget (Storyteller), aka
    Nahiyeeł, He Dreamed It, and Marine veteran
Curly *Dichoshé*, old Shaggy, president of *Mescalero* Apache Tribal
    Council
Albert Silentman, All Clans Museum director and Marine veteran

Characters in Mexico

Blue Mountain People
Dzilthdaklizhéndé, Grandmother, plus 17 children, ages 4–17
Shiwóyé, Grandmother aka *Báyání* (the elderly one, the last adult)

Girls

Binat'izh, Eyebrows, age 5

Biyoo', Her Beads, age 17, aka Ella, wears her mother's black and white beads

Dahsts'aa', Strawberry, age 9, knee-length hair worn in braid tucked in belt

Gidi, Cat, age 4, youngest of the Blue Mountain People

In'łt'áni, Cricket, age 10, has a rough, raspy voice

Izee, Medicine (Plant), age 8

Łichii, Red One, age 7

Yaa', Louse, age 6

Zhonne, Pretty One, age 11, "mother figure" to younger children

Girls on Training Mission (will appear in Vol. 3)

Ch'a banné, Big Ears (word describing Bats), age 7

Jeeh, Piñon Pitch, age 11

Boys

Baishan, Knife, age 9

Bee eshgané, Left Hand, age 9

Bikécho, His Big Toe, age 10, has a "wall eye"

Ch'anáidił'įį, He Hides It, age 6

Naadiktaz, It Wiggles, age 12 (group leader when *Biyoo'* is not present)

Na'iłtł'oolé, Spider/Tarantula, age 7

At Rancho Garcia, Sonora (west side of Sierra Madre Range aka Blue Mountains)

Esteban Garcia, owner of Rancho Garcia

Ignacio Garcia, son of Esteban

At Suiza Colonia, Chihuahua (east side of Sierra Madre Range aka Blue Mountains)

Elder Rafael Ellsworth, leader of Colonia Suiza, a religious colony

Lucero Gonzales, foreman at Colonia Suiza

APACHE VOCABULARY AND PHRASES

ąął: done, finished

ánaazhátah: finally (old term)

Ashch'ishégo: small one

Baishan: Knife, a personal nickname

Béshbijád: Metal Legs, a personal nickname

Béshnaghái: metal wagon (pick-up truck or automobile)

bidahłenistł'ooni: fences/fence (literally "that which goes around them")

Bikécho: His Big Toe, a personal nickname

Bitsizíl hisdlos: Curly-Hair, a personal nickname and/or descriptor

Biyoo': Her Beads, a personal nickname

chagosh'oh: brush shelter for cooking, shade

Ch'anáidił'įį: He Hides It, a personal nickname

ch'idagozteel: wide valley

Ch'igoná'ái nitis dahsol'ees hela': Don't let the sun step over you, i.e., rise early, be self-disciplined and industrious

ch'iin: ghost, spirit

ch'ikii: girls

Chiricahua: One of the six major Apache bands. Also, the name of a mountain range in Cochise County, Arizona, referred to as "the Cheery-cows" by local modern ranchers

Chokonen: a Chiricahua sub-band, literally "the Rising Sun People," led by Cochise. Other sub-bands are: Chihenne (Red Paint People), Nednhi (Enemy People), Bedonkohe (In the Front of the End people).

dá'áiyee: correct

dá'ánii: it's true

Dabik'ehyu ansht'ee nnzi: You know I'm right!

dadét'įį: Let us go look.

dagot'é: hello

dah: no

Dahnodaa doo hwaa gońch'aa da (PL): Sit and be still! (Said before a storytelling) *da'izháí'*: stop; Stop right at that place.

Daká gozhǫ́ǫ́ nt'éé: Everything will turn out right for her; lucky

dants'ag: We understand.

dédí'iléí: soft

Dichoshé: Shaggy, a personal nickname

dikohe: apprentice warrior

diyééhinee: This is yours.

dołkáh: You (plural) go!

Doo bígonsįh da: I don't know.

doo' dadozhéh le': Let us go hunting.

Doo dágoyá dago ádaadii: They don't know what they say (they're crazy).

doo dat'įį dah: That Which Can't Be Seen, invisible

Doo jád da: No Legs, a personal nickname

Doo łikąą golįh da: It doesn't taste sweet (good).

Doo ts'iziłhee da: Don't kill him.

Doo yidah da: He Does Not Forget, a personal nickname

dzaneezi: the one with ears long and slender (mule)

Dzil Nii'leezhé Bigowa: Prairie Dogs' (or Ground Squirrels') Home Mountain

Dzilth dotł'izh: Blue Mountains of Mexico (Sierra Madre Mountains Occidental)

Dzilthdaklizhéndé: the Blue Mountain People

édįhi: missing or dead

enjuh: good

gah: rabbit

Gidi: a personal nickname (or just a cat)

gocho': That place is bad.

goshe: dog

gową: home

ha'ah: yes

hadín láhi díí: Who can this be?

Hadínyaa?: Where are you going?

Hasdziih: I will speak.

Hikah doleeł: They are coming.

hoddentin: cattail pollen

Indah: literally, the Living (White People, the Pale Eyes, the Enemy)

Indah ch'iidn: enemy ghosts (a raiding and warfare term for the enemy)

Iniwozh: dry gully

Intin digiz: crooked path, Zig Zag Trail

itsį' isgá': jerky, dried meat

Izee' ágan: Medicine House (hospital)

izee' déncho'i: harmful medicine, poison

izee' libaahí: dull-colored plant medicine

k'ad: right now (immediately)

kíh: building or house; an enclosed space

kuughą: home (long poles leaned together, covered in hides, blankets, or grasses)

Ła'ihíí: the Other, a personal nickname

Łankah: we come together and meet

lashí: maybe

Łichii: the Red One, a personal nickname (or just the color red)

łįį': horse

łikąą golįh: literally, it tastes sweet (good)

ná: here (take it)

Naadiktaz: It Wiggles, a personal nickname

nadah: agave (agave hearts roasted underground for two days and pounded into transportable cakes)

nadask'igí diłhił: dark or black hills, Peloncillo Mountains, which divide Arizona and New Mexico

Náhikah: We are coming back.

nah-leen: a maiden; a maiden's hairstyle: gathered into a flat dumbbell shape, covered with red, and studded in place with metal buttons

Nakaiyé: Those Who Walk (the Mexicans)

Nakaiyé nowik'edandiihi: our enemies that walk around (the Mexicans)

Naki gozłíí' néé: We are twins (literally, two-born).

Nayidi'aah: He Lifts It (as in lifting a rock), personal nickname

Ncho'go natsíńkees da!: Don't think unpleasant thoughts!

Ndaa': white men

Ndaa' bidiyégé – white man's clothes

Ndee: literally, the Dead (the Real People), Apaches

Ndee ndaaye': A human enemy is coming.

Ndee Nnaahi: the Nameless Ones, "Bronco" or wild Apaches

Netdahe: the wild ones, those who remained in the Sierra Madre; Broncos

Nlááyú: Over there

nowik'edandiihi Nakaiyé: our enemies that walk around (Mexicans)

Nzhoo: nice, good, beautiful

Nzhooonigo: very nice

Sąh: Listen!

shash: bear

Shibéhé: my uncle

Shich'ą' ch'a'okíí.: I lost the people.

Shichóyé: my grandfather

Shidee: my older sister

Shidizhé: my younger sister

Shigo shk'anni sidja: Here lies my yucca fruit. (Traditional way to end a story; approximately equals "That's my story.")

shiłt'ii: my friend (man speaking to man)

Shiwóyé: grandmother

Shizhaazhé: my son

siladáá: soldiers

Ti'i: Go on.

ts'aał: cradleboard, used to carry and protect infants

tseebitu': water naturally held in rock tanks or pools

Tséé Naadadn' áhá yu ágodzaa: It happened at Scattered Rocks Stand Straight Up, at that exact place. (Traditional way to begin and end a story by describing the location.)

Tséyi' Łigai: White Rocks, a place name

Tingui: the four card used to play the card game called Monte in Spanish

Ussen: the Creator; God

Yidah: he forgets

Yaa': Louse, a personal nickname (or just a louse)

Zhonne: Pretty One, a personal nickname

SPANISH VOCABULARY AND PHRASES

a sus órdenes: at your service

cabron: goat (slang: bastard, asshole, cuckold)

Chapo: Shorty, a nickname

chido: cool (slang)

chile rellenos: Ortega chiles stuffed with cheese, coated in flour, and fried in oil

chingado: f - - k

claro que si: of course

colonia: colony, a group of farmers, ranchers, or tradesmen who group together

corridos: traditional Mexican ballads with lyrics of Mexican history

coyote: a canine, wild animal (slang for guide of illegal immigrants to cross border)

cuidado: Be careful.

D'accuerdo: I agree.

Enmedios: In the Middle, a place name

Falta: It's lacking.

federales: the Mexican national police

Hacendado: land grant from the Spanish crown

hermano: brother

hombre: man

huarache: a woven leather sandal, often with tire rubber soles

La Forastera: the outsider

La Migra: the U.S. Border Patrol

La Sartén: the skillet, a slender ridge connecting *Juh's* Stronghold to the Sierra Madre Range

¡Levántate!: Get up!

¿Listo?: Ready?

Los Muchachos: aka LM, The Friends, a fictional drug cartel

mijo/mija: my son, my daughter

narcotraficantes: those who deal in growing, selling, business of drugs

patrón: the boss

pendejo: idiot, fool (slang). Exact meaning is 'pubic hair'.

perdóneme: pardon me

pollo: chicken (slang for illegal immigrants, led by a guide often called a coyote)

primo: cousin

pues: well

puta: whore

¡Que loca!: How crazy!

querida: darling

San Enebro: St. Juniper (fictional New Mexican town)

segundo: second in command

señor: sir or mister

señora: married woman

señorita: unmarried woman

tia: aunt

tinajas: rock pools, aka tanks, sometimes hold water for days and weeks

ABOUT THE AUTHOR

LYNN GALVIN graduated from the University of Wyoming with a BA in history and a law degree. She has worked as an attorney for the Navajo Nation, and as a legal advisor, teacher and administrator for universities in Puerto Rico, Spain, Germany, and various states. She lived in the Chiricahua Apache homeland in today's Cochise County, Arizona where she developed a deep interest in Apache history and culture. She is a teacher consultant with the Arizona Geographic Alliance.